ADRIATIC SEA

ITALY

OTTOMAN

Monte
negro

Albania

Saloniki

Berat

Epirus

Ioannina

Gardiki
Gravia

Arta

Messolonghi

Dervenakia

Tripoli

Peloponnesus

Nafplio

Monemvasia

Athens

Chios

Smyrna

Constantinople

EMPIRE

Cyprus

Candia

Naples

Palermo

SICILY

Malta

MEDITERRANEAN SEA

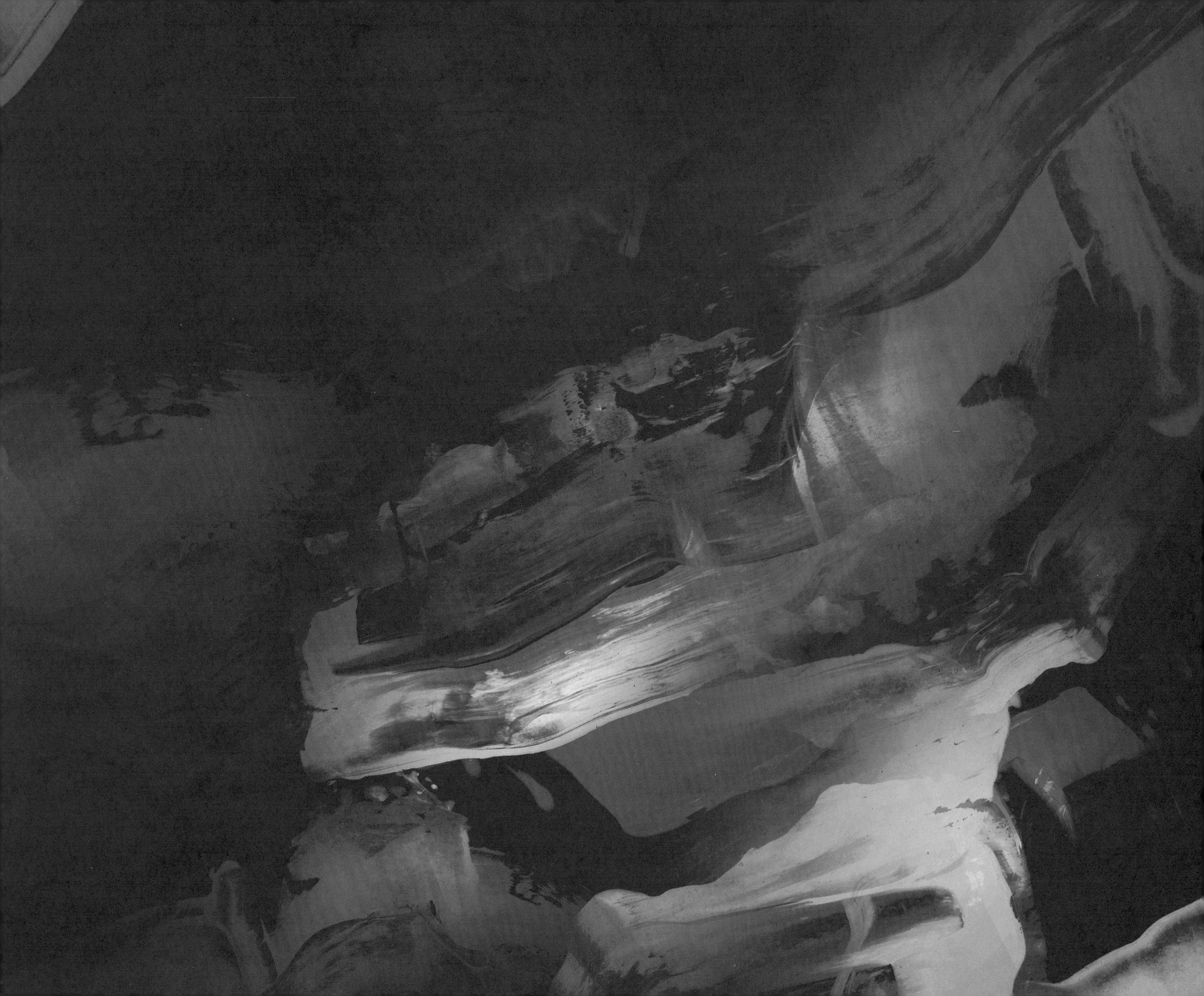

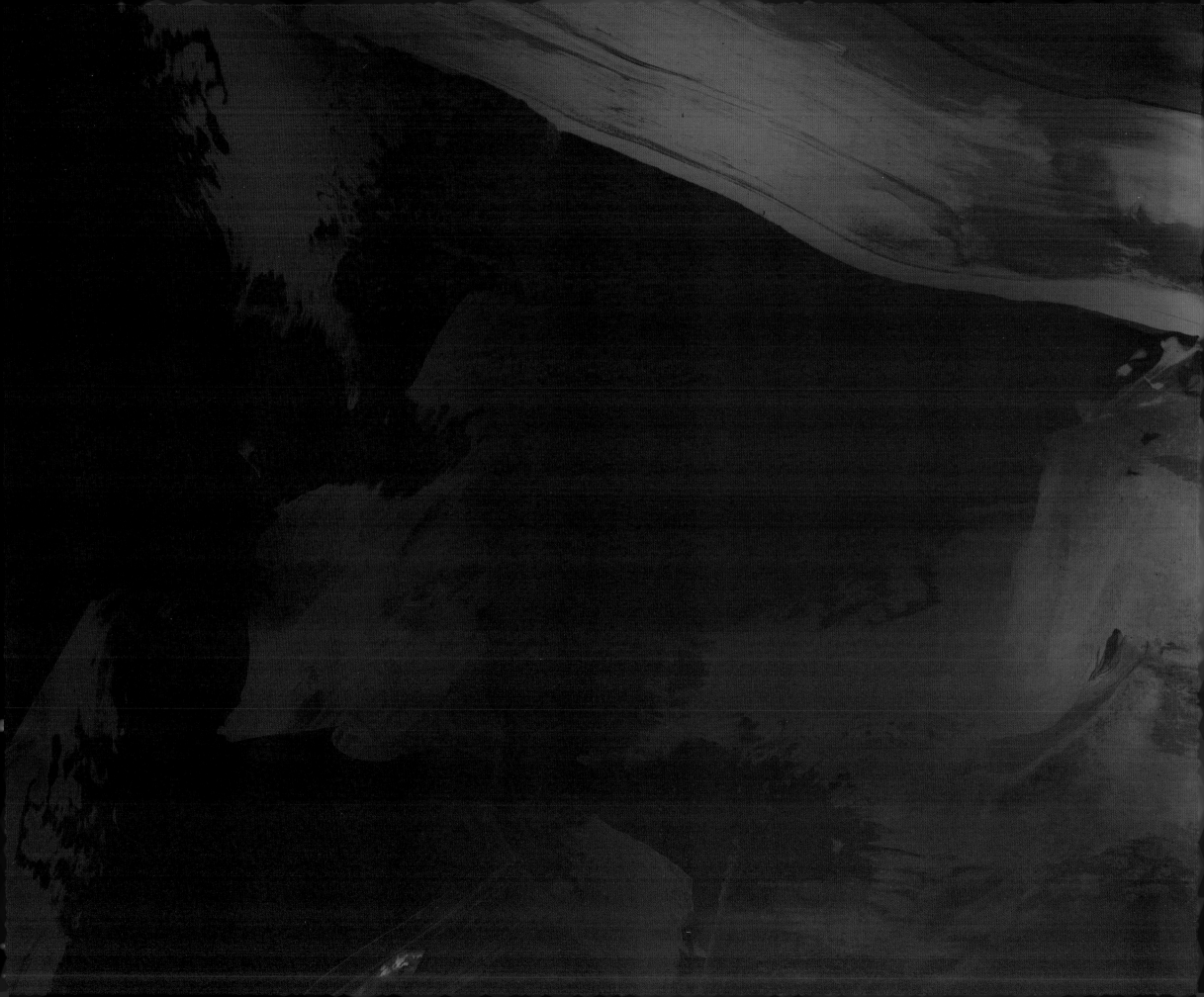

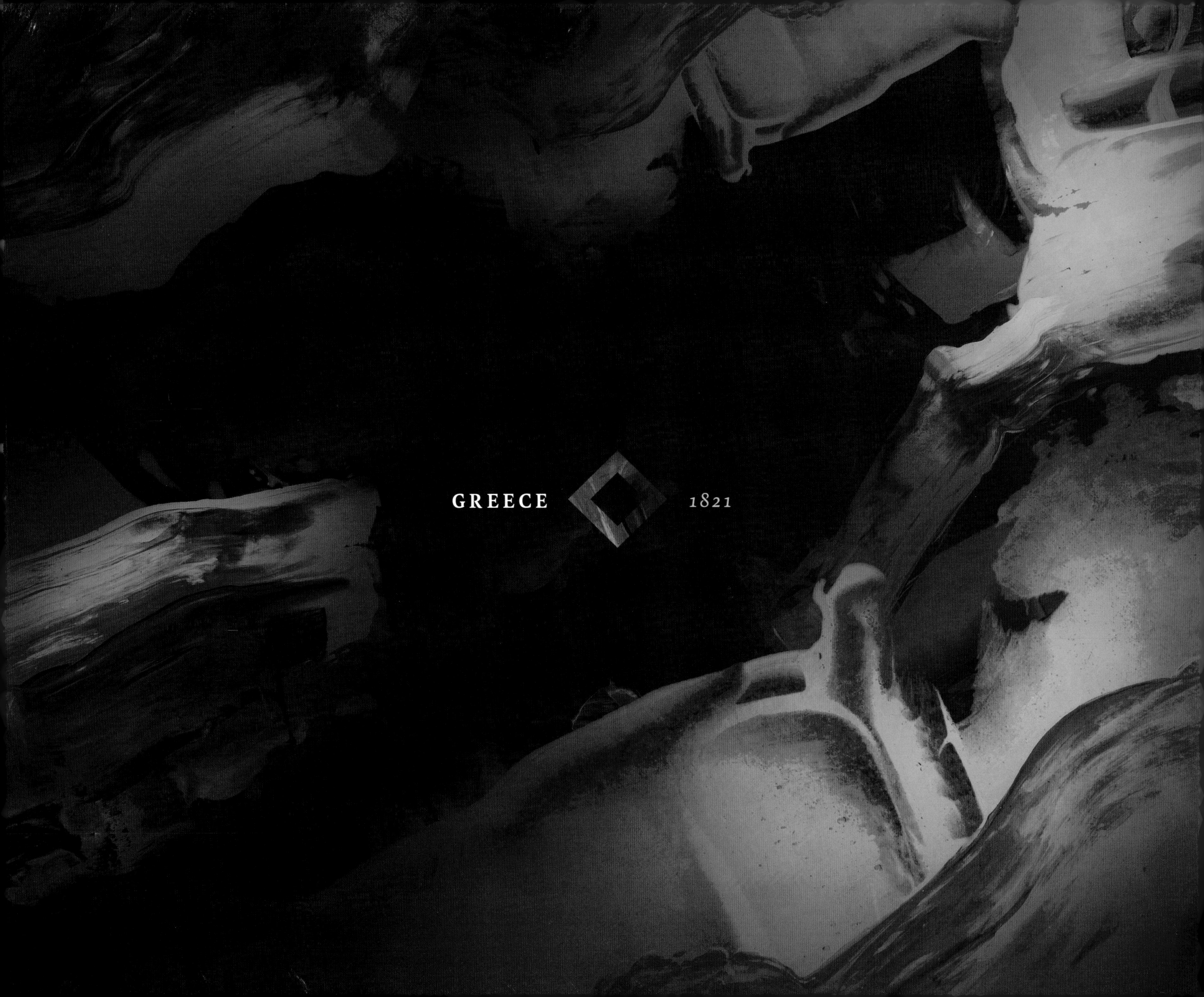
GREECE 1821

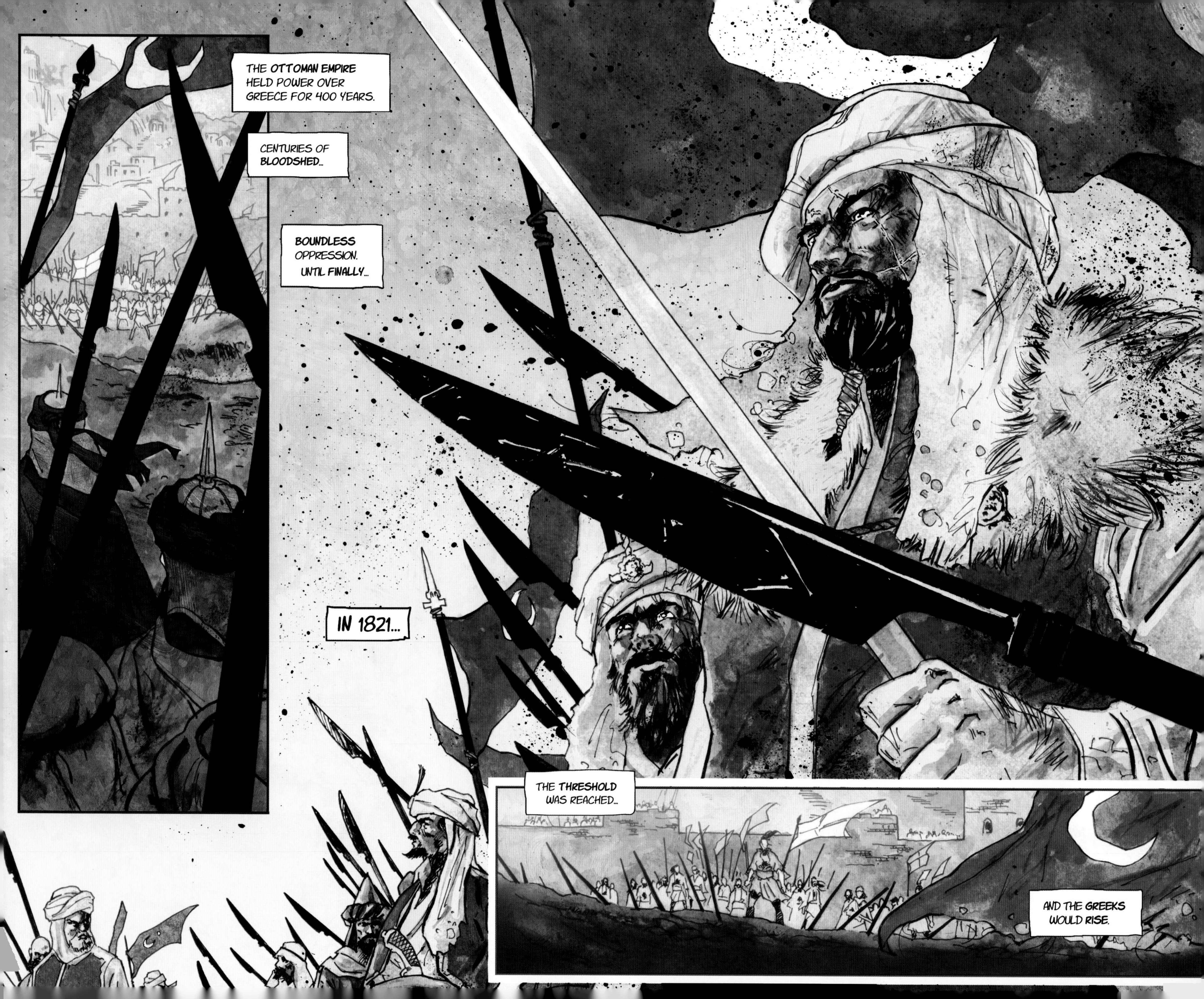
THE OTTOMAN EMPIRE HELD POWER OVER GREECE FOR 400 YEARS.
CENTURIES OF BLOODSHED...
BOUNDLESS OPPRESSION. UNTIL FINALLY...
IN 1821...
THE THRESHOLD WAS REACHED...
AND THE GREEKS WOULD RISE.

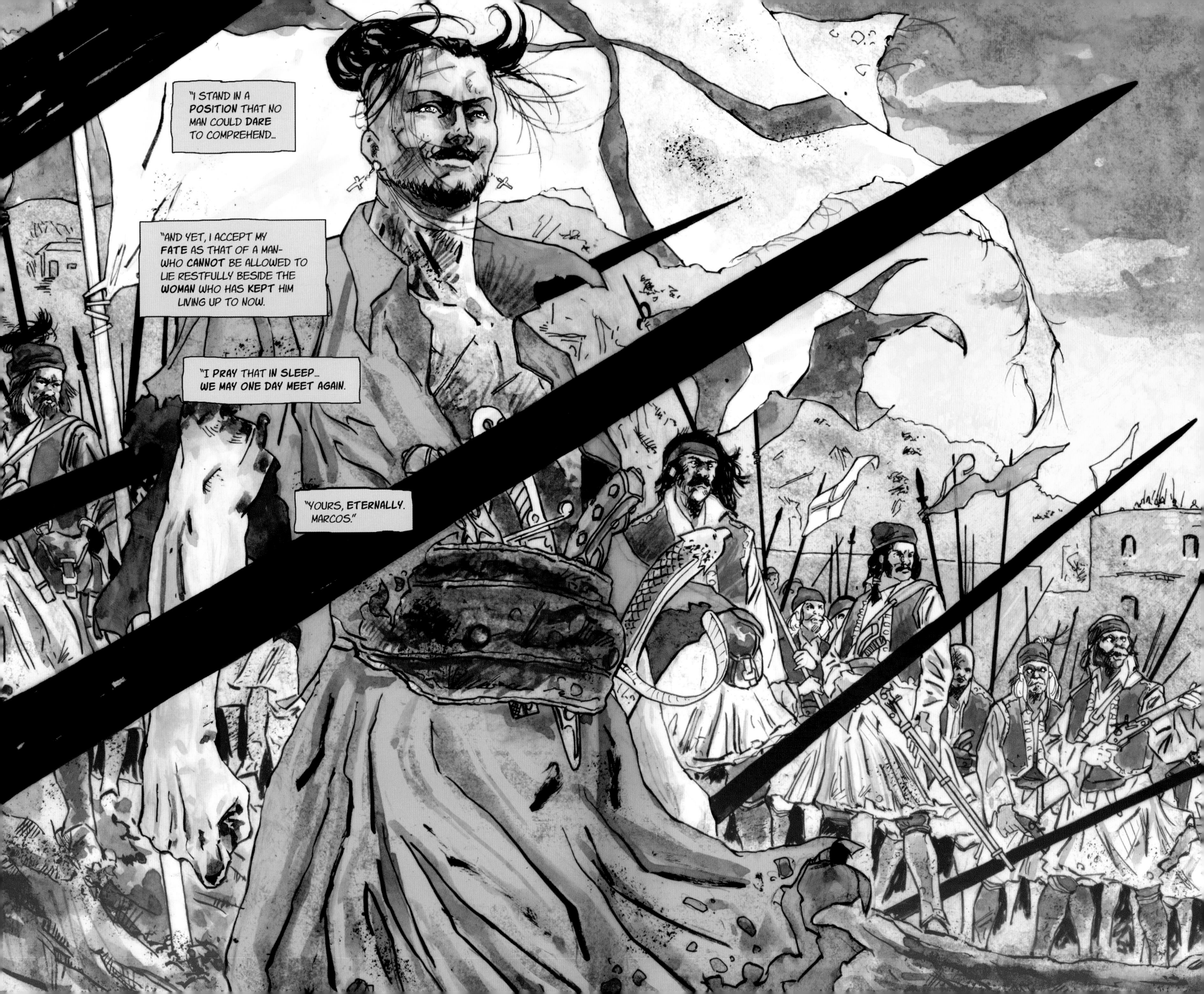
"I STAND IN A POSITION THAT NO MAN COULD DARE TO COMPREHEND...
"AND YET, I ACCEPT MY FATE AS THAT OF A MAN-WHO CANNOT BE ALLOWED TO LIE RESTFULLY BESIDE THE WOMAN WHO HAS KEPT HIM LIVING UP TO NOW.
"I PRAY THAT IN SLEEP... WE MAY ONE DAY MEET AGAIN.
"YOURS, ETERNALLY. MARCOS."

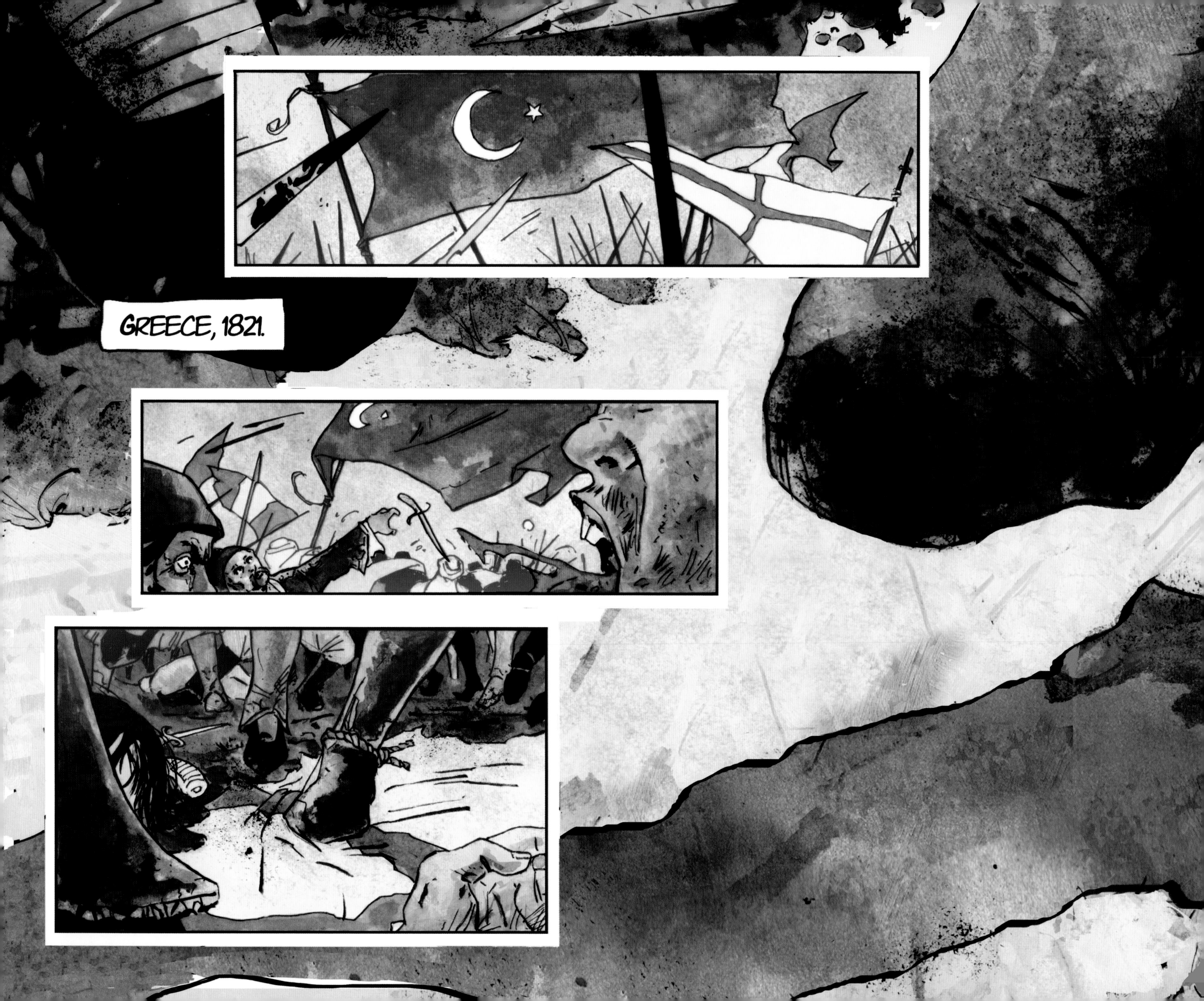
GREECE, 1821.

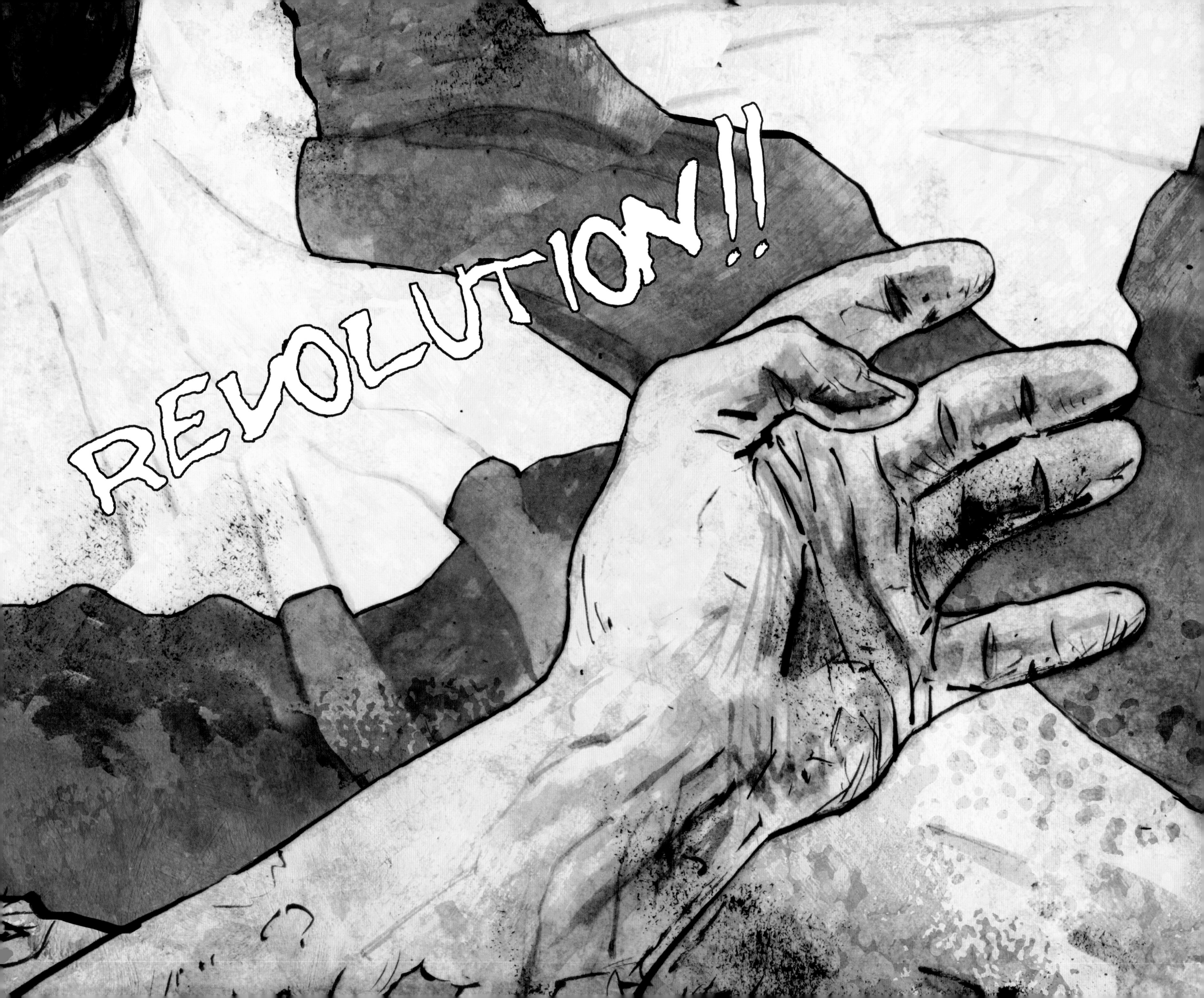
REVOLUTION!!

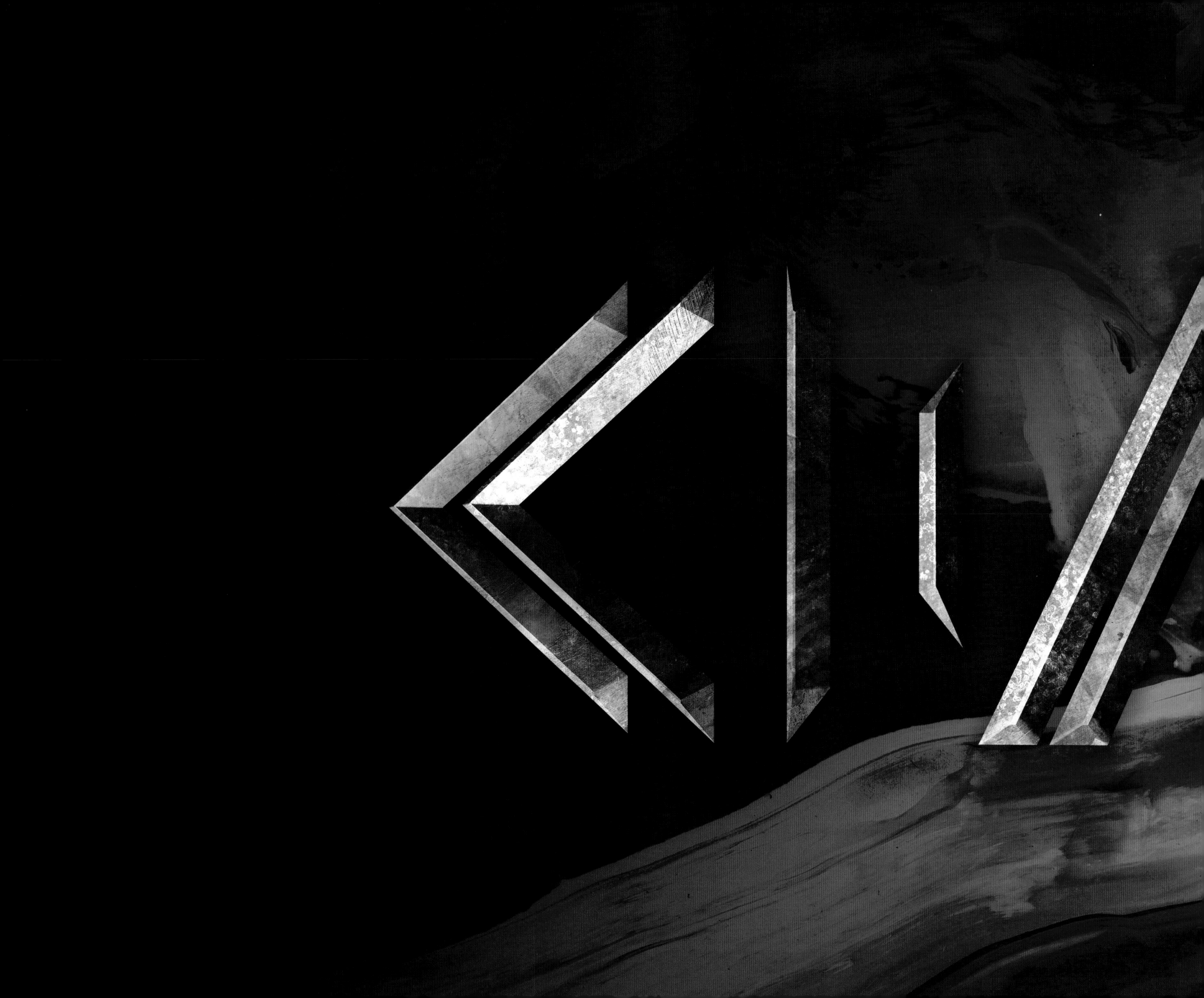

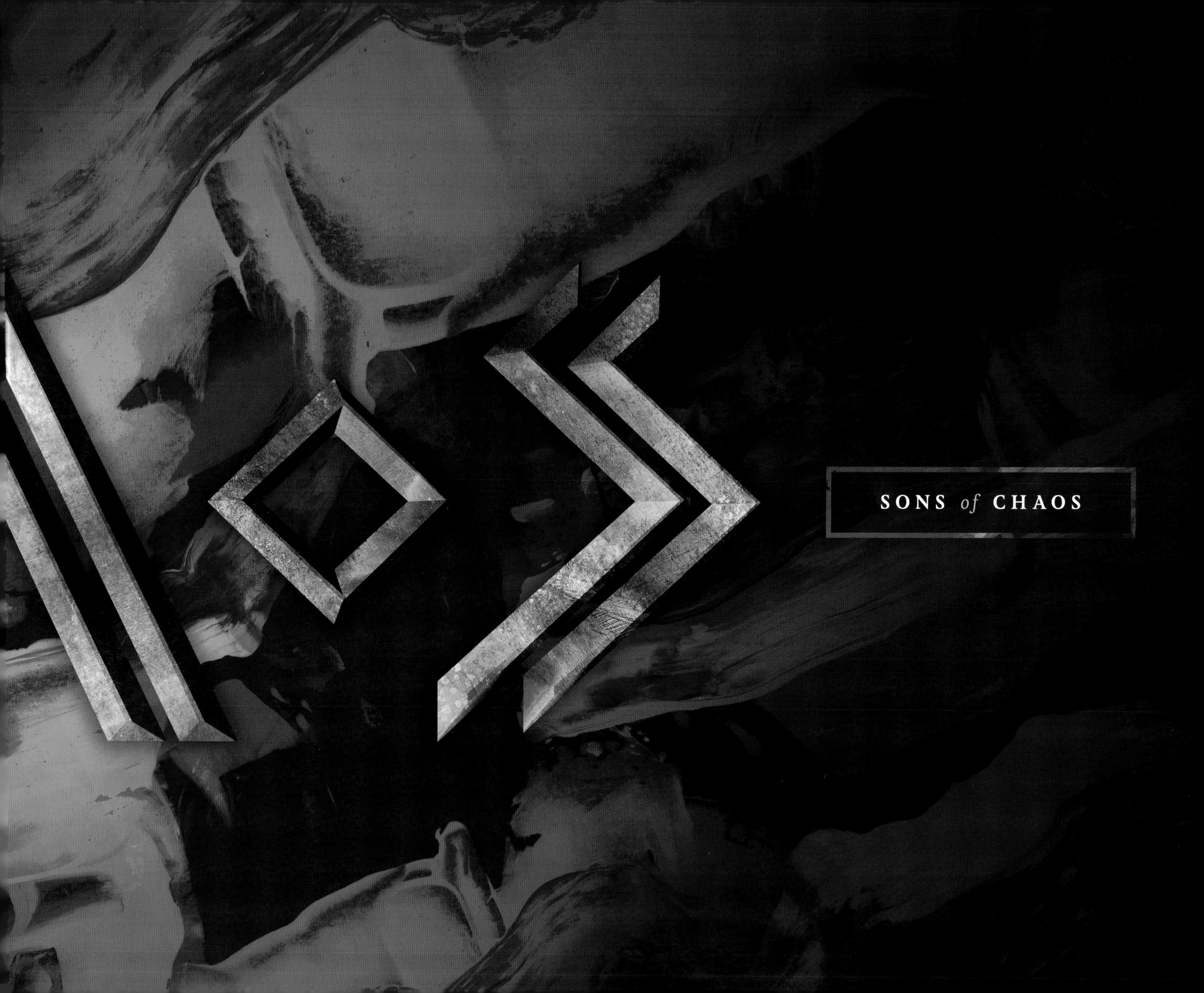
SONS *of* CHAOS

ISBN: 978-1-68405-479-4   22 21 20 19   1 2 3 4

COLLECTION EDITS BY
JUSTIN EISINGER AND
ALONZO SIMON

PRODUCTION BY
RON ESTEVEZ

Chris Ryall, President, Publisher, and Chief Creative Officer
John Barber, Editor-In-Chief
Robbie Robbins, EVP/Sr. Art Director
Cara Morrison, Chief Financial Officer
Matt Ruzicka, Chief Accounting Officer
David Hedgecock, Associate Publisher
Jerry Bennington, VP of New Product Development
Lorelei Bunjes, VP of Digital Services
Justin Eisinger, Editorial Director, Graphic Novels & Collections
Eric Moss, Senior Director, Licensing and Business Development

Ted Adams, IDW Founder

CHAOS

SONS *of* CHAOS

Written & Produced By
Chris Jaymes

Art By
Ale Aragon

Color By
Hi-Fi Design

Letters and Map By
Pablo Ayala

Story By
Chris Jaymes & Jordan Beckett

Editor
M. Huehner

Cover Art By
David Palumbo

Design and Logo By
Cody Tilson

Executive Producers
Nick Lambrou & Michael Wortsman

From Levendis Entertainment & Hollywood Laundromat

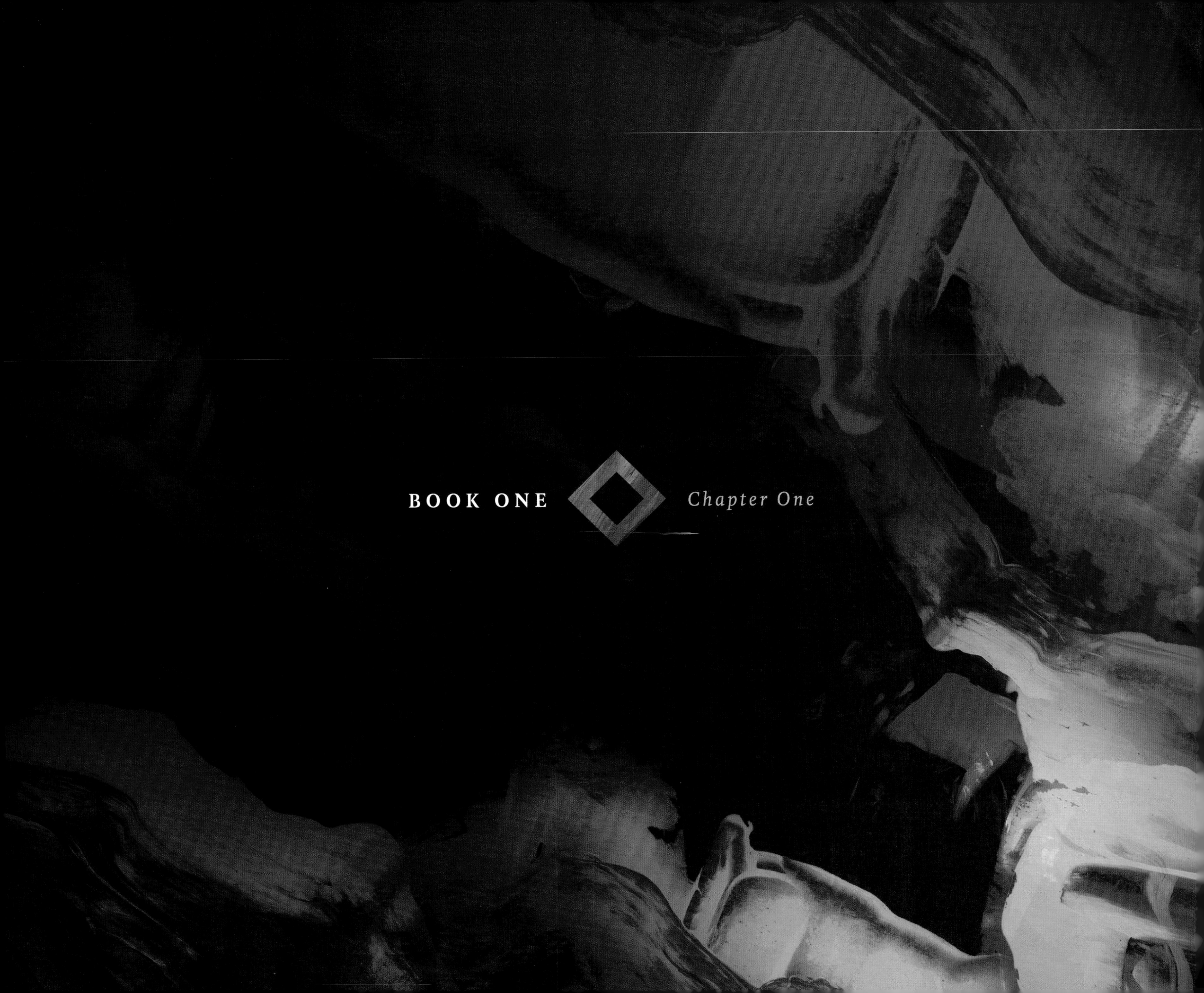

BOOK ONE ◇ *Chapter One*

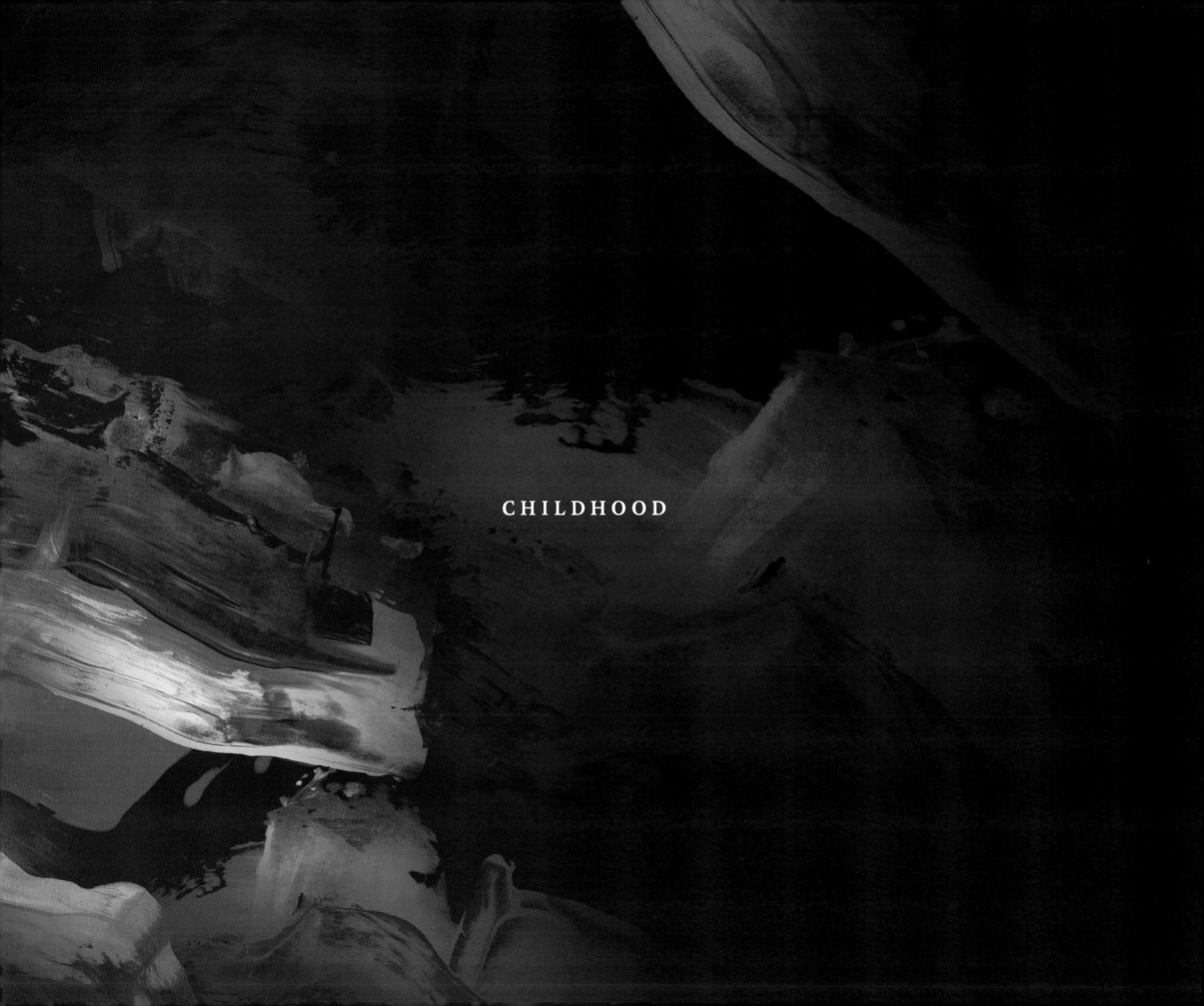

CHILDHOOD

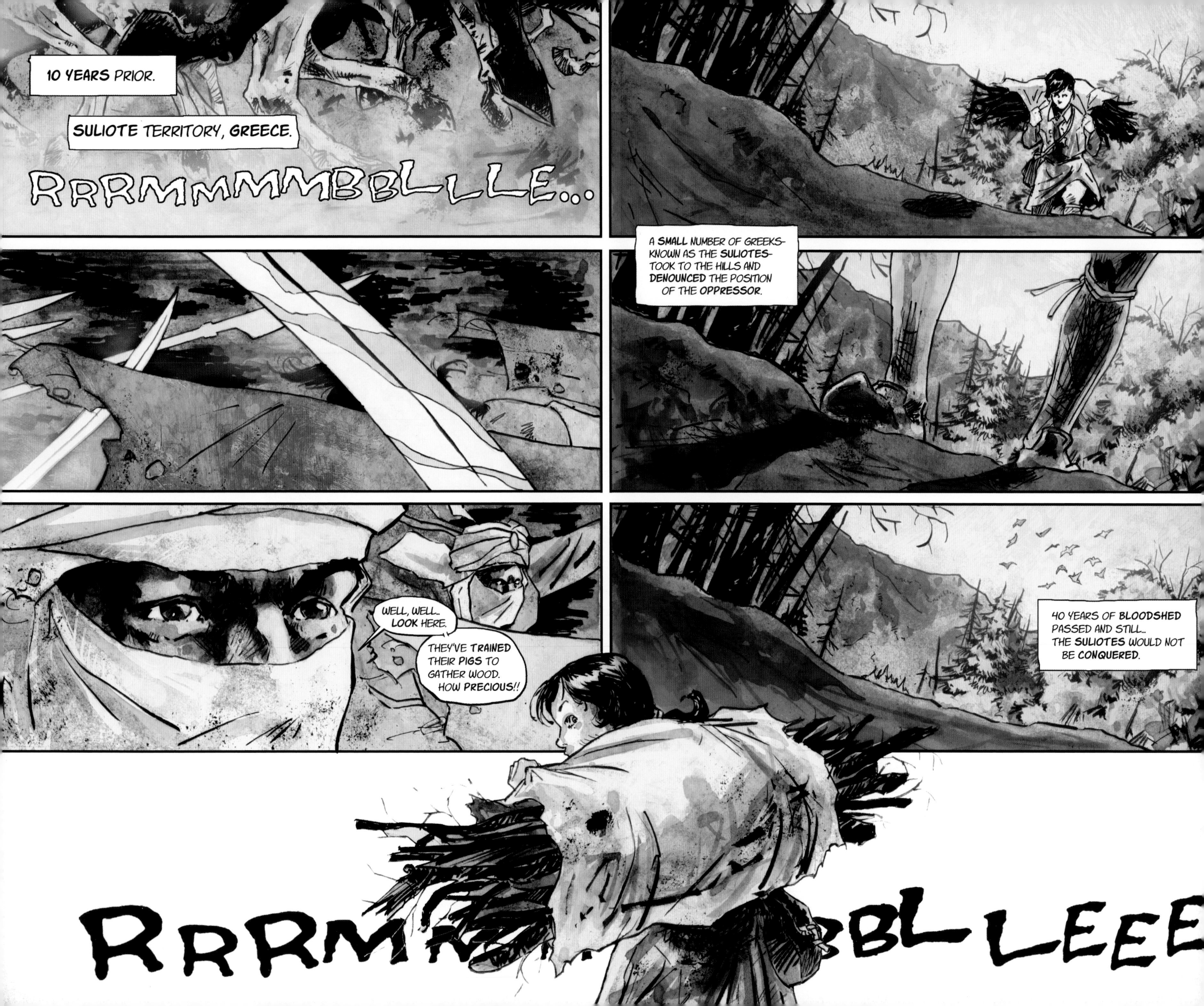
10 YEARS PRIOR.
SULIOTE TERRITORY, GREECE.
RRRMMMMMBBLLLE...
A SMALL NUMBER OF GREEKS- KNOWN AS THE SULIOTES- TOOK TO THE HILLS AND DENOUNCED THE POSITION OF THE OPPRESSOR.
WELL, WELL... LOOK HERE.
THEY'VE TRAINED THEIR PIGS TO GATHER WOOD. HOW PRECIOUS!!
40 YEARS OF BLOODSHED PASSED AND STILL... THE SULIOTES WOULD NOT BE CONQUERED.
RRRM
BBLLEEE

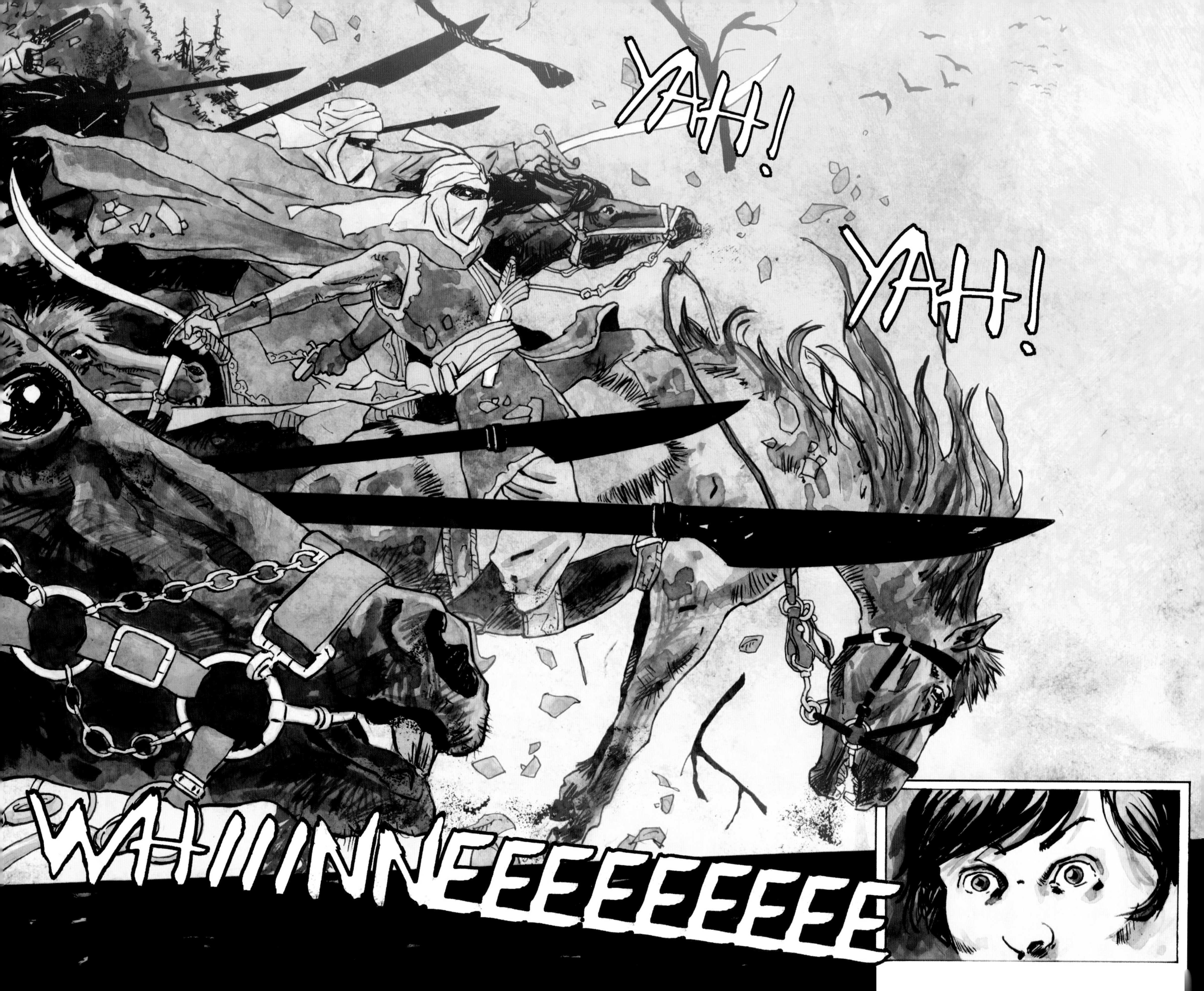

YAH!
YAH!
WHIIIINNEEEEEEEEE

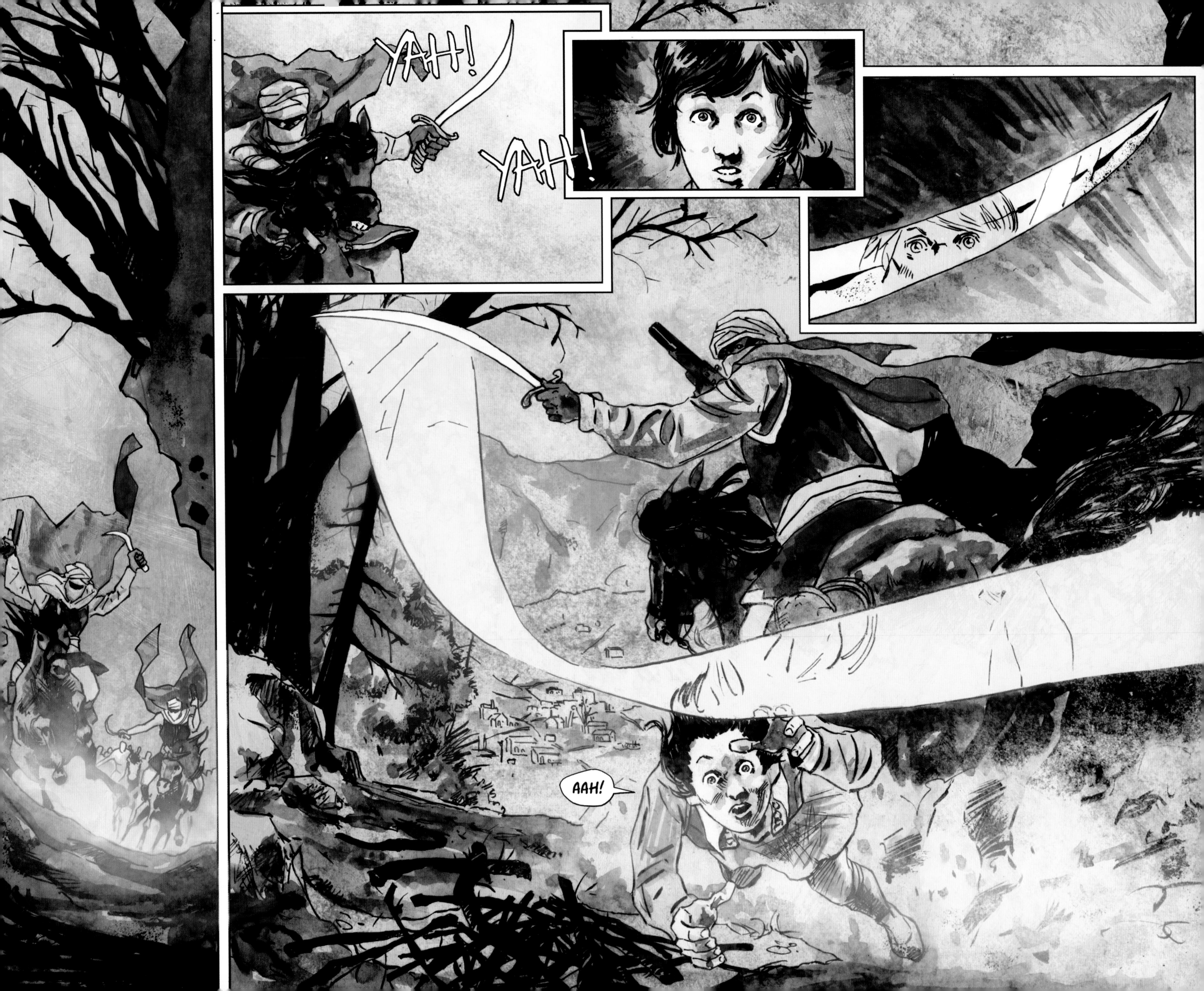
YAH!
YAH!
AAH!

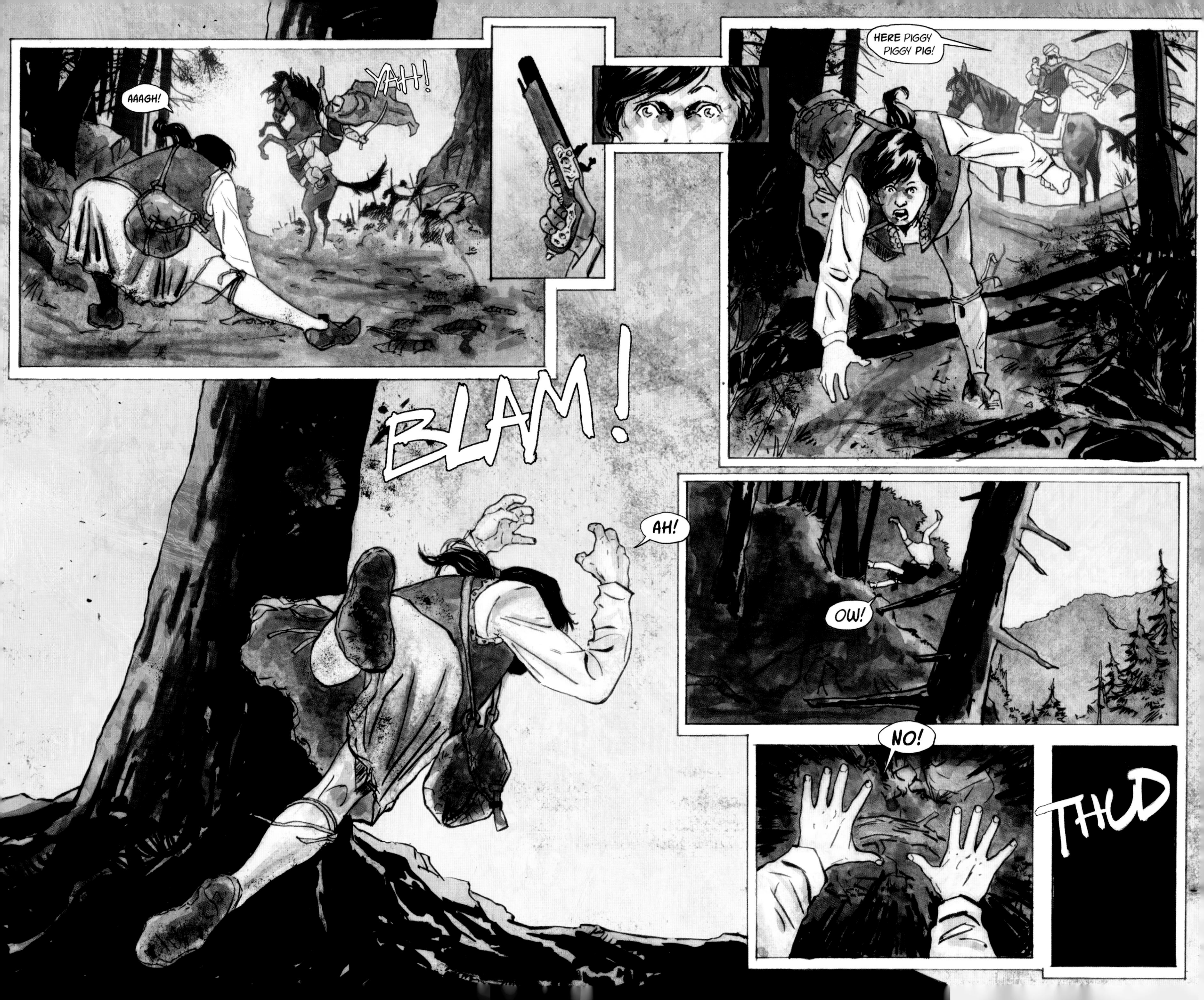
AAAGH!
YAH!
HERE PIGGY PIGGY PIG!
BLAM!
AH!
OW!
NO!
THUD

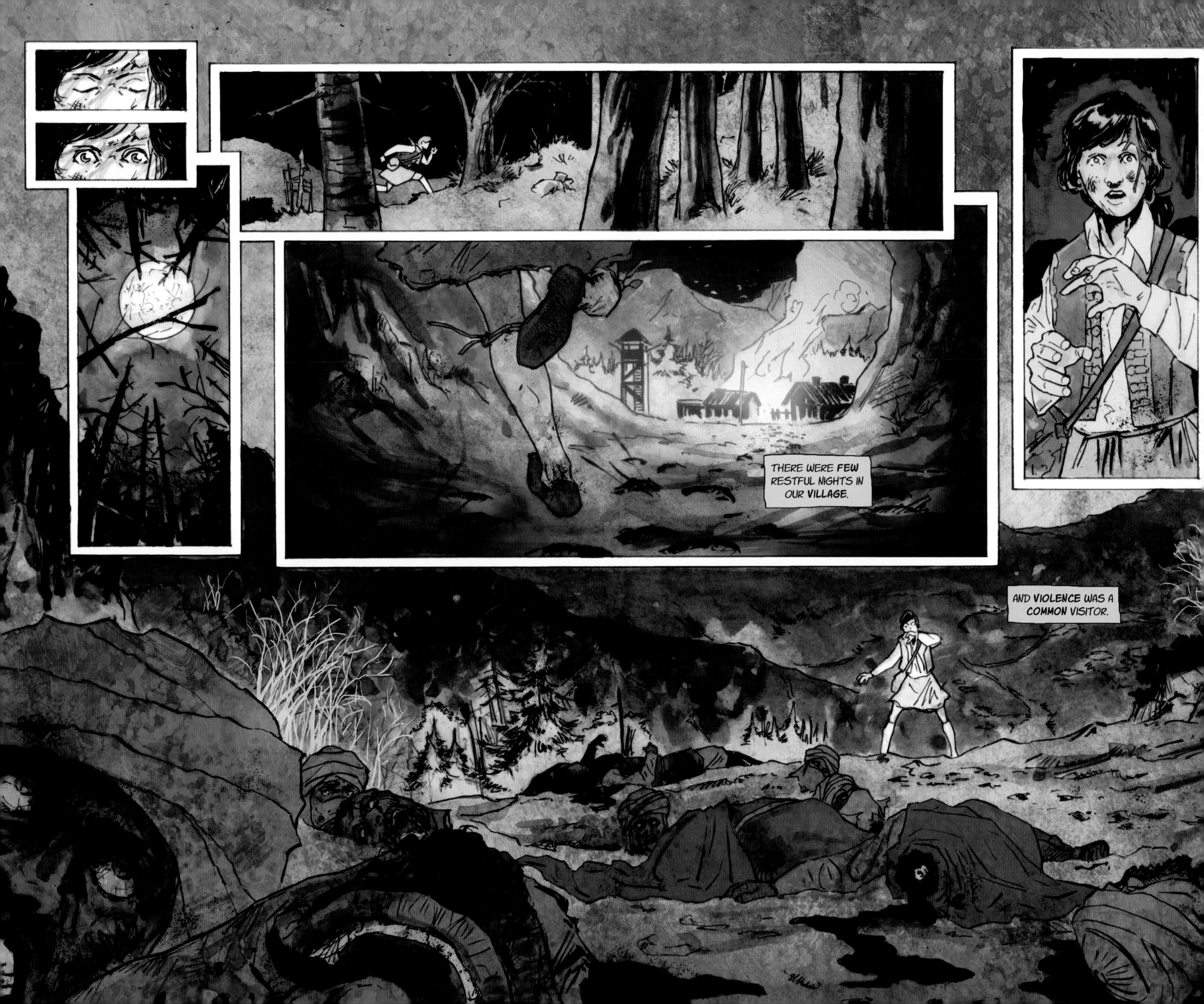
THERE WERE FEW RESTFUL NIGHTS IN OUR VILLAGE.
AND VIOLENCE WAS A COMMON VISITOR.

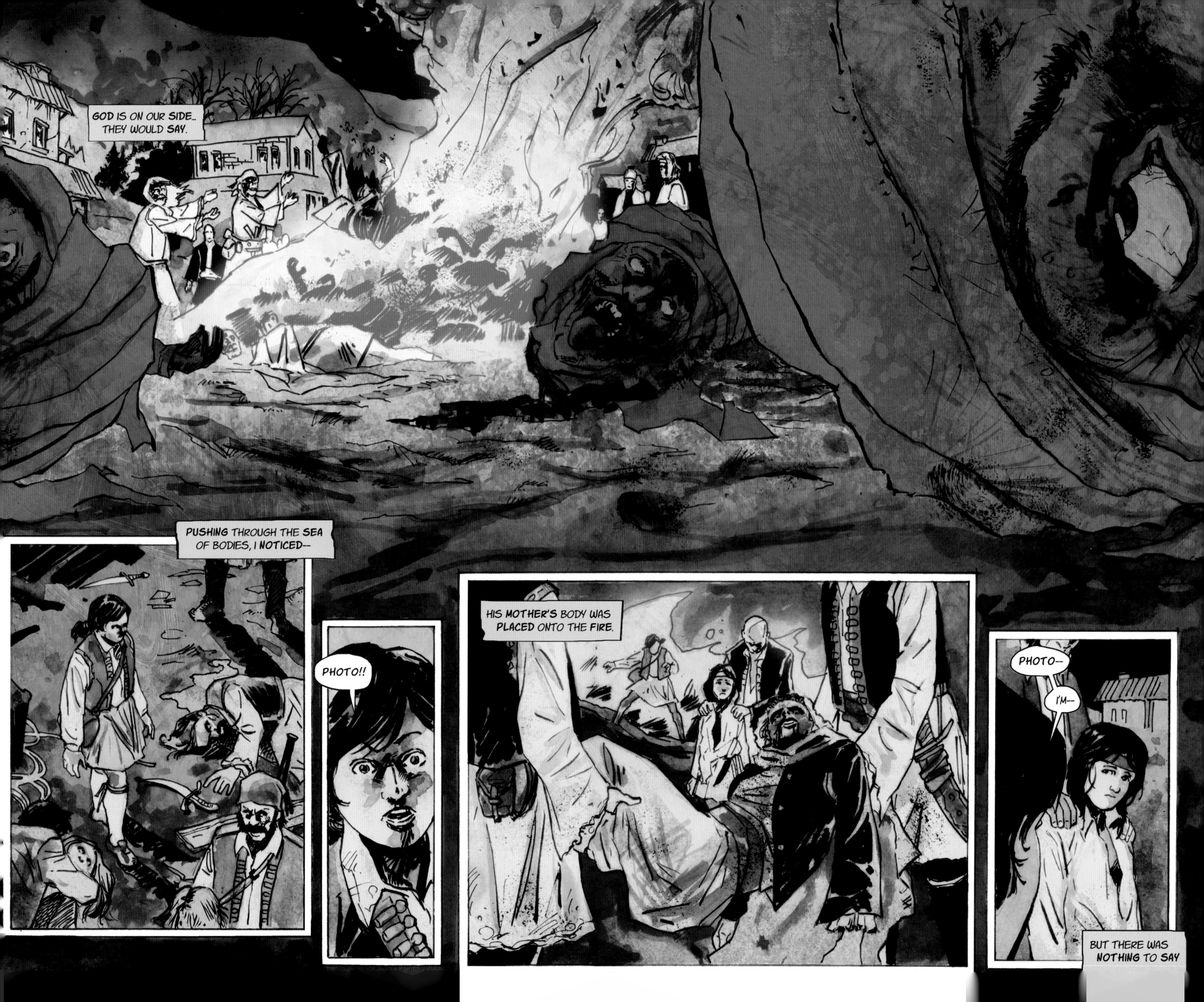
GOD IS ON OUR SIDE... THEY WOULD SAY.
PUSHING THROUGH THE SEA OF BODIES, I NOTICED--
PHOTO!!
HIS MOTHER'S BODY WAS PLACED ONTO THE FIRE.
PHOTO--
I'M--
BUT THERE WAS NOTHING TO SAY

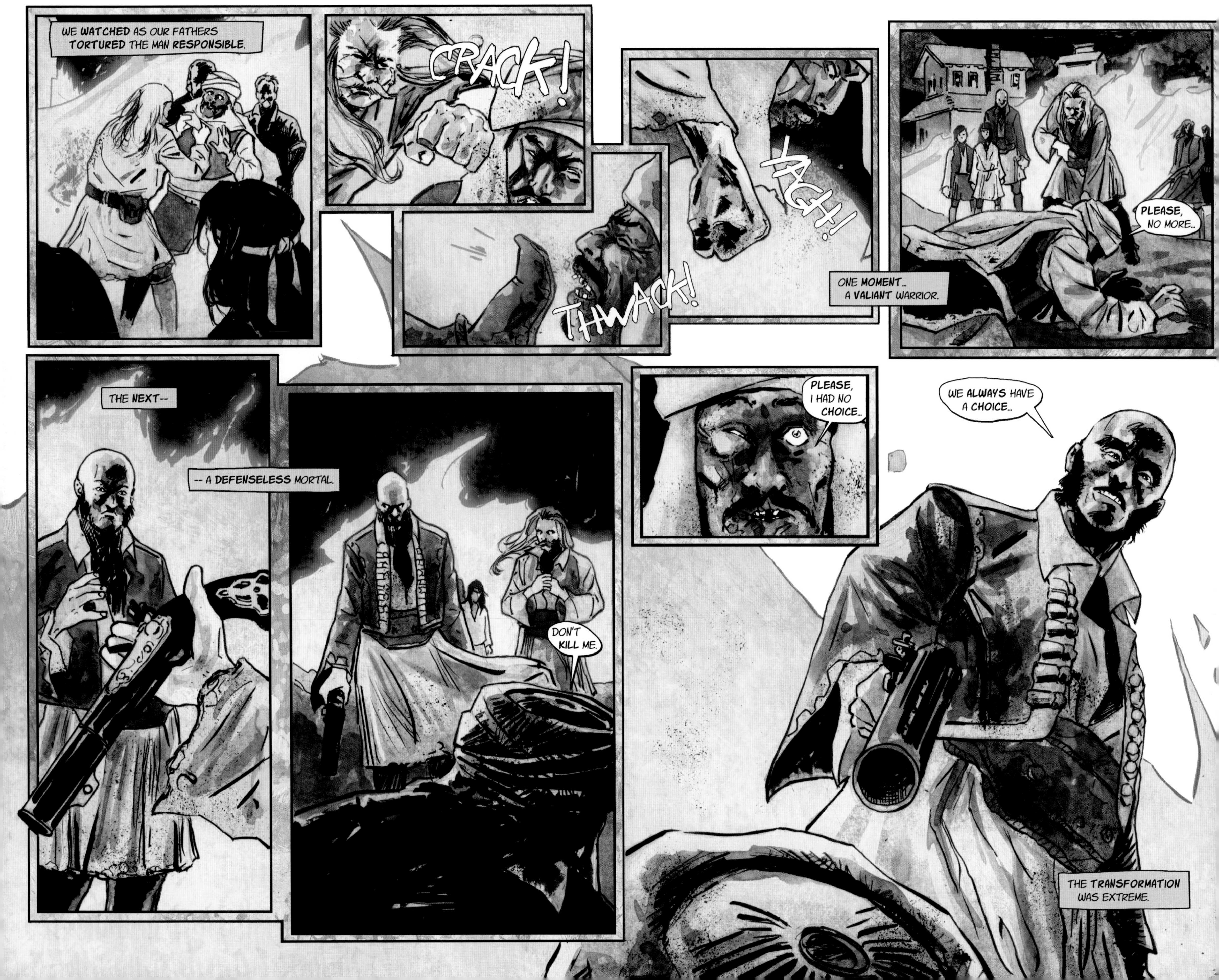

WE WATCHED AS OUR FATHERS TORTURED THE MAN RESPONSIBLE.
CRACK!
THWACK!
YAGH!
ONE MOMENT... A VALIANT WARRIOR.
PLEASE, NO MORE...
THE NEXT--
-- A DEFENSELESS MORTAL.
DON'T KILL ME.
PLEASE, I HAD NO CHOICE...
WE ALWAYS HAVE A CHOICE...
THE TRANSFORMATION WAS EXTREME.

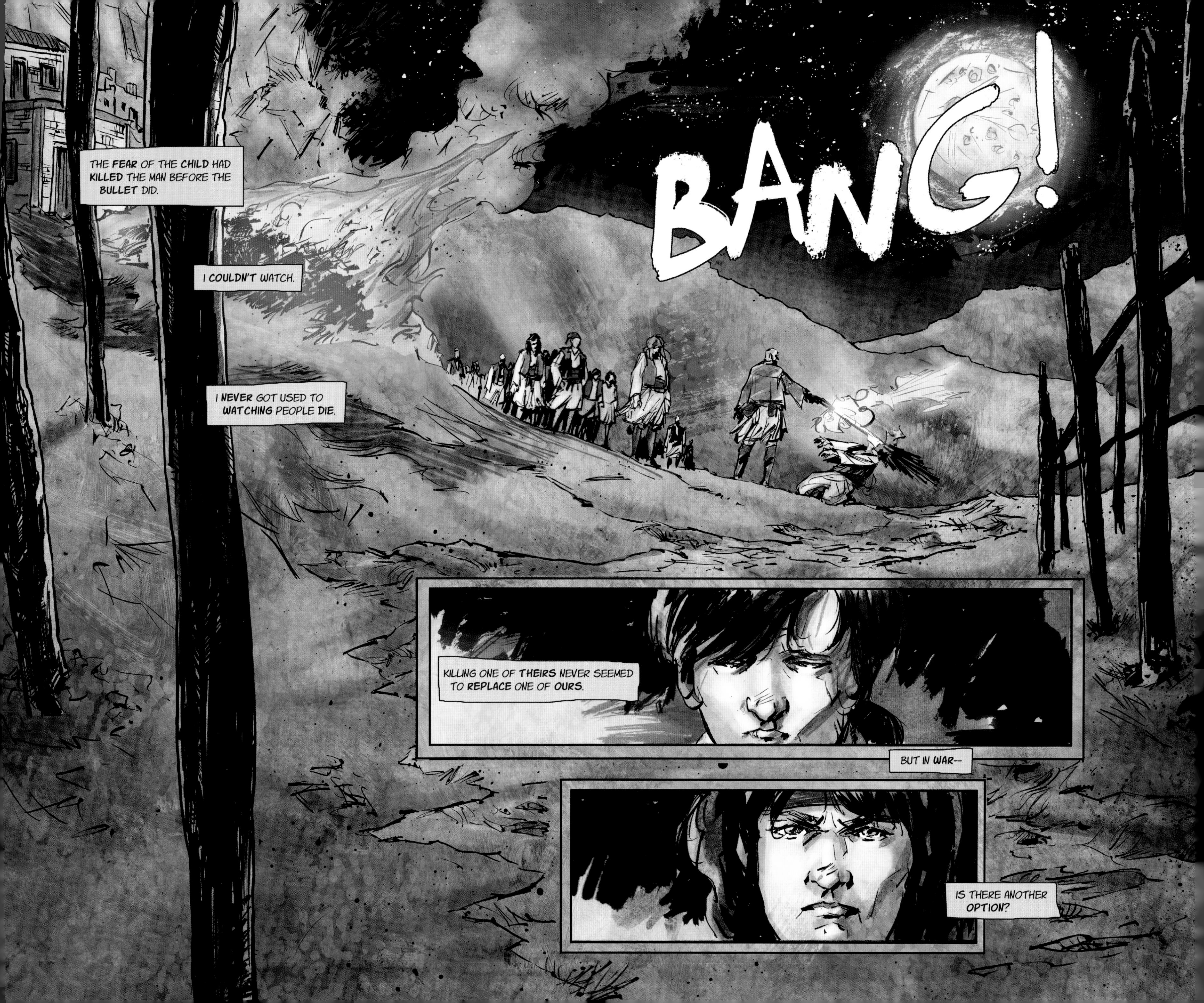
THE FEAR OF THE CHILD HAD KILLED THE MAN BEFORE THE BULLET DID.
I COULDN'T WATCH.
I NEVER GOT USED TO WATCHING PEOPLE DIE.
BANG!
KILLING ONE OF THEIRS NEVER SEEMED TO REPLACE ONE OF OURS.
BUT IN WAR--
IS THERE ANOTHER OPTION?

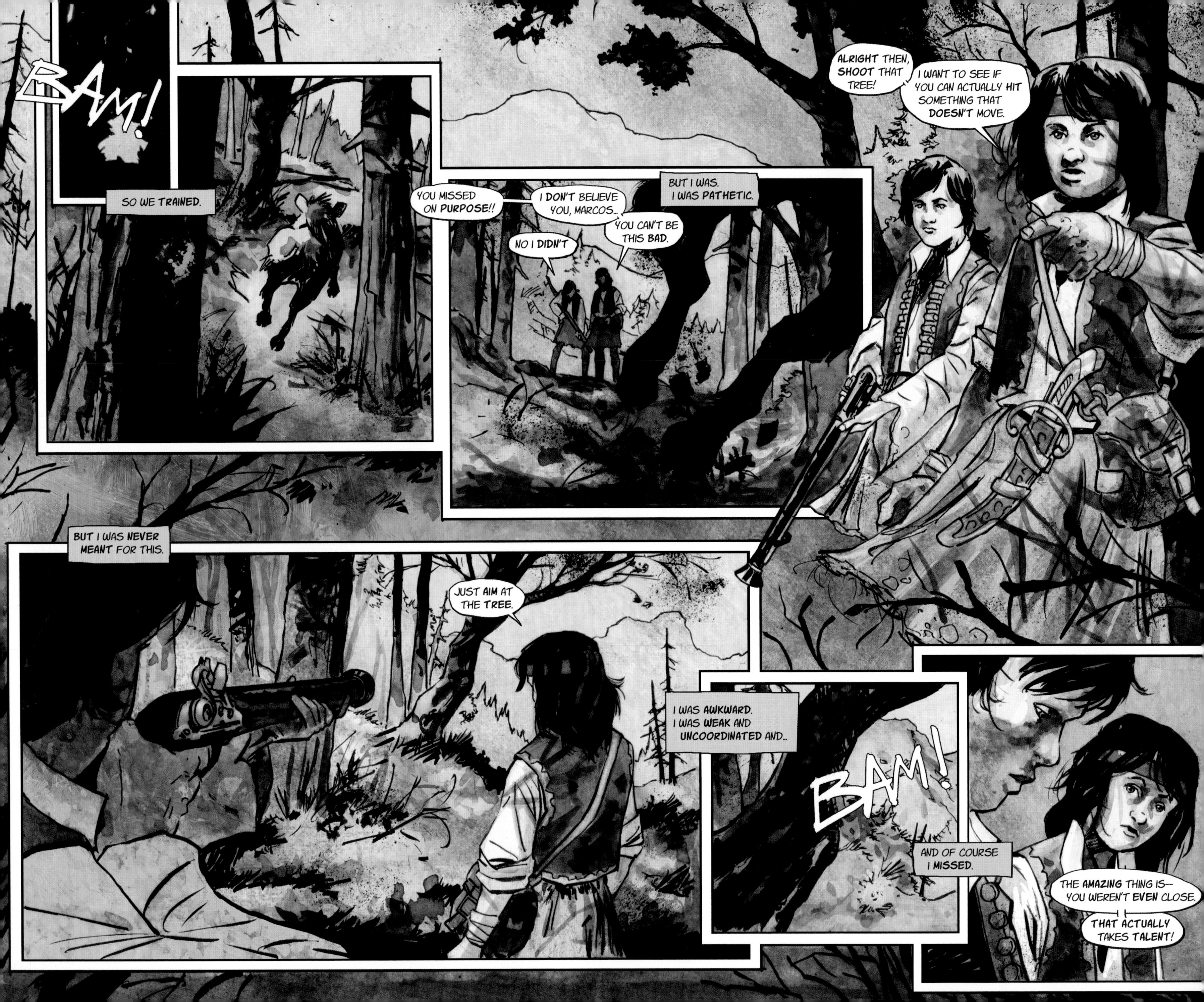

BAM!
SO WE TRAINED.
ALRIGHT THEN, SHOOT THAT TREE!
I WANT TO SEE IF YOU CAN ACTUALLY HIT SOMETHING THAT DOESN'T MOVE.
YOU MISSED ON PURPOSE!!
I DON'T BELIEVE YOU, MARCOS...
NO I DIDN'T
YOU CAN'T BE THIS BAD.
BUT I WAS. I WAS PATHETIC.
BUT I WAS NEVER MEANT FOR THIS.
JUST AIM AT THE TREE.
I WAS AWKWARD. I WAS WEAK AND UNCOORDINATED AND...
BAM!
AND OF COURSE I MISSED.
THE AMAZING THING IS-- YOU WEREN'T EVEN CLOSE.
THAT ACTUALLY TAKES TALENT!

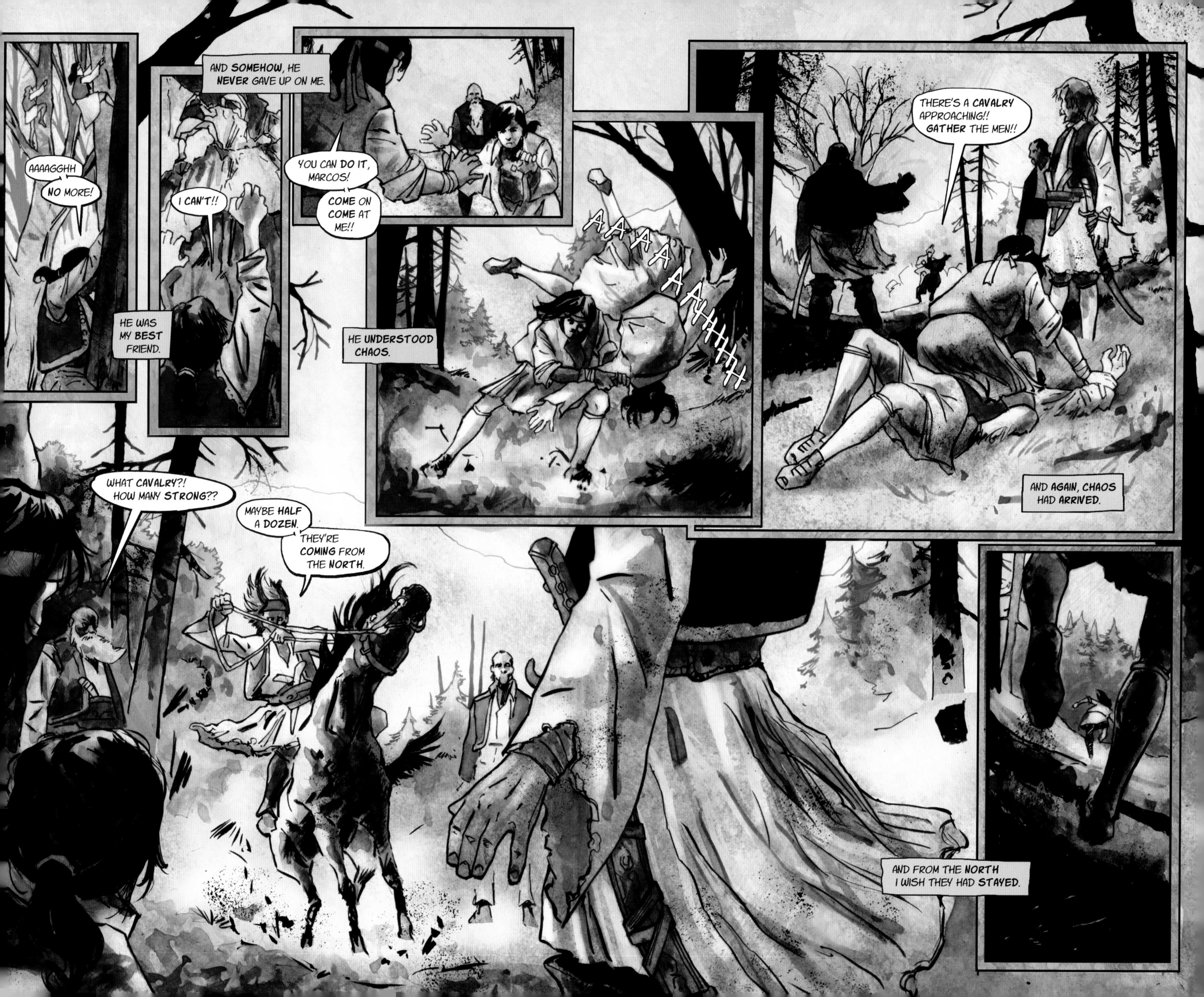
AAAAGGHH
NO MORE!
AND SOMEHOW, HE NEVER GAVE UP ON ME.
I CAN'T!!
HE WAS MY BEST FRIEND.
YOU CAN DO IT, MARCOS!
COME ON COME AT ME!!
HE UNDERSTOOD CHAOS.
AAAAAAAHHHHH
THERE'S A CAVALRY APPROACHING!! GATHER THE MEN!!
AND AGAIN, CHAOS HAD ARRIVED.
WHAT CAVALRY?! HOW MANY STRONG??
MAYBE HALF A DOZEN.
THEY'RE COMING FROM THE NORTH.
AND FROM THE NORTH I WISH THEY HAD STAYED.

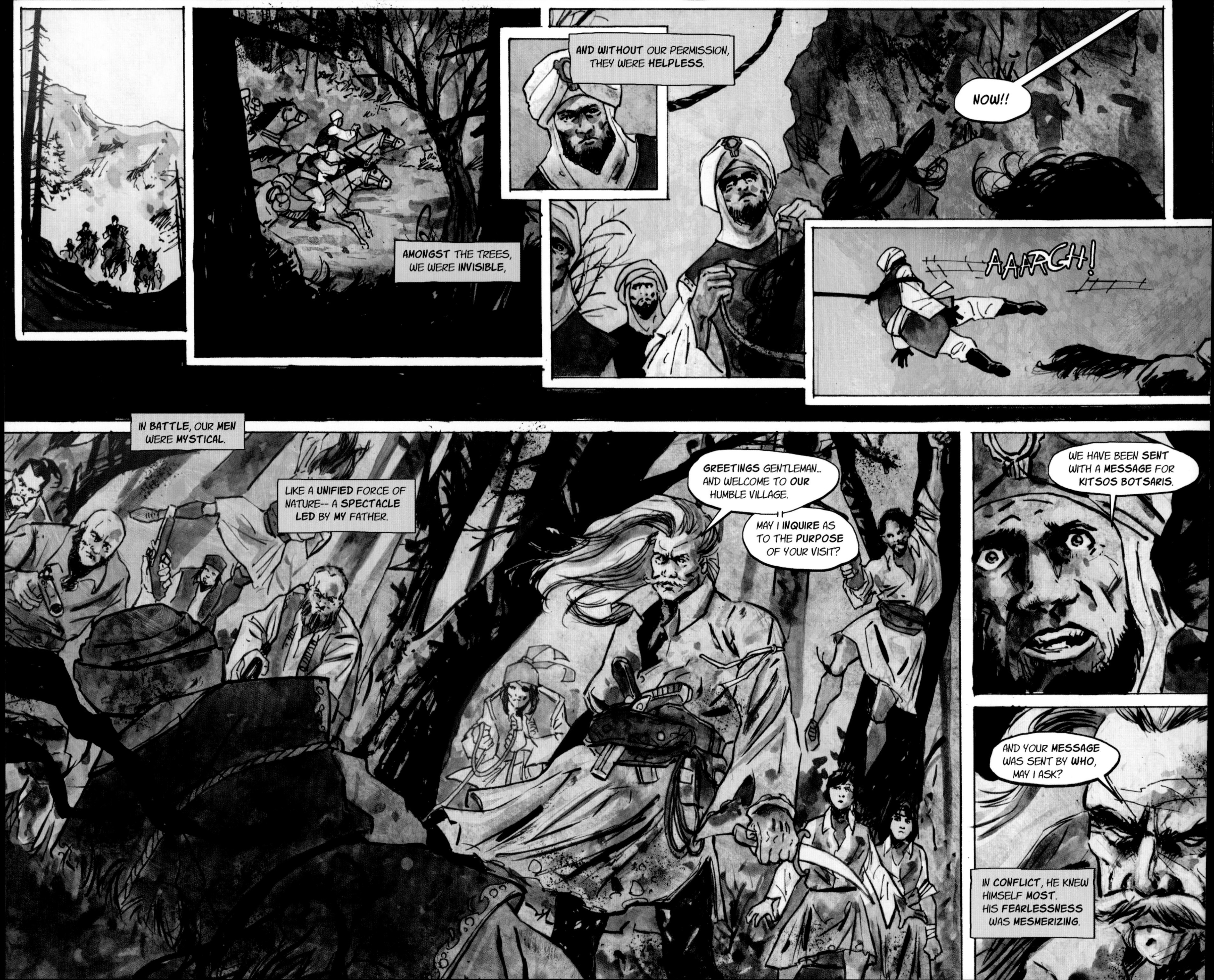
AMONGST THE TREES, WE WERE INVISIBLE,
AND WITHOUT OUR PERMISSION, THEY WERE HELPLESS.
NOW!!
AAARGH!
IN BATTLE, OUR MEN WERE MYSTICAL.
LIKE A UNIFIED FORCE OF NATURE-- A SPECTACLE LED BY MY FATHER.
GREETINGS GENTLEMAN... AND WELCOME TO OUR HUMBLE VILLAGE.
MAY I INQUIRE AS TO THE PURPOSE OF YOUR VISIT?
WE HAVE BEEN SENT WITH A MESSAGE FOR KITSOS BOTSARIS.
AND YOUR MESSAGE WAS SENT BY WHO, MAY I ASK?
IN CONFLICT, HE KNEW HIMSELF MOST. HIS FEARLESSNESS WAS MESMERIZING.

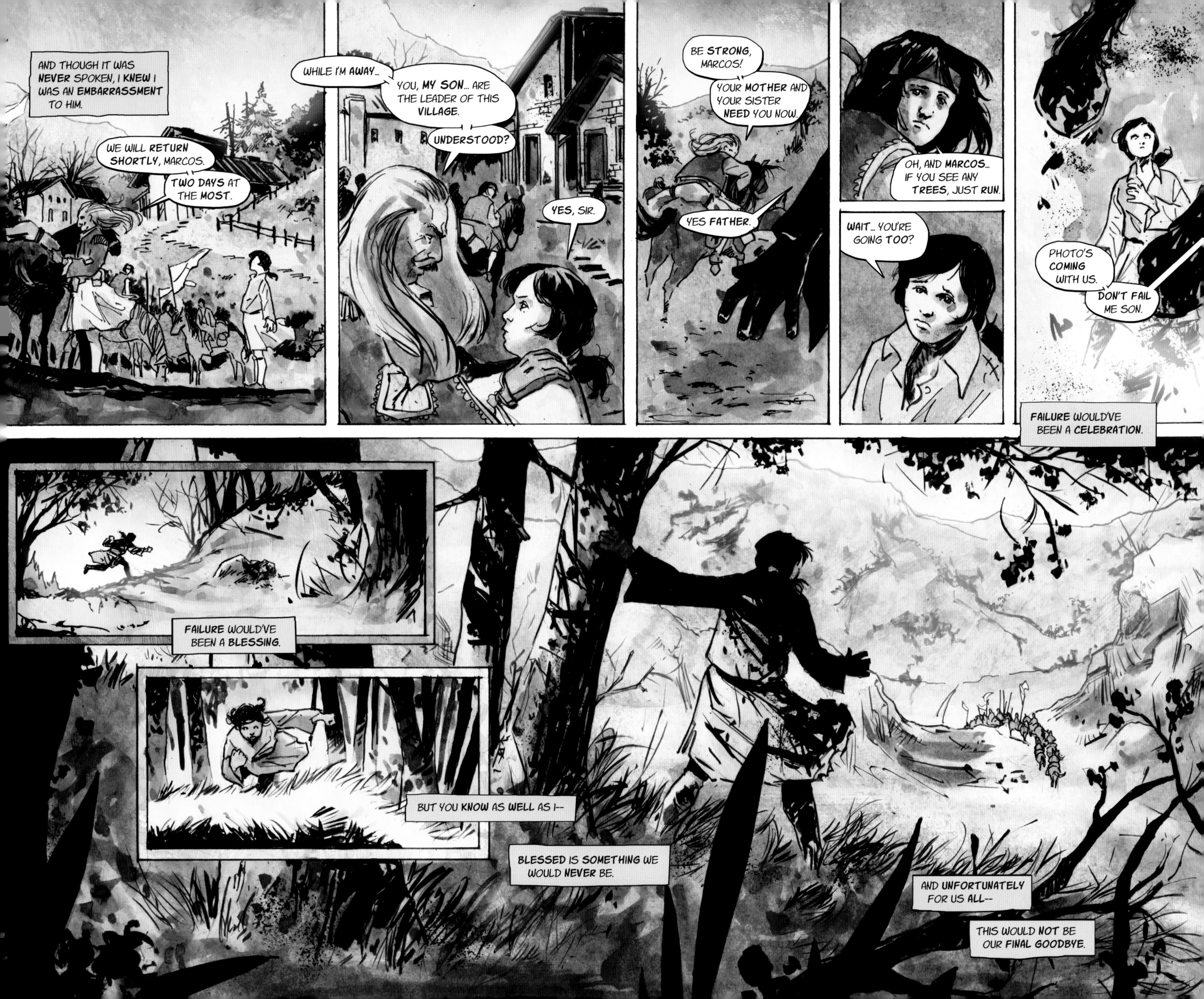
AND THOUGH IT WAS NEVER SPOKEN, I KNEW I WAS AN EMBARRASSMENT TO HIM.
WE WILL RETURN SHORTLY, MARCOS.
TWO DAYS AT THE MOST.
WHILE I'M AWAY...
YOU, MY SON... ARE THE LEADER OF THIS VILLAGE.
UNDERSTOOD?
YES, SIR.
BE STRONG, MARCOS!
YOUR MOTHER AND YOUR SISTER NEED YOU NOW.
YES FATHER.
OH, AND MARCOS... IF YOU SEE ANY TREES, JUST RUN.
WAIT... YOU'RE GOING TOO?
PHOTO'S COMING WITH US.
DON'T FAIL ME SON.
FAILURE WOULD'VE BEEN A CELEBRATION.
FAILURE WOULD'VE BEEN A BLESSING.
BUT YOU KNOW AS WELL AS I--
BLESSED IS SOMETHING WE WOULD NEVER BE.
AND UNFORTUNATELY FOR US ALL--
THIS WOULD NOT BE OUR FINAL GOODBYE.

BOOK ONE ◇ *Chapter Two*

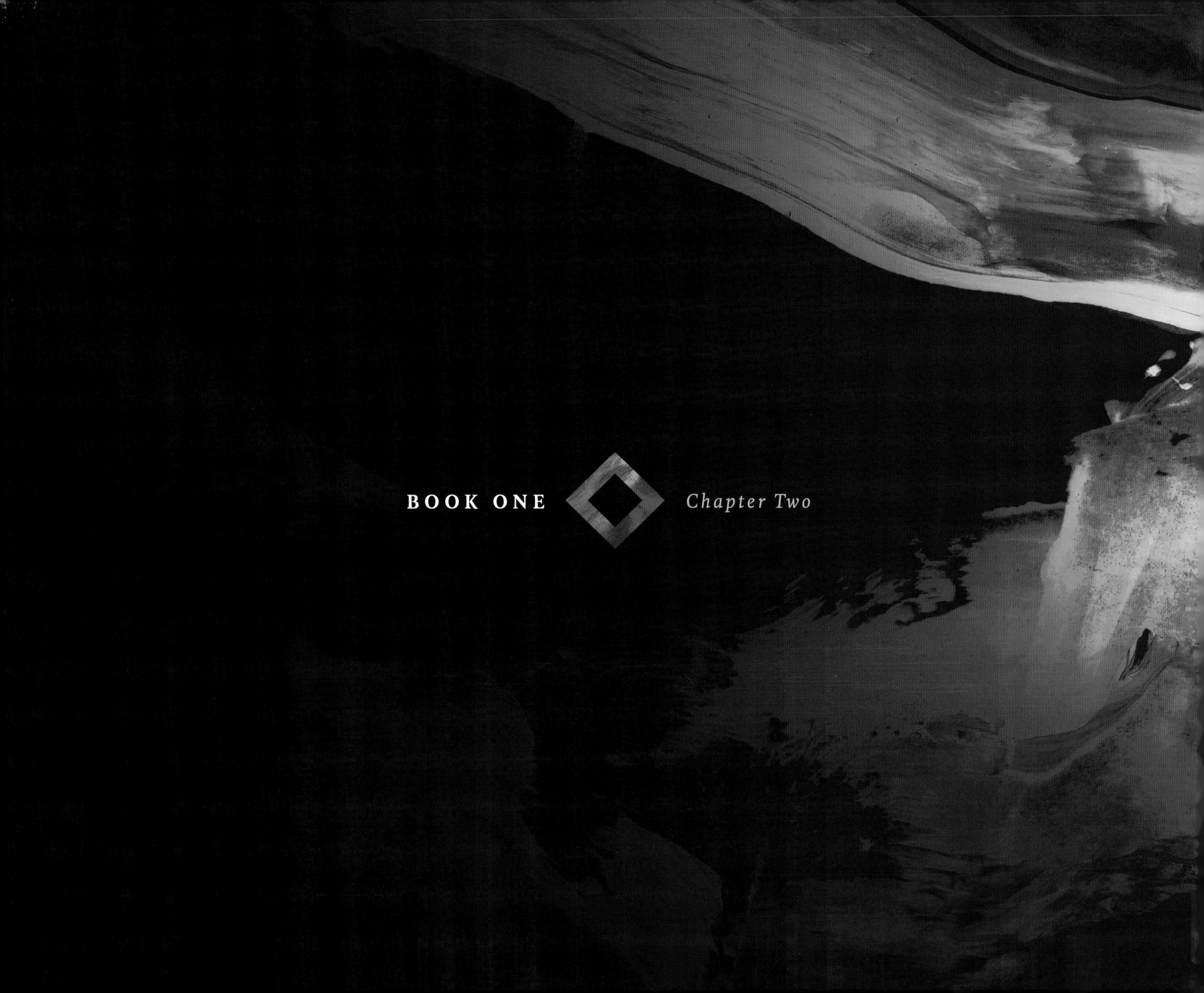

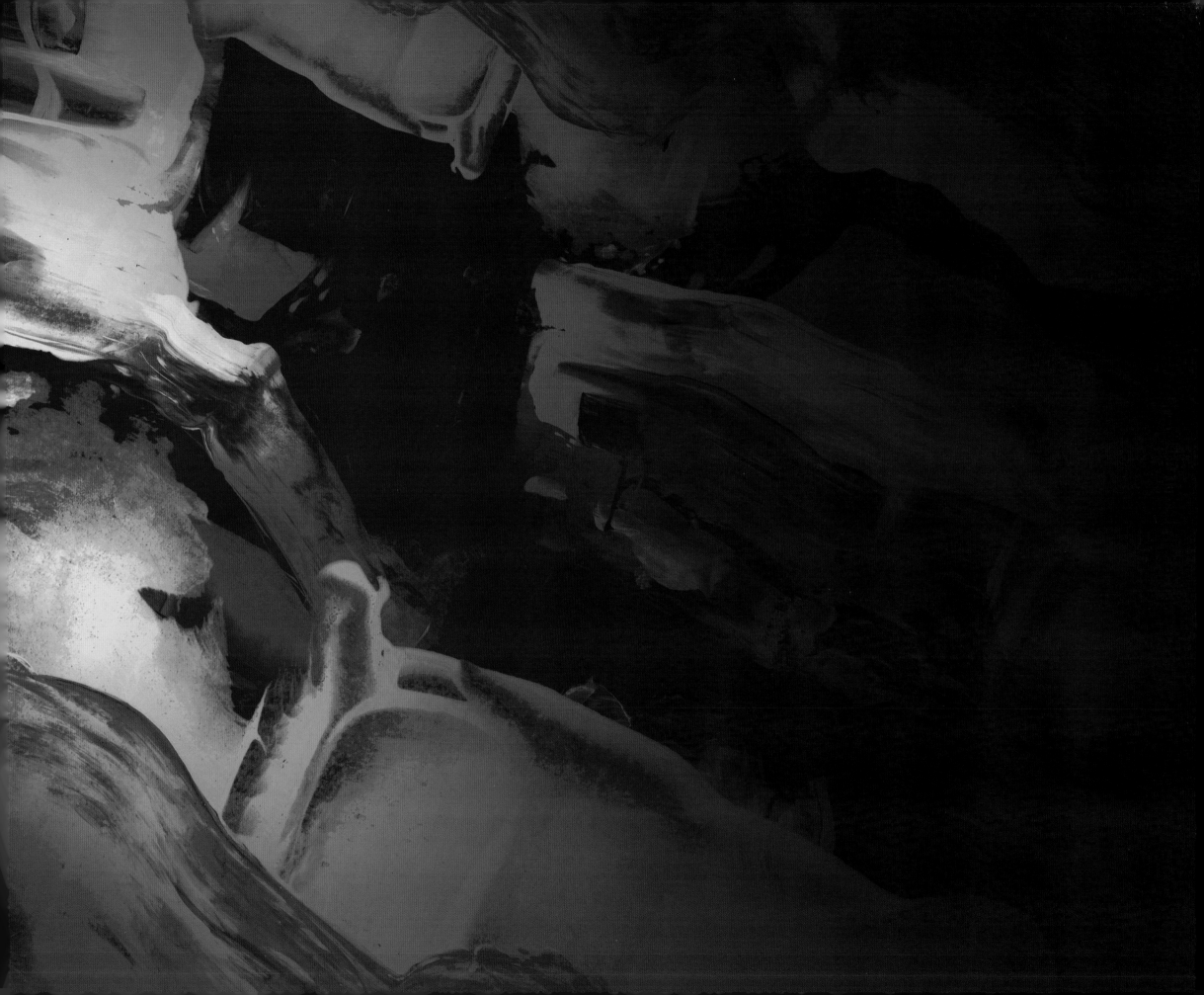

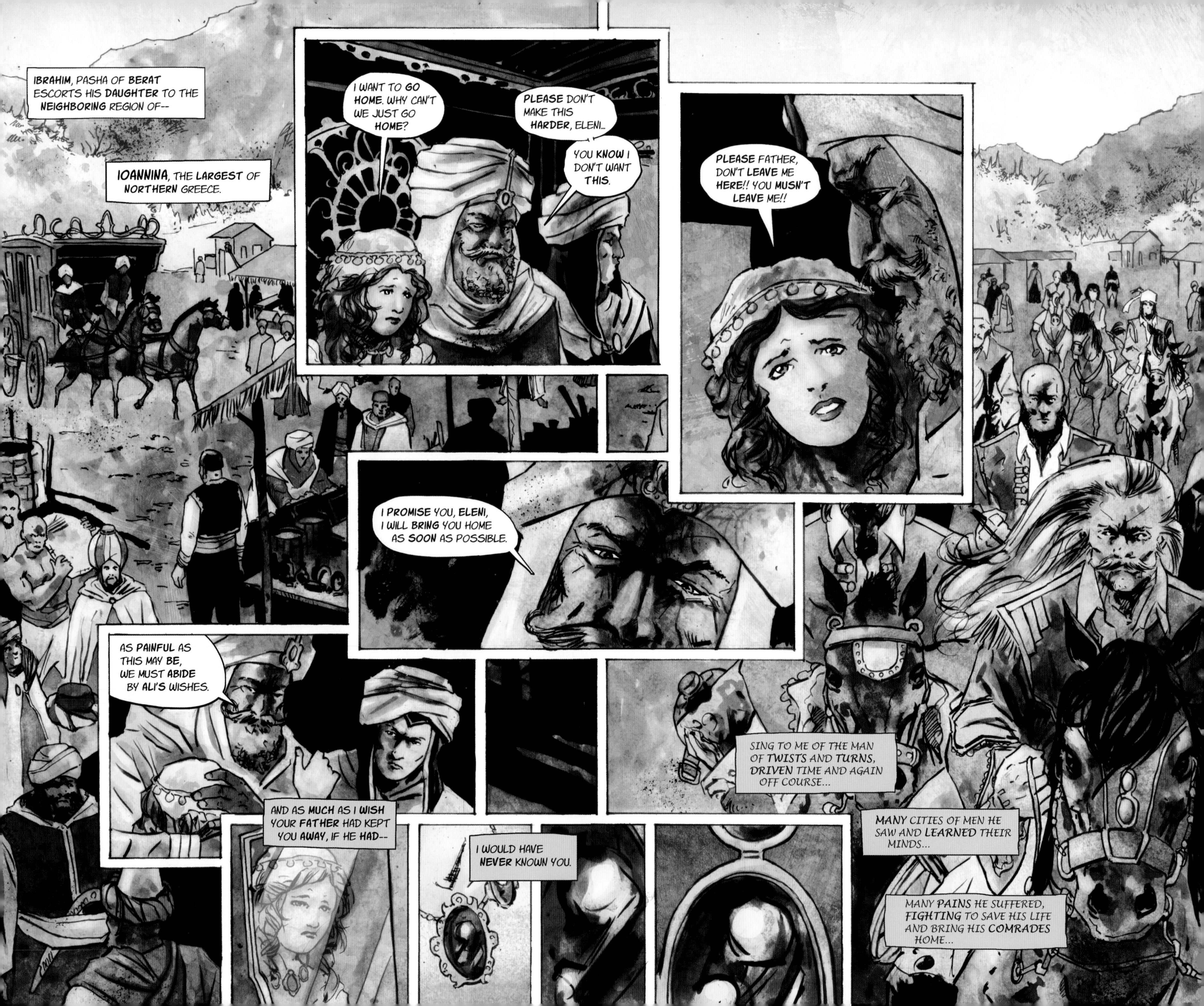
IBRAHIM, PASHA OF BERAT ESCORTS HIS DAUGHTER TO THE NEIGHBORING REGION OF--
IOANNINA, THE LARGEST OF NORTHERN GREECE.
I WANT TO GO HOME. WHY CAN'T WE JUST GO HOME?
PLEASE DON'T MAKE THIS HARDER, ELENI...
YOU KNOW I DON'T WANT THIS.
PLEASE FATHER, DON'T LEAVE ME HERE!! YOU MUSN'T LEAVE ME!!
I PROMISE YOU, ELENI, I WILL BRING YOU HOME AS SOON AS POSSIBLE.
AS PAINFUL AS THIS MAY BE, WE MUST ABIDE BY ALI'S WISHES.
AND AS MUCH AS I WISH YOUR FATHER HAD KEPT YOU AWAY, IF HE HAD--
I WOULD HAVE NEVER KNOWN YOU.
SING TO ME OF THE MAN OF TWISTS AND TURNS, DRIVEN TIME AND AGAIN OFF COURSE...
MANY CITIES OF MEN HE SAW AND LEARNED THEIR MINDS...
MANY PAINS HE SUFFERED, FIGHTING TO SAVE HIS LIFE AND BRING HIS COMRADES HOME...

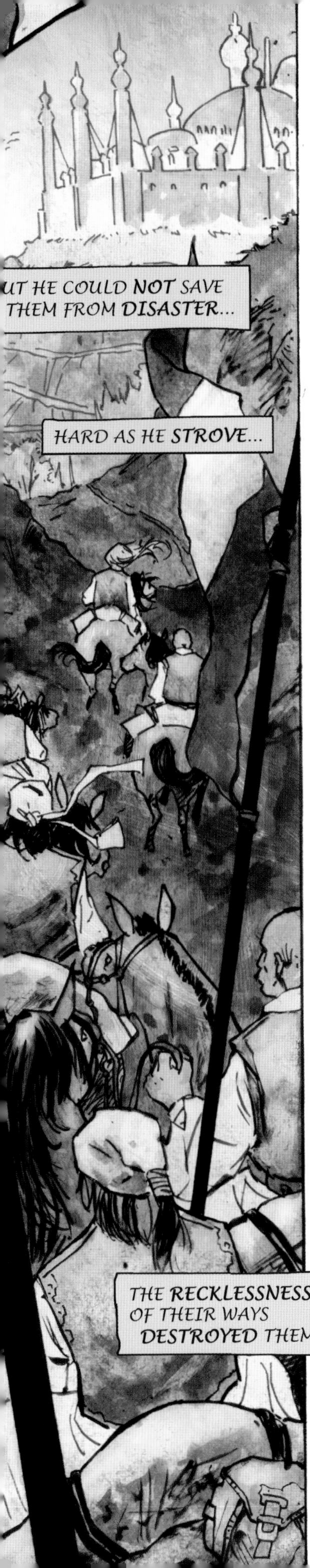
UT HE COULD NOT SAVE THEM FROM DISASTER...
HARD AS HE STROVE...
THE RECKLESSNESS OF THEIR WAYS DESTROYED THEM ALL.

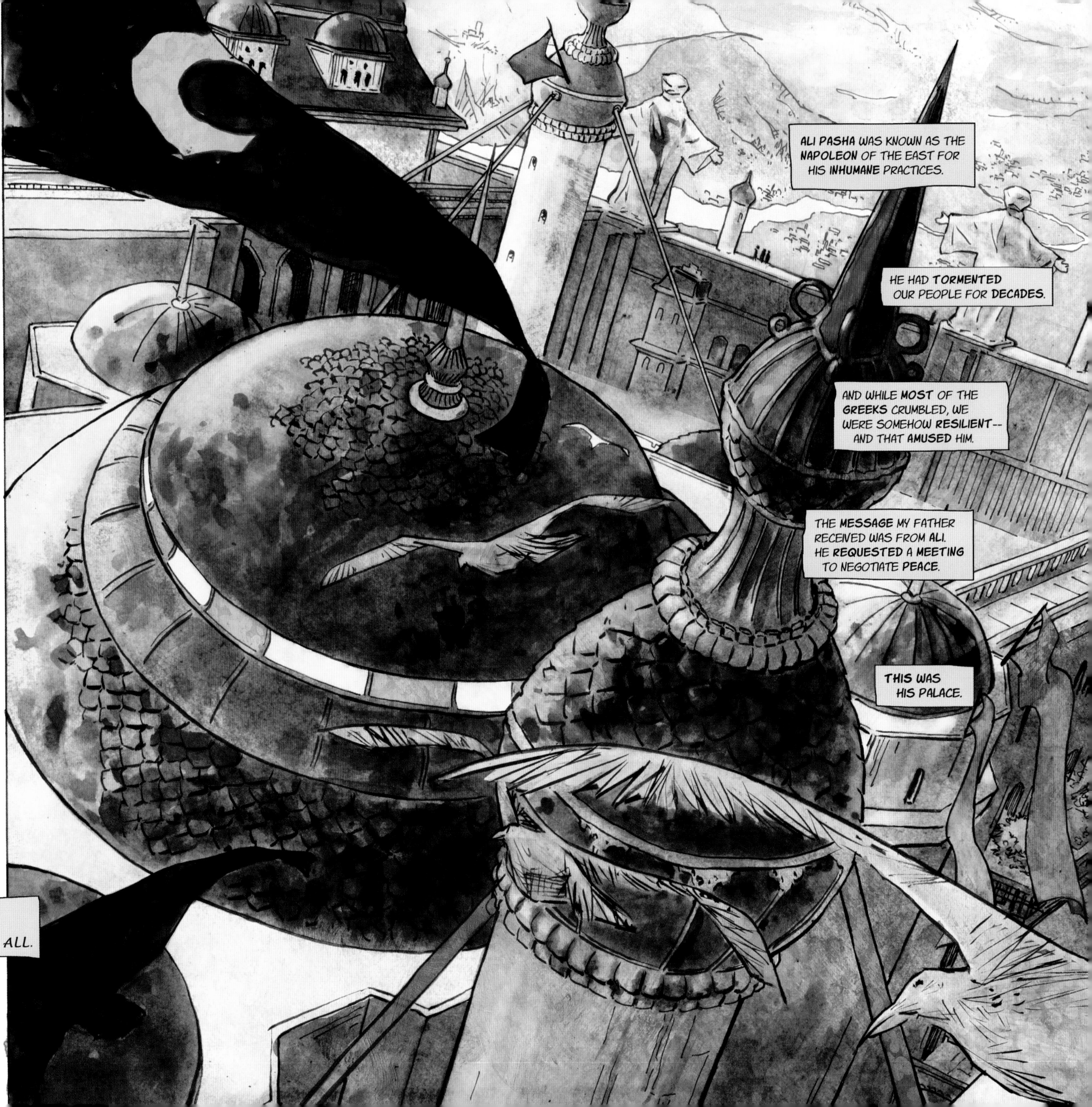
ALI PASHA WAS KNOWN AS THE NAPOLEON OF THE EAST FOR HIS INHUMANE PRACTICES.
HE HAD TORMENTED OUR PEOPLE FOR DECADES.
AND WHILE MOST OF THE GREEKS CRUMBLED, WE WERE SOMEHOW RESILIENT-- AND THAT AMUSED HIM.
THE MESSAGE MY FATHER RECEIVED WAS FROM ALI. HE REQUESTED A MEETING TO NEGOTIATE PEACE.
THIS WAS HIS PALACE.

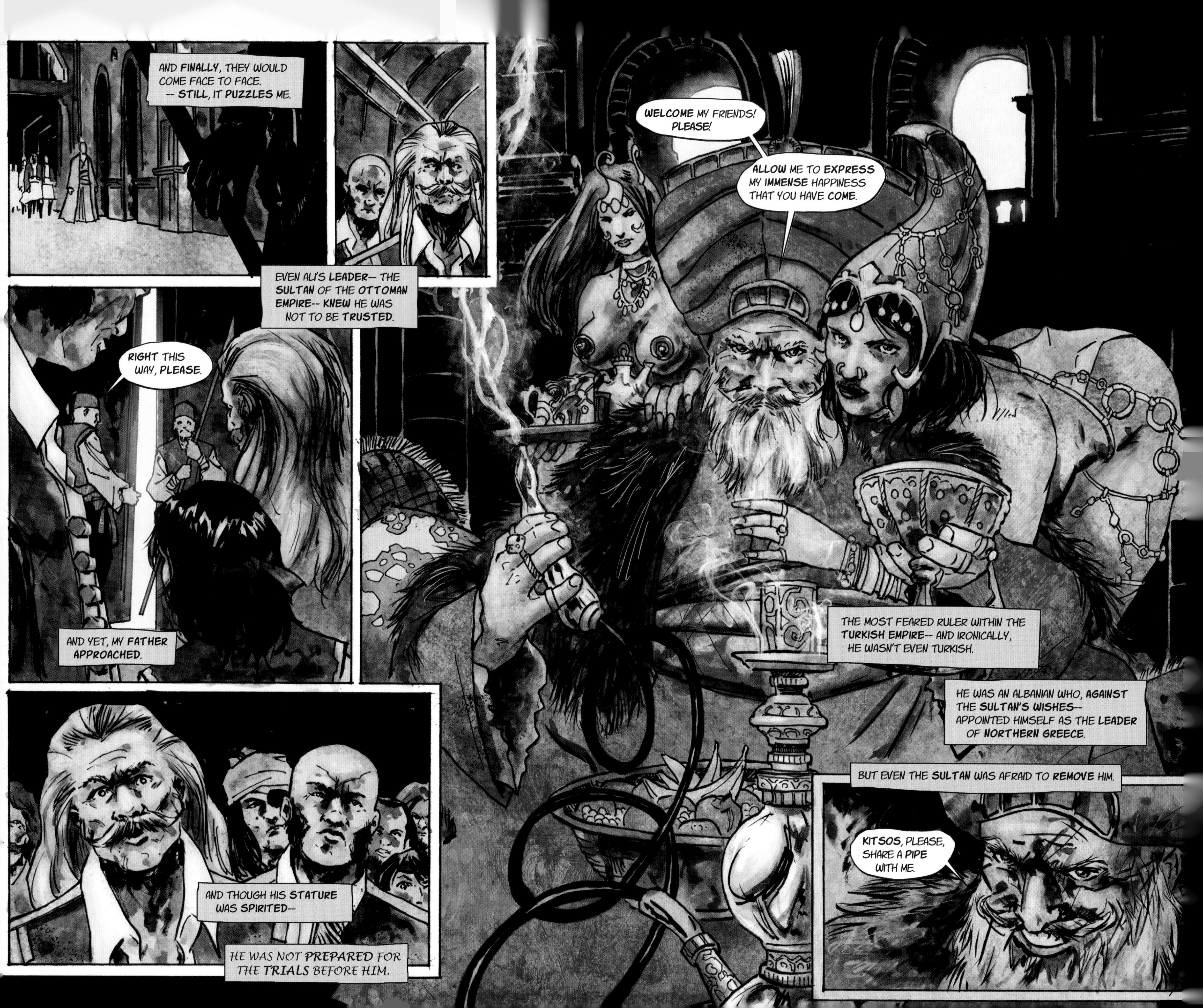

AND FINALLY, THEY WOULD COME FACE TO FACE. -- STILL, IT PUZZLES ME.
EVEN ALI'S LEADER-- THE SULTAN OF THE OTTOMAN EMPIRE-- KNEW HE WAS NOT TO BE TRUSTED.
RIGHT THIS WAY, PLEASE.
AND YET, MY FATHER APPROACHED.
AND THOUGH HIS STATURE WAS SPIRITED--
HE WAS NOT PREPARED FOR THE TRIALS BEFORE HIM.
WELCOME MY FRIENDS! PLEASE!
ALLOW ME TO EXPRESS MY IMMENSE HAPPINESS THAT YOU HAVE COME.
THE MOST FEARED RULER WITHIN THE TURKISH EMPIRE-- AND IRONICALLY, HE WASN'T EVEN TURKISH.
HE WAS AN ALBANIAN WHO, AGAINST THE SULTAN'S WISHES-- APPOINTED HIMSELF AS THE LEADER OF NORTHERN GREECE.
BUT EVEN THE SULTAN WAS AFRAID TO REMOVE HIM.
KITSOS, PLEASE, SHARE A PIPE WITH ME.

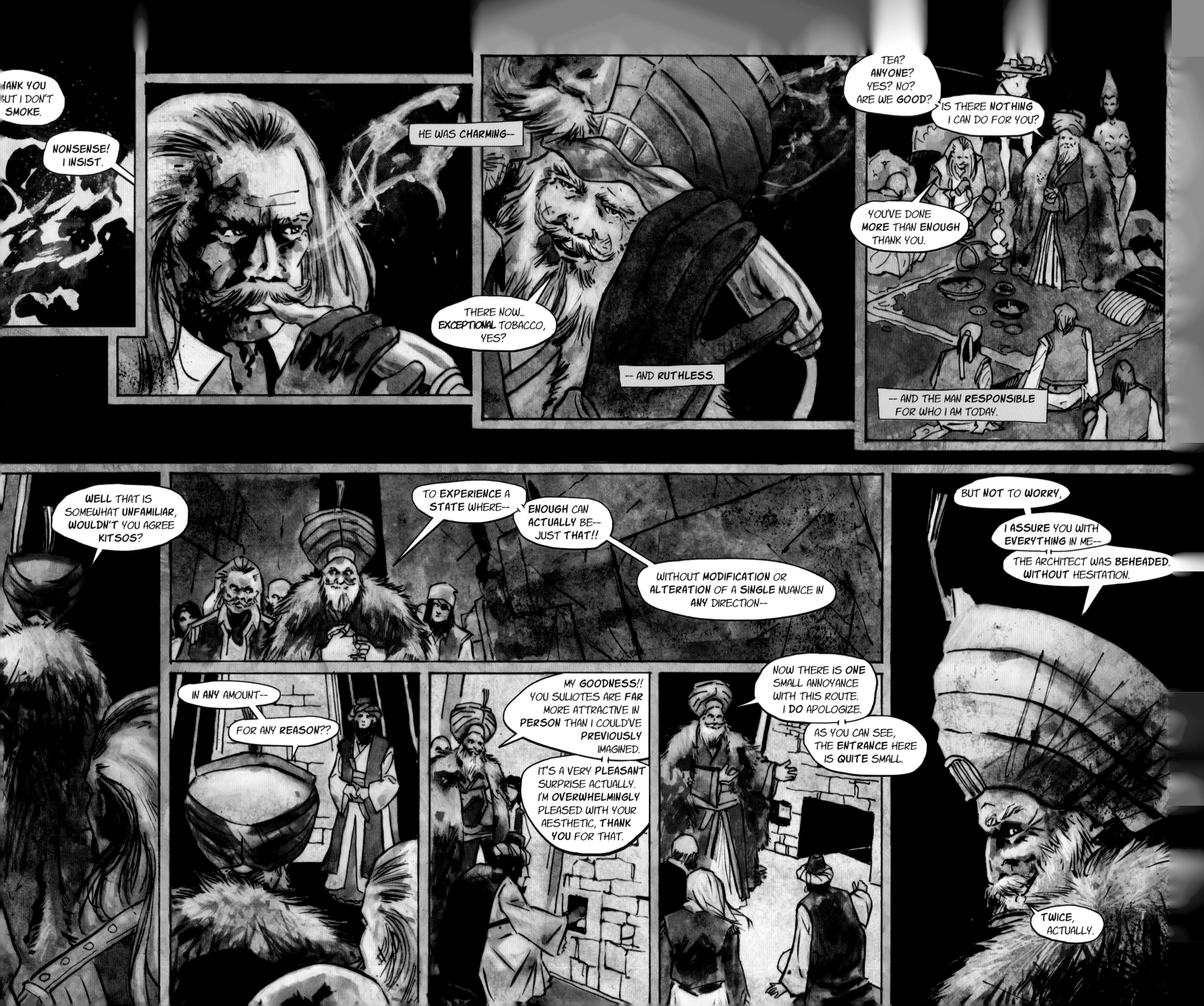

HANK YOU BUT I DON'T SMOKE.
NONSENSE! I INSIST.
HE WAS CHARMING--
THERE NOW... EXCEPTIONAL TOBACCO, YES?
-- AND RUTHLESS.
TEA? ANYONE? YES? NO? ARE WE GOOD?
IS THERE NOTHING I CAN DO FOR YOU?
YOU'VE DONE MORE THAN ENOUGH THANK YOU.
-- AND THE MAN RESPONSIBLE FOR WHO I AM TODAY.
WELL THAT IS SOMEWHAT UNFAMILIAR, WOULDN'T YOU AGREE KITSOS?
TO EXPERIENCE A STATE WHERE--
ENOUGH CAN ACTUALLY BE-- JUST THAT!!
WITHOUT MODIFICATION OR ALTERATION OF A SINGLE NUANCE IN ANY DIRECTION--
IN ANY AMOUNT--
FOR ANY REASON??
MY GOODNESS!! YOU SULIOTES ARE FAR MORE ATTRACTIVE IN PERSON THAN I COULD'VE PREVIOUSLY IMAGINED.
IT'S A VERY PLEASANT SURPRISE ACTUALLY. I'M OVERWHELMINGLY PLEASED WITH YOUR AESTHETIC, THANK YOU FOR THAT.
NOW THERE IS ONE SMALL ANNOYANCE WITH THIS ROUTE. I DO APOLOGIZE.
AS YOU CAN SEE, THE ENTRANCE HERE IS QUITE SMALL.
BUT NOT TO WORRY,
I ASSURE YOU WITH EVERYTHING IN ME--
THE ARCHITECT WAS BEHEADED. WITHOUT HESITATION.
TWICE, ACTUALLY.

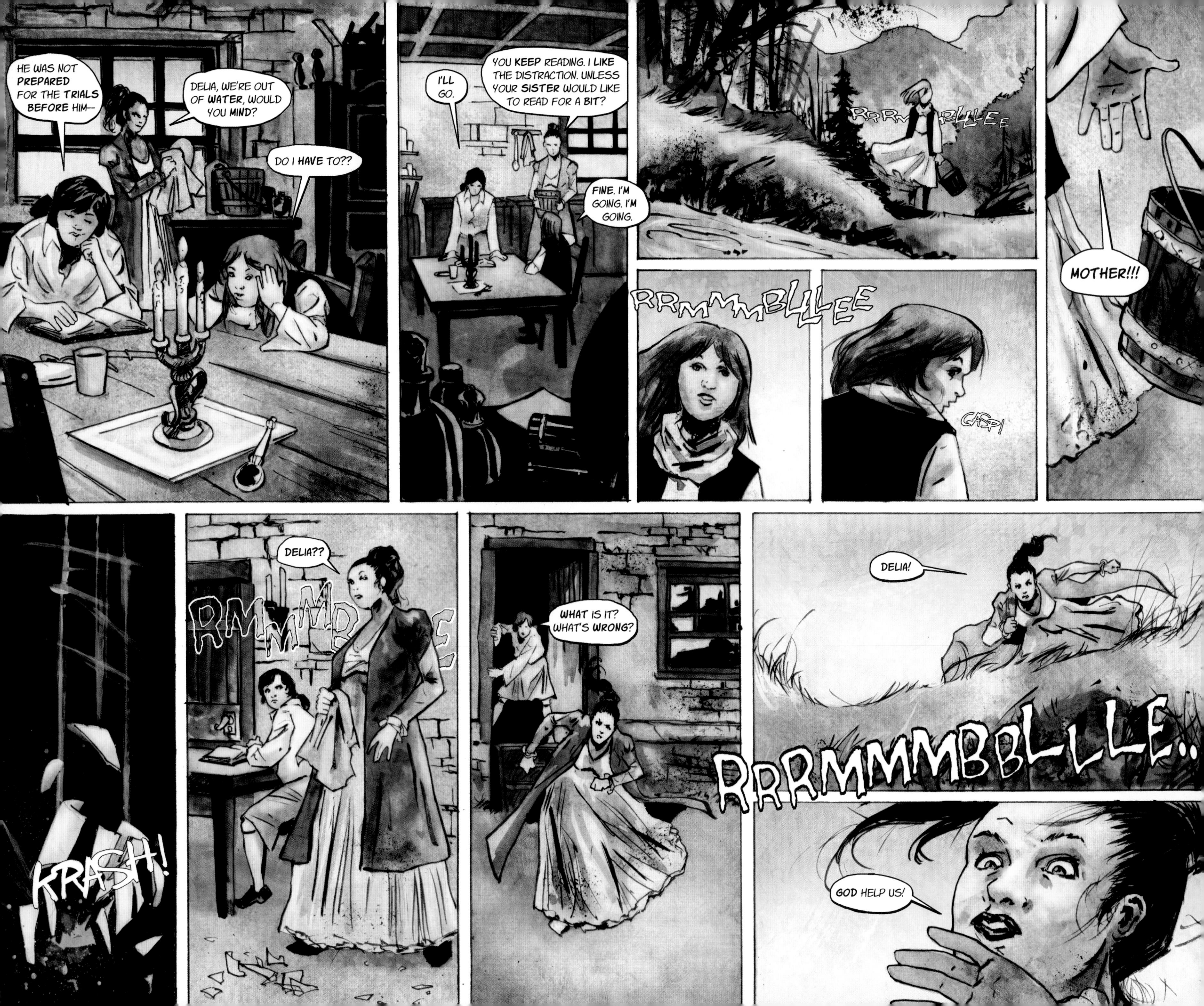

HE WAS NOT PREPARED FOR THE TRIALS BEFORE HIM--
DELIA, WE'RE OUT OF WATER, WOULD YOU MIND?
DO I HAVE TO??
I'LL GO.
YOU KEEP READING. I LIKE THE DISTRACTION. UNLESS YOUR SISTER WOULD LIKE TO READ FOR A BIT?
FINE. I'M GOING. I'M GOING.
RRRMMMBLLEE
RRMMMMBLLLEE
GASP!
MOTHER!!!
KRASH!
DELIA??
RMMMMBLLE
WHAT IS IT? WHAT'S WRONG?
DELIA!
RRRMMMMBBLLLE..
GOD HELP US!

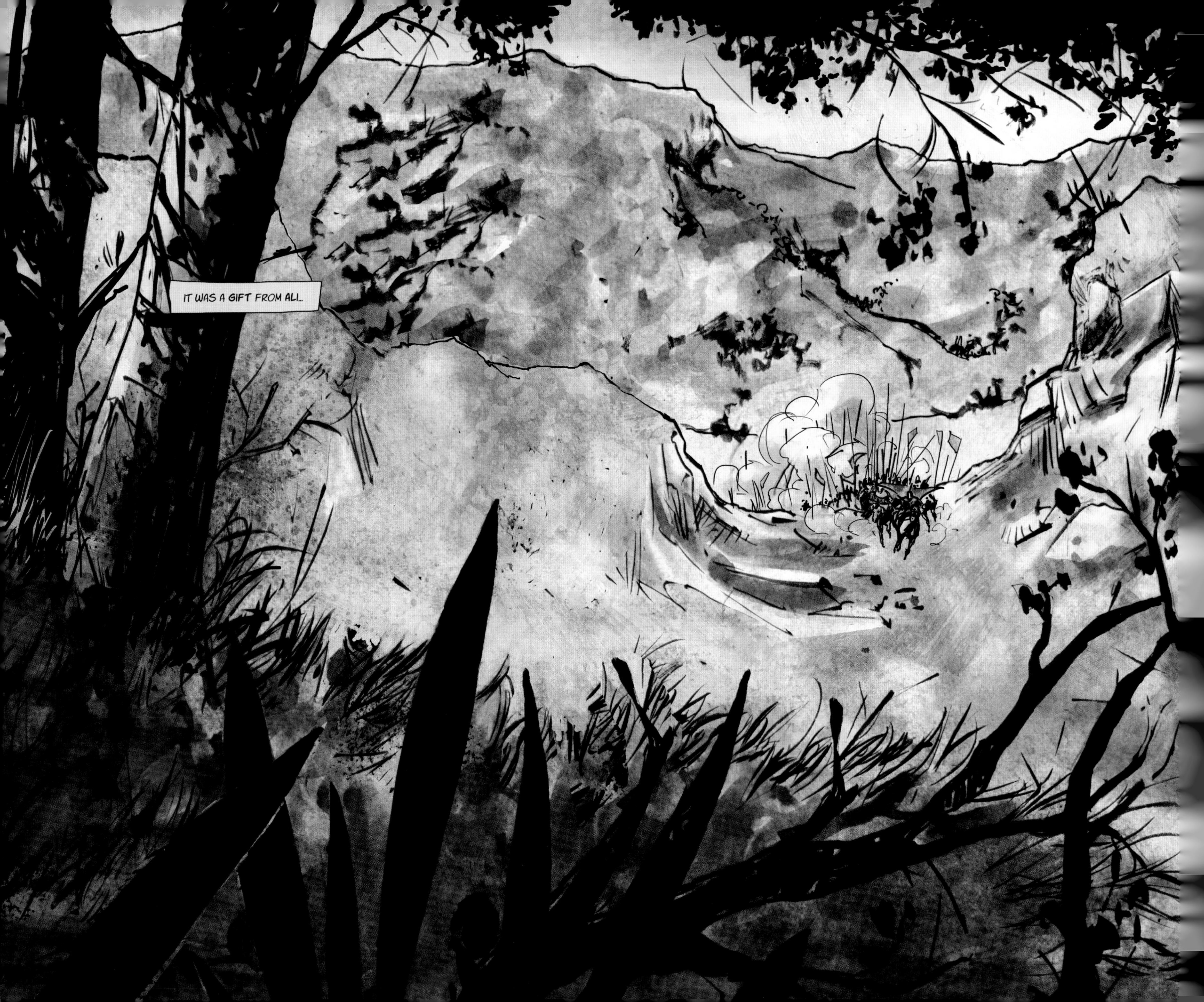
IT WAS A GIFT FROM ALI...

A SMALL SYMBOL OF MY GRATITUDE.

IF NOT FOR YOU, MY PERSONAL EVOLUTION WOULD HAVE REMAINED THAT OF A DULL AND MISERLY PASHA...

AND BECAUSE OF YOU... THAT IS ABSOLUTELY NOT THE CASE.

COME, I MUST INTRODUCE YOU.

IBRAHIM! SO WONDERFUL TO SEE YOU.

I'D LIKE YOU TO MEET THE EVER-SO-DISTINGUISHED KITSOS BOTSARIS THAT WE'VE ADMIRED FROM AFAR FOR SO MANY YEARS.

AND KITSOS, IT'S MY PLEASURE TO INTRODUCE YOU TO IBRAHIM OF BERAT, THE CELEBRATED LEGEND AND FATHER OF MY SOON TO BE, DANGEROUSLY ADORABLE DAUGHTER-IN-LAW--

THE GRACEFUL ELENI- WHO WILL BE JOINING HANDS WITH MY FINE YOUNG SON, MUHKTAR...

WHO IS REGRETTABLY UNABLE TO JOIN US THIS EVENING.

PLEASURE TO MEET YOU, KITSOS. I'VE HEARD MANY RESPECTABLE THINGS.

AND HIS MASCULINE YOUNG SON, ISMAEL.

PLEASURE.

IT WAS IBRAHIM WHO PERSUADED ME THAT THE MOST EFFECTIVE ROUTE OF OVERCOMING OUR SORDID PAST WAS UNIFICATION.

AND HE WAS CORRECT.

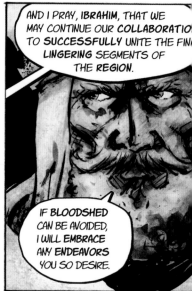

AND I PRAY, IBRAHIM, THAT WE MAY CONTINUE OUR COLLABORATION TO SUCCESSFULLY UNITE THE FINAL LINGERING SEGMENTS OF THE REGION.

IF BLOODSHED CAN BE AVOIDED, I WILL EMBRACE ANY ENDEAVORS YOU SO DESIRE.

THE PERFECT WORDS FROM THE PERFECT TONGUE.

LET ALL ENDEAVORS FROM HERE FORWARD BE THOSE OF PEACE. IN THE PUREST SENSE OF THE WORD.

AT LEAST THOSE WITH MY NAME. ATTACHED.

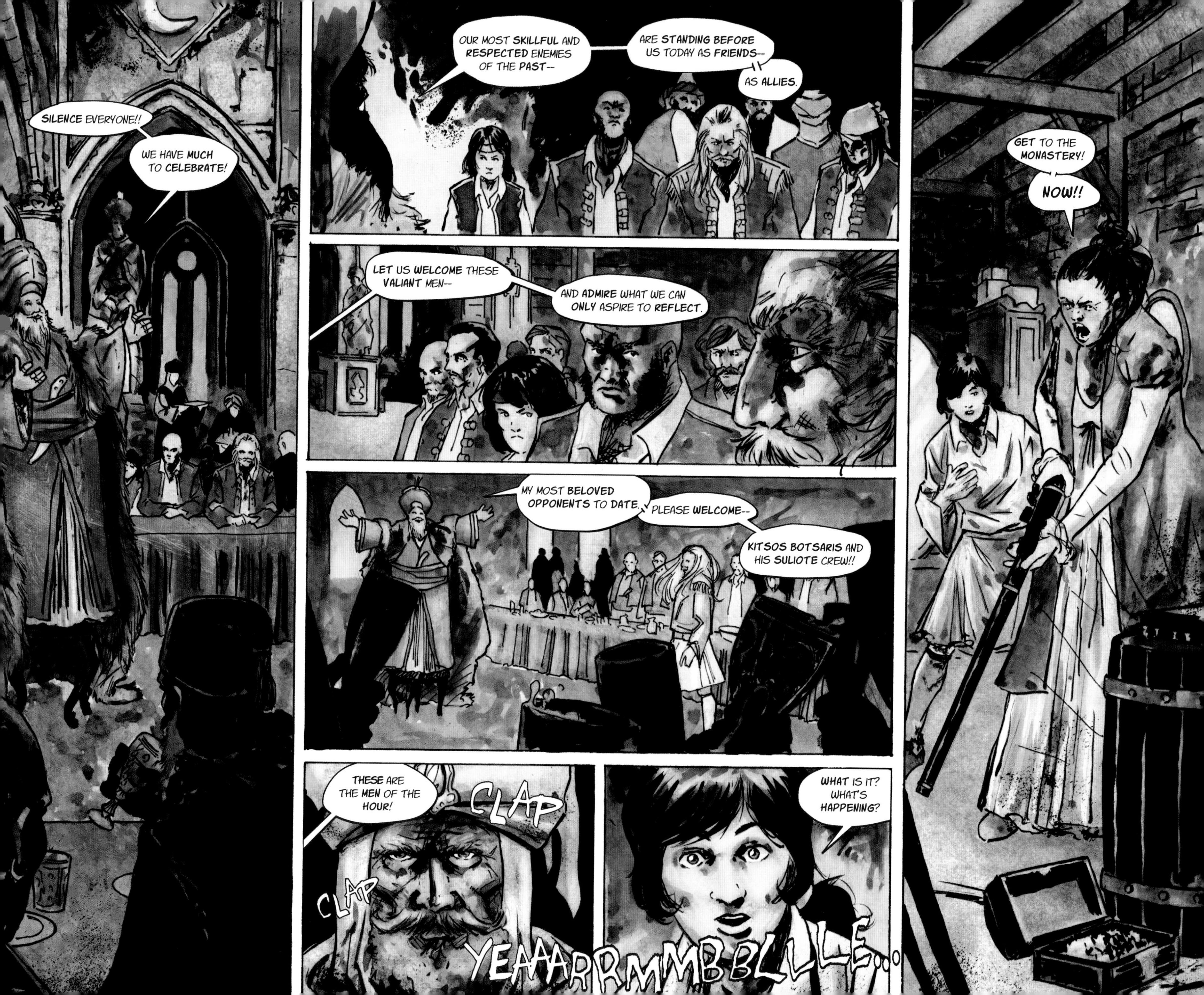
SILENCE EVERYONE!!
WE HAVE MUCH TO CELEBRATE!
OUR MOST SKILLFUL AND RESPECTED ENEMIES OF THE PAST--
ARE STANDING BEFORE US TODAY AS FRIENDS--
AS ALLIES.
LET US WELCOME THESE VALIANT MEN--
AND ADMIRE WHAT WE CAN ONLY ASPIRE TO REFLECT.
MY MOST BELOVED OPPONENTS TO DATE.
PLEASE WELCOME--
KITSOS BOTSARIS AND HIS SULIOTE CREW!!
THESE ARE THE MEN OF THE HOUR!
CLAP
CLAP
WHAT IS IT? WHAT'S HAPPENING?
YEAAARRMMBBLLLE...
GET TO THE MONASTERY!
NOW!!

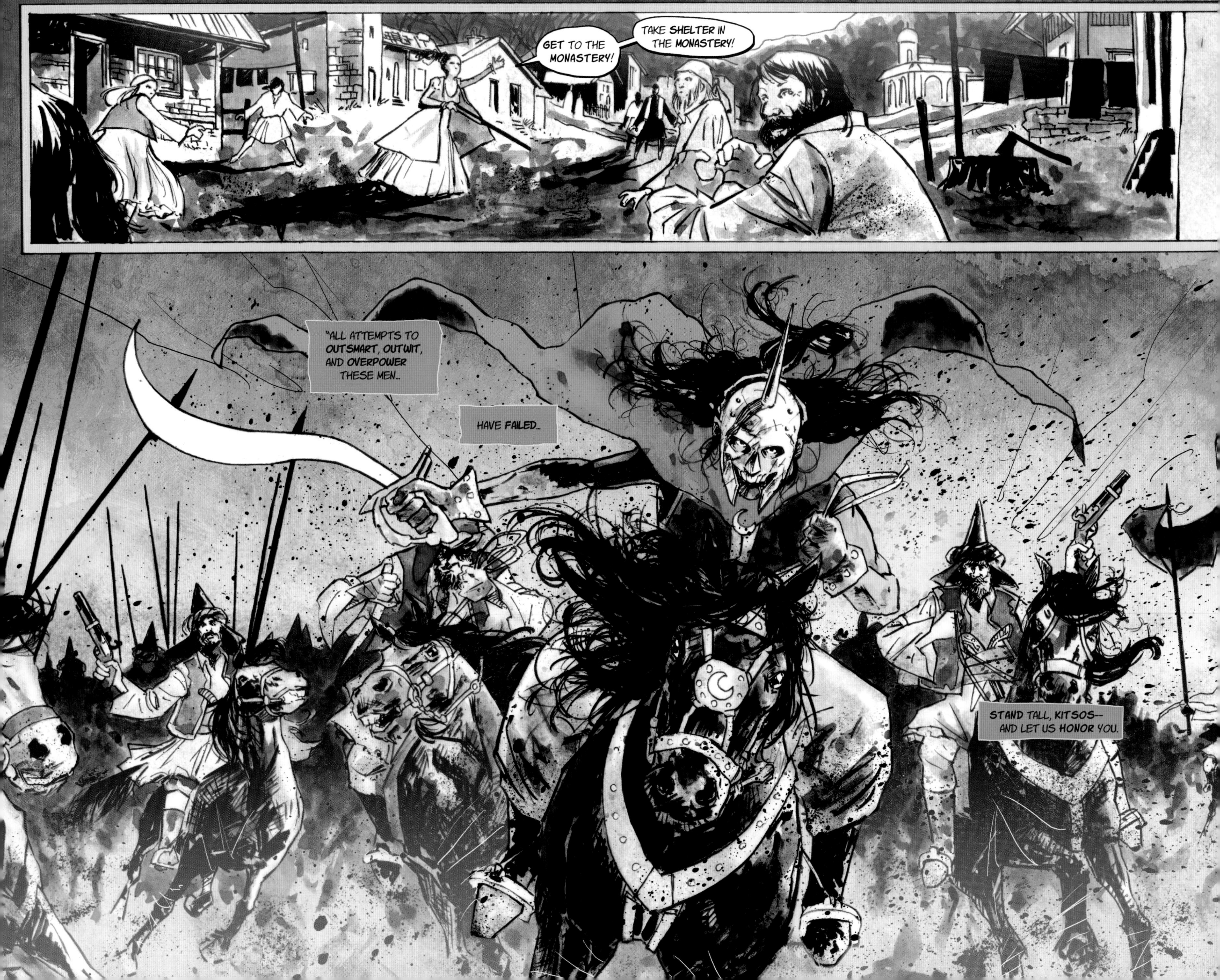
GET TO THE MONASTERY!
TAKE SHELTER IN THE MONASTERY!
"ALL ATTEMPTS TO OUTSMART, OUTWIT, AND OVERPOWER THESE MEN...
HAVE FAILED...
STAND TALL, KITSOS— AND LET US HONOR YOU.

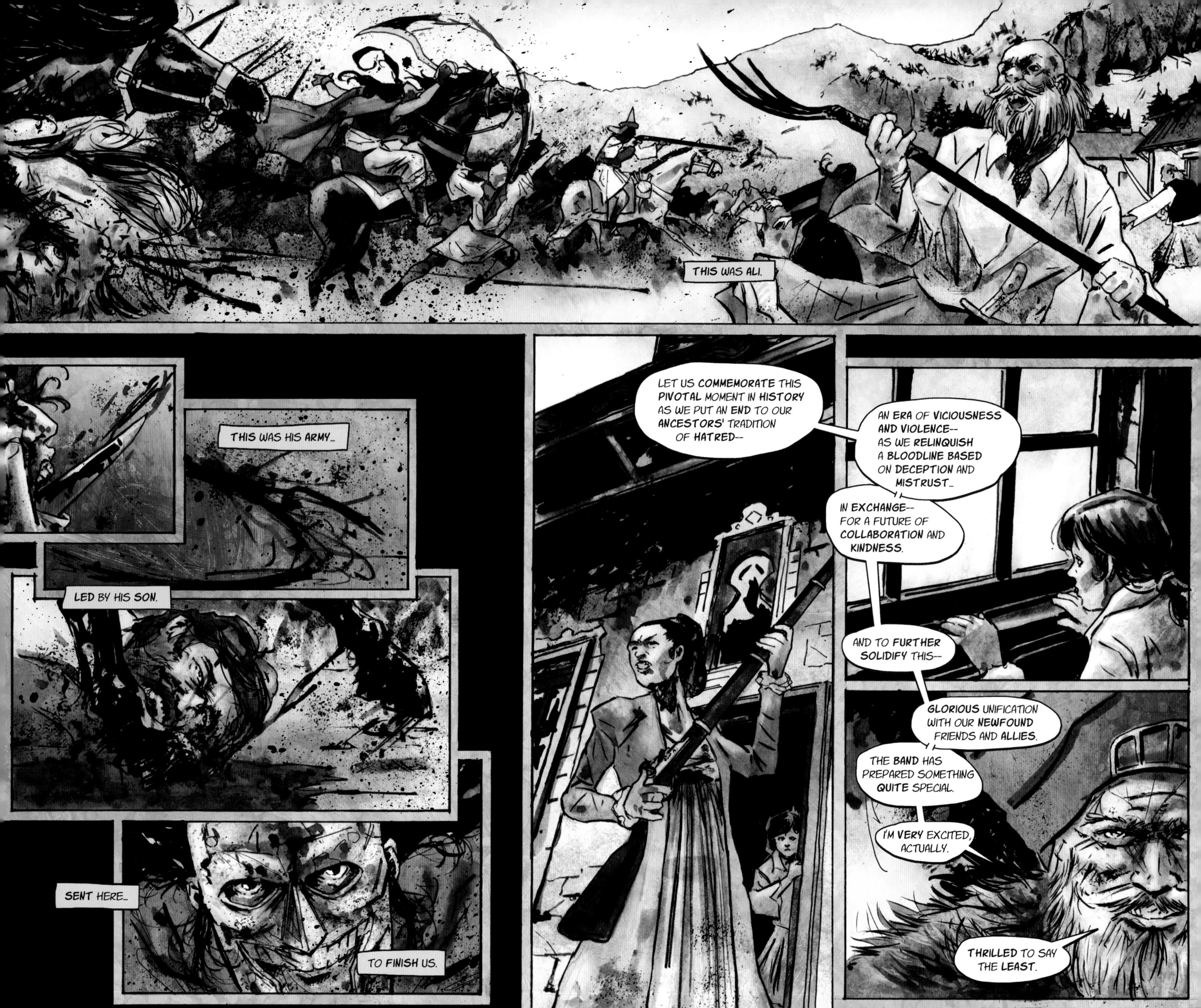
THIS WAS ALI.
THIS WAS HIS ARMY...
LED BY HIS SON.
SENT HERE...
TO FINISH US.
LET US COMMEMORATE THIS PIVOTAL MOMENT IN HISTORY AS WE PUT AN END TO OUR ANCESTORS' TRADITION OF HATRED--
AN ERA OF VICIOUSNESS AND VIOLENCE-- AS WE RELINQUISH A BLOODLINE BASED ON DECEPTION AND MISTRUST...
IN EXCHANGE-- FOR A FUTURE OF COLLABORATION AND KINDNESS.
AND TO FURTHER SOLIDIFY THIS--
GLORIOUS UNIFICATION WITH OUR NEWFOUND FRIENDS AND ALLIES.
THE BAND HAS PREPARED SOMETHING QUITE SPECIAL.
I'M VERY EXCITED, ACTUALLY.
THRILLED TO SAY THE LEAST.

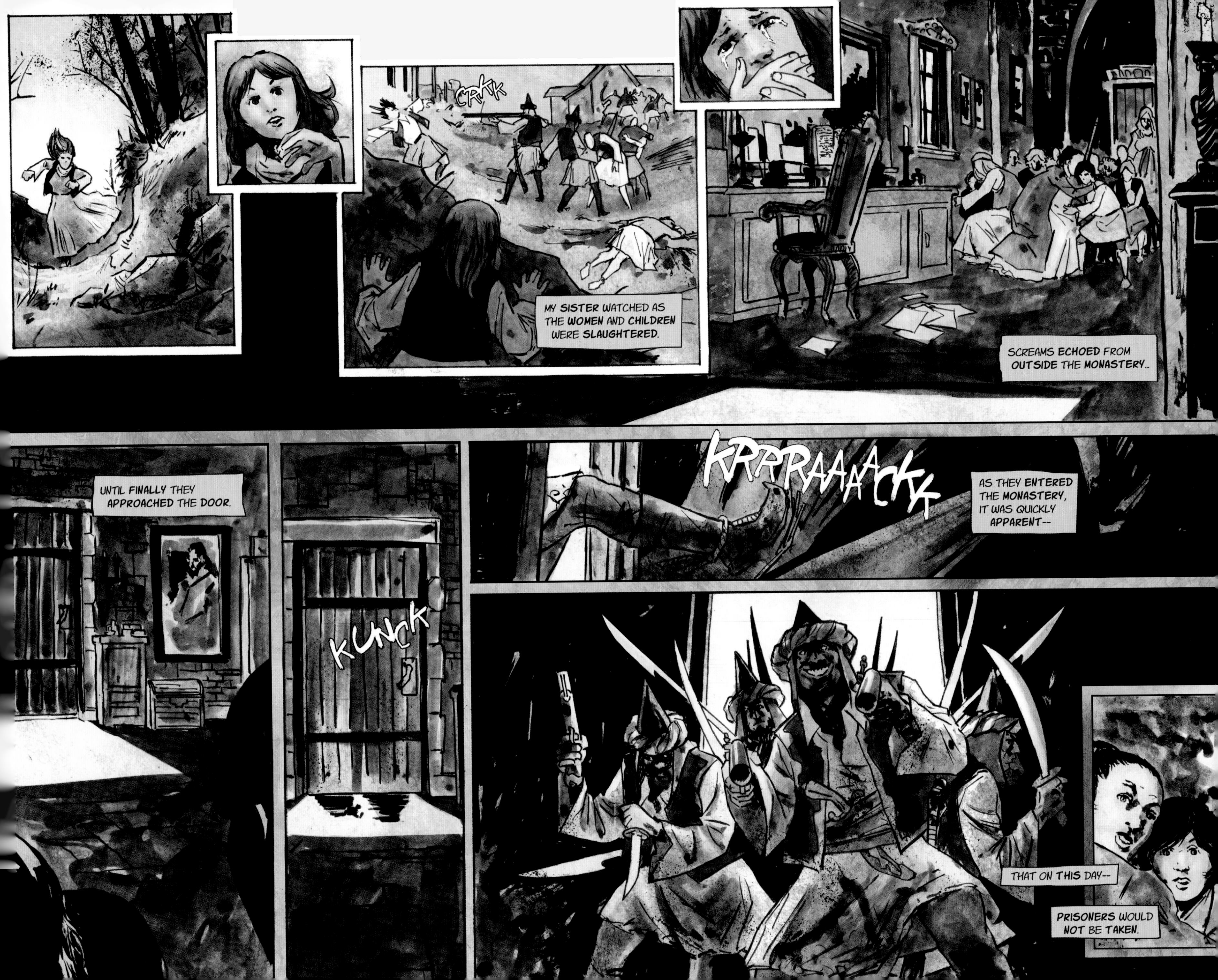
CRKK
MY SISTER WATCHED AS THE WOMEN AND CHILDREN WERE SLAUGHTERED.
SCREAMS ECHOED FROM OUTSIDE THE MONASTERY...
UNTIL FINALLY THEY APPROACHED THE DOOR.
KUNCK
KRRRAAAACKK
AS THEY ENTERED THE MONASTERY, IT WAS QUICKLY APPARENT--
THAT ON THIS DAY--
PRISONERS WOULD NOT BE TAKEN.

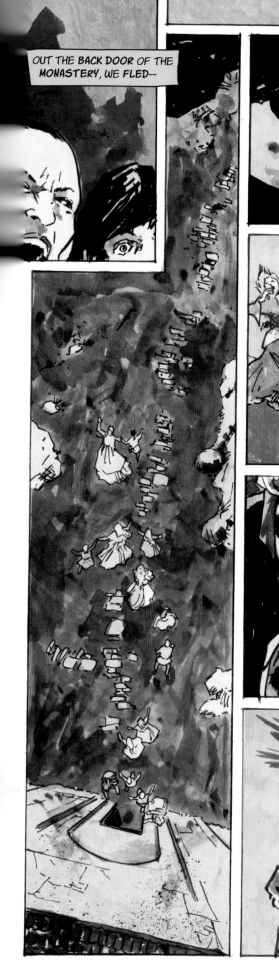

OUT THE BACK DOOR OF THE MONASTERY, WE FLED—

AND UP TO THE HIGHEST PEAK OF ZALONGO.

BUT THERE WAS NO ESCAPE.

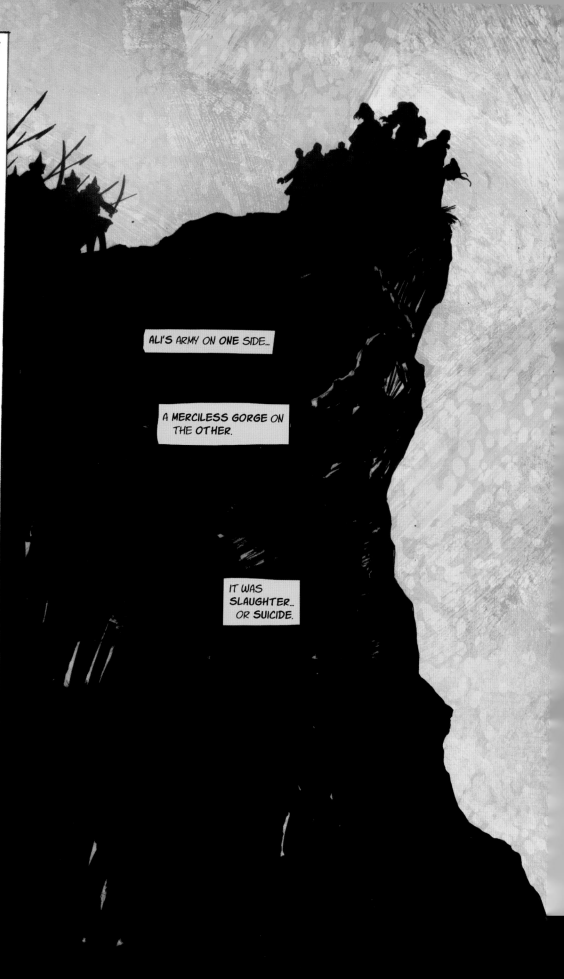

ALI'S ARMY ON ONE SIDE...

A MERCILESS GORGE ON THE OTHER.

IT WAS SLAUGHTER... OR SUICIDE.

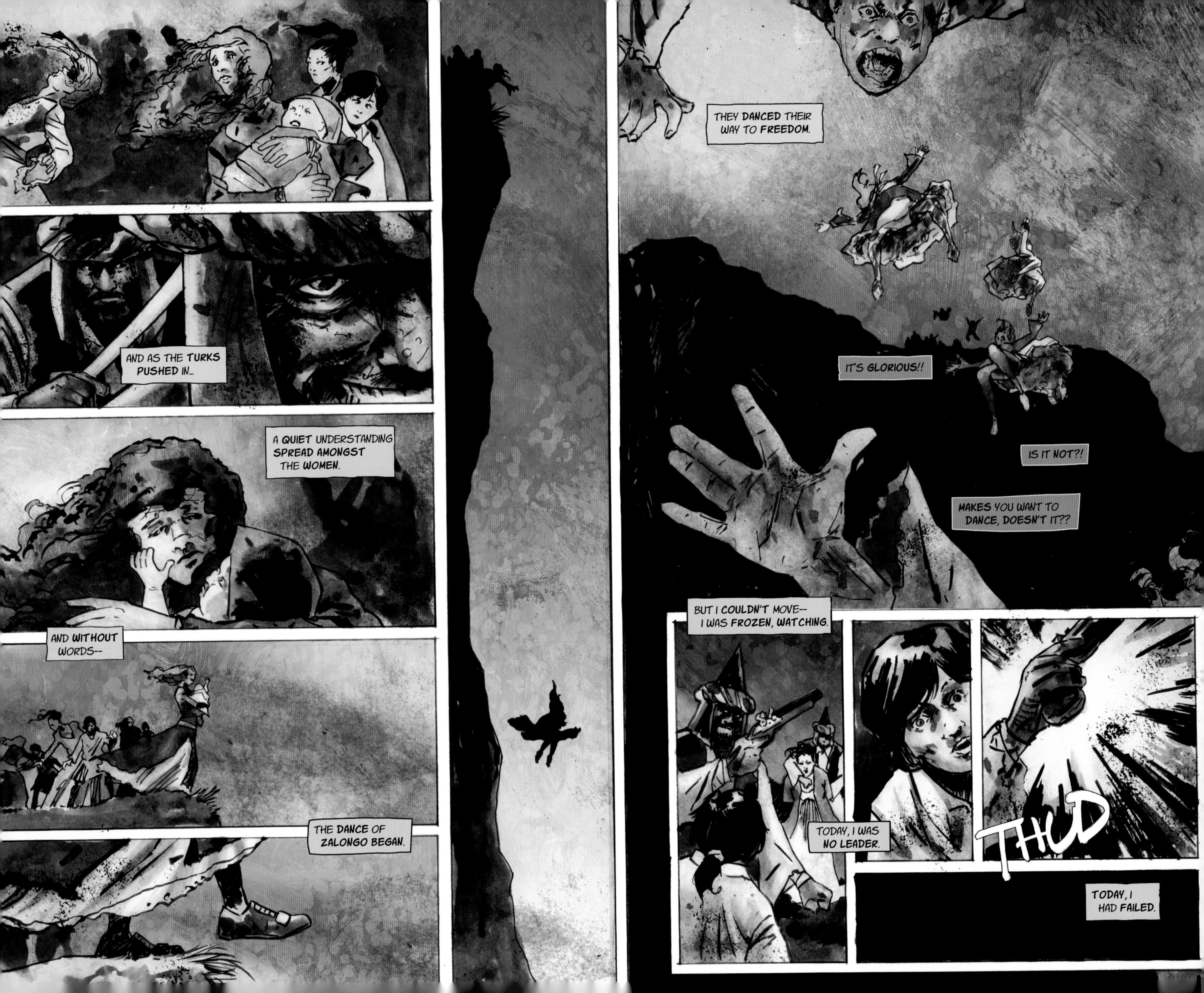
AND AS THE TURKS PUSHED IN...
A QUIET UNDERSTANDING SPREAD AMONGST THE WOMEN.
AND WITHOUT WORDS--
THE DANCE OF ZALONGO BEGAN.
THEY DANCED THEIR WAY TO FREEDOM.
IT'S GLORIOUS!!
IS IT NOT?!
MAKES YOU WANT TO DANCE, DOESN'T IT??
BUT I COULDN'T MOVE-- I WAS FROZEN, WATCHING.
TODAY, I WAS NO LEADER.
THUD
TODAY, I HAD FAILED.

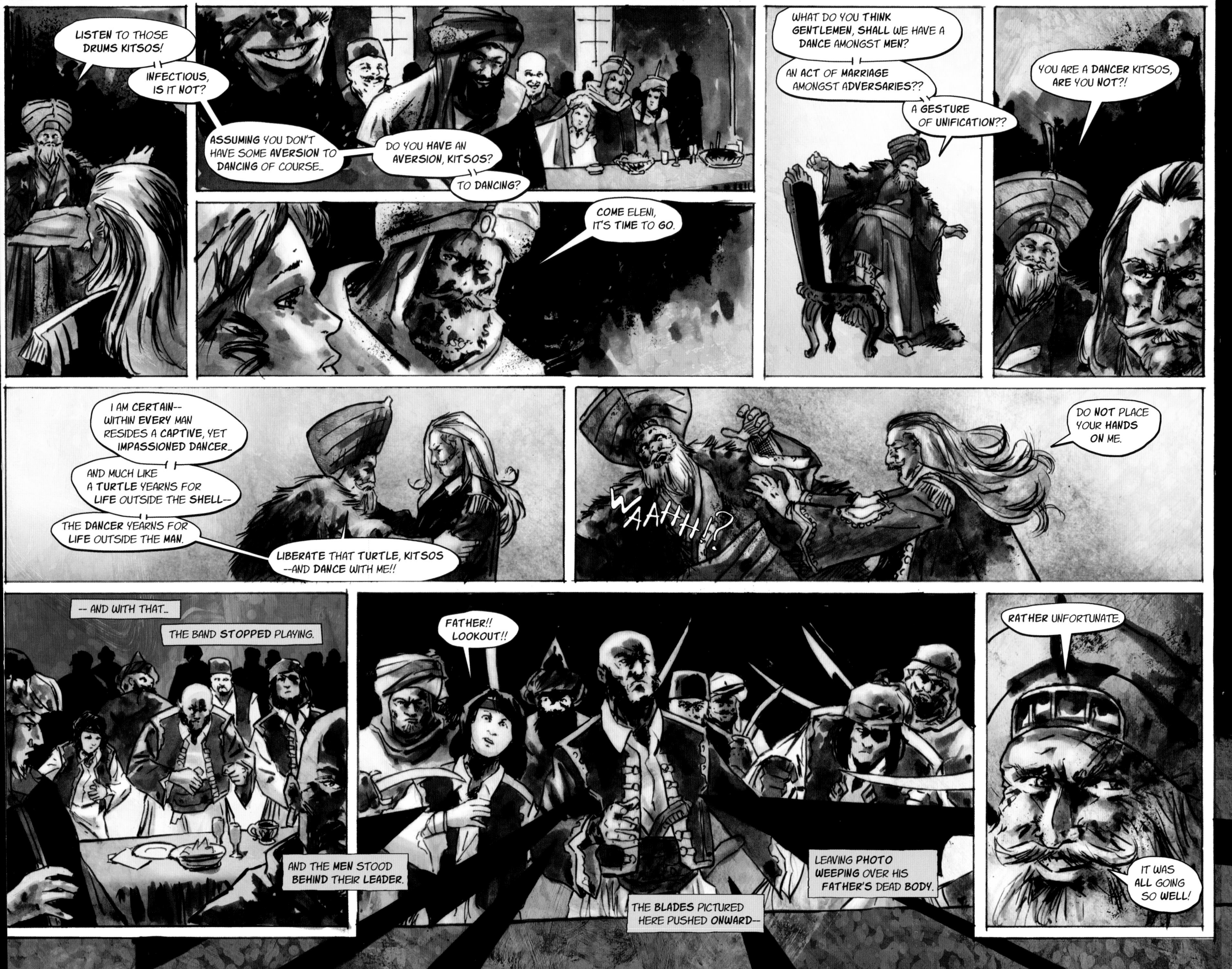

LISTEN TO THOSE DRUMS KITSOS!
INFECTIOUS, IS IT NOT?
ASSUMING YOU DON'T HAVE SOME AVERSION TO DANCING OF COURSE...
DO YOU HAVE AN AVERSION, KITSOS?
TO DANCING?
COME ELENI, IT'S TIME TO GO.
WHAT DO YOU THINK GENTLEMEN, SHALL WE HAVE A DANCE AMONGST MEN?
AN ACT OF MARRIAGE AMONGST ADVERSARIES??
A GESTURE OF UNIFICATION??
YOU ARE A DANCER KITSOS, ARE YOU NOT?!
I AM CERTAIN-- WITHIN EVERY MAN RESIDES A CAPTIVE, YET IMPASSIONED DANCER...
AND MUCH LIKE A TURTLE YEARNS FOR LIFE OUTSIDE THE SHELL--
THE DANCER YEARNS FOR LIFE OUTSIDE THE MAN.
LIBERATE THAT TURTLE, KITSOS --AND DANCE WITH ME!!
WAAHH!?
DO NOT PLACE YOUR HANDS ON ME.
-- AND WITH THAT...
THE BAND STOPPED PLAYING.
AND THE MEN STOOD BEHIND THEIR LEADER.
FATHER!! LOOKOUT!!
THE BLADES PICTURED HERE PUSHED ONWARD--
LEAVING PHOTO WEEPING OVER HIS FATHER'S DEAD BODY.
RATHER UNFORTUNATE.
IT WAS ALL GOING SO WELL!

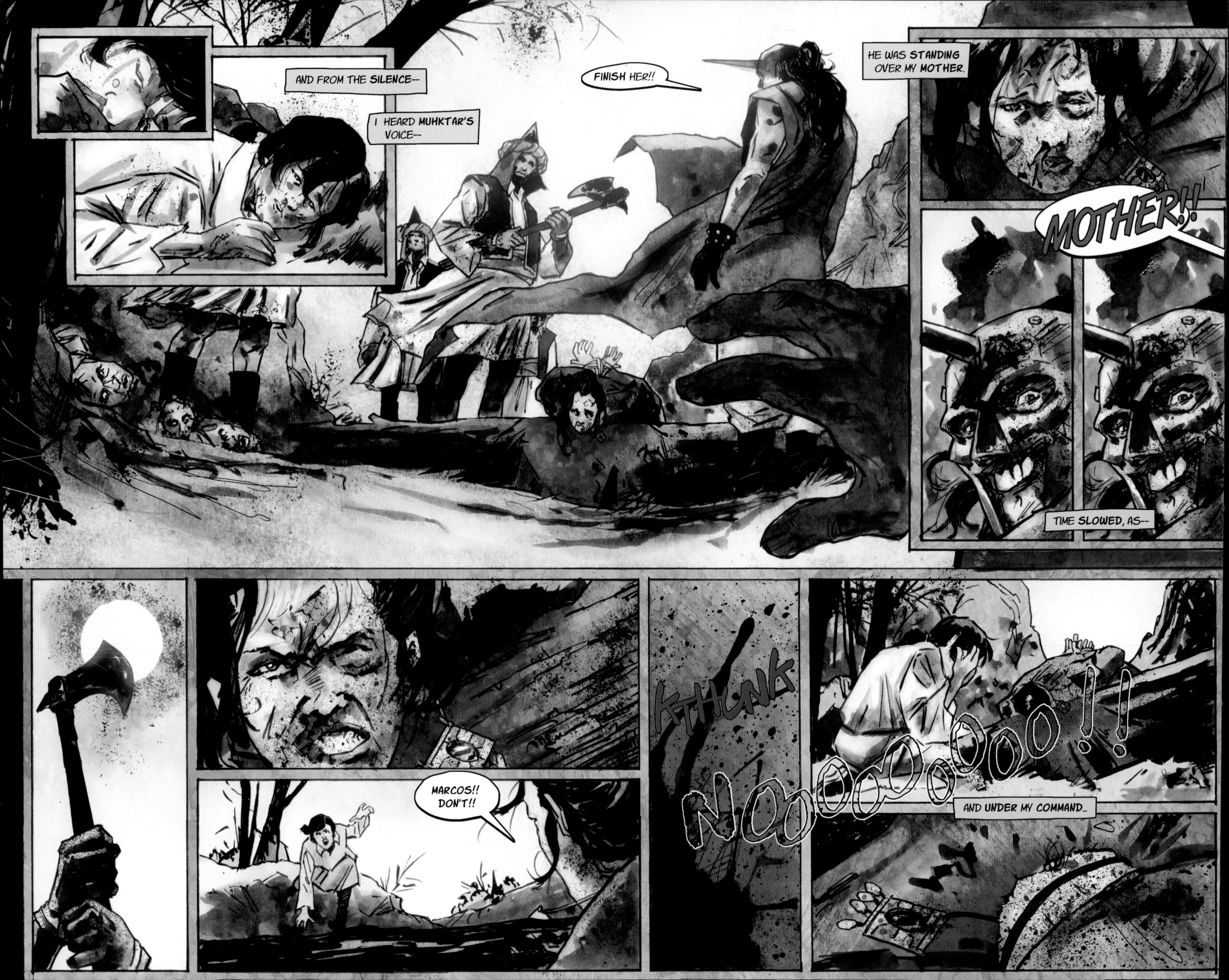
AND FROM THE SILENCE--
I HEARD MUHKTAR'S VOICE--
FINISH HER!!
HE WAS STANDING OVER MY MOTHER.
MOTHER!!
TIME SLOWED, AS--
MARCOS!! DON'T!!
KTHUNK
NOOOOOOOOO!!
AND UNDER MY COMMAND...

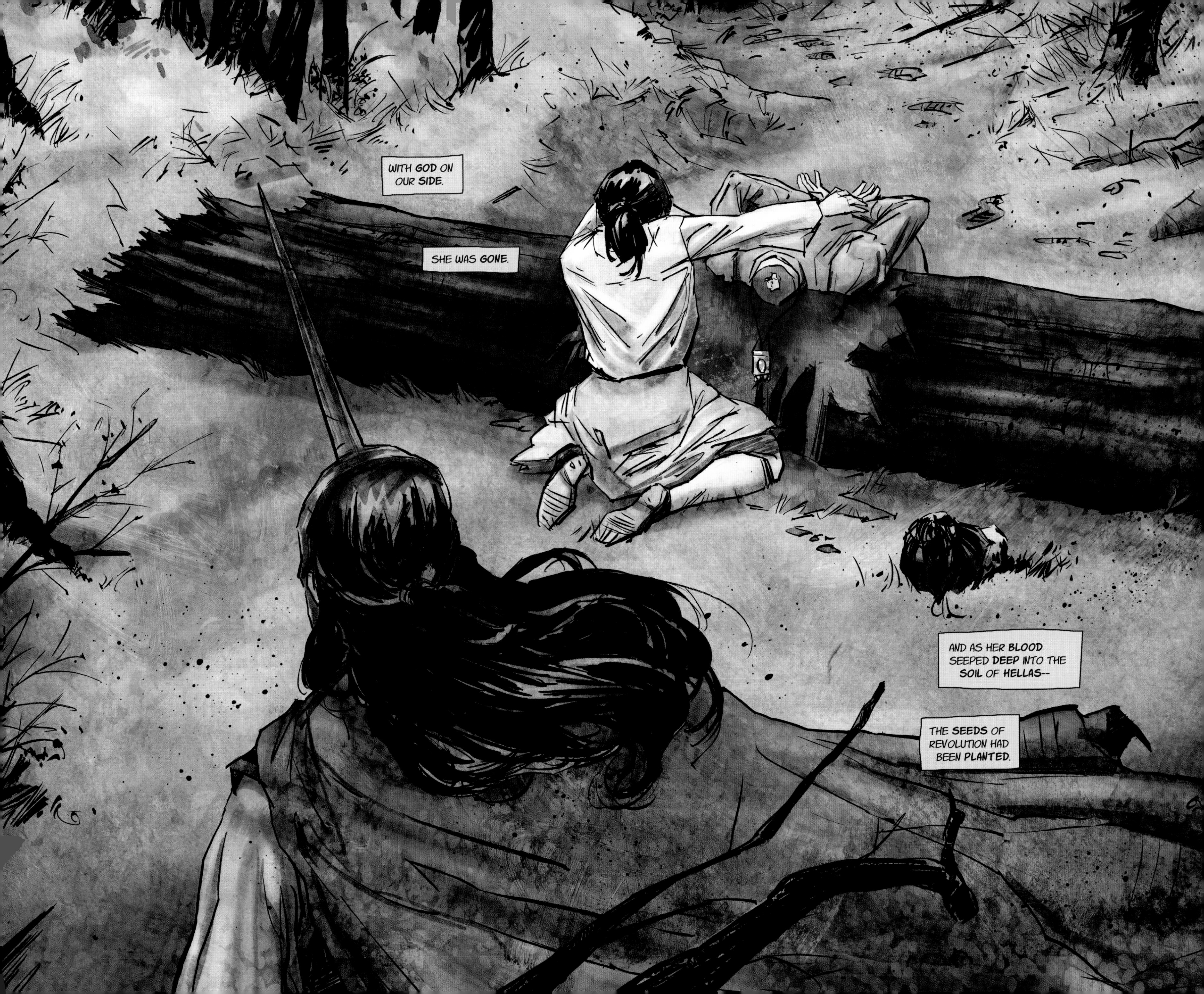
WITH GOD ON OUR SIDE.
SHE WAS GONE.
AND AS HER BLOOD SEEPED DEEP INTO THE SOIL OF HELLAS--
THE SEEDS OF REVOLUTION HAD BEEN PLANTED.

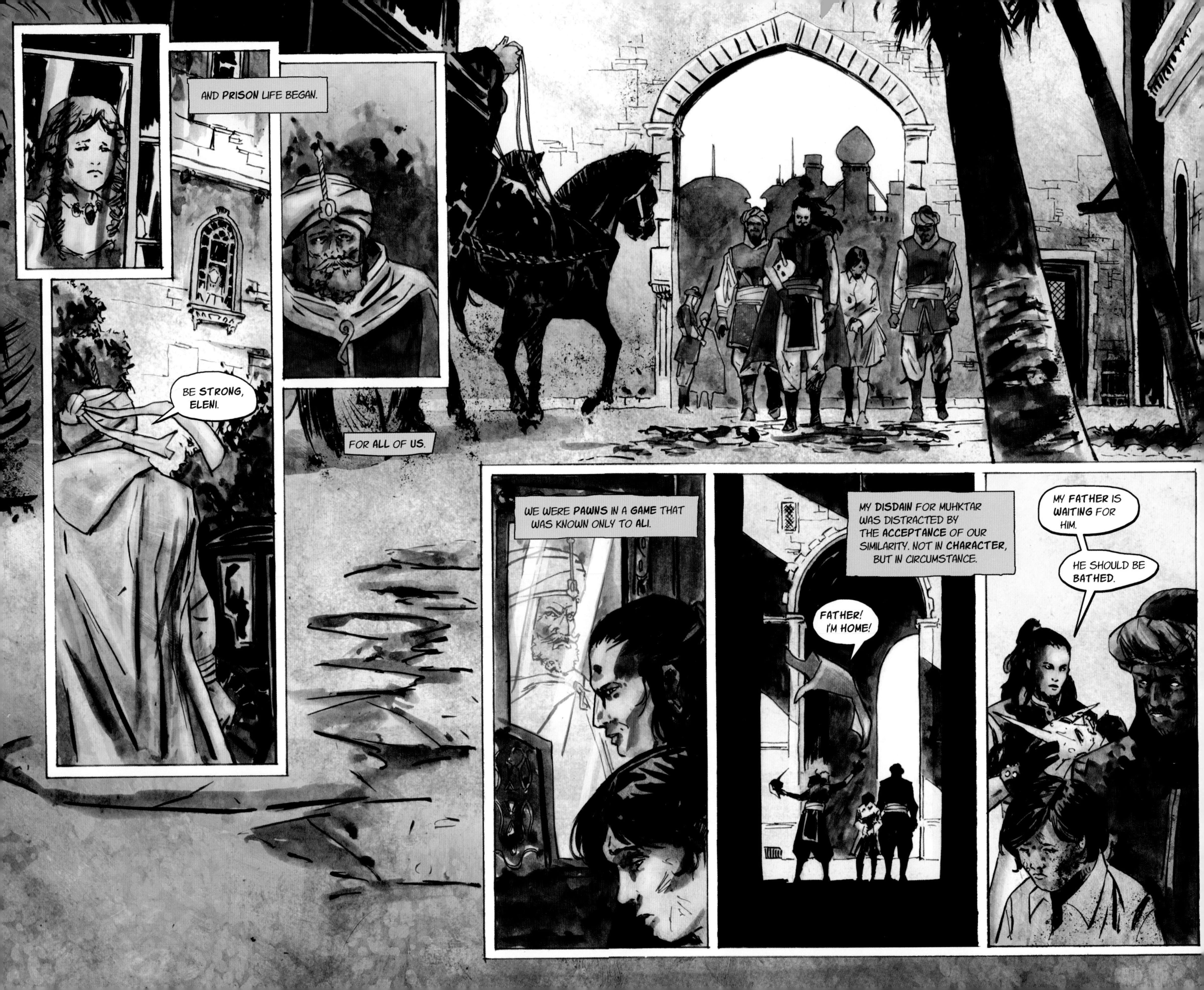

AND PRISON LIFE BEGAN.
BE STRONG, ELENI.
FOR ALL OF US.
WE WERE PAWNS IN A GAME THAT WAS KNOWN ONLY TO ALI.
MY DISDAIN FOR MUHKTAR WAS DISTRACTED BY THE ACCEPTANCE OF OUR SIMILARITY. NOT IN CHARACTER, BUT IN CIRCUMSTANCE.
FATHER! I'M HOME!
MY FATHER IS WAITING FOR HIM.
HE SHOULD BE BATHED.

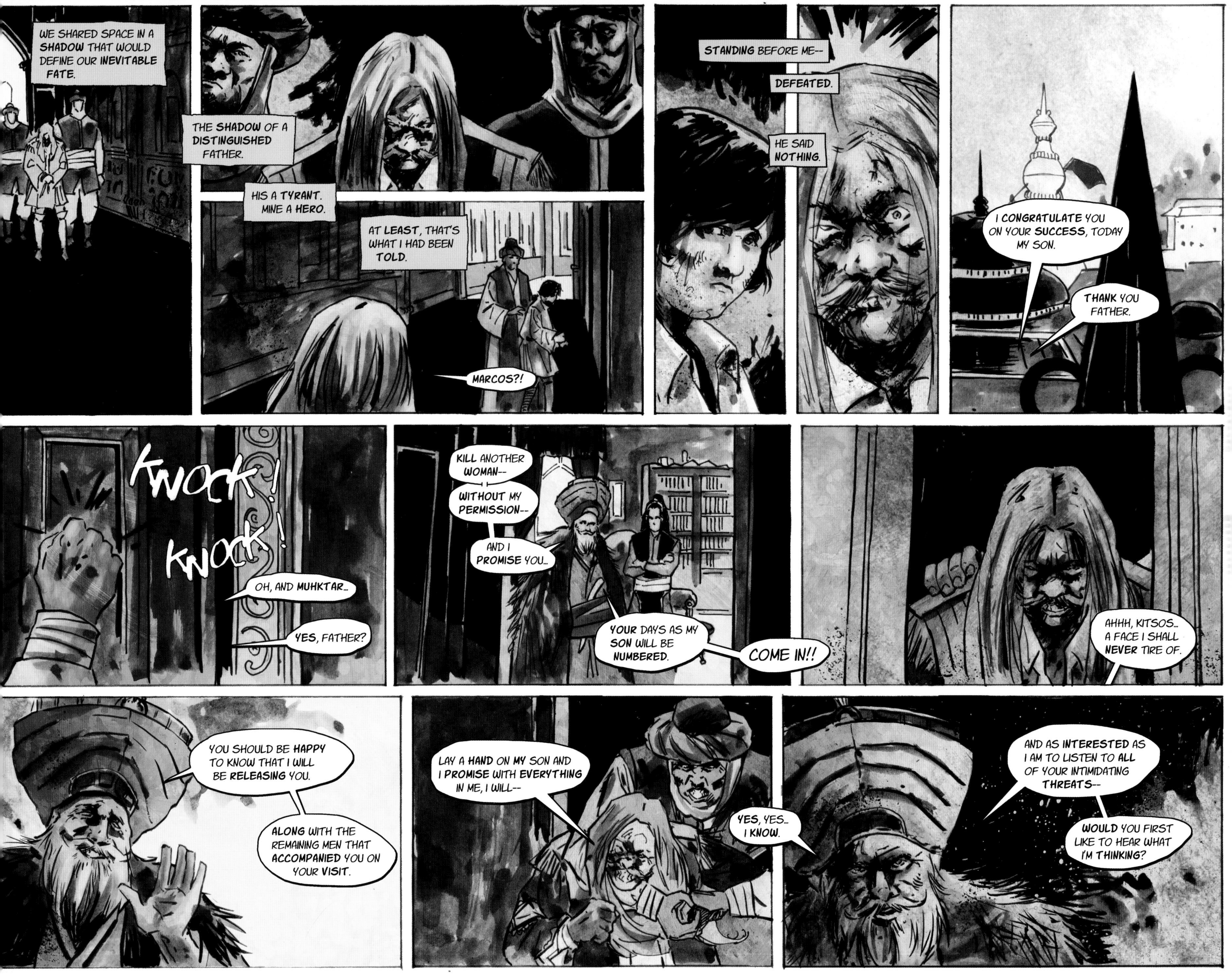
WE SHARED SPACE IN A SHADOW THAT WOULD DEFINE OUR INEVITABLE FATE.
THE SHADOW OF A DISTINGUISHED FATHER.
HIS A TYRANT. MINE A HERO.
AT LEAST, THAT'S WHAT I HAD BEEN TOLD.
MARCOS?!
STANDING BEFORE ME--
DEFEATED.
HE SAID NOTHING.
I CONGRATULATE YOU ON YOUR SUCCESS, TODAY MY SON.
THANK YOU FATHER.
KNOCK! KNOCK!
OH, AND MUHKTAR...
YES, FATHER?
KILL ANOTHER WOMAN--
WITHOUT MY PERMISSION--
AND I PROMISE YOU...
YOUR DAYS AS MY SON WILL BE NUMBERED.
COME IN!!
AHHH, KITSOS... A FACE I SHALL NEVER TIRE OF.
YOU SHOULD BE HAPPY TO KNOW THAT I WILL BE RELEASING YOU.
ALONG WITH THE REMAINING MEN THAT ACCOMPANIED YOU ON YOUR VISIT.
LAY A HAND ON MY SON AND I PROMISE WITH EVERYTHING IN ME, I WILL--
YES, YES... I KNOW.
AND AS INTERESTED AS I AM TO LISTEN TO ALL OF YOUR INTIMIDATING THREATS--
WOULD YOU FIRST LIKE TO HEAR WHAT I'M THINKING?

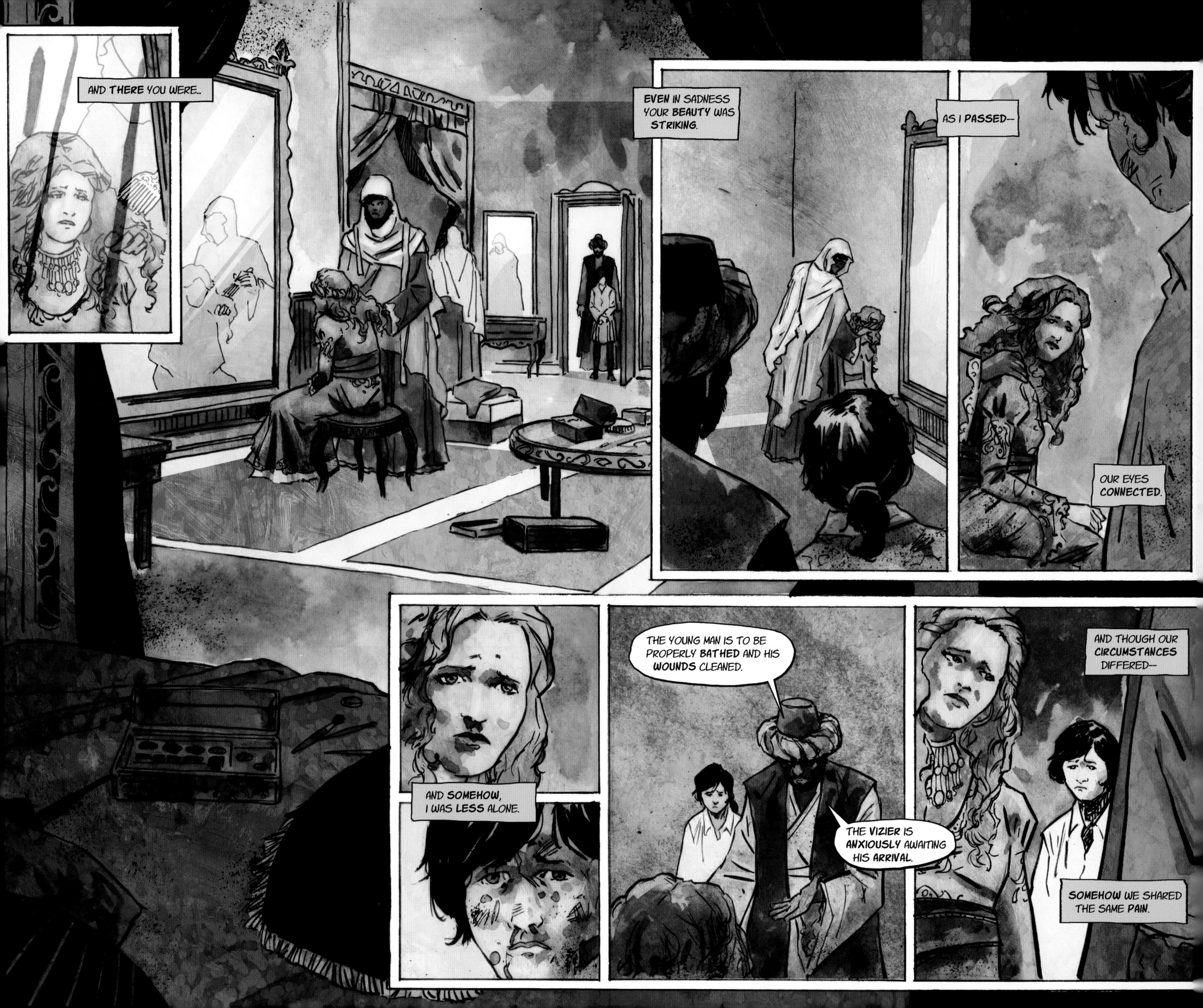

AND THERE YOU WERE...
EVEN IN SADNESS YOUR BEAUTY WAS STRIKING.
AS I PASSED--
OUR EYES CONNECTED.
AND SOMEHOW, I WAS LESS ALONE.
THE YOUNG MAN IS TO BE PROPERLY BATHED AND HIS WOUNDS CLEANED.
THE VIZIER IS ANXIOUSLY AWAITING HIS ARRIVAL.
AND THOUGH OUR CIRCUMSTANCES DIFFERED--
SOMEHOW WE SHARED THE SAME PAIN.

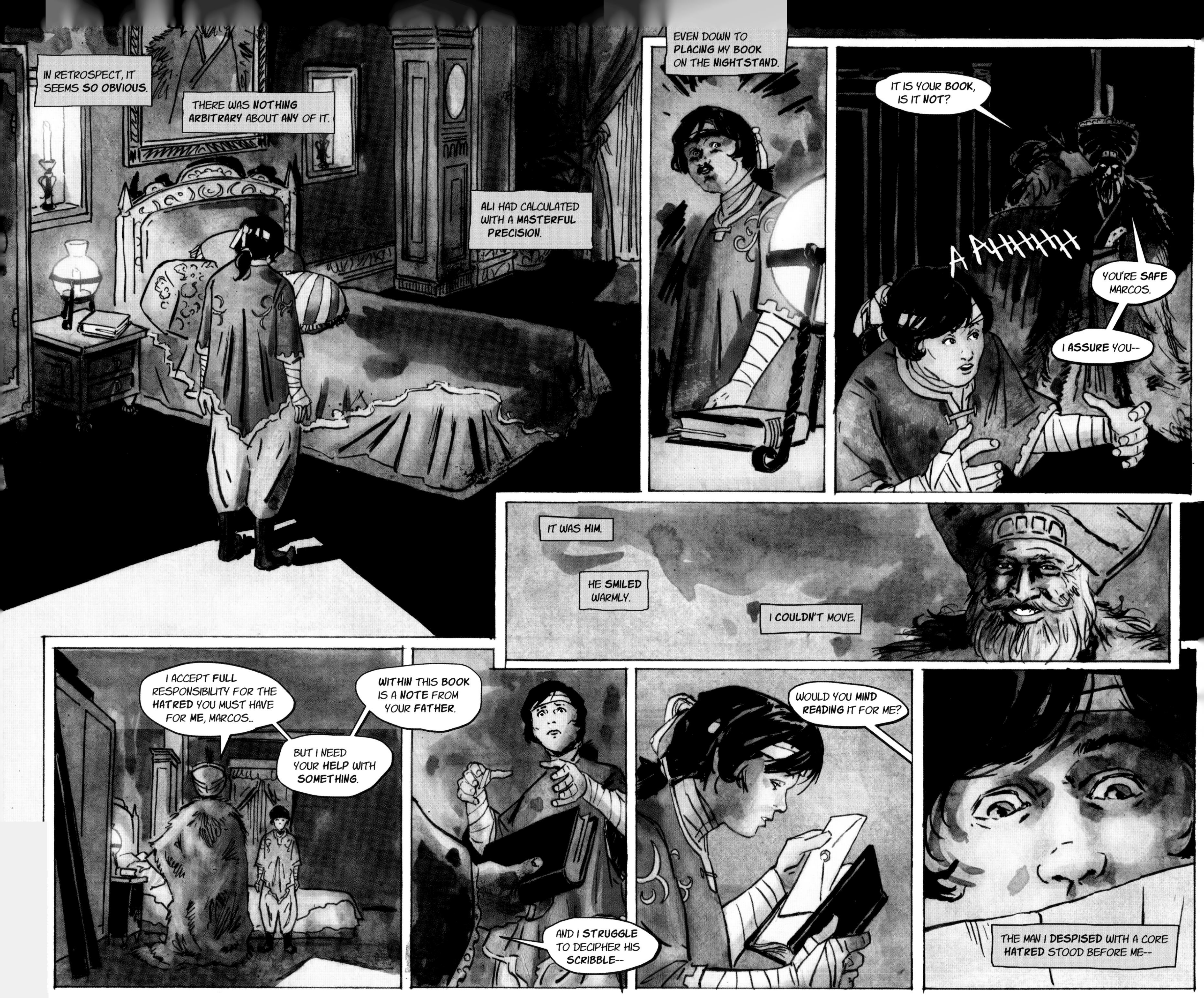
IN RETROSPECT, IT SEEMS SO OBVIOUS.
THERE WAS NOTHING ARBITRARY ABOUT ANY OF IT.
ALI HAD CALCULATED WITH A MASTERFUL PRECISION.
EVEN DOWN TO PLACING MY BOOK ON THE NIGHTSTAND.
IT IS YOUR BOOK, IS IT NOT?
AAHHHHH
YOU'RE SAFE MARCOS.
I ASSURE YOU--
IT WAS HIM.
HE SMILED WARMLY.
I COULDN'T MOVE.
I ACCEPT FULL RESPONSIBILITY FOR THE HATRED YOU MUST HAVE FOR ME, MARCOS...
BUT I NEED YOUR HELP WITH SOMETHING.
WITHIN THIS BOOK IS A NOTE FROM YOUR FATHER.
AND I STRUGGLE TO DECIPHER HIS SCRIBBLE--
WOULD YOU MIND READING IT FOR ME?
THE MAN I DESPISED WITH A CORE HATRED STOOD BEFORE ME--

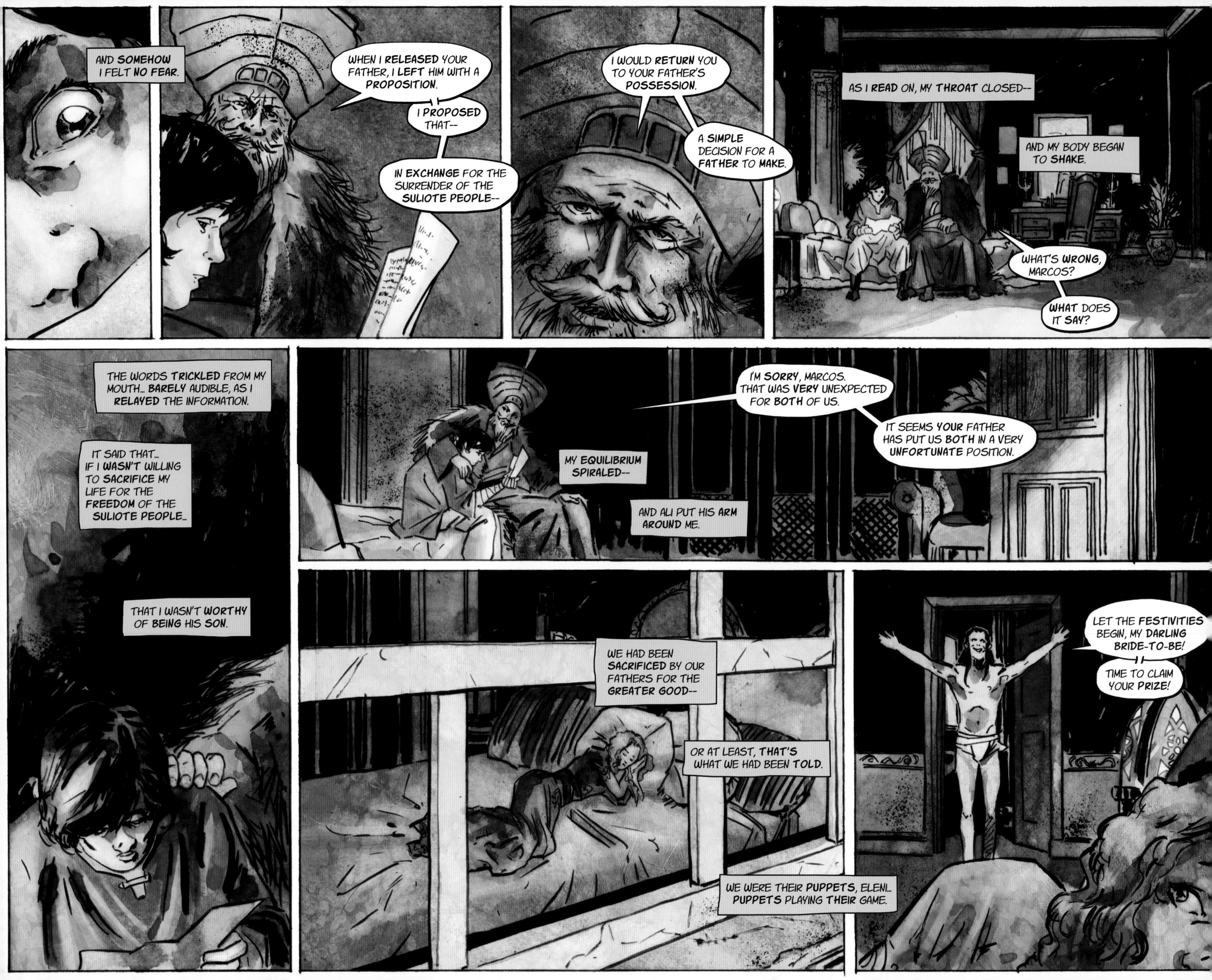
AND SOMEHOW I FELT NO FEAR.
WHEN I RELEASED YOUR FATHER, I LEFT HIM WITH A PROPOSITION.
I PROPOSED THAT--
IN EXCHANGE FOR THE SURRENDER OF THE SULIOTE PEOPLE--
I WOULD RETURN YOU TO YOUR FATHER'S POSSESSION.
A SIMPLE DECISION FOR A FATHER TO MAKE.
AS I READ ON, MY THROAT CLOSED--
AND MY BODY BEGAN TO SHAKE.
WHAT'S WRONG, MARCOS?
WHAT DOES IT SAY?
THE WORDS TRICKLED FROM MY MOUTH... BARELY AUDIBLE, AS I RELAYED THE INFORMATION.
IT SAID THAT... IF I WASN'T WILLING TO SACRIFICE MY LIFE FOR THE FREEDOM OF THE SULIOTE PEOPLE...
THAT I WASN'T WORTHY OF BEING HIS SON.
I'M SORRY, MARCOS. THAT WAS VERY UNEXPECTED FOR BOTH OF US.
IT SEEMS YOUR FATHER HAS PUT US BOTH IN A VERY UNFORTUNATE POSITION.
MY EQUILIBRIUM SPIRALED--
AND ALI PUT HIS ARM AROUND ME.
WE HAD BEEN SACRIFICED BY OUR FATHERS FOR THE GREATER GOOD--
OR AT LEAST, THAT'S WHAT WE HAD BEEN TOLD.
WE WERE THEIR PUPPETS, ELENI... PUPPETS PLAYING THEIR GAME.
LET THE FESTIVITIES BEGIN, MY DARLING BRIDE-TO-BE!
TIME TO CLAIM YOUR PRIZE!

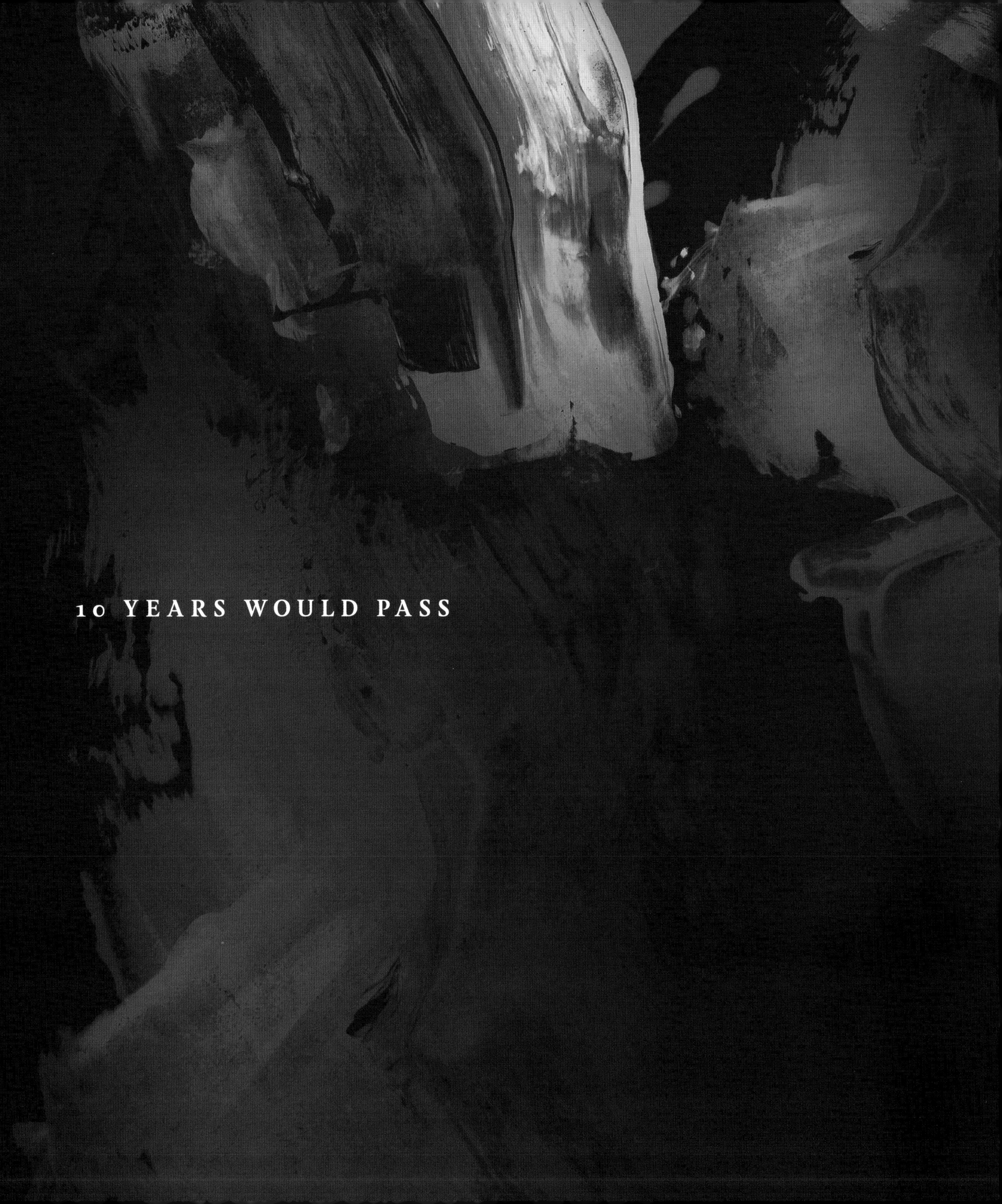

10 YEARS WOULD PASS

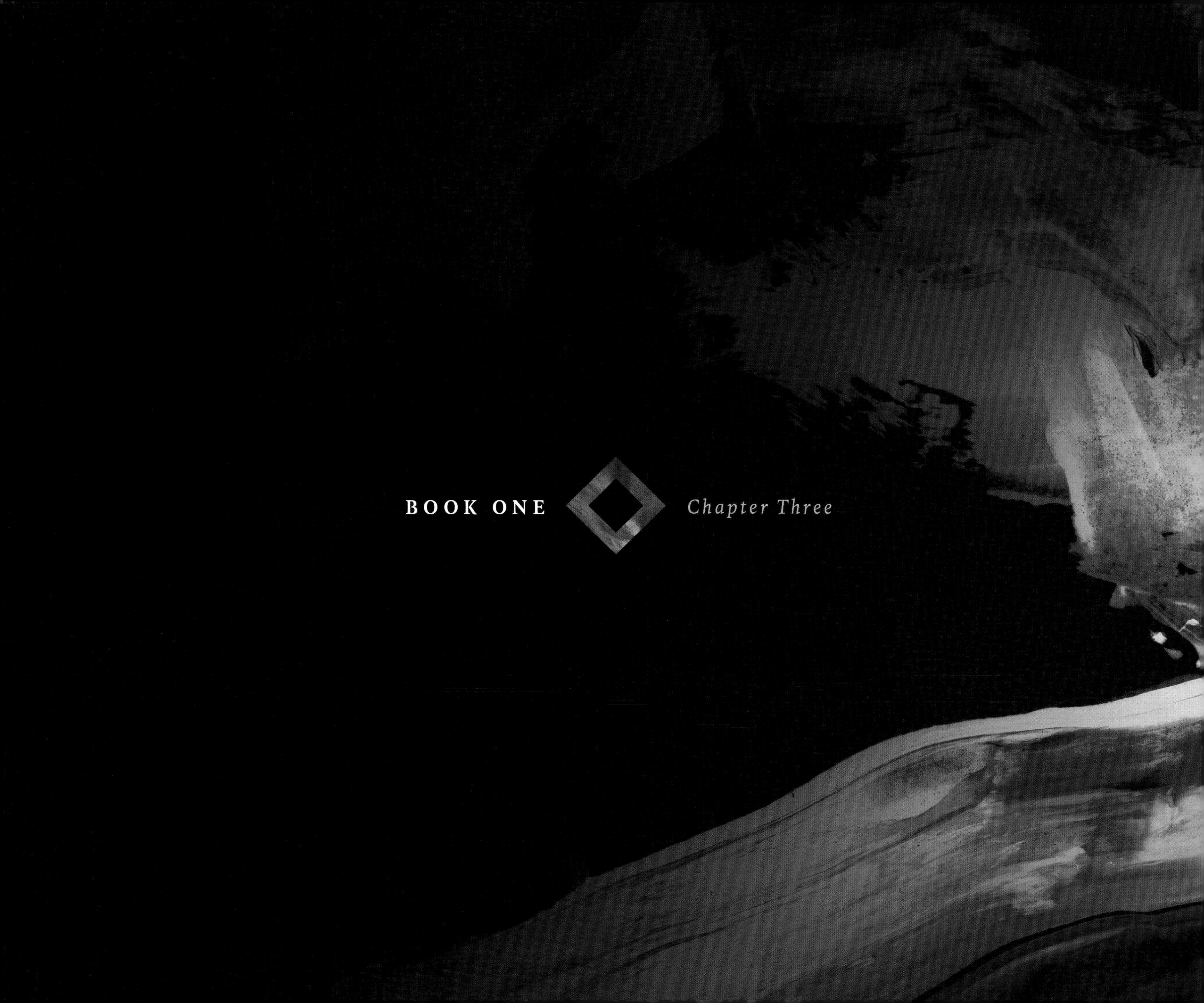

BOOK ONE ◇ *Chapter Three*

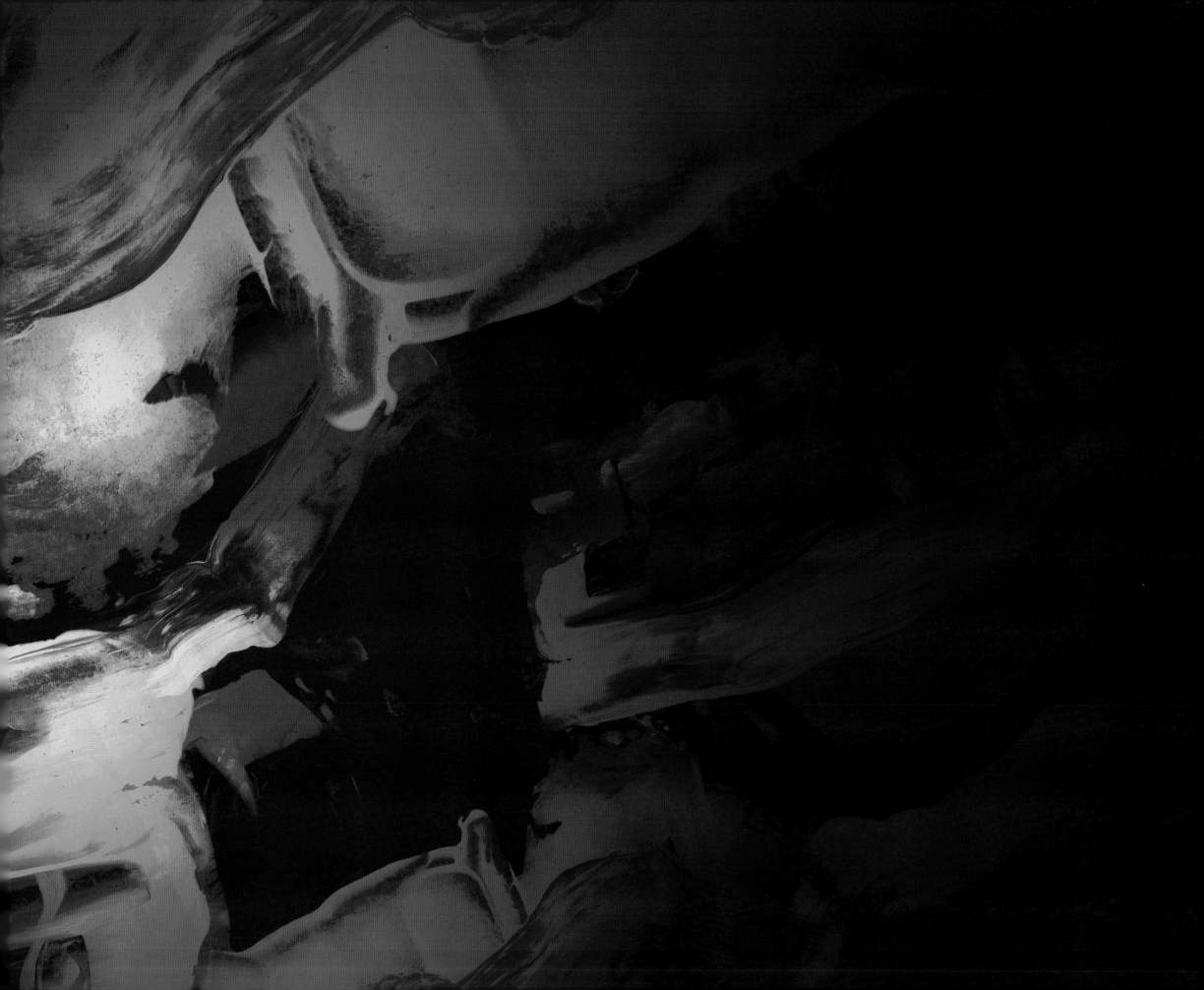

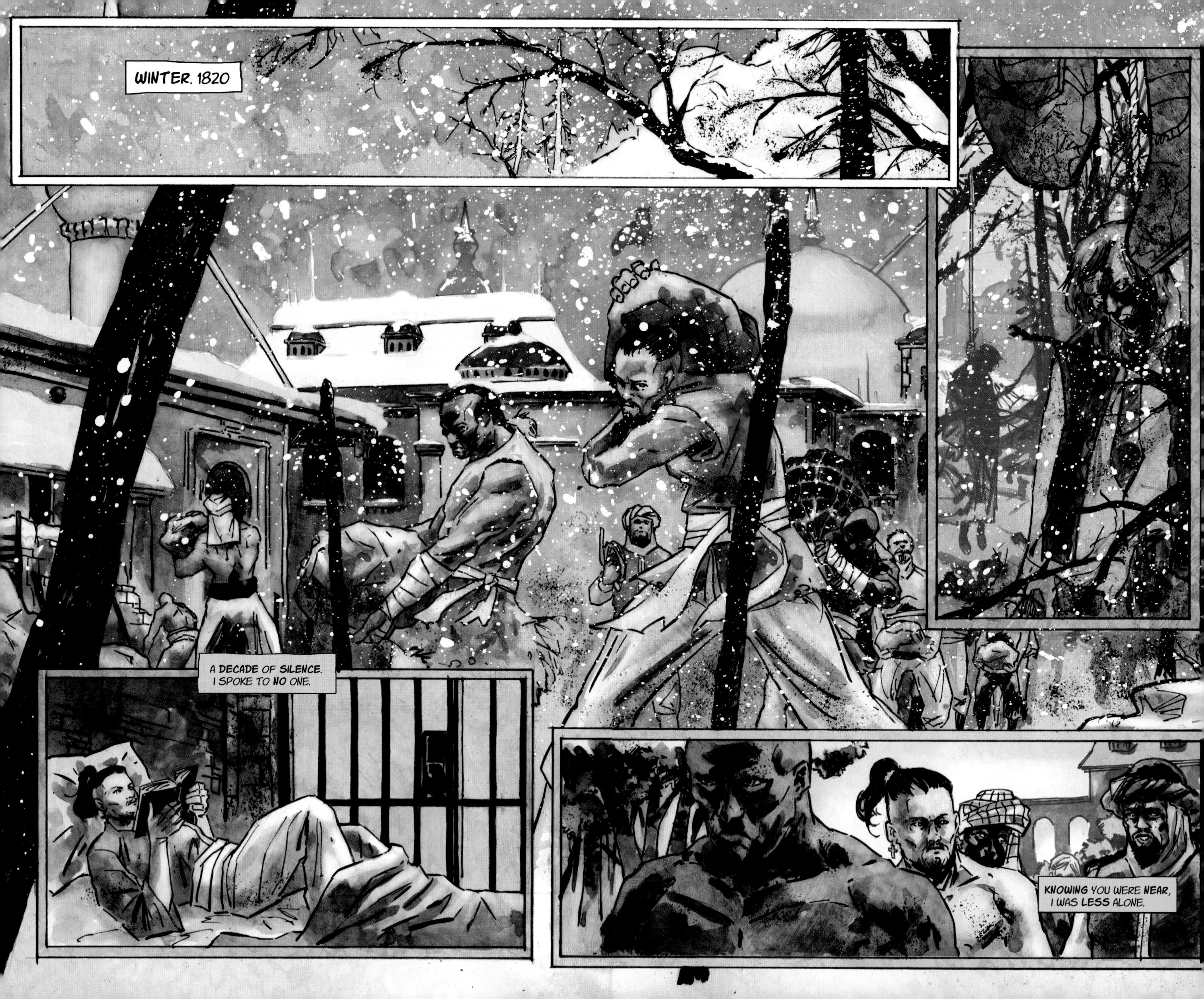
WINTER. 1820
A DECADE OF SILENCE. I SPOKE TO NO ONE.
KNOWING YOU WERE NEAR, I WAS LESS ALONE.

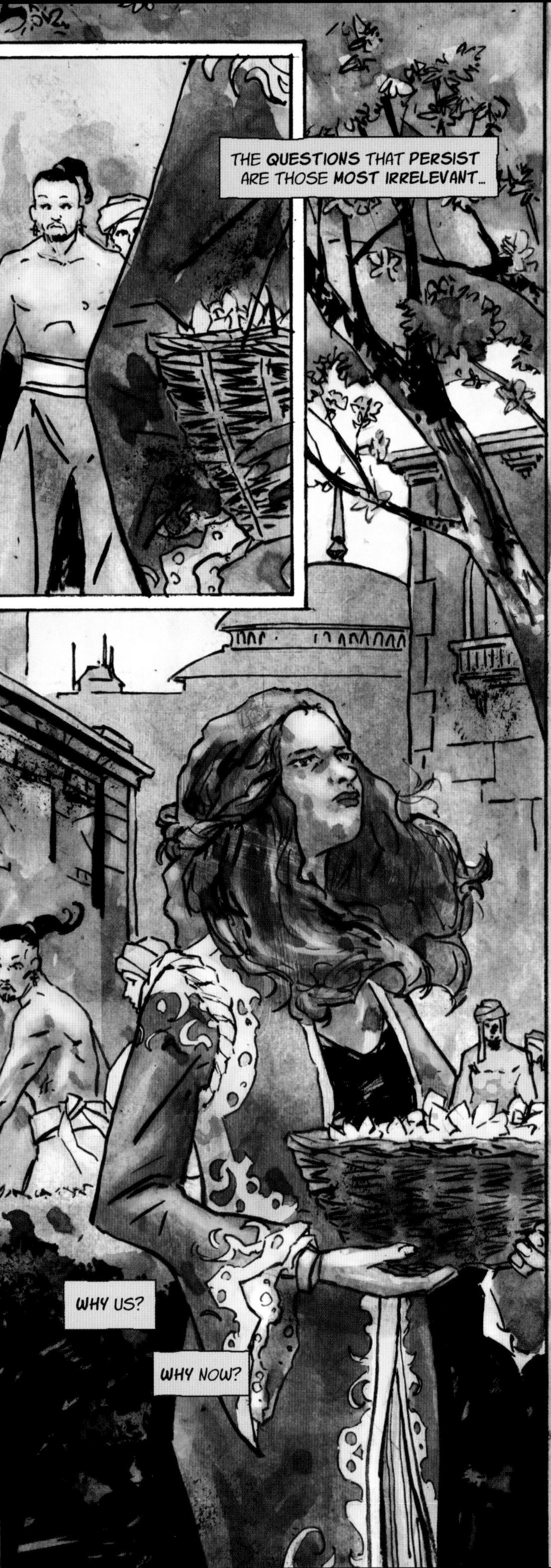
THE QUESTIONS THAT PERSIST ARE THOSE MOST IRRELEVANT...
WHY US?
WHY NOW?

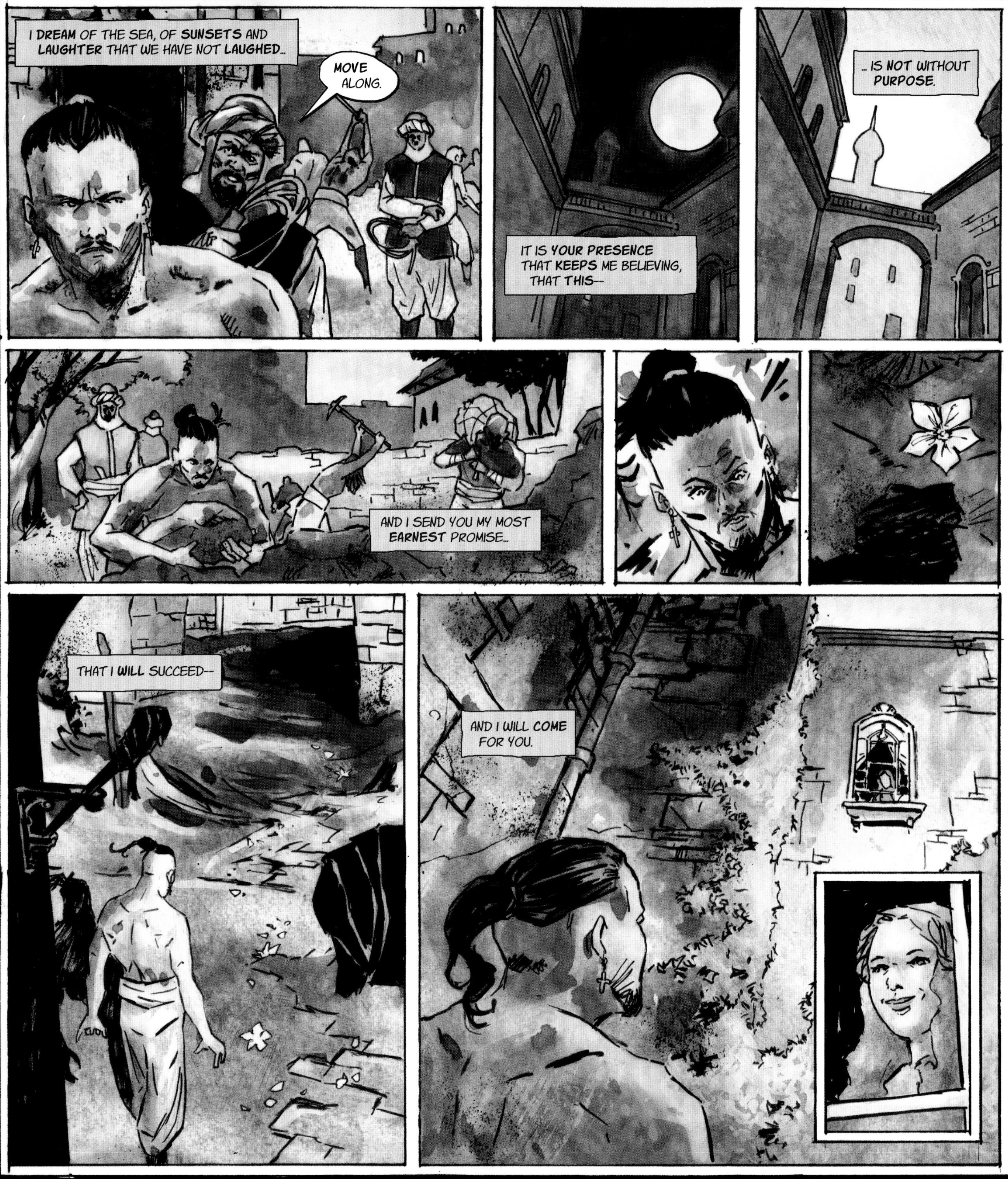
I DREAM OF THE SEA, OF SUNSETS AND LAUGHTER THAT WE HAVE NOT LAUGHED...
MOVE ALONG.
IT IS YOUR PRESENCE THAT KEEPS ME BELIEVING, THAT THIS--
...IS NOT WITHOUT PURPOSE.
AND I SEND YOU MY MOST EARNEST PROMISE...
THAT I WILL SUCCEED--
AND I WILL COME FOR YOU.

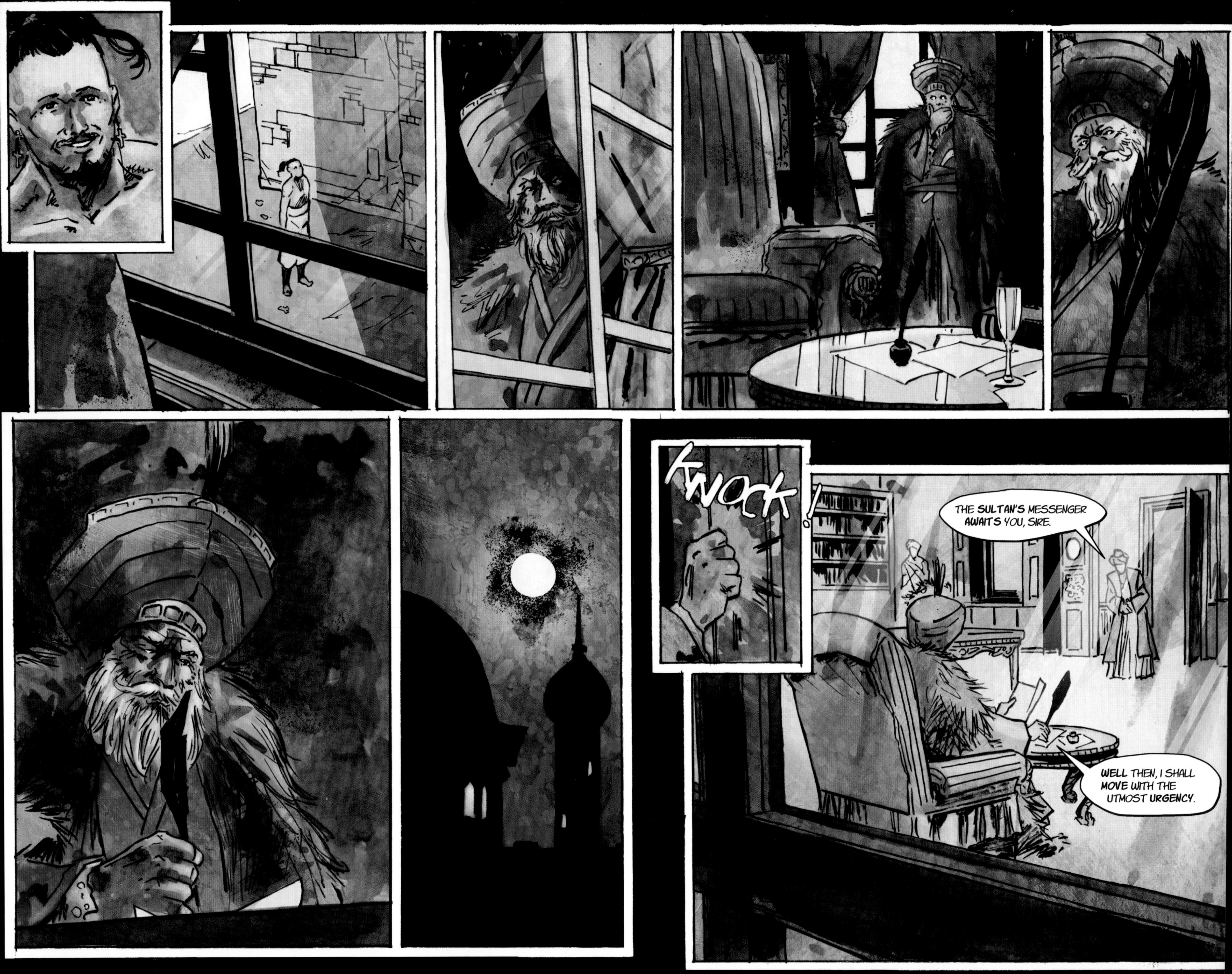
KNOCK!
THE SULTAN'S MESSENGER AWAITS YOU, SIRE.
WELL THEN, I SHALL MOVE WITH THE UTMOST URGENCY.

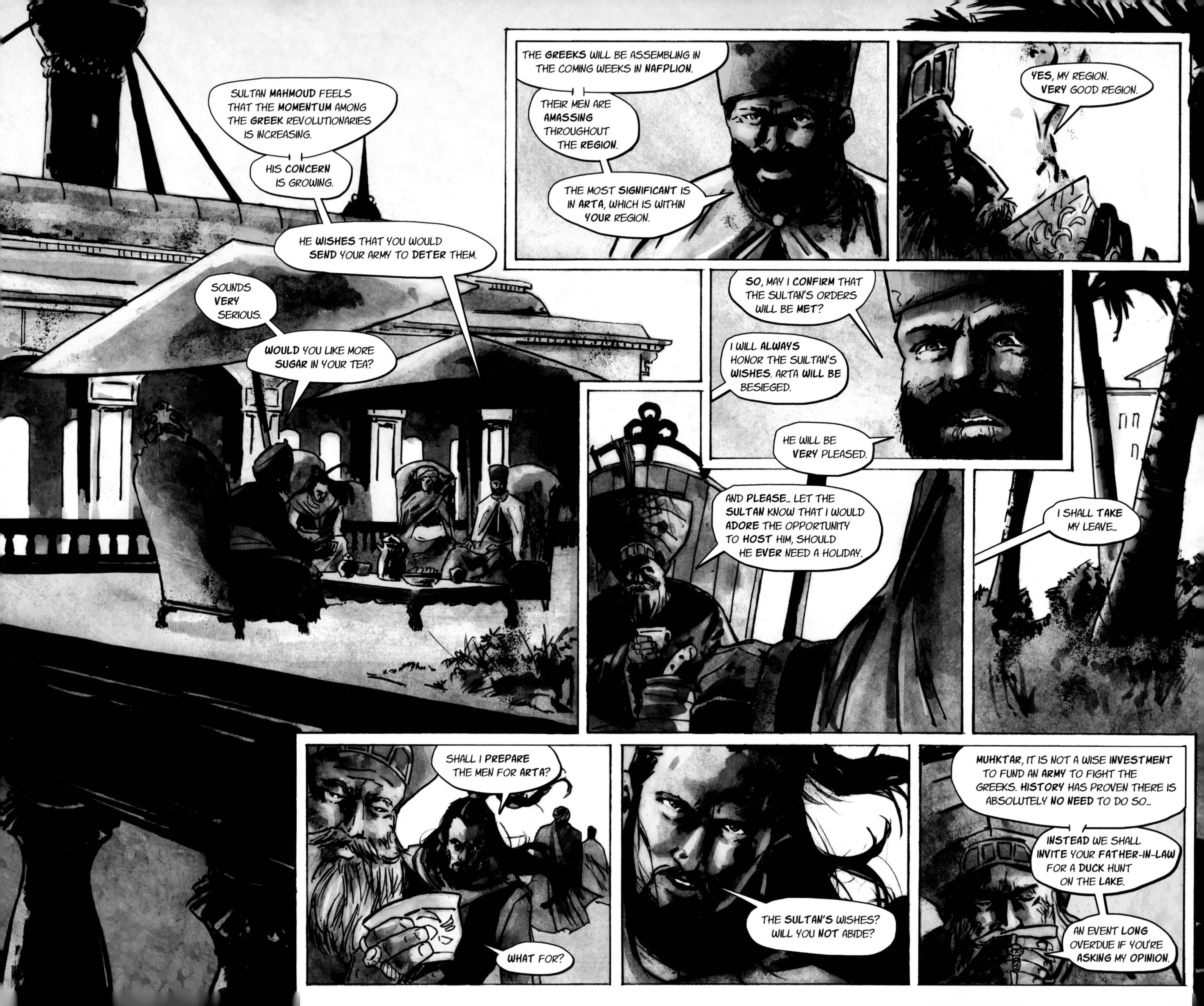
SULTAN MAHMOUD FEELS THAT THE MOMENTUM AMONG THE GREEK REVOLUTIONARIES IS INCREASING.
HIS CONCERN IS GROWING.
HE WISHES THAT YOU WOULD SEND YOUR ARMY TO DETER THEM.
SOUNDS VERY SERIOUS.
WOULD YOU LIKE MORE SUGAR IN YOUR TEA?
THE GREEKS WILL BE ASSEMBLING IN THE COMING WEEKS IN NAFPLION.
THEIR MEN ARE AMASSING THROUGHOUT THE REGION.
THE MOST SIGNIFICANT IS IN ARTA, WHICH IS WITHIN YOUR REGION.
YES, MY REGION. VERY GOOD REGION.
SO, MAY I CONFIRM THAT THE SULTAN'S ORDERS WILL BE MET?
I WILL ALWAYS HONOR THE SUILTAN'S WISHES. ARTA WILL BE BESIEGED.
HE WILL BE VERY PLEASED.
AND PLEASE... LET THE SULTAN KNOW THAT I WOULD ADORE THE OPPORTUNITY TO HOST HIM, SHOULD HE EVER NEED A HOLIDAY.
I SHALL TAKE MY LEAVE...
SHALL I PREPARE THE MEN FOR ARTA?
WHAT FOR?
THE SULTAN'S WISHES? WILL YOU NOT ABIDE?
MUHKTAR, IT IS NOT A WISE INVESTMENT TO FUND AN ARMY TO FIGHT THE GREEKS. HISTORY HAS PROVEN THERE IS ABSOLUTELY NO NEED TO DO SO...
INSTEAD WE SHALL INVITE YOUR FATHER-IN-LAW FOR A DUCK HUNT ON THE LAKE.
AN EVENT LONG OVERDUE IF YOU'RE ASKING MY OPINION.

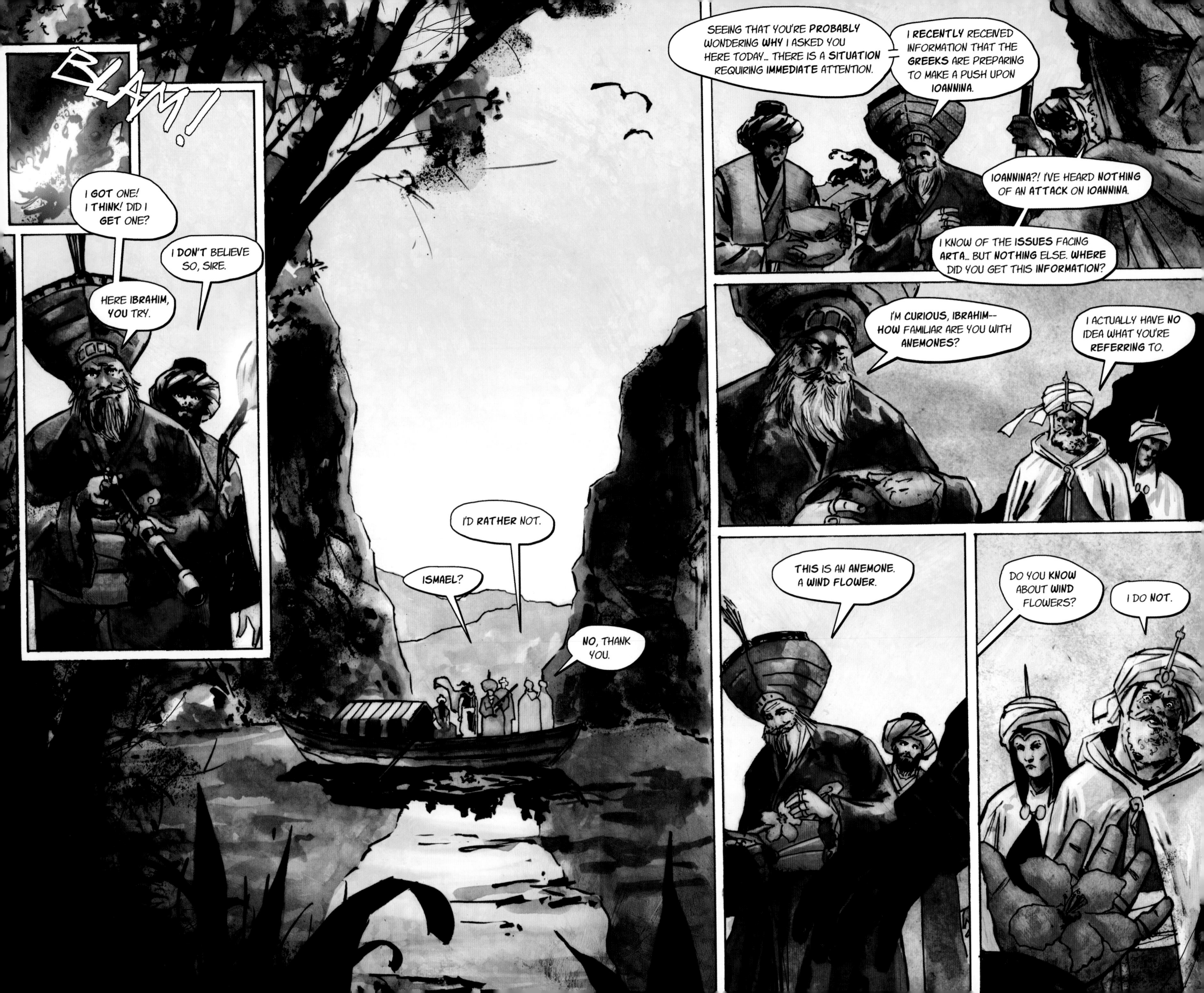
BLAM!
I GOT ONE! I THINK! DID I GET ONE?
I DON'T BELIEVE SO, SIRE.
HERE IBRAHIM, YOU TRY.
ISMAEL?
I'D RATHER NOT.
NO, THANK YOU.
SEEING THAT YOU'RE PROBABLY WONDERING WHY I ASKED YOU HERE TODAY... THERE IS A SITUATION REQUIRING IMMEDIATE ATTENTION.
I RECENTLY RECEIVED INFORMATION THAT THE GREEKS ARE PREPARING TO MAKE A PUSH UPON IOANNINA.
IOANNINA?! I'VE HEARD NOTHING OF AN ATTACK ON IOANNINA.
I KNOW OF THE ISSUES FACING ARTA... BUT NOTHING ELSE. WHERE DID YOU GET THIS INFORMATION?
I'M CURIOUS, IBRAHIM-- HOW FAMILIAR ARE YOU WITH ANEMONES?
I ACTUALLY HAVE NO IDEA WHAT YOU'RE REFERRING TO.
THIS IS AN ANEMONE. A WIND FLOWER.
DO YOU KNOW ABOUT WIND FLOWERS?
I DO NOT.

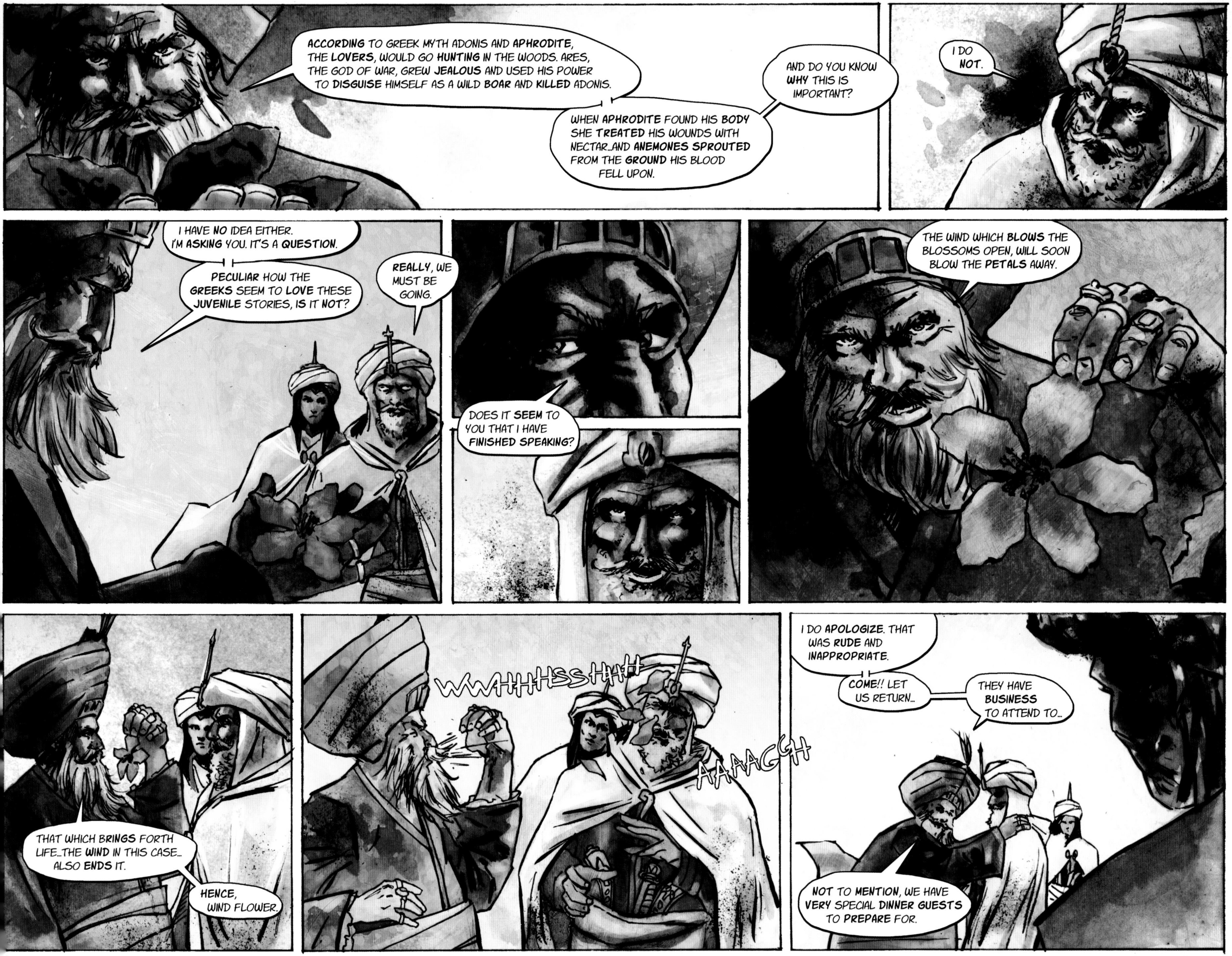
ACCORDING TO GREEK MYTH ADONIS AND APHRODITE, THE LOVERS, WOULD GO HUNTING IN THE WOODS. ARES, THE GOD OF WAR, GREW JEALOUS AND USED HIS POWER TO DISGUISE HIMSELF AS A WILD BOAR AND KILLED ADONIS.
WHEN APHRODITE FOUND HIS BODY SHE TREATED HIS WOUNDS WITH NECTAR...AND ANEMONES SPROUTED FROM THE GROUND HIS BLOOD FELL UPON.
AND DO YOU KNOW WHY THIS IS IMPORTANT?
I DO NOT.
I HAVE NO IDEA EITHER. I'M ASKING YOU. IT'S A QUESTION.
PECULIAR HOW THE GREEKS SEEM TO LOVE THESE JUVENILE STORIES, IS IT NOT?
REALLY, WE MUST BE GOING.
DOES IT SEEM TO YOU THAT I HAVE FINISHED SPEAKING?
THE WIND WHICH BLOWS THE BLOSSOMS OPEN, WILL SOON BLOW THE PETALS AWAY.
THAT WHICH BRINGS FORTH LIFE...THE WIND IN THIS CASE... ALSO ENDS IT.
HENCE, WIND FLOWER.
WWAHHHSSHHH
AAAAGGH
I DO APOLOGIZE. THAT WAS RUDE AND INAPPROPRIATE.
COME!! LET US RETURN...
THEY HAVE BUSINESS TO ATTEND TO...
NOT TO MENTION, WE HAVE VERY SPECIAL DINNER GUESTS TO PREPARE FOR.

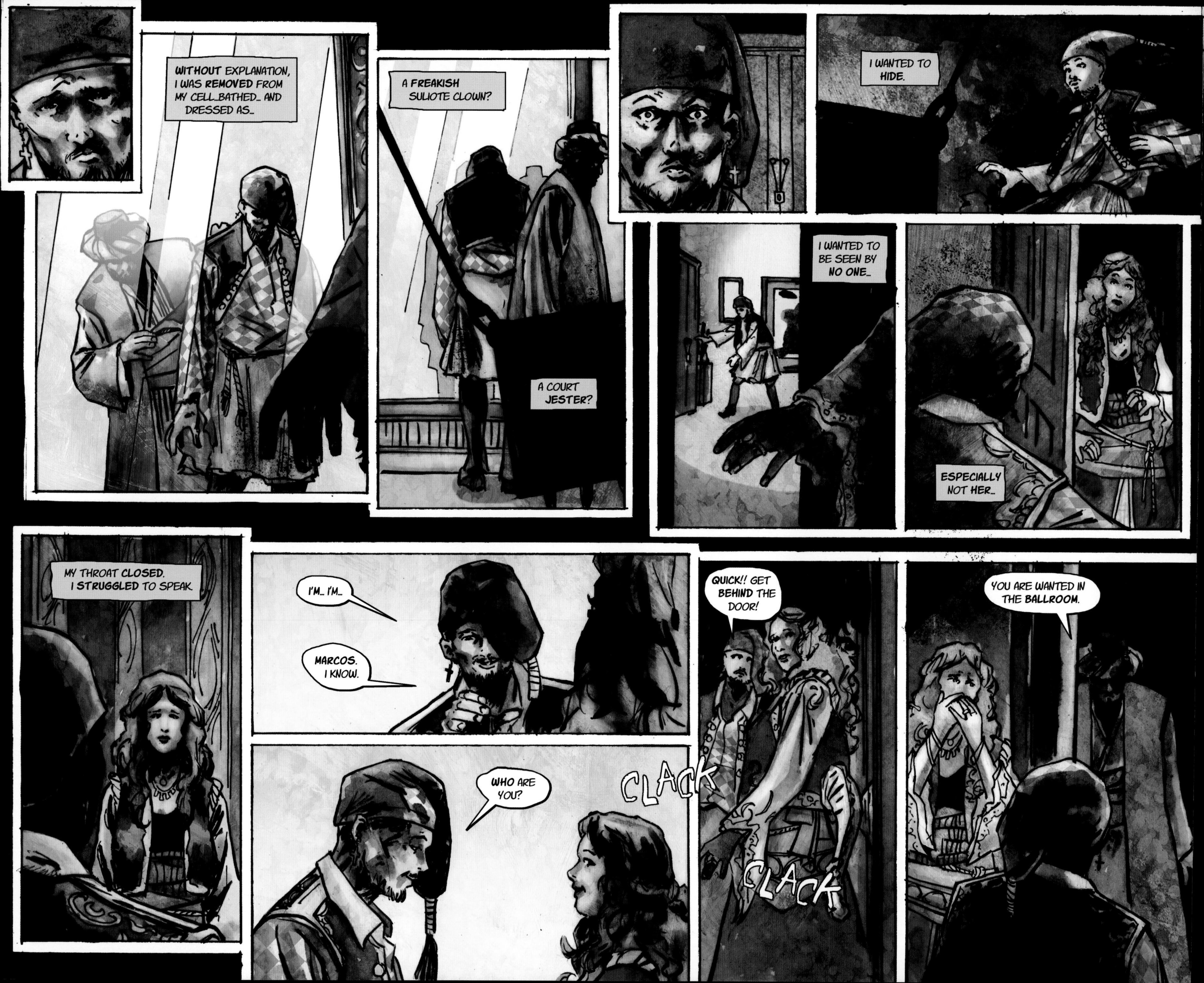
WITHOUT EXPLANATION, I WAS REMOVED FROM MY CELL...BATHED... AND DRESSED AS...
A FREAKISH SULIOTE CLOWN?
A COURT JESTER?
I WANTED TO HIDE.
I WANTED TO BE SEEN BY NO ONE...
ESPECIALLY NOT HER...
MY THROAT CLOSED. I STRUGGLED TO SPEAK.
I'M... I'M...
MARCOS. I KNOW.
WHO ARE YOU?
QUICK!! GET BEHIND THE DOOR!
CLACK
CLACK
YOU ARE WANTED IN THE BALLROOM.

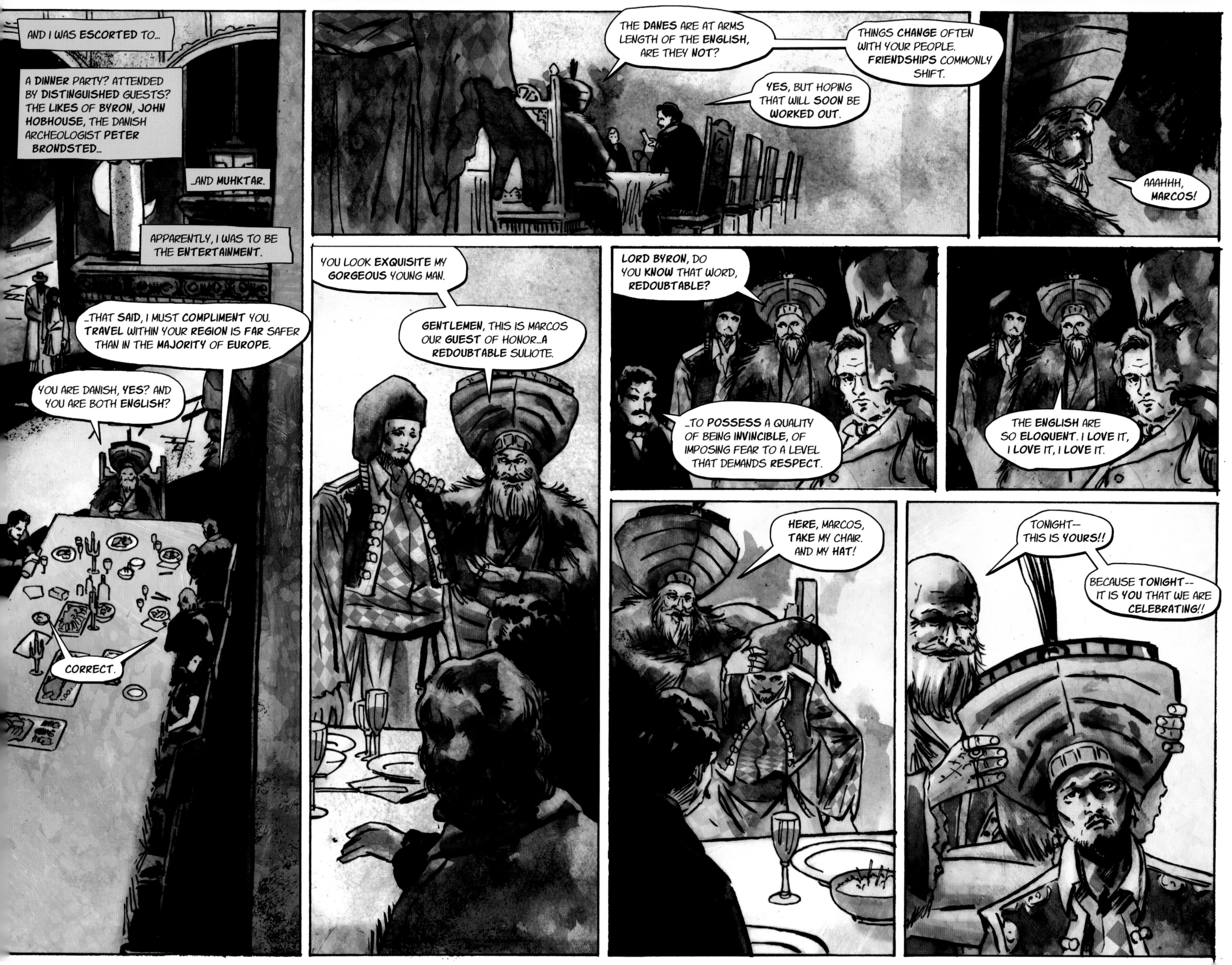
AND I WAS ESCORTED TO...
A DINNER PARTY? ATTENDED BY DISTINGUISHED GUESTS? THE LIKES OF BYRON, JOHN HOBHOUSE, THE DANISH ARCHEOLOGIST PETER BRONDSTED...
...AND MUHKTAR.
APPARENTLY, I WAS TO BE THE ENTERTAINMENT.
...THAT SAID, I MUST COMPLIMENT YOU. TRAVEL WITHIN YOUR REGION IS FAR SAFER THAN IN THE MAJORITY OF EUROPE.
YOU ARE DANISH, YES? AND YOU ARE BOTH ENGLISH?
CORRECT.
THE DANES ARE AT ARMS LENGTH OF THE ENGLISH, ARE THEY NOT?
THINGS CHANGE OFTEN WITH YOUR PEOPLE. FRIENDSHIPS COMMONLY SHIFT.
YES, BUT HOPING THAT WILL SOON BE WORKED OUT.
AAAHHH, MARCOS!
YOU LOOK EXQUISITE MY GORGEOUS YOUNG MAN.
GENTLEMEN, THIS IS MARCOS OUR GUEST OF HONOR...A REDOUBTABLE SULIOTE.
LORD BYRON, DO YOU KNOW THAT WORD, REDOUBTABLE?
...TO POSSESS A QUALITY OF BEING INVINCIBLE, OF IMPOSING FEAR TO A LEVEL THAT DEMANDS RESPECT.
THE ENGLISH ARE SO ELOQUENT. I LOVE IT, I LOVE IT, I LOVE IT.
HERE, MARCOS, TAKE MY CHAIR. AND MY HAT!
TONIGHT-- THIS IS YOURS!!
BECAUSE TONIGHT-- IT IS YOU THAT WE ARE CELEBRATING!!

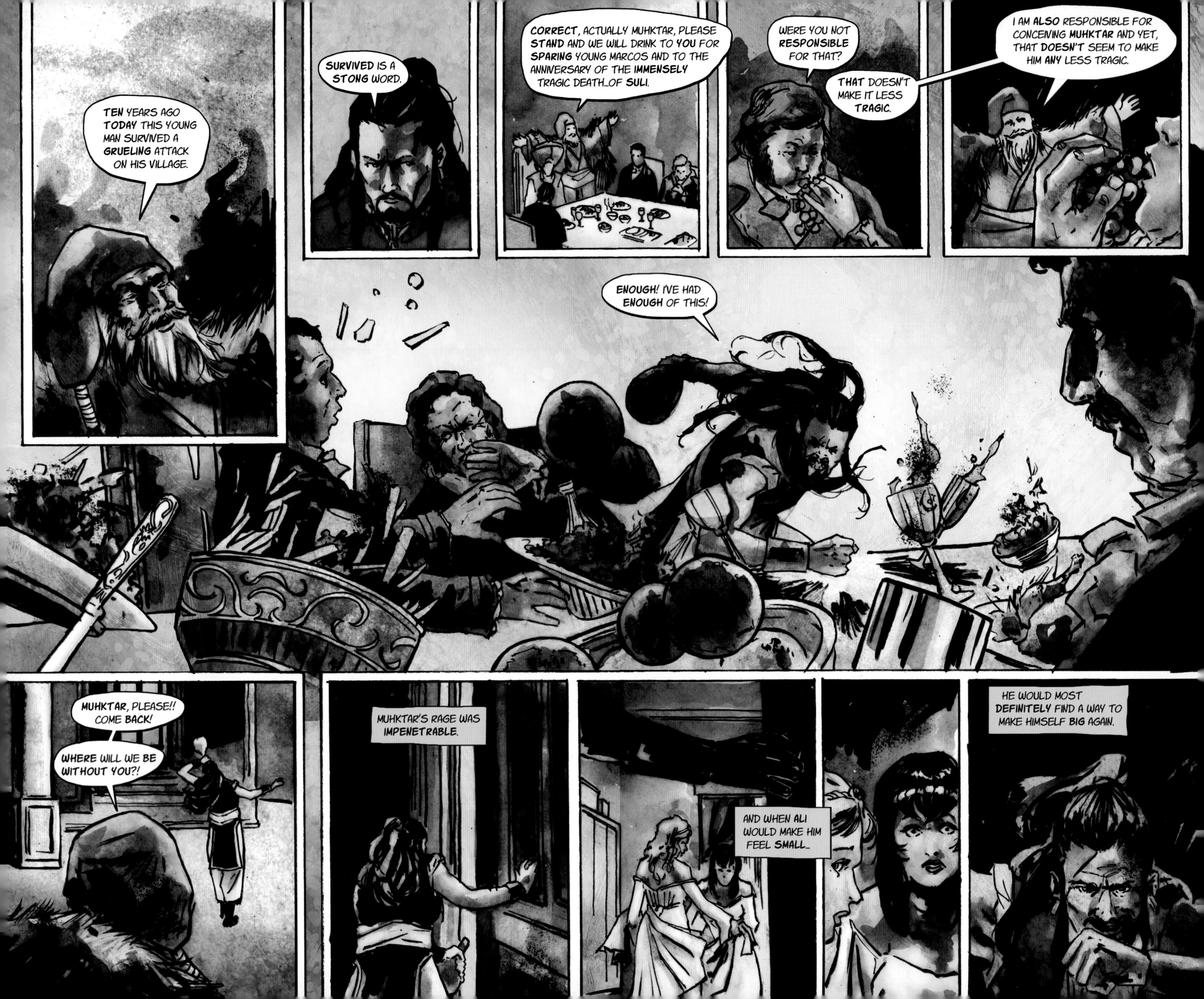

TEN YEARS AGO TODAY THIS YOUNG MAN SURVIVED A GRUELING ATTACK ON HIS VILLAGE.
SURVIVED IS A STONG WORD.
CORRECT, ACTUALLY MUHKTAR, PLEASE STAND AND WE WILL DRINK TO YOU FOR SPARING YOUNG MARCOS AND TO THE ANNIVERSARY OF THE IMMENSELY TRAGIC DEATH...OF SULI.
WERE YOU NOT RESPONSIBLE FOR THAT?
THAT DOESN'T MAKE IT LESS TRAGIC.
I AM ALSO RESPONSIBLE FOR CONCEIVING MUHKTAR AND YET, THAT DOESN'T SEEM TO MAKE HIM ANY LESS TRAGIC.
ENOUGH! I'VE HAD ENOUGH OF THIS!
MUHKTAR, PLEASE!! COME BACK!
WHERE WILL WE BE WITHOUT YOU?!
MUHKTAR'S RAGE WAS IMPENETRABLE.
AND WHEN ALI WOULD MAKE HIM FEEL SMALL...
HE WOULD MOST DEFINITELY FIND A WAY TO MAKE HIMSELF BIG AGAIN.

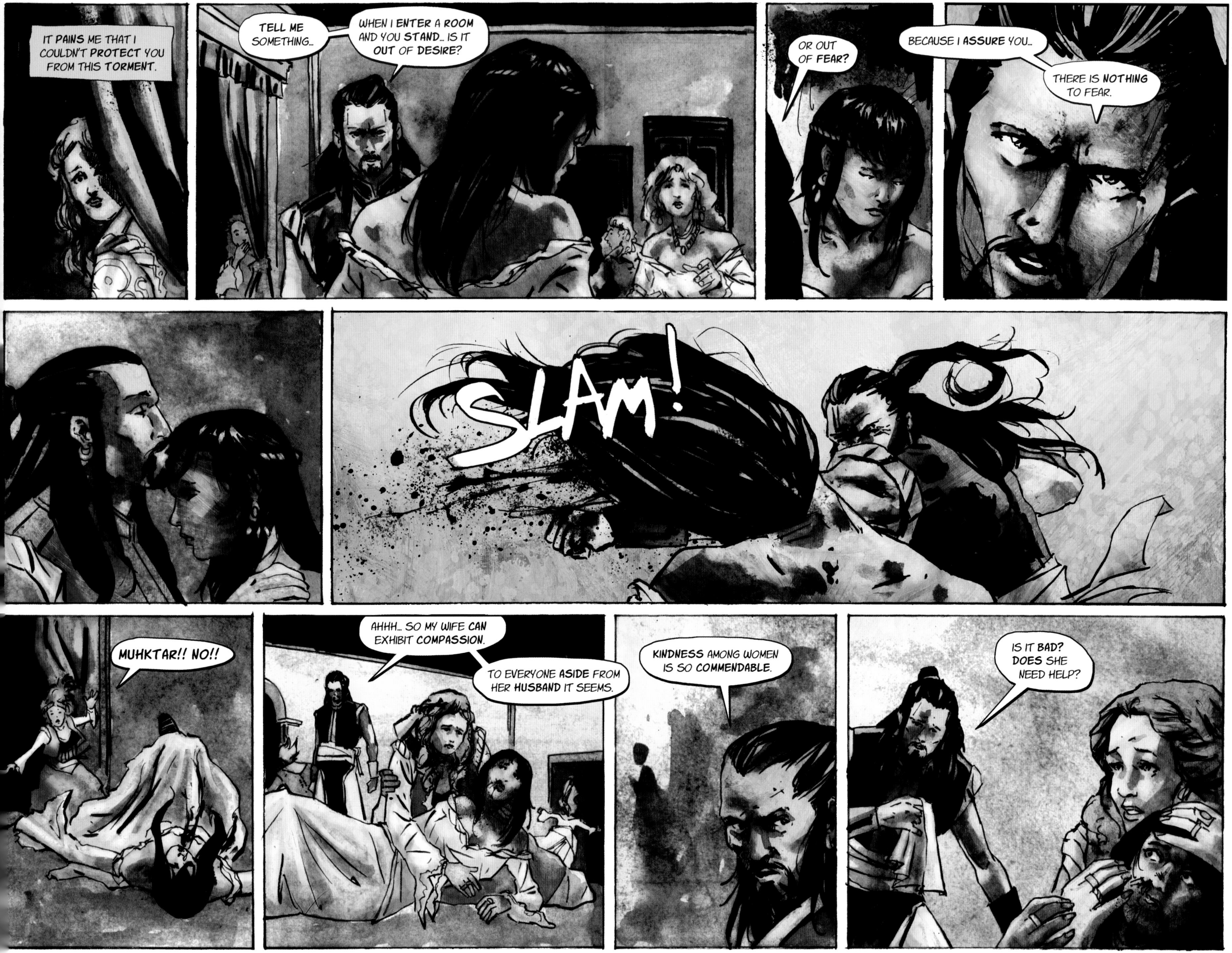
IT PAINS ME THAT I COULDN'T PROTECT YOU FROM THIS TORMENT.
TELL ME SOMETHING...
WHEN I ENTER A ROOM AND YOU STAND... IS IT OUT OF DESIRE?
OR OUT OF FEAR?
BECAUSE I ASSURE YOU...
THERE IS NOTHING TO FEAR.
SLAM!
MUHKTAR!! NO!!
AHHH... SO MY WIFE CAN EXHIBIT COMPASSION.
TO EVERYONE ASIDE FROM HER HUSBAND IT SEEMS.
KINDNESS AMONG WOMEN IS SO COMMENDABLE.
IS IT BAD? DOES SHE NEED HELP?

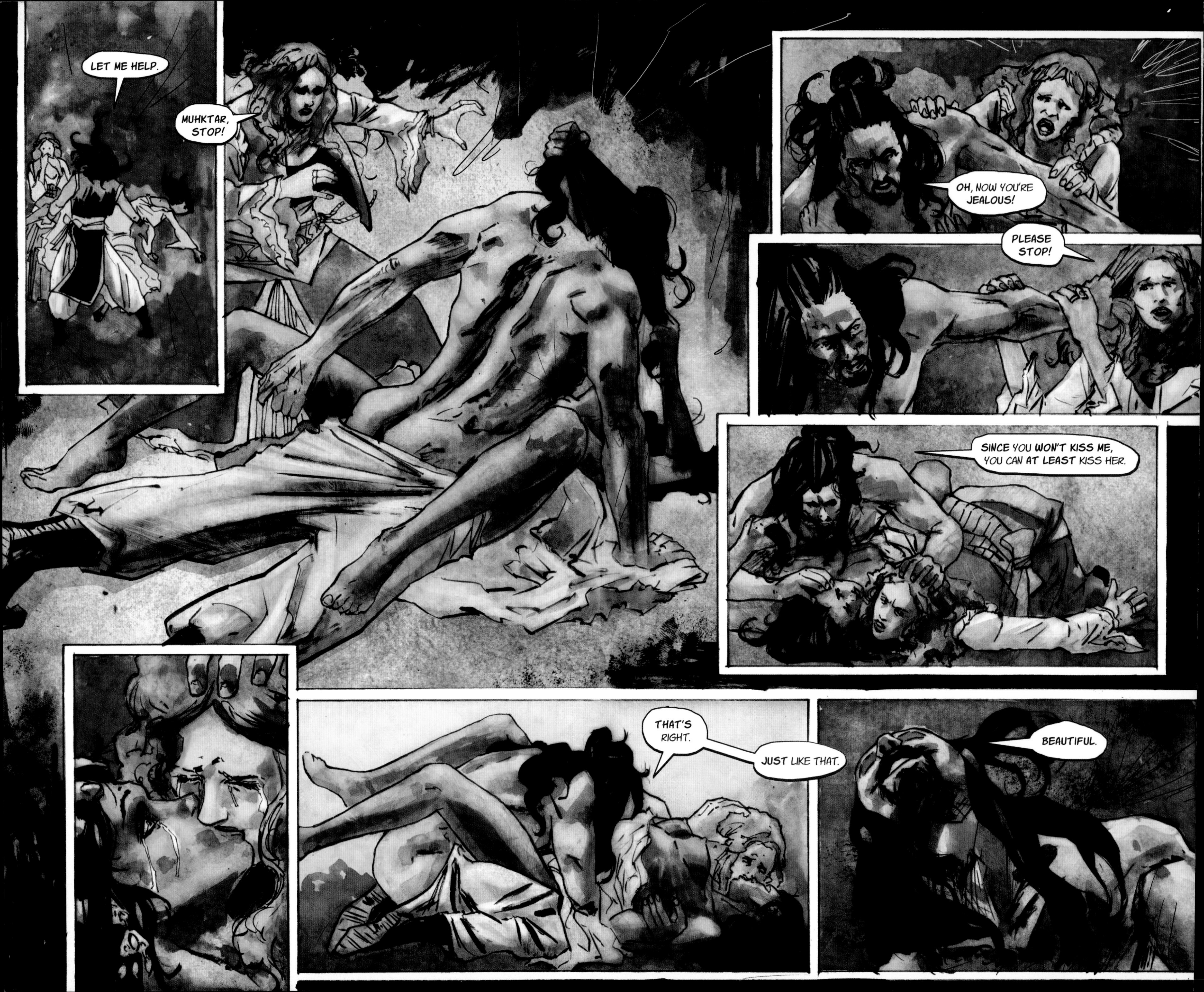

LET ME HELP.
MUHKTAR, STOP!
OH, NOW YOU'RE JEALOUS!
PLEASE STOP!
SINCE YOU WON'T KISS ME, YOU CAN AT LEAST KISS HER.
THAT'S RIGHT.
JUST LIKE THAT.
BEAUTIFUL.

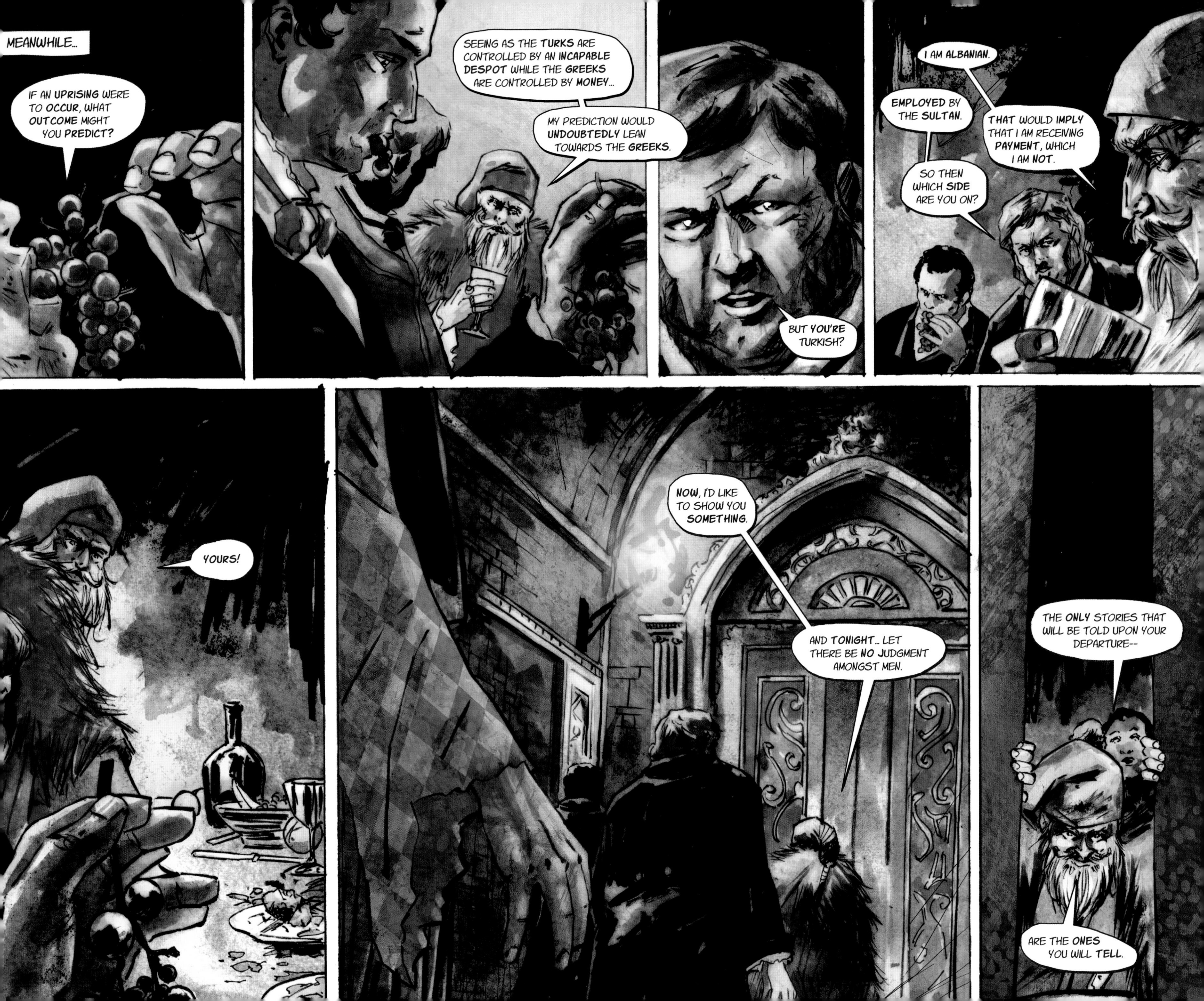
MEANWHILE...
IF AN UPRISING WERE TO OCCUR, WHAT OUTCOME MIGHT YOU PREDICT?
SEEING AS THE TURKS ARE CONTROLLED BY AN INCAPABLE DESPOT WHILE THE GREEKS ARE CONTROLLED BY MONEY...
MY PREDICTION WOULD UNDOUBTEDLY LEAN TOWARDS THE GREEKS.
BUT YOU'RE TURKISH?
I AM ALBANIAN.
EMPLOYED BY THE SULTAN.
THAT WOULD IMPLY THAT I AM RECEIVING PAYMENT, WHICH I AM NOT.
SO THEN WHICH SIDE ARE YOU ON?
YOURS!
NOW, I'D LIKE TO SHOW YOU SOMETHING.
AND TONIGHT... LET THERE BE NO JUDGMENT AMONGST MEN.
THE ONLY STORIES THAT WILL BE TOLD UPON YOUR DEPARTURE--
ARE THE ONES YOU WILL TELL.

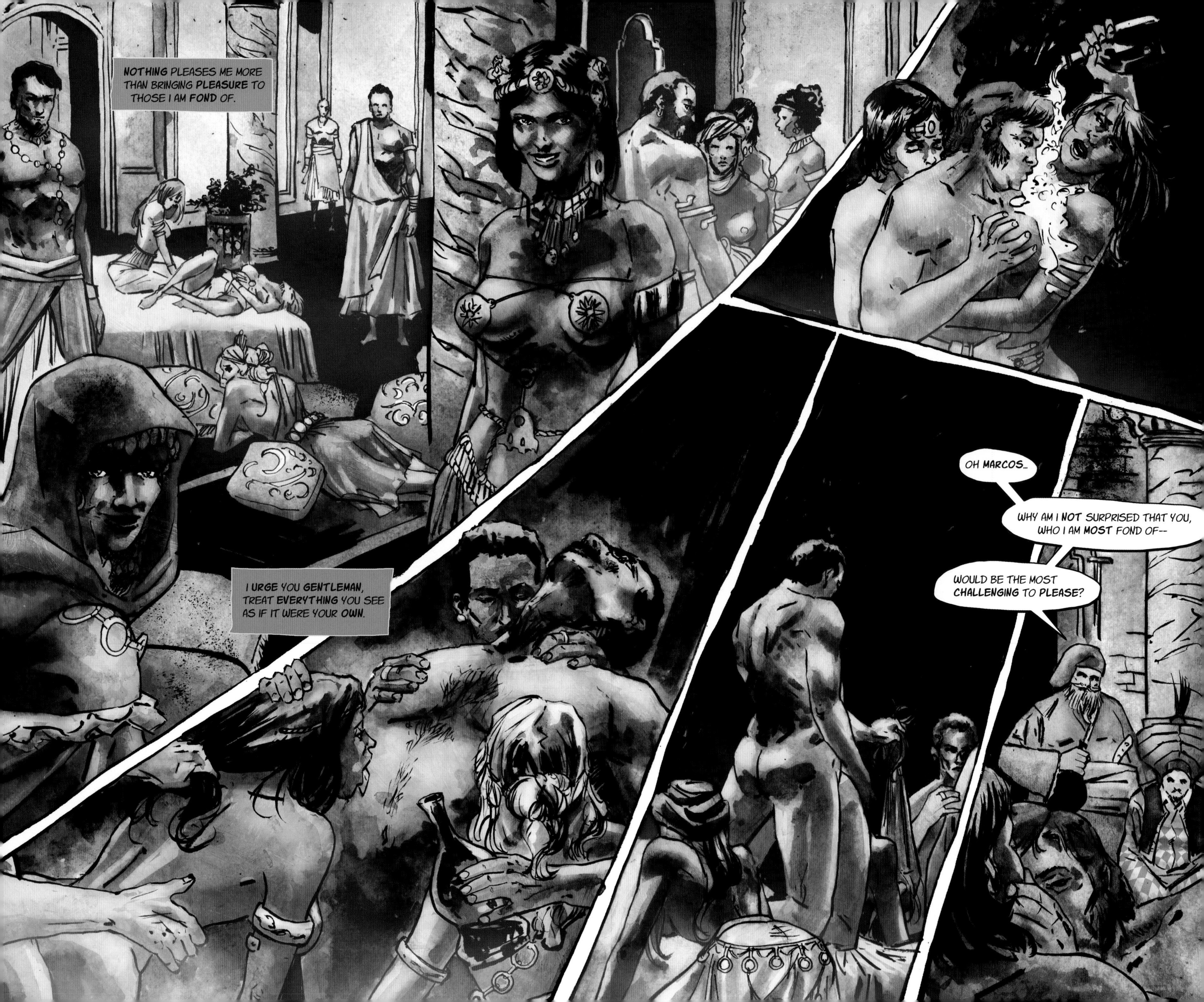
NOTHING PLEASES ME MORE THAN BRINGING PLEASURE TO THOSE I AM FOND OF.
I URGE YOU GENTLEMAN, TREAT EVERYTHING YOU SEE AS IF IT WERE YOUR OWN.
OH MARCOS...
WHY AM I NOT SURPRISED THAT YOU, WHO I AM MOST FOND OF--
WOULD BE THE MOST CHALLENGING TO PLEASE?

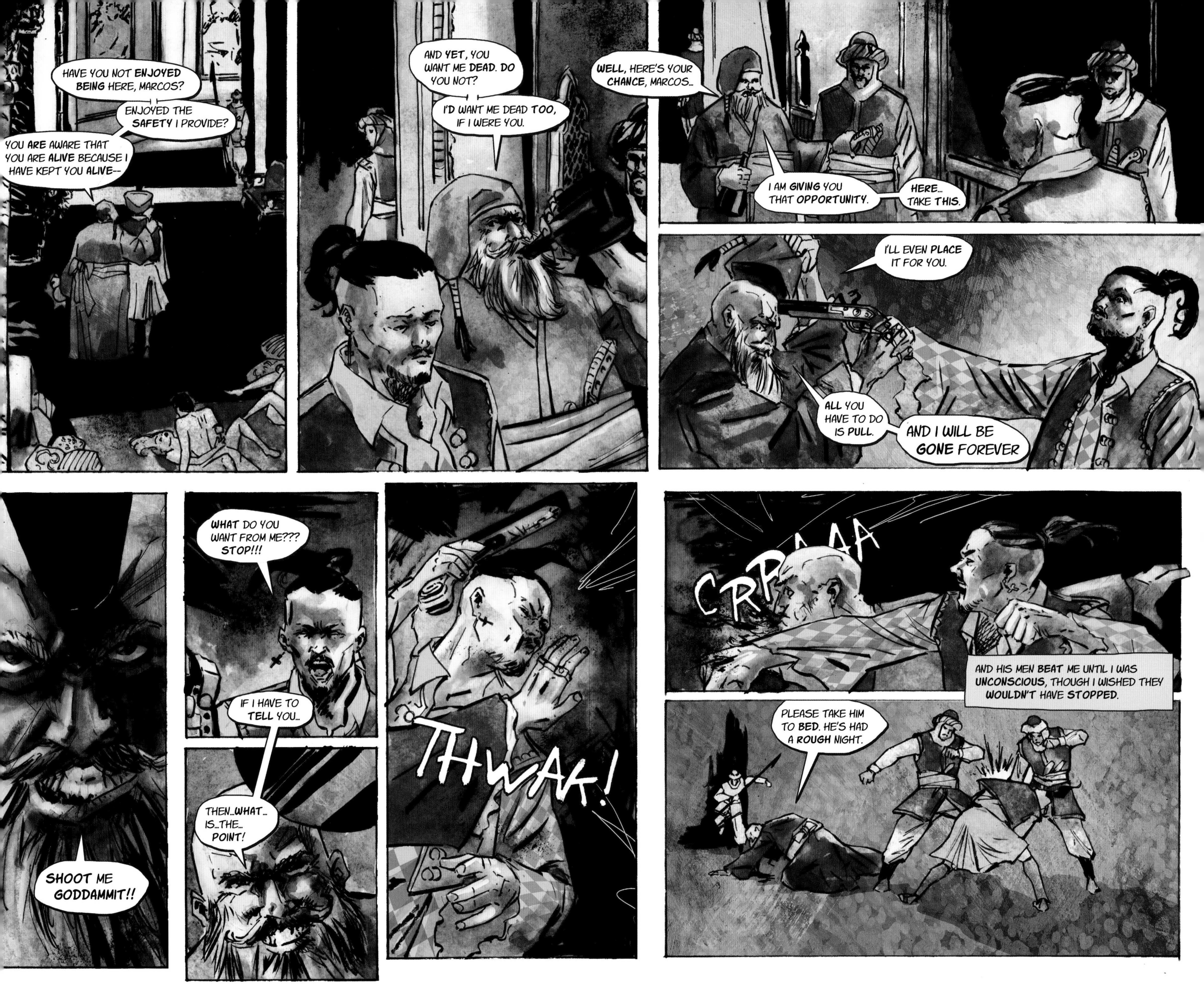

HAVE YOU NOT ENJOYED BEING HERE, MARCOS?
ENJOYED THE SAFETY I PROVIDE?
YOU ARE AWARE THAT YOU ARE ALIVE BECAUSE I HAVE KEPT YOU ALIVE--
AND YET, YOU WANT ME DEAD. DO YOU NOT?
I'D WANT ME DEAD TOO, IF I WERE YOU.
WELL, HERE'S YOUR CHANCE, MARCOS...
I AM GIVING YOU THAT OPPORTUNITY.
HERE... TAKE THIS.
I'LL EVEN PLACE IT FOR YOU.
ALL YOU HAVE TO DO IS PULL.
AND I WILL BE GONE FOREVER
SHOOT ME GODDAMMIT!!
WHAT DO YOU WANT FROM ME??? STOP!!!
IF I HAVE TO TELL YOU...
THEN...WHAT... IS...THE... POINT!
THWAK!
CRPAAA
AND HIS MEN BEAT ME UNTIL I WAS UNCONSCIOUS, THOUGH I WISHED THEY WOULDN'T HAVE STOPPED.
PLEASE TAKE HIM TO BED. HE'S HAD A ROUGH NIGHT.

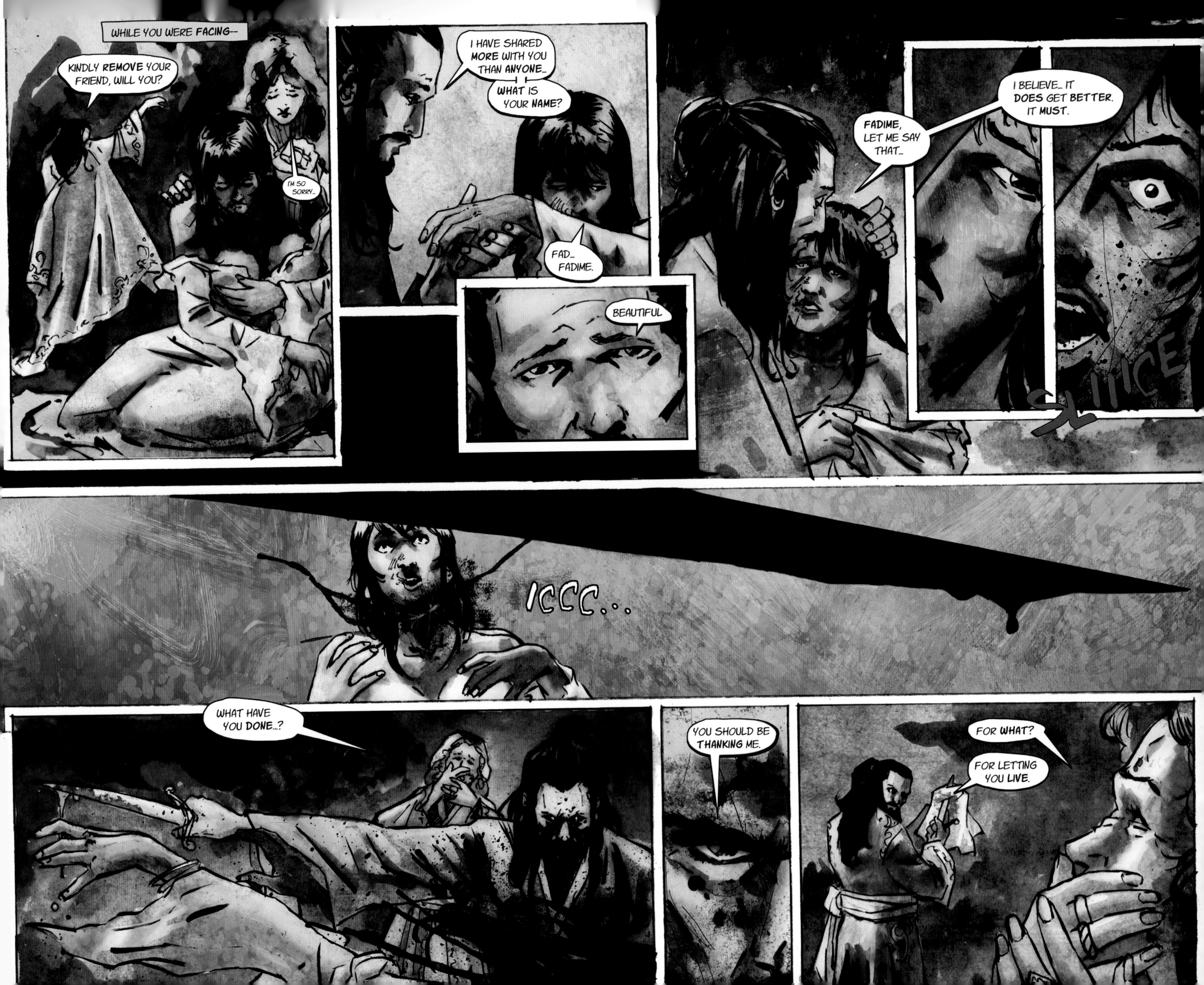
WHILE YOU WERE FACING--
KINDLY REMOVE YOUR FRIEND, WILL YOU?
I'M SO SORRY...
I HAVE SHARED MORE WITH YOU THAN ANYONE...
WHAT IS YOUR NAME?
FAD... FADIME.
BEAUTIFUL
FADIME, LET ME SAY THAT...
I BELIEVE... IT DOES GET BETTER. IT MUST.
SKLIIICE
ICCC...
WHAT HAVE YOU DONE...?
YOU SHOULD BE THANKING ME.
FOR WHAT?
FOR LETTING YOU LIVE.

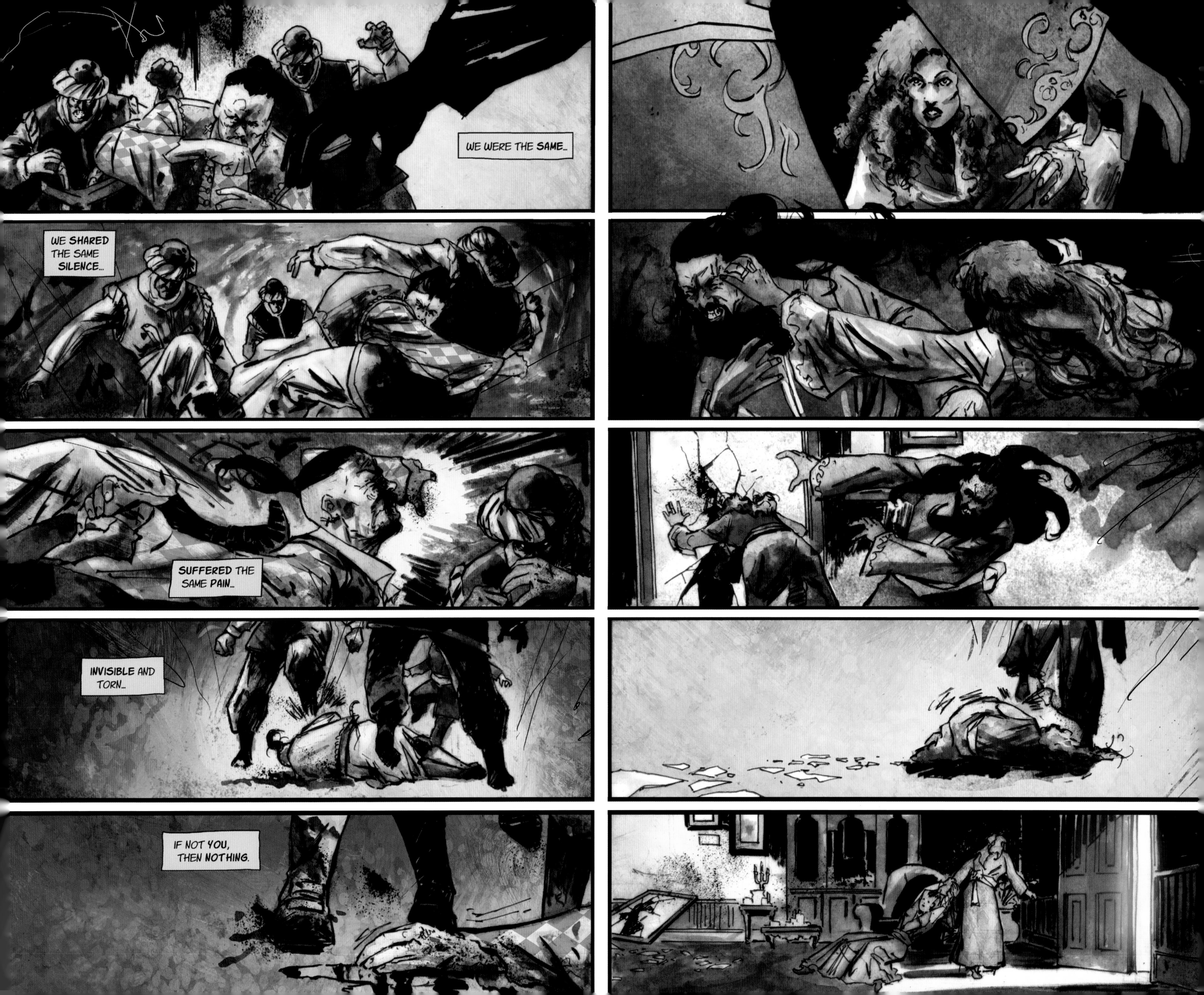
WE WERE THE SAME...
WE SHARED THE SAME SILENCE...
SUFFERED THE SAME PAIN...
INVISIBLE AND TORN...
IF NOT YOU, THEN NOTHING.

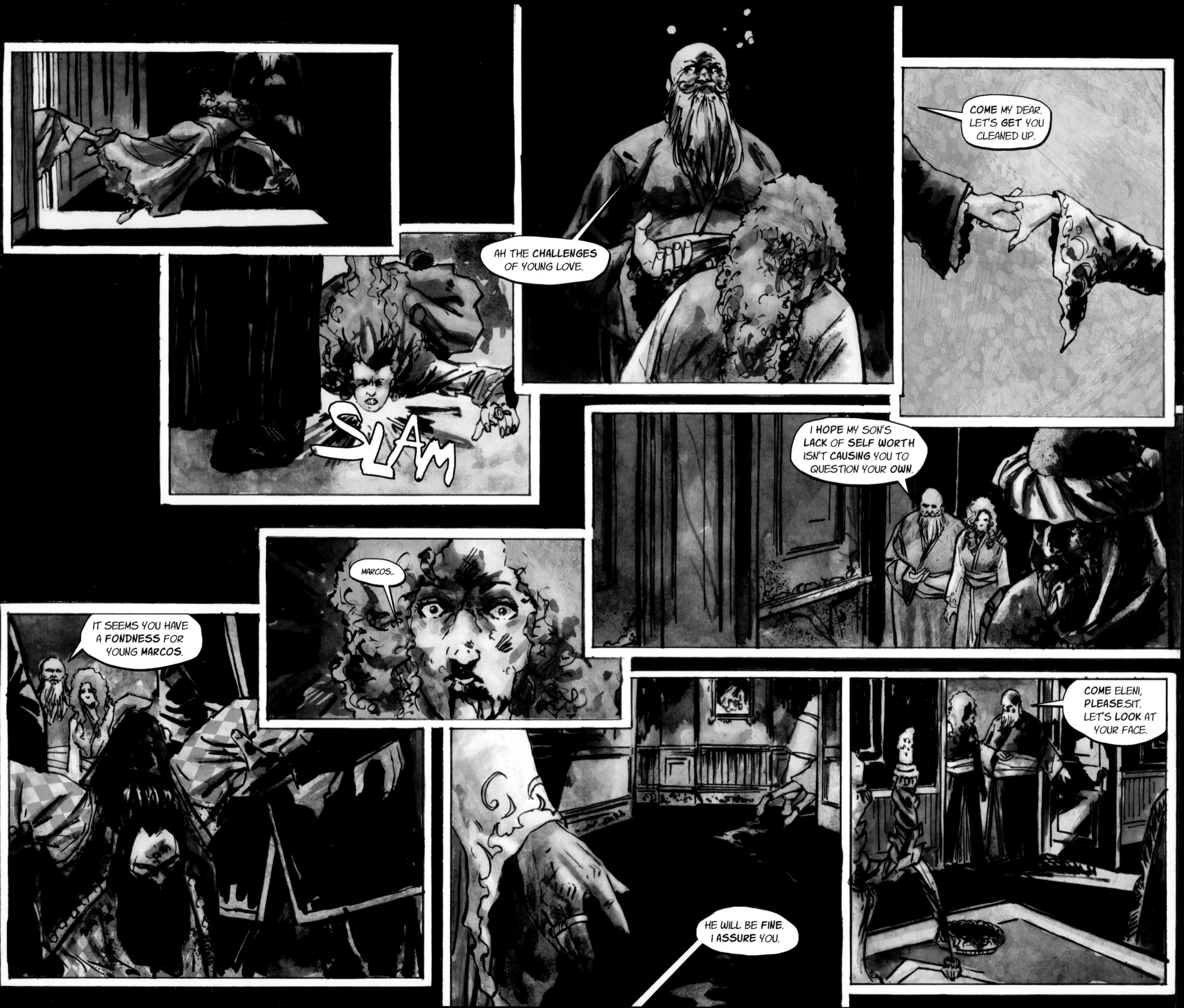
SLAM
AH THE CHALLENGES OF YOUNG LOVE.
COME MY DEAR. LET'S GET YOU CLEANED UP.
I HOPE MY SON'S LACK OF SELF WORTH ISN'T CAUSING YOU TO QUESTION YOUR OWN.
MARCOS...
IT SEEMS YOU HAVE A FONDNESS FOR YOUNG MARCOS.
HE WILL BE FINE. I ASSURE YOU.
COME ELENI, PLEASE.SIT. LET'S LOOK AT YOUR FACE.

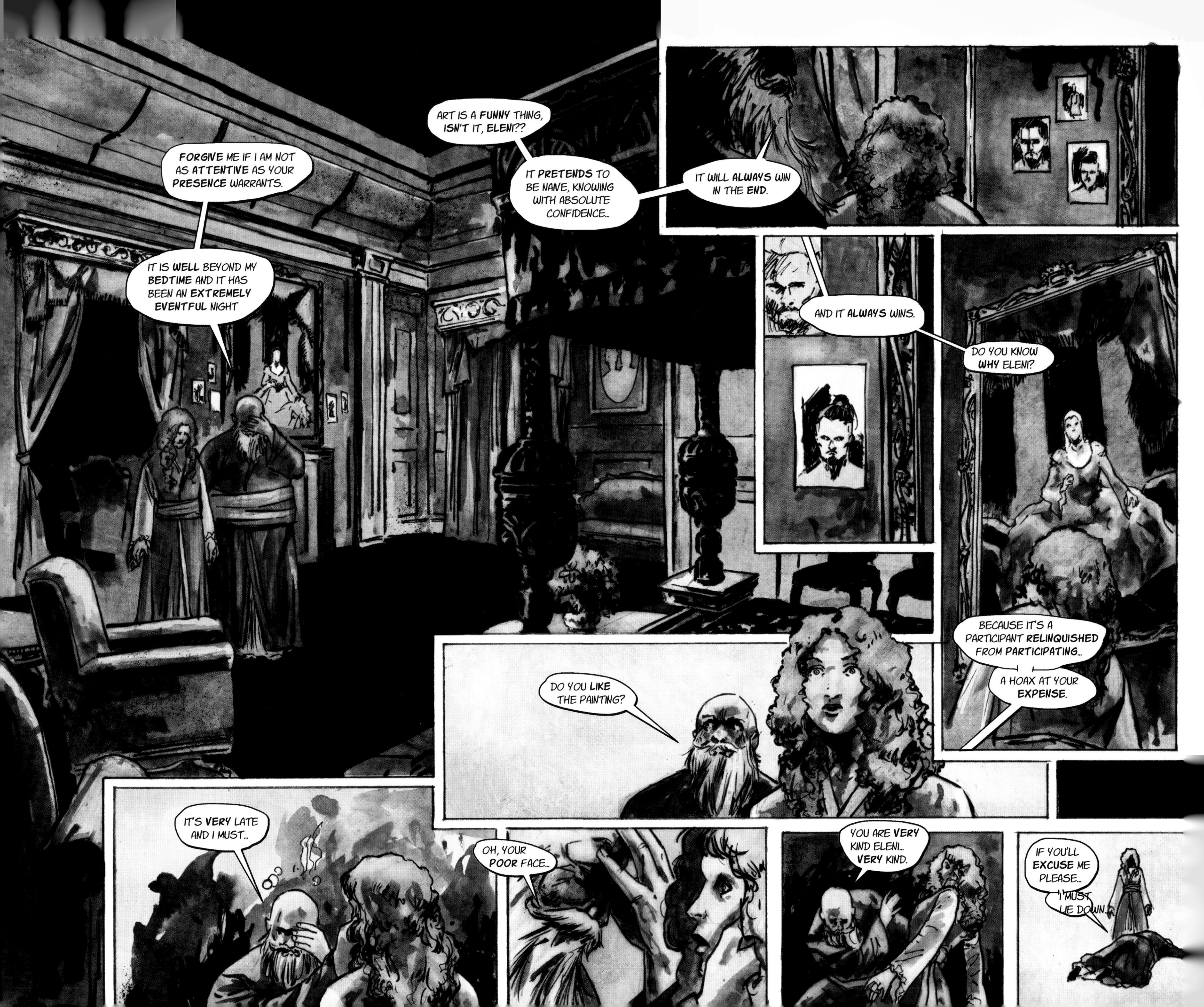
FORGIVE ME IF I AM NOT AS ATTENTIVE AS YOUR PRESENCE WARRANTS.
IT IS WELL BEYOND MY BEDTIME AND IT HAS BEEN AN EXTREMELY EVENTFUL NIGHT
ART IS A FUNNY THING, ISN'T IT, ELENI??
IT PRETENDS TO BE NAIVE, KNOWING WITH ABSOLUTE CONFIDENCE...
IT WILL ALWAYS WIN IN THE END.
AND IT ALWAYS WINS.
DO YOU KNOW WHY ELENI?
BECAUSE IT'S A PARTICIPANT RELINQUISHED FROM PARTICIPATING...
A HOAX AT YOUR EXPENSE.
DO YOU LIKE THE PAINTING?
IT'S VERY LATE AND I MUST...
OH, YOUR POOR FACE...
YOU ARE VERY KIND ELENI... VERY KIND.
IF YOU'LL EXCUSE ME PLEASE...
I MUST LIE DOWN.

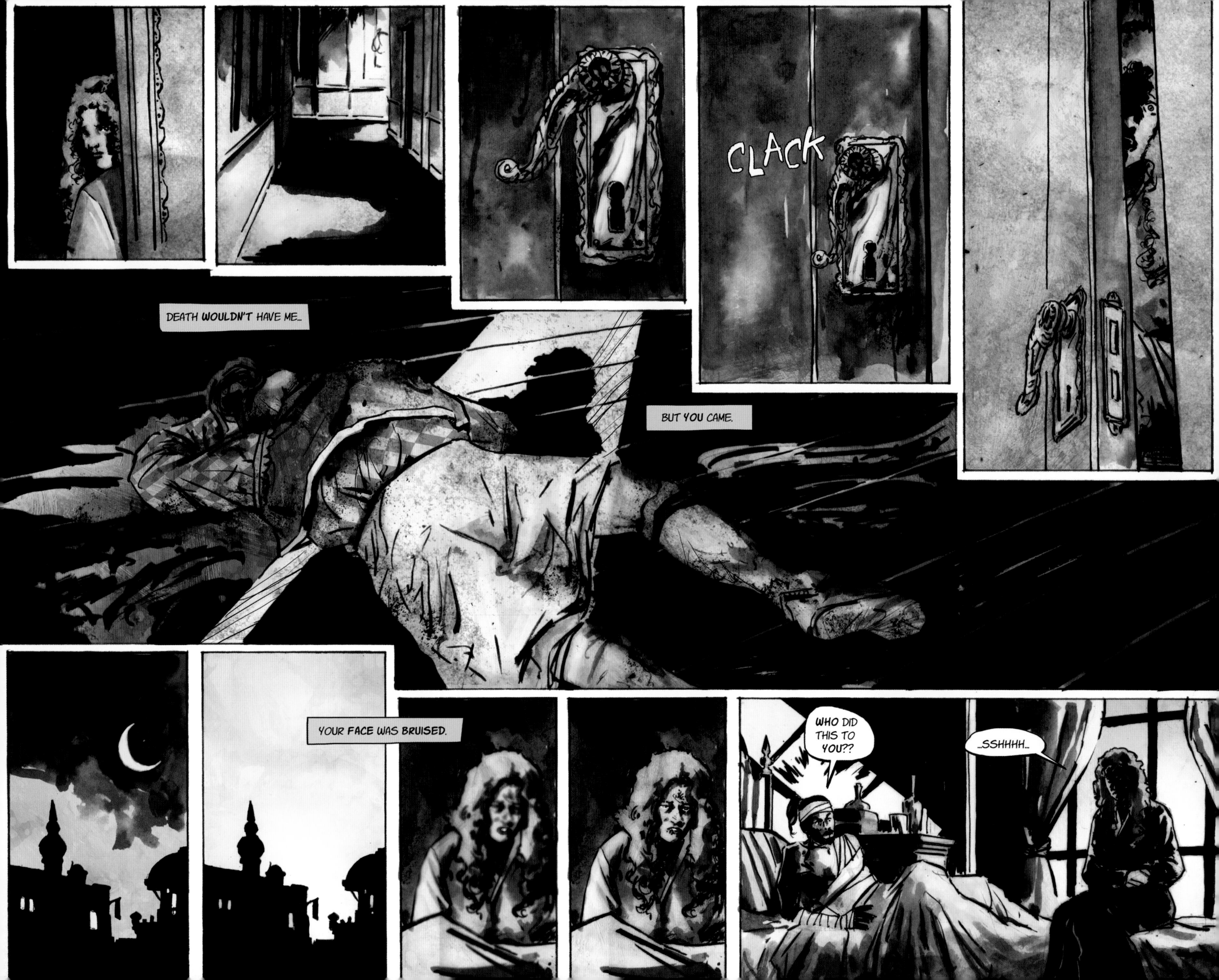
CLACK
DEATH WOULDN'T HAVE ME...
BUT YOU CAME.
YOUR FACE WAS BRUISED.
WHO DID THIS TO YOU??
...SSHHHH...

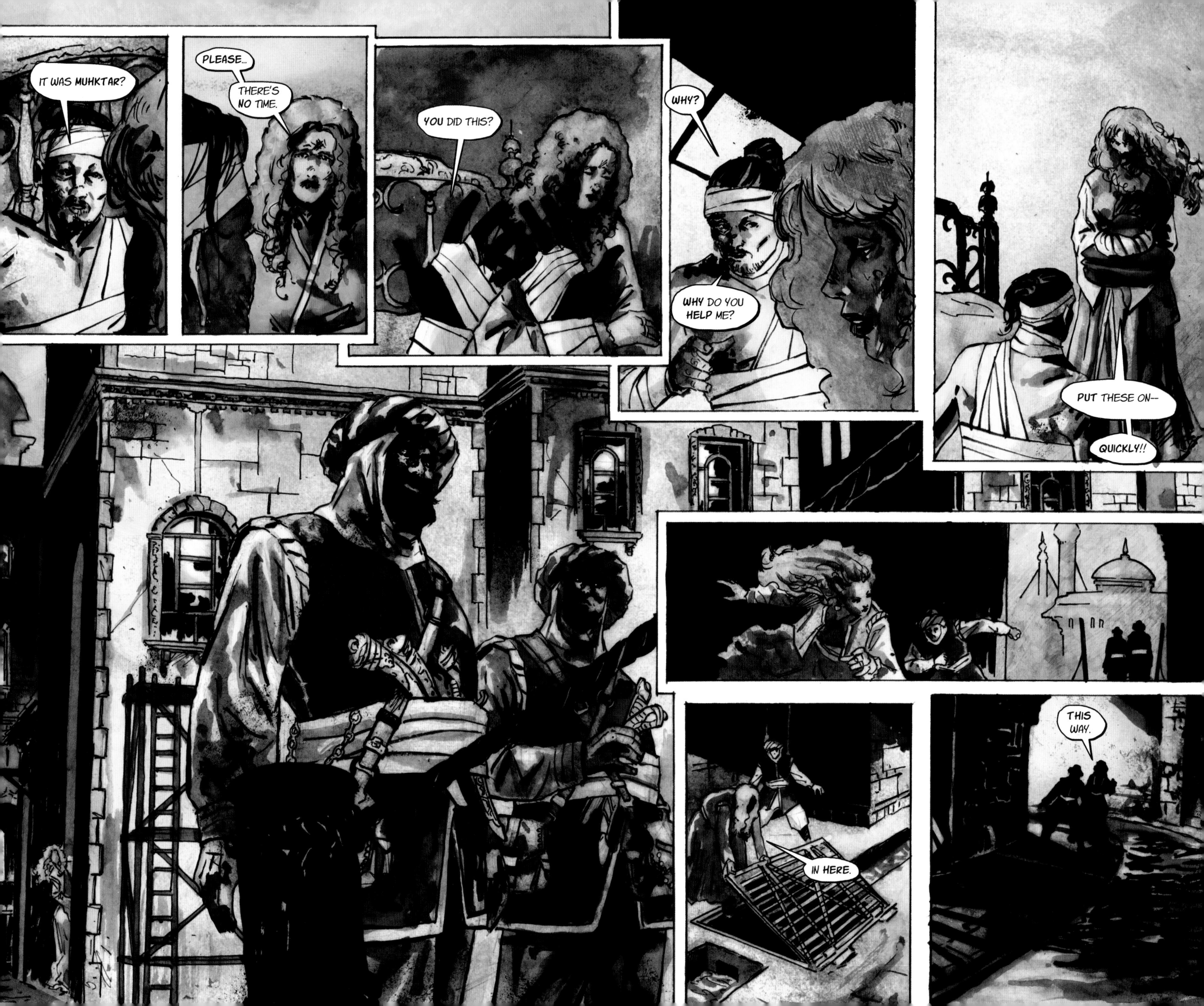
IT WAS MUHKTAR?
PLEASE...
THERE'S NO TIME.
YOU DID THIS?
WHY?
WHY DO YOU HELP ME?
PUT THESE ON--
QUICKLY!!
IN HERE.
THIS WAY.

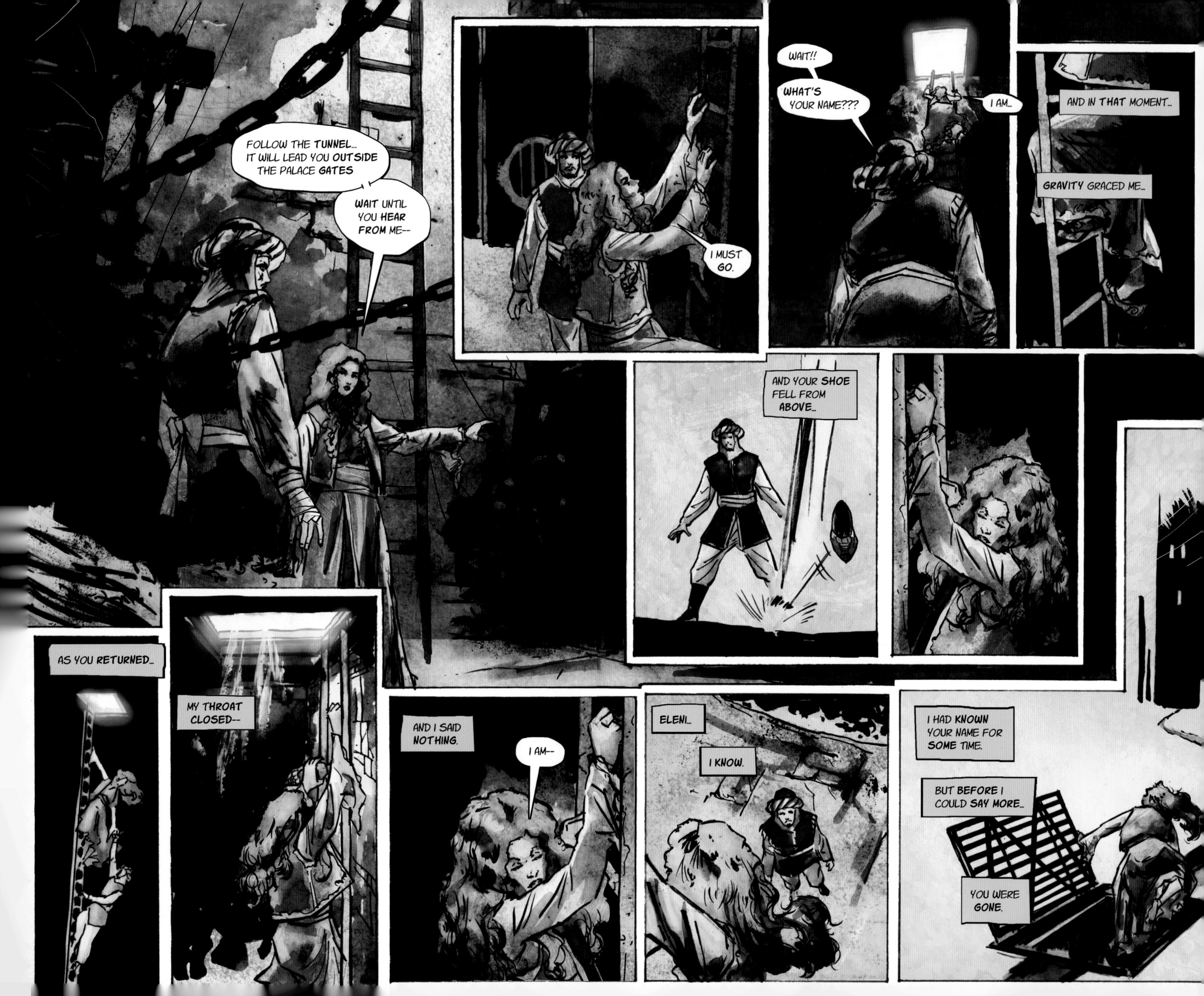
FOLLOW THE TUNNEL... IT WILL LEAD YOU OUTSIDE THE PALACE GATES
WAIT UNTIL YOU HEAR FROM ME--
I MUST GO.
WAIT!!
WHAT'S YOUR NAME???
I AM...
AND IN THAT MOMENT...
GRAVITY GRACED ME...
AND YOUR SHOE FELL FROM ABOVE...
AS YOU RETURNED...
MY THROAT CLOSED--
AND I SAID NOTHING.
I AM--
ELENI...
I KNOW.
I HAD KNOWN YOUR NAME FOR SOME TIME.
BUT BEFORE I COULD SAY MORE...
YOU WERE GONE.

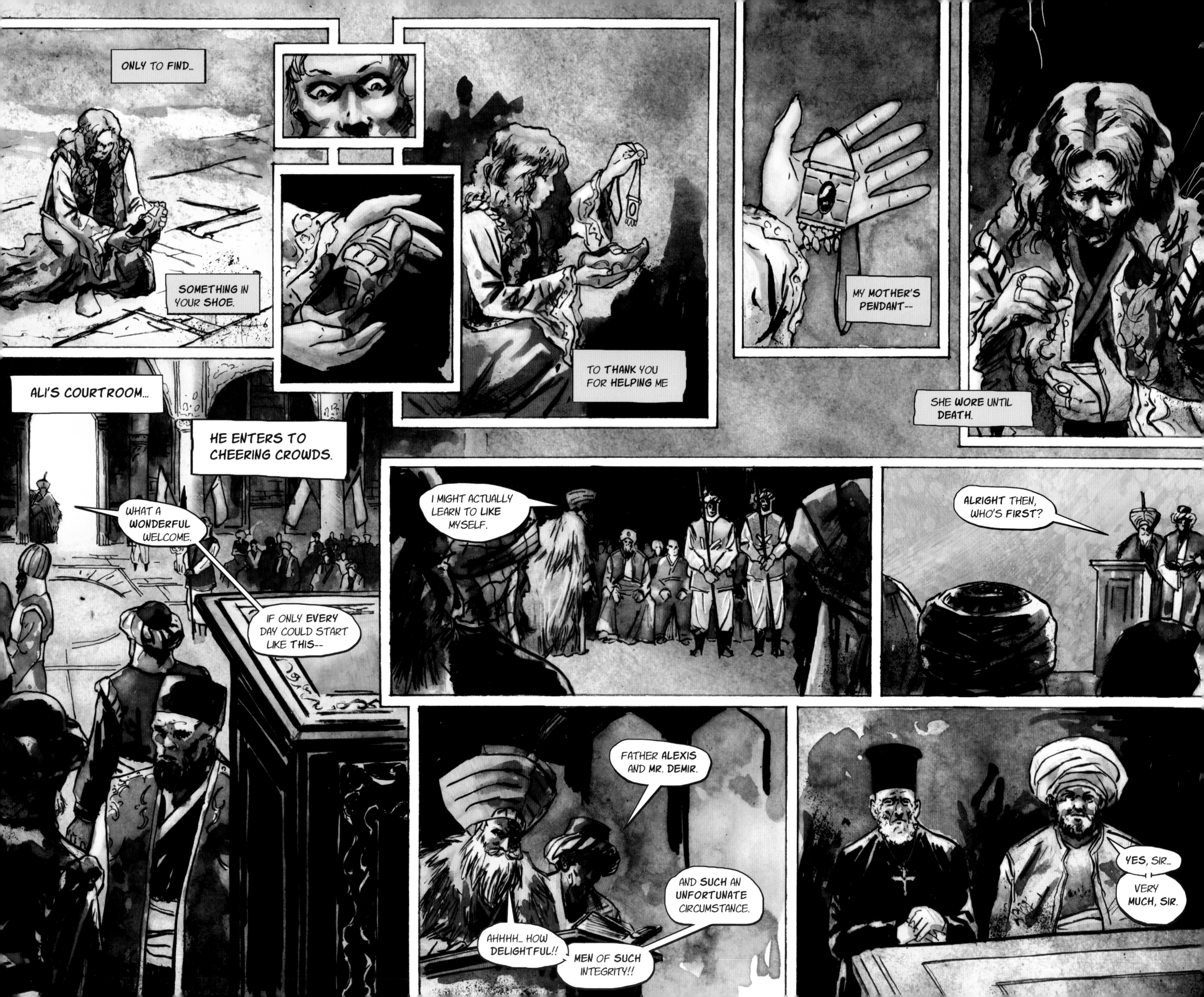
ONLY TO FIND...
SOMETHING IN YOUR SHOE.
TO THANK YOU FOR HELPING ME
MY MOTHER'S PENDANT--
SHE WORE UNTIL DEATH.
ALI'S COURTROOM...
HE ENTERS TO CHEERING CROWDS.
WHAT A WONDERFUL WELCOME.
IF ONLY EVERY DAY COULD START LIKE THIS--
I MIGHT ACTUALLY LEARN TO LIKE MYSELF.
ALRIGHT THEN, WHO'S FIRST?
FATHER ALEXIS AND MR. DEMIR.
AHHHH... HOW DELIGHTFUL!!
MEN OF SUCH INTEGRITY!!
AND SUCH AN UNFORTUNATE CIRCUMSTANCE.
YES, SIR...
VERY MUCH, SIR.

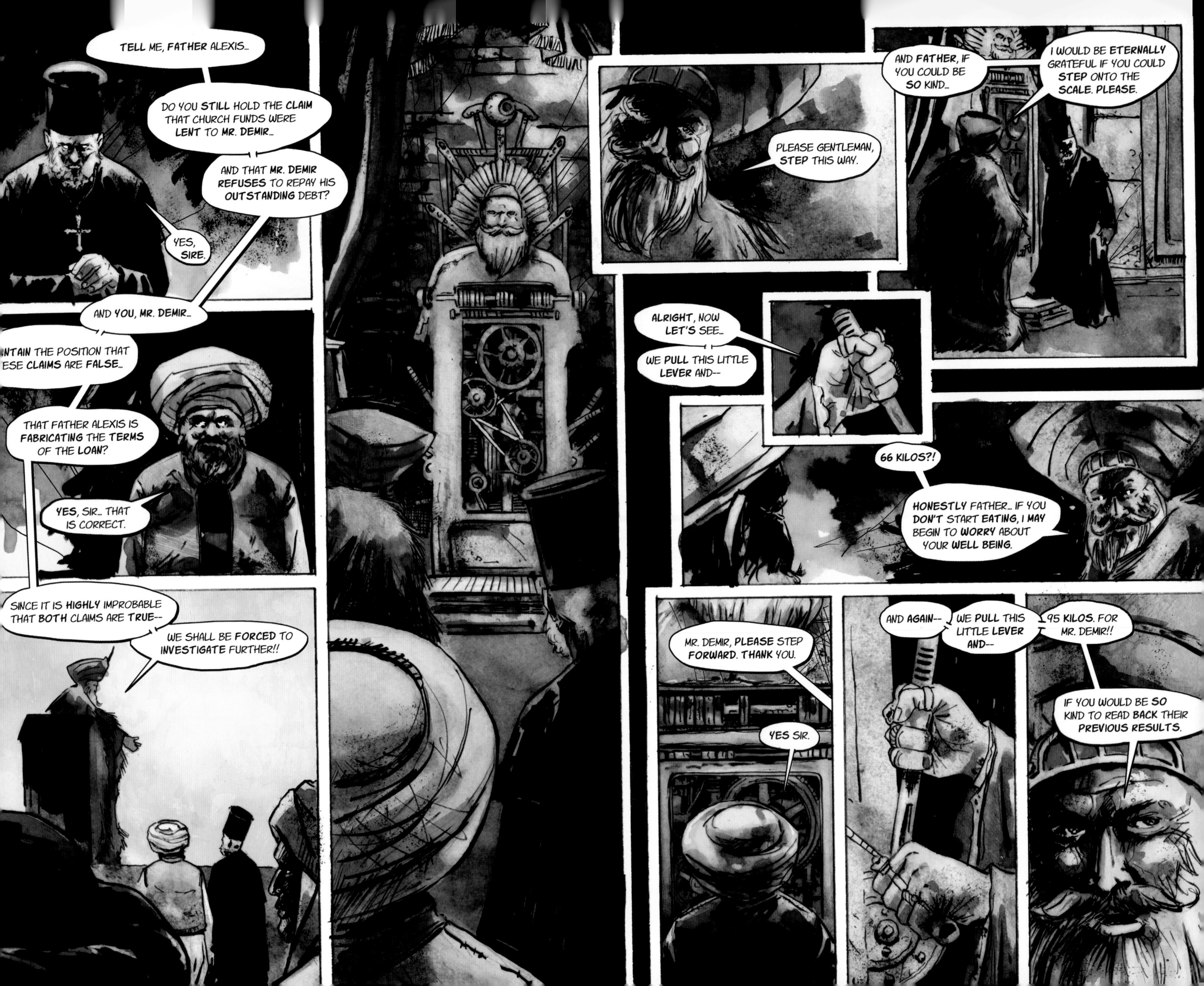
TELL ME, FATHER ALEXIS...
DO YOU STILL HOLD THE CLAIM THAT CHURCH FUNDS WERE LENT TO MR. DEMIR...
AND THAT MR. DEMIR REFUSES TO REPAY HIS OUTSTANDING DEBT?
YES, SIRE.
AND YOU, MR. DEMIR...
NTAIN THE POSITION THAT ESE CLAIMS ARE FALSE...
THAT FATHER ALEXIS IS FABRICATING THE TERMS OF THE LOAN?
YES, SIR... THAT IS CORRECT.
SINCE IT IS HIGHLY IMPROBABLE THAT BOTH CLAIMS ARE TRUE--
WE SHALL BE FORCED TO INVESTIGATE FURTHER!!
PLEASE GENTLEMAN, STEP THIS WAY.
AND FATHER, IF YOU COULD BE SO KIND...
I WOULD BE ETERNALLY GRATEFUL IF YOU COULD STEP ONTO THE SCALE. PLEASE.
ALRIGHT, NOW LET'S SEE...
WE PULL THIS LITTLE LEVER AND--
66 KILOS?!
HONESTLY FATHER... IF YOU DON'T START EATING, I MAY BEGIN TO WORRY ABOUT YOUR WELL BEING.
MR. DEMIR, PLEASE STEP FORWARD. THANK YOU.
YES SIR.
AND AGAIN--
WE PULL THIS LITTLE LEVER AND--
95 KILOS. FOR MR. DEMIR!!
IF YOU WOULD BE SO KIND TO READ BACK THEIR PREVIOUS RESULTS.

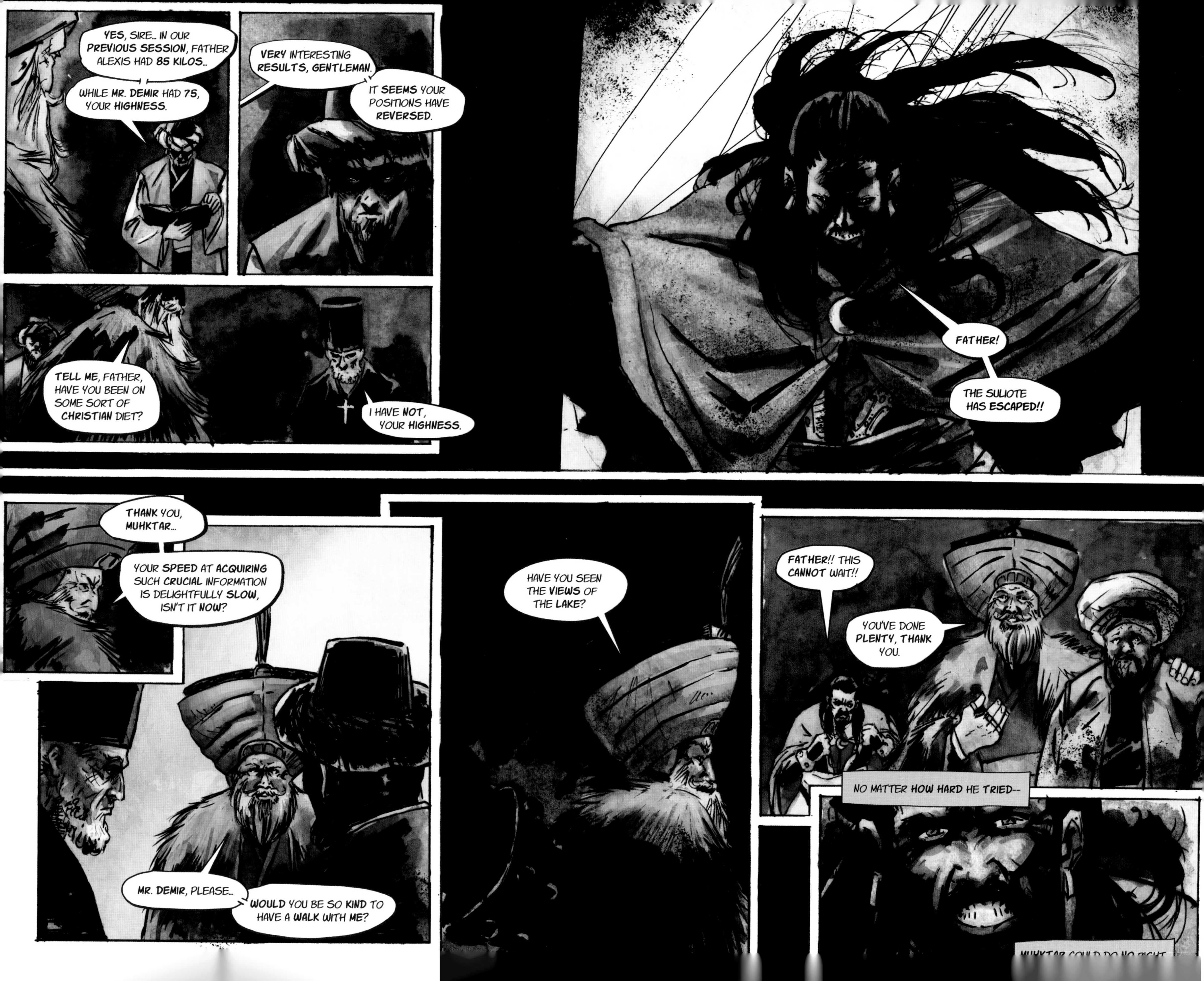
YES, SIRE... IN OUR PREVIOUS SESSION, FATHER ALEXIS HAD 85 KILOS...
WHILE MR. DEMIR HAD 75, YOUR HIGHNESS.
VERY INTERESTING RESULTS, GENTLEMAN.
IT SEEMS YOUR POSITIONS HAVE REVERSED.
TELL ME, FATHER, HAVE YOU BEEN ON SOME SORT OF CHRISTIAN DIET?
I HAVE NOT, YOUR HIGHNESS.
THANK YOU, MUHKTAR...
YOUR SPEED AT ACQUIRING SUCH CRUCIAL INFORMATION IS DELIGHTFULLY SLOW, ISN'T IT NOW?
MR. DEMIR, PLEASE...
WOULD YOU BE SO KIND TO HAVE A WALK WITH ME?
FATHER!
THE SULIOTE HAS ESCAPED!!
HAVE YOU SEEN THE VIEWS OF THE LAKE?
FATHER!! THIS CANNOT WAIT!!
YOU'VE DONE PLENTY, THANK YOU.
NO MATTER HOW HARD HE TRIED--

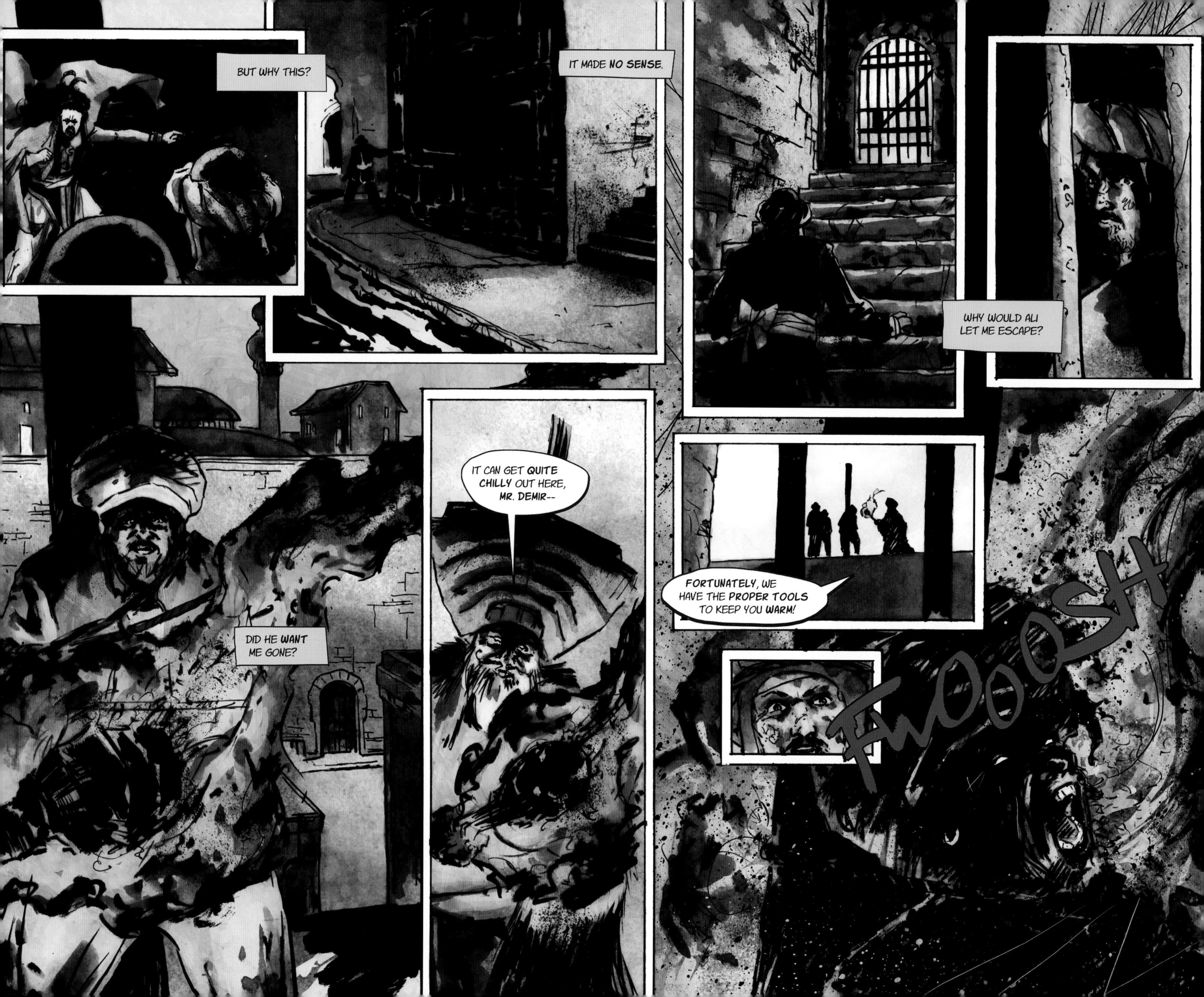
BUT WHY THIS?
IT MADE NO SENSE.
WHY WOULD ALI LET ME ESCAPE?
DID HE WANT ME GONE?
IT CAN GET QUITE CHILLY OUT HERE, MR. DEMIR--
FORTUNATELY, WE HAVE THE PROPER TOOLS TO KEEP YOU WARM!
FWOOOSH

THERE WERE NO MISTAKES WITH ALI.

IT WAS CALCULATED.

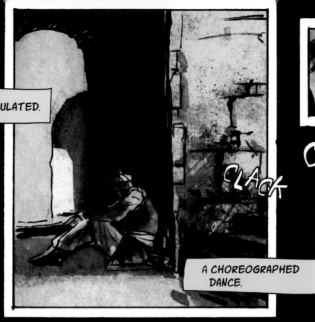

A CHOREOGRAPHED DANCE.

CLACK CLACK

CLACK

AS YOUR SIGNAL ARRIVED, SO DID MY FEAR.

THE WORLD OUTSIDE DID NOT BRING COMFORT.

AND THE IDEA OF FREEDOM??

IS THERE SUCH A THING?

ESCAPE FROM ONE PASHA AND HEAD TO THE HOME OF ANOTHER?

Do not leave tonight. you will be spotted. Depart just upon sunrise.

Suli no longer exists, going there will only put you in danger.

Go to my father, Ibrahim of Berat, and he will give you support. I will tell him you are coming and will visit as soon as i can.

Yours,
Eleni

DID I HAVE A CHOICE?

I AM A STRANGER OUTSIDE THESE WALLS--

ASIDE FROM YOU, THERE IS NO ONE.

SO FROM HERE FORWARD...

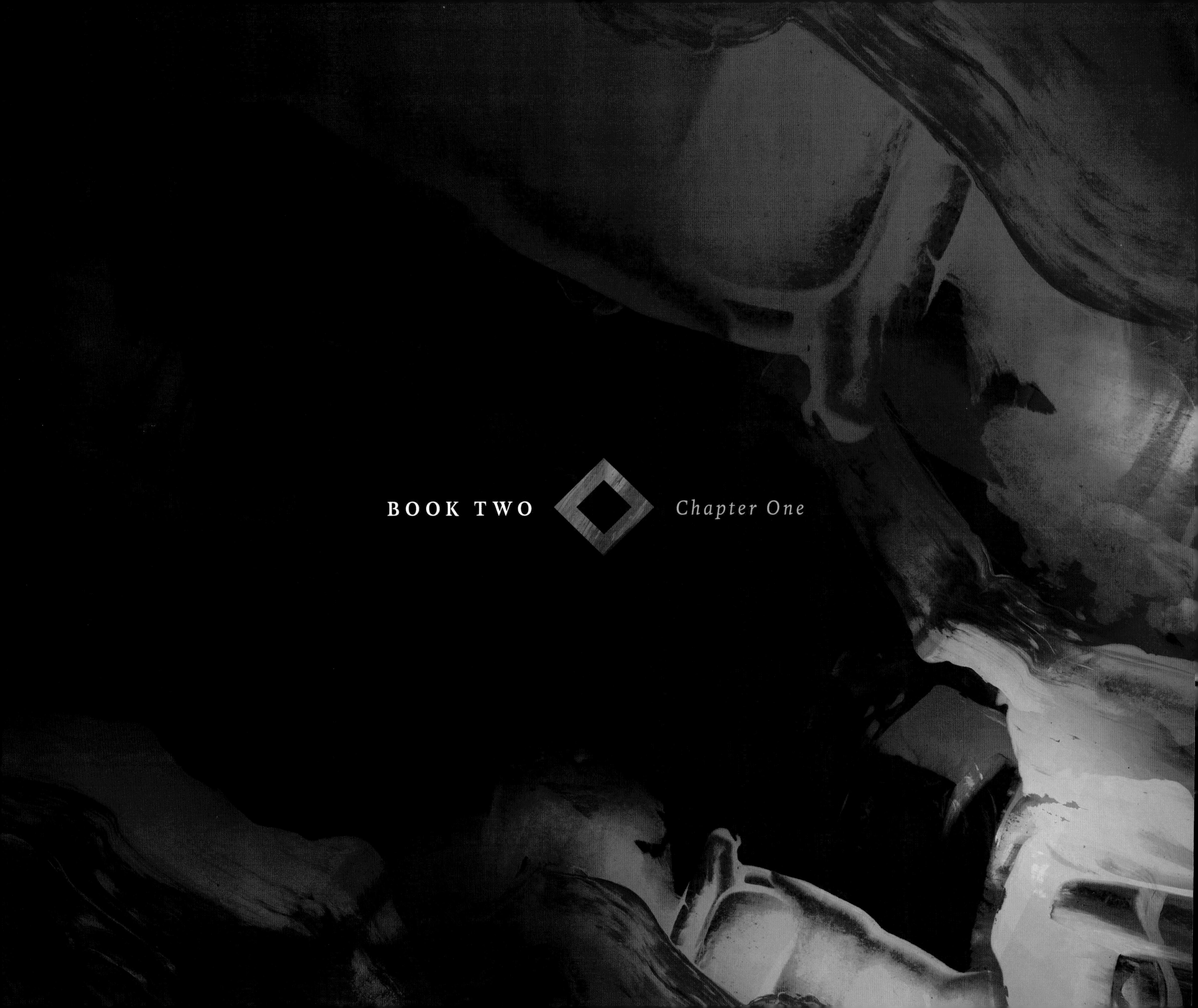

BOOK TWO

Chapter One

ADOLESCENCE

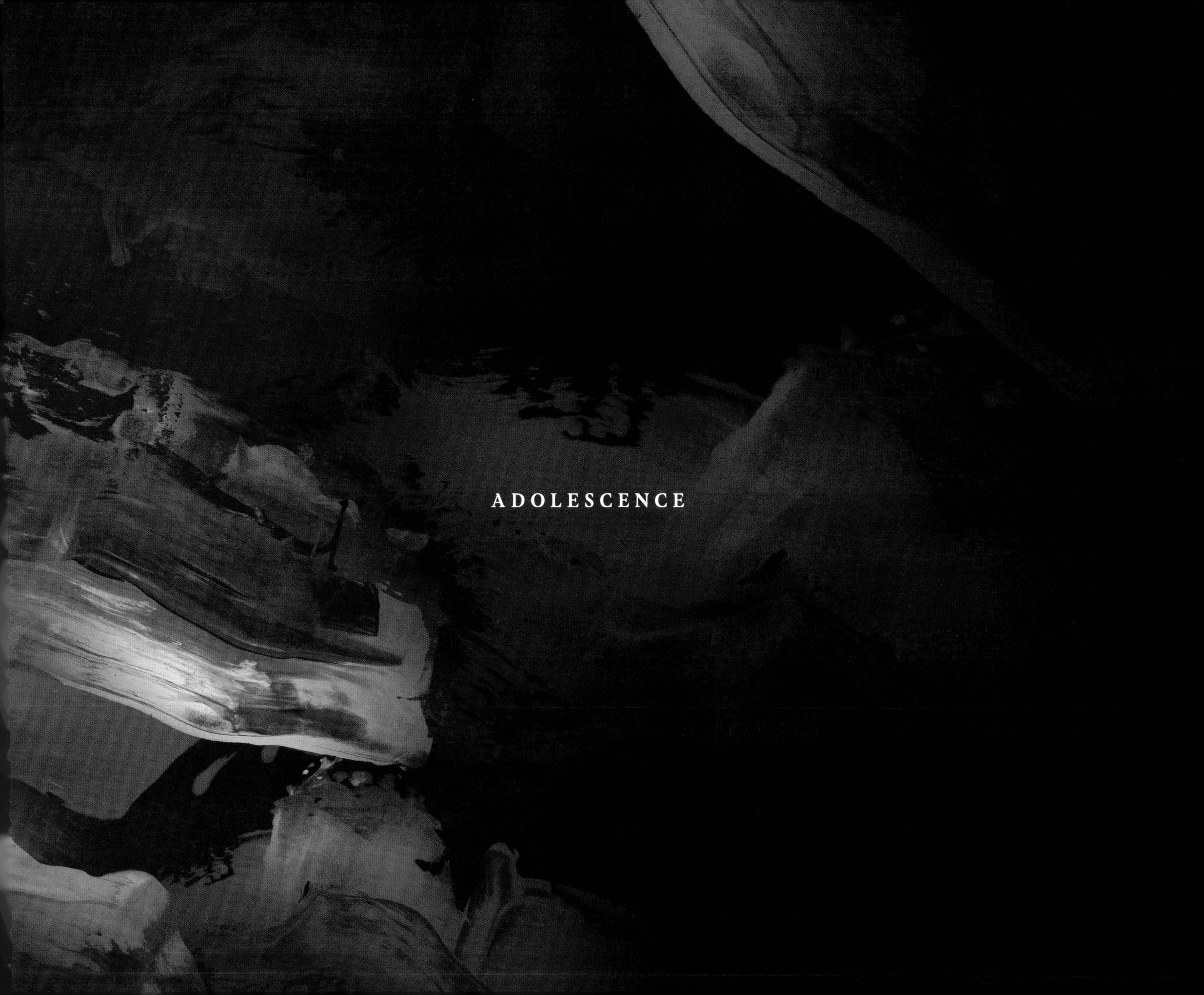

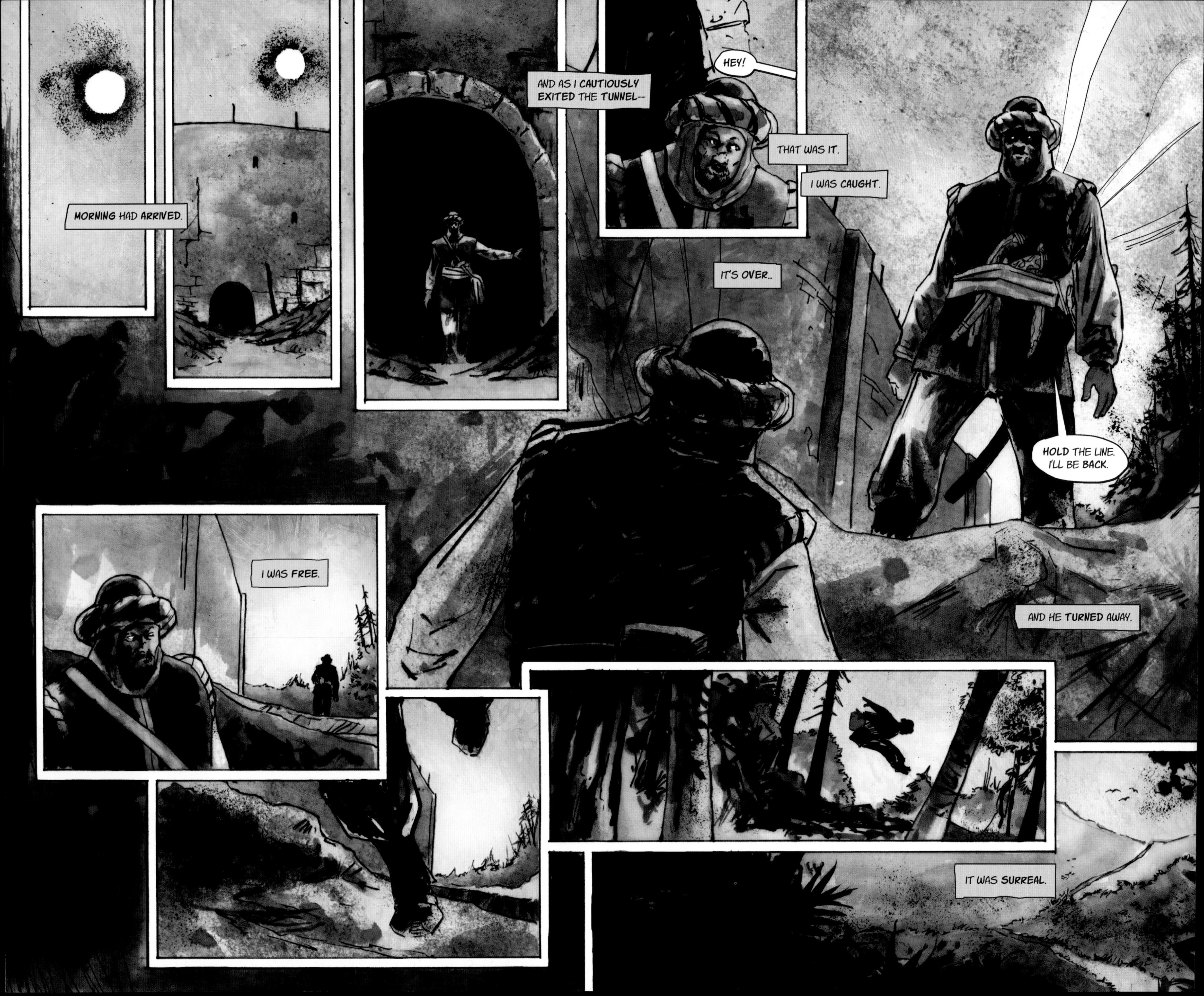
MORNING HAD ARRIVED.
AND AS I CAUTIOUSLY EXITED THE TUNNEL--
HEY!
THAT WAS IT.
I WAS CAUGHT.
IT'S OVER...
HOLD THE LINE. I'LL BE BACK.
AND HE TURNED AWAY.
I WAS FREE.
IT WAS SURREAL.

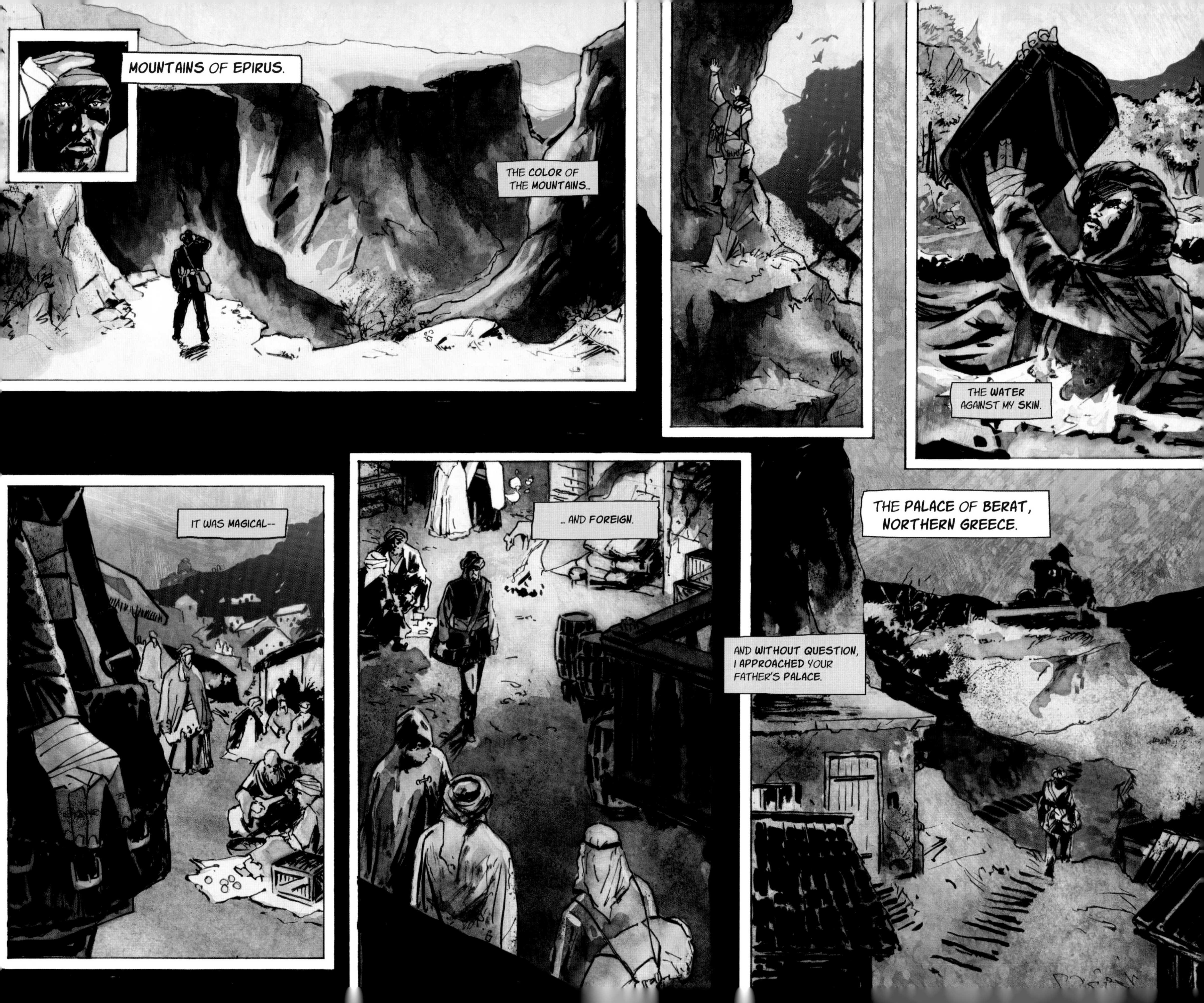
MOUNTAINS OF EPIRUS.
THE COLOR OF THE MOUNTAINS...
THE WATER AGAINST MY SKIN.
IT WAS MAGICAL--
...AND FOREIGN.
THE PALACE OF BERAT, NORTHERN GREECE.
AND WITHOUT QUESTION, I APPROACHED YOUR FATHER'S PALACE.

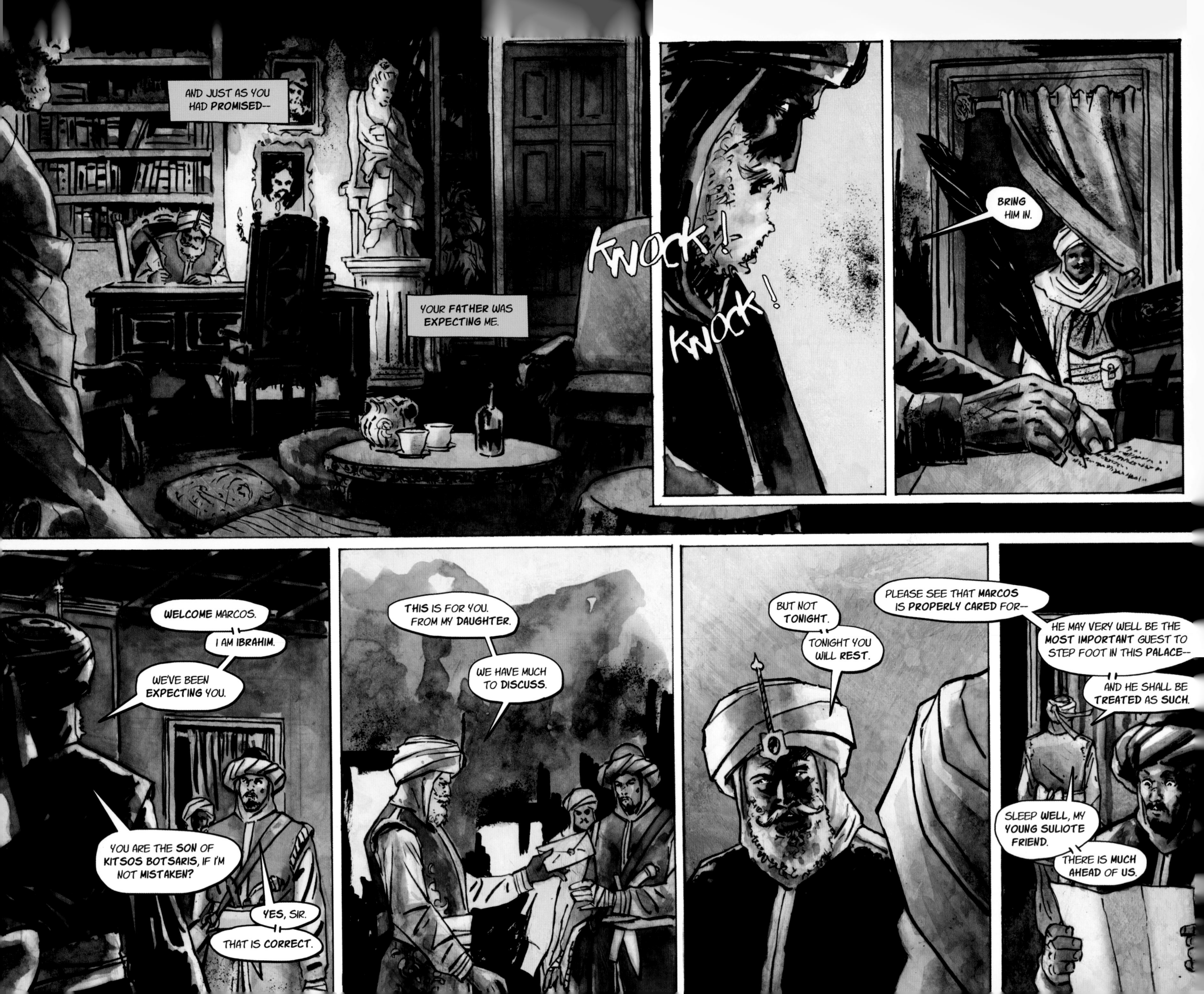
AND JUST AS YOU HAD PROMISED--
YOUR FATHER WAS EXPECTING ME.
KNOCK!
KNOCK!
BRING HIM IN.
WELCOME MARCOS.
I AM IBRAHIM.
WE'VE BEEN EXPECTING YOU.
YOU ARE THE SON OF KITSOS BOTSARIS, IF I'M NOT MISTAKEN?
YES, SIR.
THAT IS CORRECT.
THIS IS FOR YOU. FROM MY DAUGHTER.
WE HAVE MUCH TO DISCUSS.
BUT NOT TONIGHT.
TONIGHT YOU WILL REST.
PLEASE SEE THAT MARCOS IS PROPERLY CARED FOR--
HE MAY VERY WELL BE THE MOST IMPORTANT GUEST TO STEP FOOT IN THIS PALACE--
AND HE SHALL BE TREATED AS SUCH.
SLEEP WELL, MY YOUNG SULIOTE FRIEND.
THERE IS MUCH AHEAD OF US.

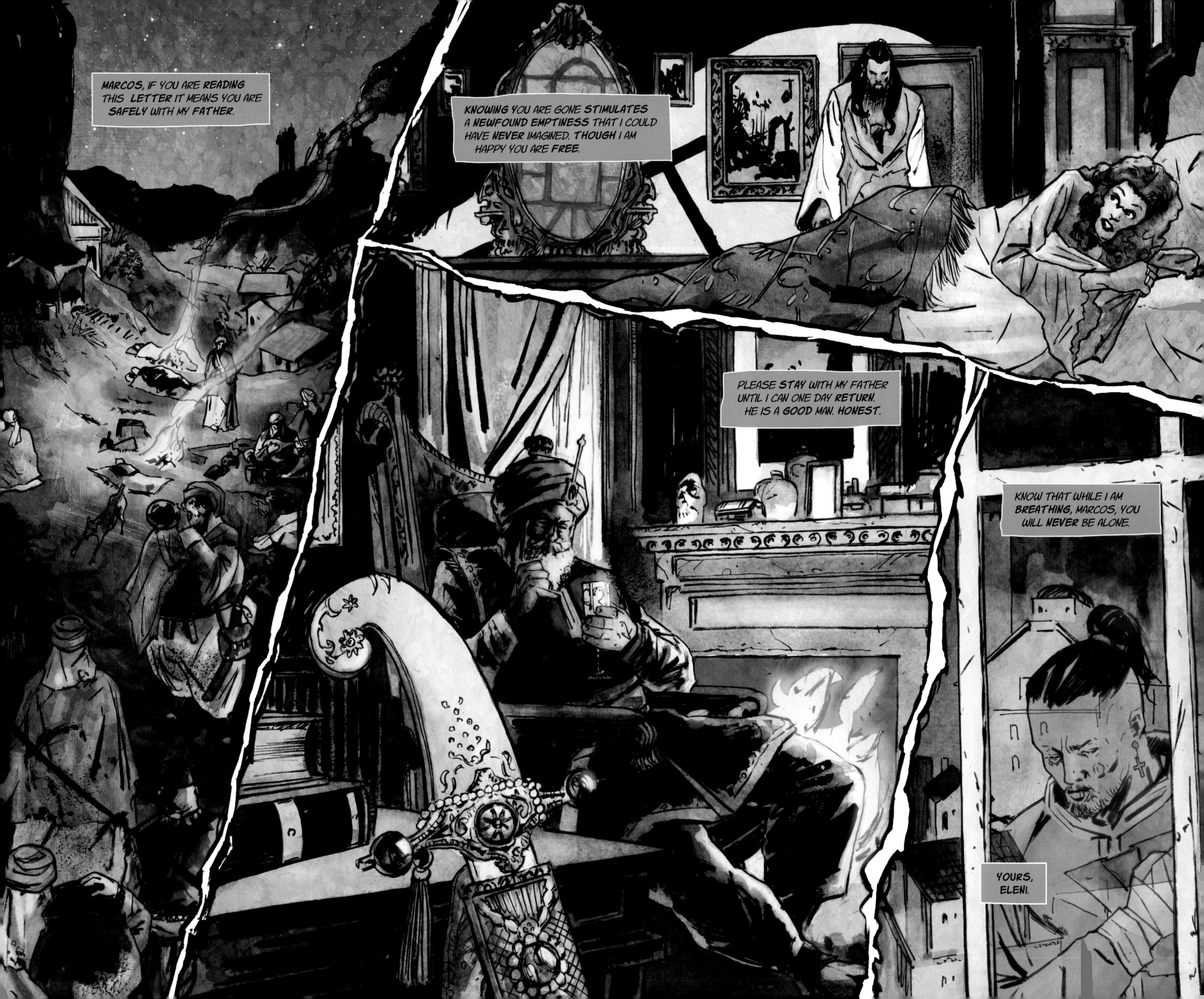
MARCOS, IF YOU ARE READING THIS LETTER IT MEANS YOU ARE SAFELY WITH MY FATHER.
KNOWING YOU ARE GONE STIMULATES A NEWFOUND EMPTINESS THAT I COULD HAVE NEVER IMAGINED. THOUGH I AM HAPPY YOU ARE FREE.
PLEASE STAY WITH MY FATHER UNTIL I CAN ONE DAY RETURN. HE IS A GOOD MAN. HONEST.
KNOW THAT WHILE I AM BREATHING, MARCOS, YOU WILL NEVER BE ALONE.
YOURS, ELENI.

MORNING

WHY IS HE STILL WEARING THAT HIDEOUS OUTFIT?

HAS NO ONE OFFERED A CHANGE OF CLOTHES?

YES, SIR. THEY DID.

BUT I CANNOT ACCEPT.

UNFORTUNATELY, I MUST BE GOING.

AND WHERE MIGHT YOU GO?

BEYOND YOUR RESPONSIBILITY, SIR.

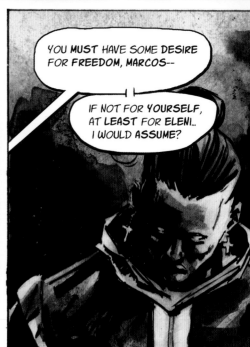

BEING THE SON OF A MAN LIKE YOUR FATHER PUTS YOU IN A PROMINENT POSITION.

I HAVE NO INTEREST IN THAT POSITION.

BUT YOU HAVE AN INTEREST IN MY DAUGHTER?

EXCUSE ME?

NOW, MORE THAN EVER, GREECE NEEDS A LEADER.

WHAT GREECE NEEDS IS SOMETHING FAR BEYOND WHAT I CAN PROVIDE...

I'M SORRY TO DISAPPOINT YOU— BUT I'M NO LEADER.

AND MAYBE THAT'S TRUE MARCOS...

BUT WHAT'S THE ALTERNATIVE??

SPEND YOUR LIFE IN HIDING?

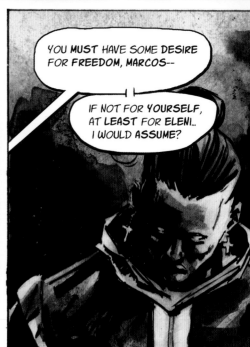

YOU MUST HAVE SOME DESIRE FOR FREEDOM, MARCOS—

IF NOT FOR YOURSELF, AT LEAST FOR ELENI... I WOULD ASSUME?

WHEN YOU DON'T SPEAK, IS THAT TYPICALLY A GOOD THING?

YOU'RE NOT ALONE, MARCOS.

NOT IN THIS.

THIS IS MY SON, ISMAEL. YOU WILL LISTEN TO HIM.

AND HE WILL PREPARE YOU FOR WHAT IS AHEAD.

THERE IS MUCH TO ACCOMPLISH AND VERY LITTLE TIME TO DO SO.

BACK IN IOANNINA...

IS IT YOUR INTENTION TO STEAL EVERY MOMENT OF JOY FROM ME OR JUST A COINCIDENCE?

WHAT THRILLING NEWS DO YOU HAVE FOR ME NOW, MUHKTAR?

IBRAHIM OF BERAT IS HOUSING THE SULIOTE PRISONER.

OOOHHH GOODNESS

NO MUHKTAR... NOOOO!!

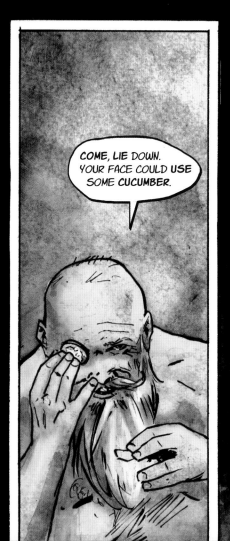

COME, LIE DOWN. YOUR FACE COULD USE SOME CUCUMBER.

DO NOT TOUCH ME!

I'M DONE WITH YOUR MOCKING!!

NO MOCKING!! JUST A FATHER CONCERNED WITH HIS SON'S COMPLEXION.

AAAAGH!!

LIKE I'VE ALWAYS SAID... HEALTHY SKIN, HEALTHY HEART!!

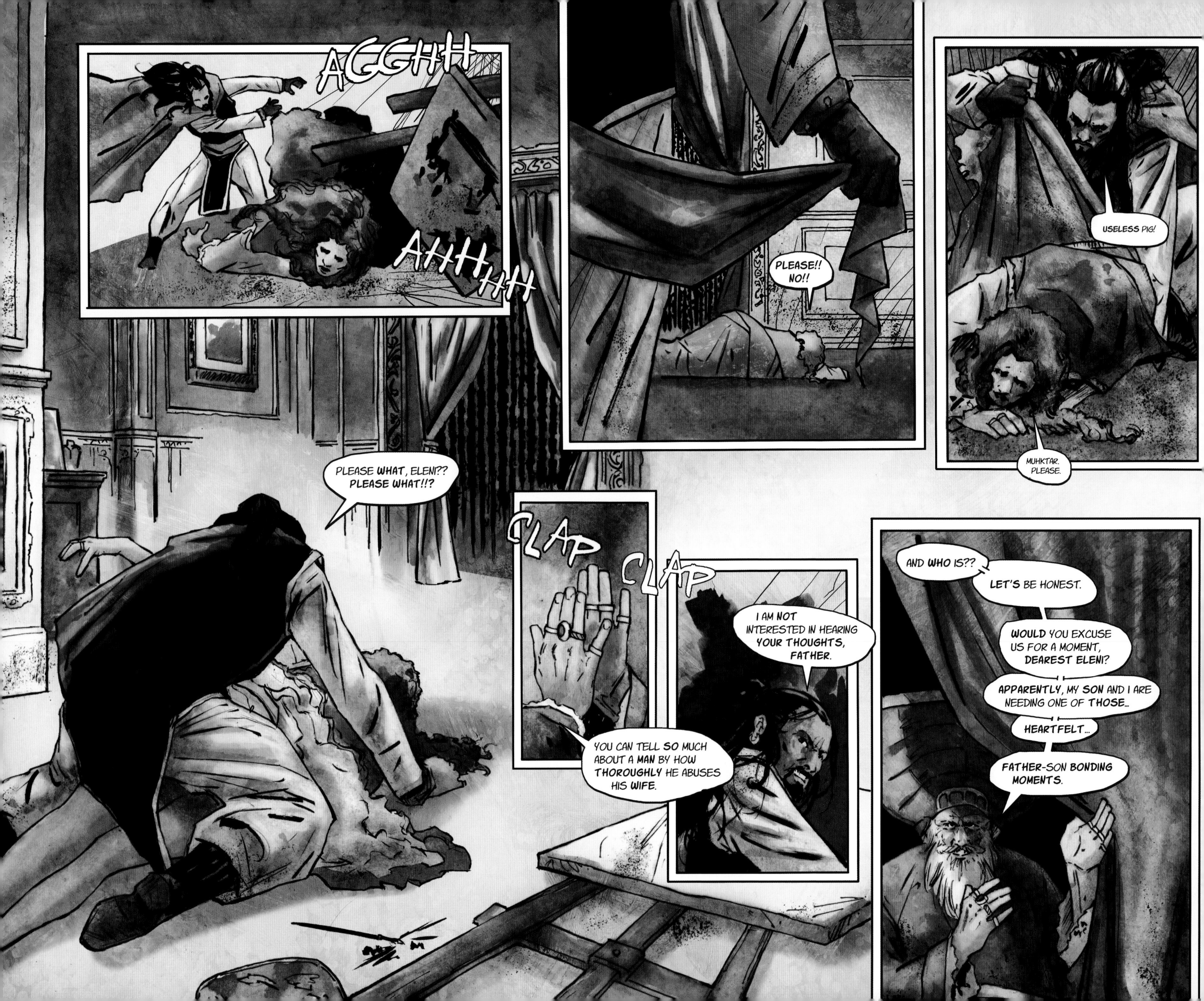
AGGHH
AHHHHH
PLEASE!! NO!!
USELESS PIG!
MUHKTAR. PLEASE.
PLEASE WHAT, ELENI?? PLEASE WHAT!!?
CLAP
CLAP
YOU CAN TELL SO MUCH ABOUT A MAN BY HOW THOROUGHLY HE ABUSES HIS WIFE.
I AM NOT INTERESTED IN HEARING YOUR THOUGHTS, FATHER.
AND WHO IS??
LET'S BE HONEST.
WOULD YOU EXCUSE US FOR A MOMENT, DEAREST ELENI?
APPARENTLY, MY SON AND I ARE NEEDING ONE OF THOSE...
HEARTFELT...
FATHER-SON BONDING MOMENTS.

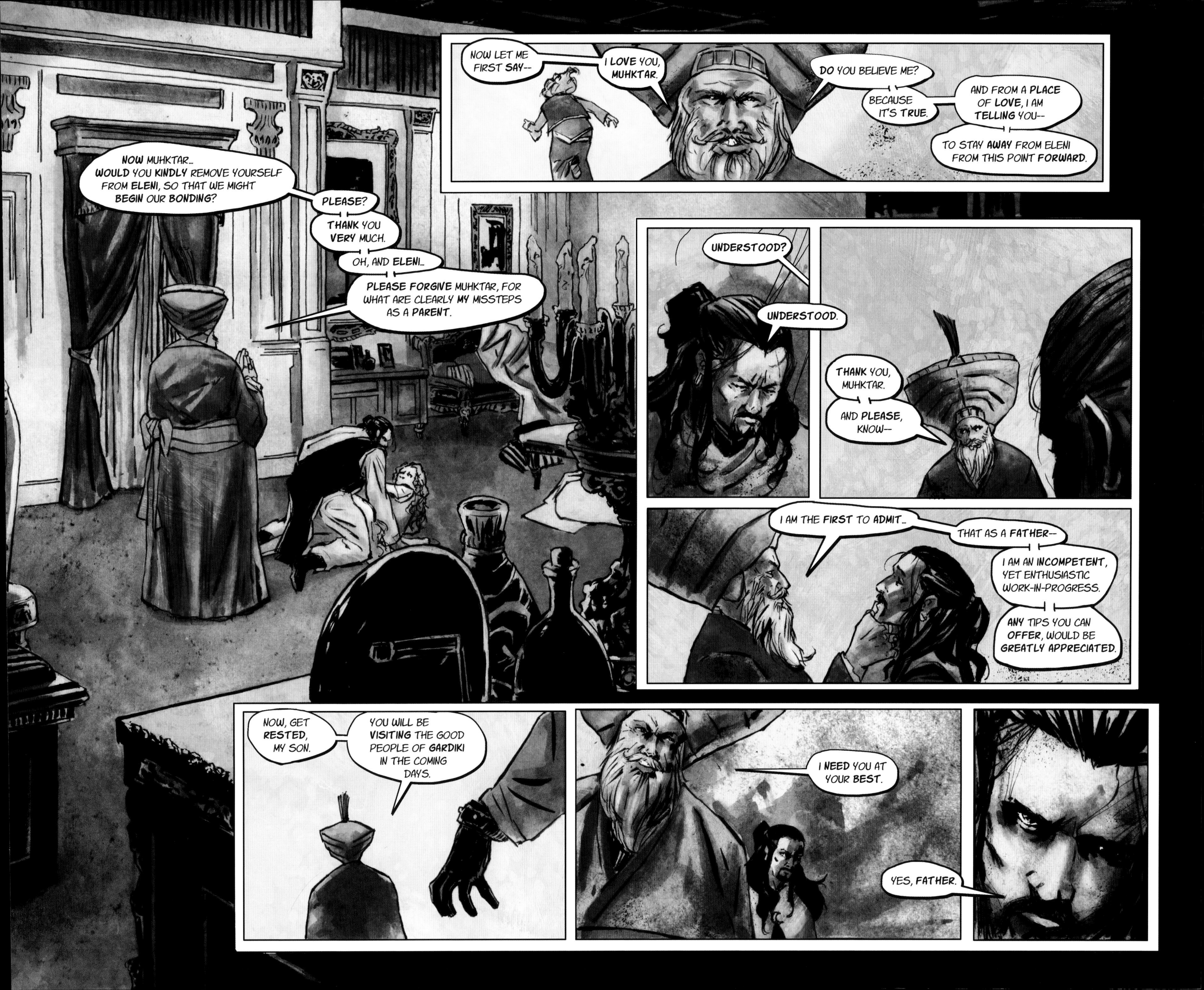
NOW MUHKTAR... WOULD YOU KINDLY REMOVE YOURSELF FROM ELENI, SO THAT WE MIGHT BEGIN OUR BONDING?
PLEASE?
THANK YOU VERY MUCH.
OH, AND ELENI...
PLEASE FORGIVE MUHKTAR, FOR WHAT ARE CLEARLY MY MISSTEPS AS A PARENT.
NOW LET ME FIRST SAY--
I LOVE YOU, MUHKTAR.
DO YOU BELIEVE ME?
BECAUSE IT'S TRUE.
AND FROM A PLACE OF LOVE, I AM TELLING YOU--
TO STAY AWAY FROM ELENI FROM THIS POINT FORWARD.
UNDERSTOOD?
UNDERSTOOD.
THANK YOU, MUHKTAR.
AND PLEASE, KNOW--
I AM THE FIRST TO ADMIT...
THAT AS A FATHER--
I AM AN INCOMPETENT, YET ENTHUSIASTIC WORK-IN-PROGRESS.
ANY TIPS YOU CAN OFFER, WOULD BE GREATLY APPRECIATED.
NOW, GET RESTED, MY SON.
YOU WILL BE VISITING THE GOOD PEOPLE OF GARDIKI IN THE COMING DAYS.
I NEED YOU AT YOUR BEST.
YES, FATHER.

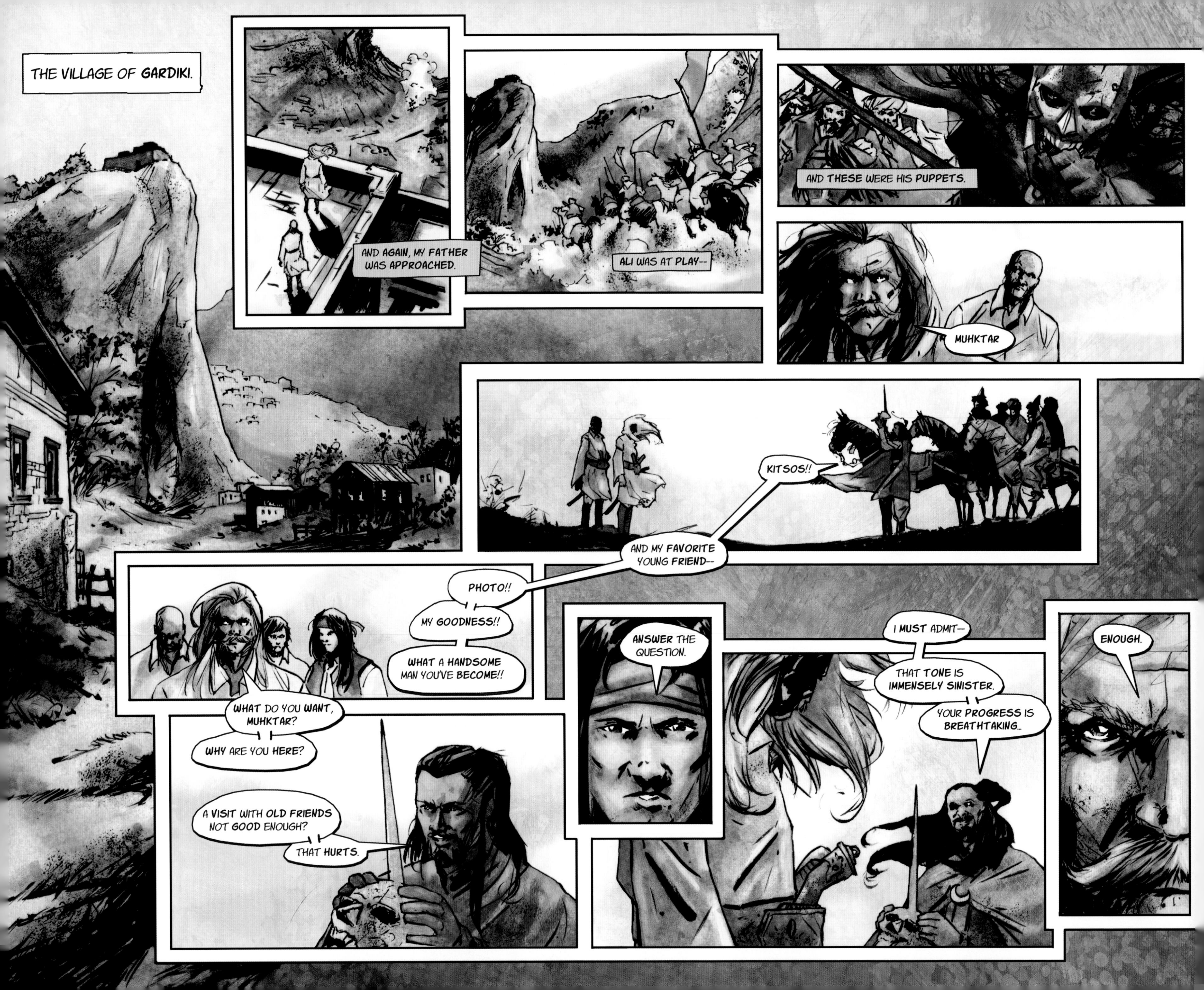
THE VILLAGE OF GARDIKI.
AND AGAIN, MY FATHER WAS APPROACHED.
ALI WAS AT PLAY--
AND THESE WERE HIS PUPPETS.
MUHKTAR
KITSOS!!
AND MY FAVORITE YOUNG FRIEND--
PHOTO!!
MY GOODNESS!!
WHAT A HANDSOME MAN YOU'VE BECOME!!
WHAT DO YOU WANT, MUHKTAR?
WHY ARE YOU HERE?
A VISIT WITH OLD FRIENDS NOT GOOD ENOUGH?
THAT HURTS.
ANSWER THE QUESTION.
I MUST ADMIT--
THAT TONE IS IMMENSELY SINISTER.
YOUR PROGRESS IS BREATHTAKING...
ENOUGH.

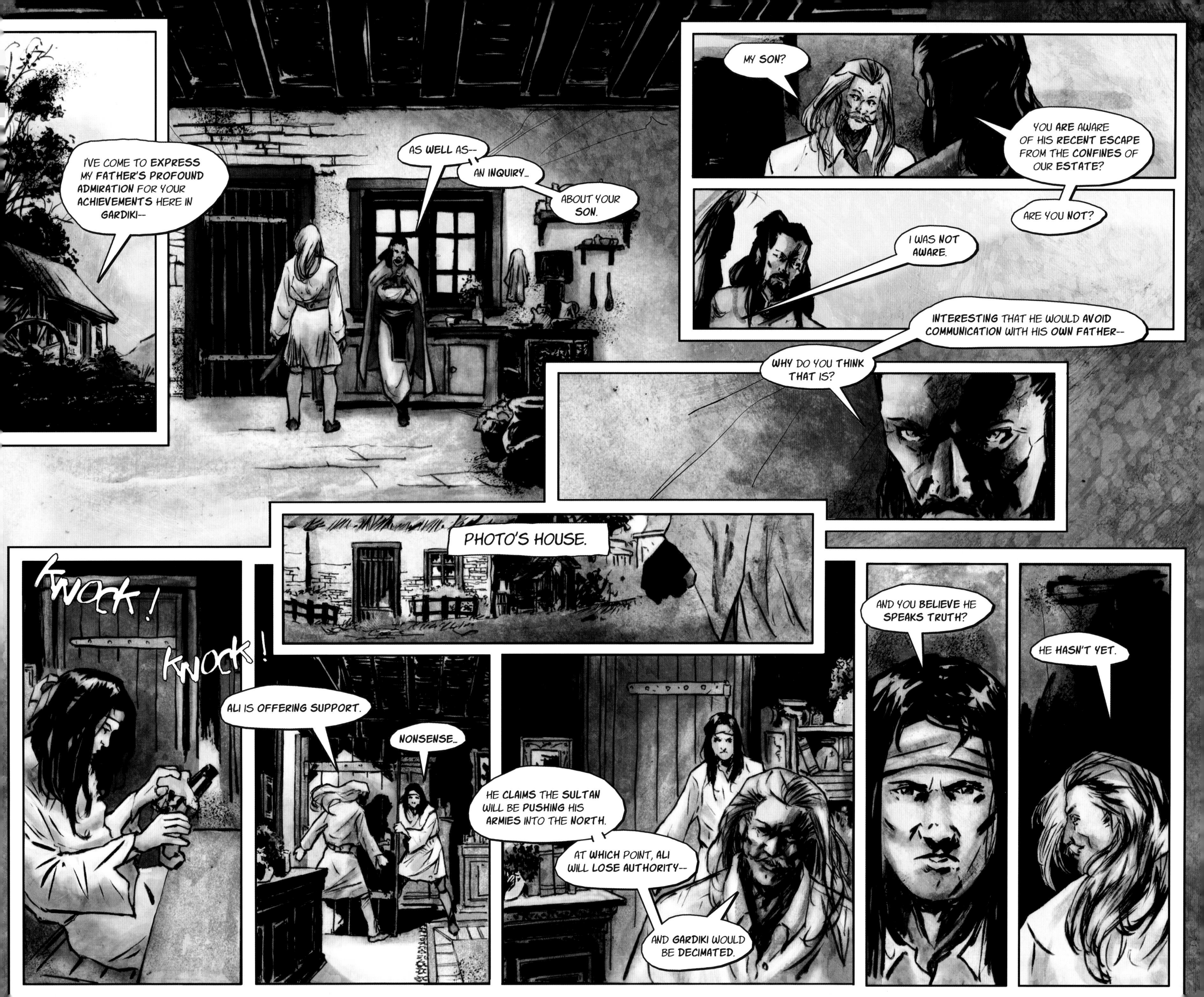
I'VE COME TO EXPRESS MY FATHER'S PROFOUND ADMIRATION FOR YOUR ACHIEVEMENTS HERE IN GARDIKI--
AS WELL AS--
AN INQUIRY...
ABOUT YOUR SON.
MY SON?
YOU ARE AWARE OF HIS RECENT ESCAPE FROM THE CONFINES OF OUR ESTATE?
ARE YOU NOT?
I WAS NOT AWARE.
INTERESTING THAT HE WOULD AVOID COMMUNICATION WITH HIS OWN FATHER--
WHY DO YOU THINK THAT IS?
PHOTO'S HOUSE.
KNOCK!
KNOCK!
ALI IS OFFERING SUPPORT.
NONSENSE...
HE CLAIMS THE SULTAN WILL BE PUSHING HIS ARMIES INTO THE NORTH.
AT WHICH POINT, ALI WILL LOSE AUTHORITY--
AND GARDIKI WOULD BE DECIMATED.
AND YOU BELIEVE HE SPEAKS TRUTH?
HE HASN'T YET.

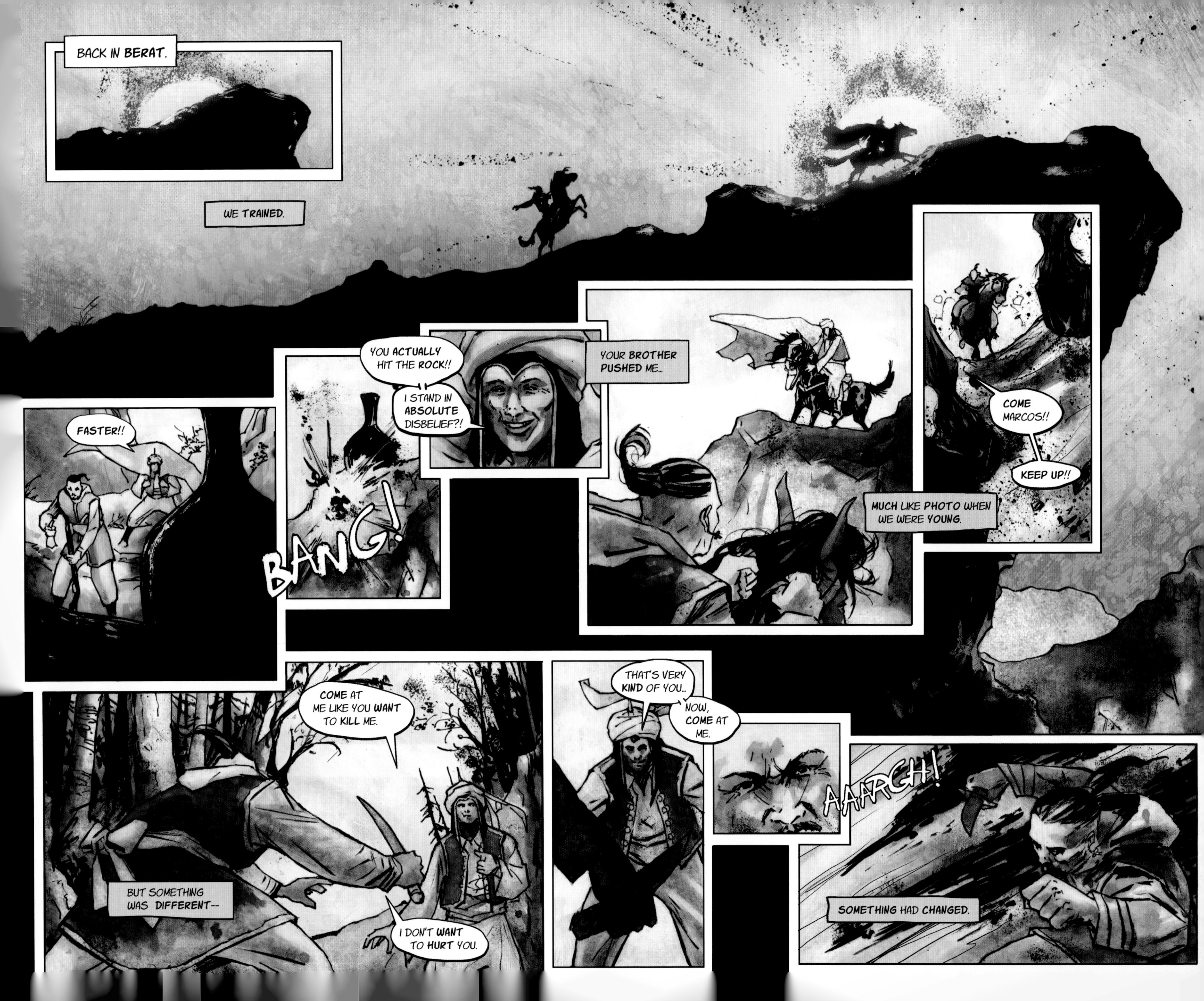
BACK IN BERAT.
WE TRAINED.
FASTER!!
YOU ACTUALLY HIT THE ROCK!!
I STAND IN ABSOLUTE DISBELIEF?!
BANG!
YOUR BROTHER PUSHED ME...
COME MARCOS!!
KEEP UP!!
MUCH LIKE PHOTO WHEN WE WERE YOUNG.
COME AT ME LIKE YOU WANT TO KILL ME.
BUT SOMETHING WAS DIFFERENT--
I DON'T WANT TO HURT YOU.
THAT'S VERY KIND OF YOU...
NOW, COME AT ME.
AAARGH!
SOMETHING HAD CHANGED.

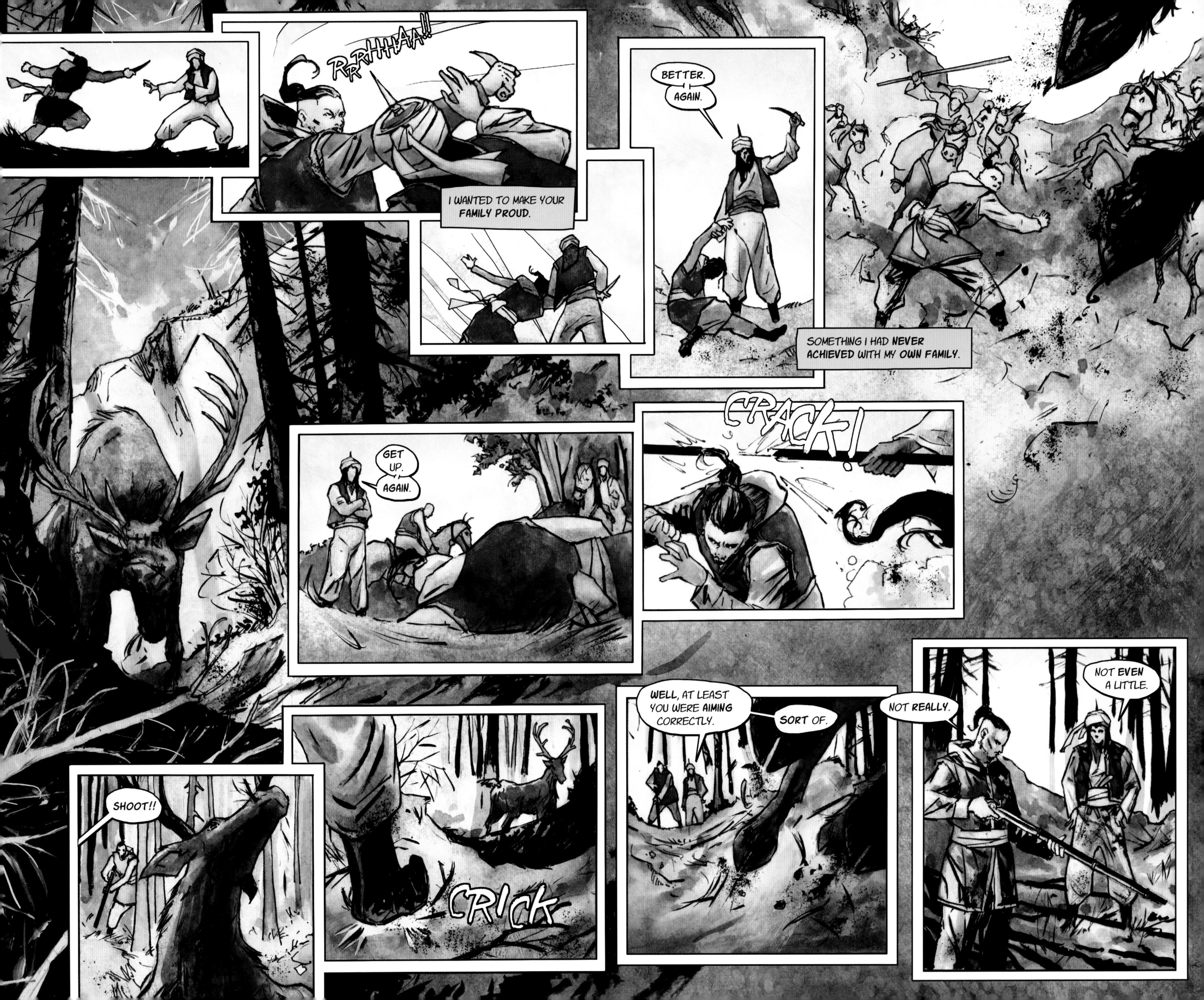
RRRHHAA!!
I WANTED TO MAKE YOUR FAMILY PROUD.
BETTER.
AGAIN.
SOMETHING I HAD NEVER ACHIEVED WITH MY OWN FAMILY.
GET UP.
AGAIN.
CRACK!
SHOOT!!
CRICK
WELL, AT LEAST YOU WERE AIMING CORRECTLY.
SORT OF.
NOT REALLY.
NOT EVEN A LITTLE.

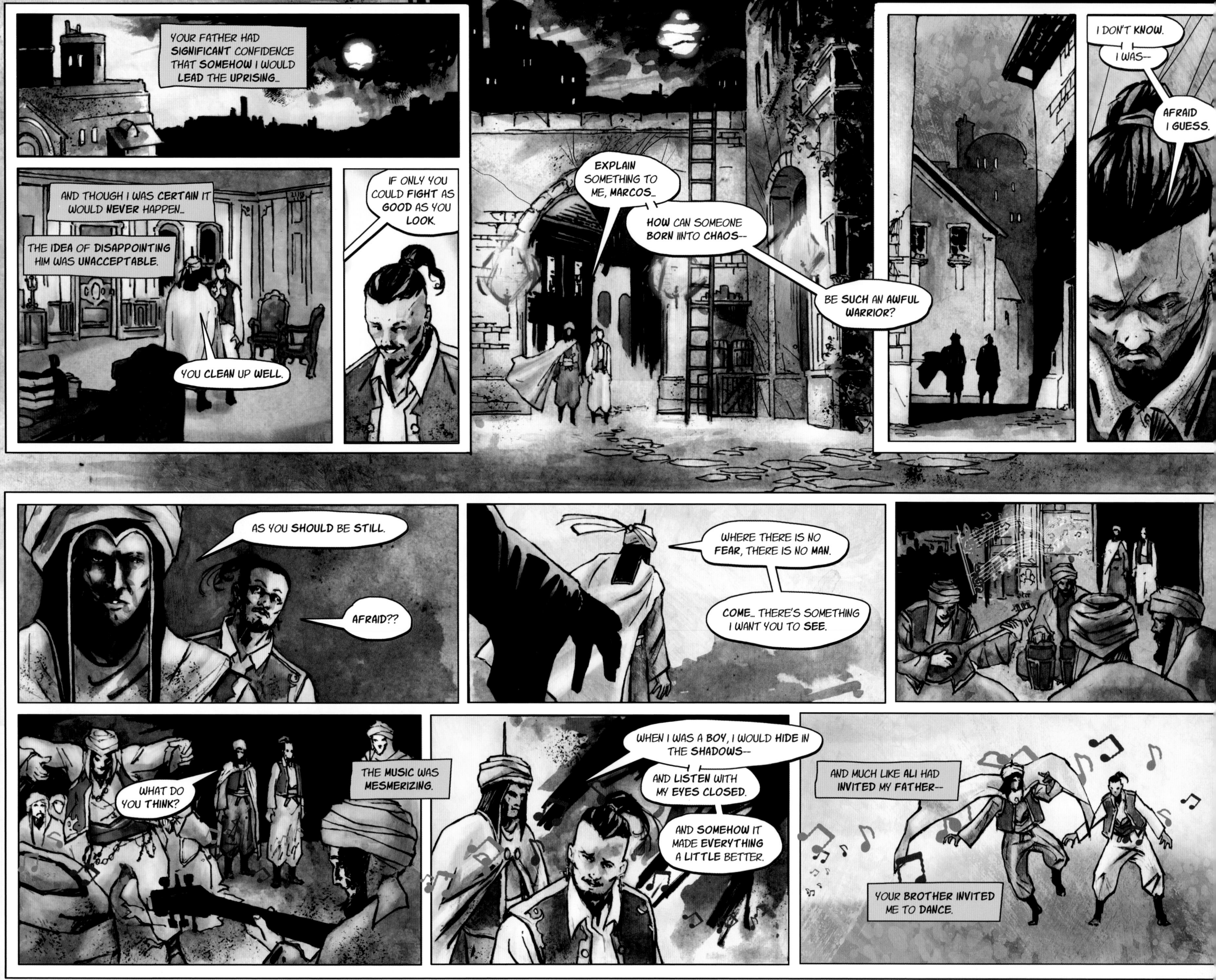
YOUR FATHER HAD SIGNIFICANT CONFIDENCE THAT SOMEHOW I WOULD LEAD THE UPRISING...
AND THOUGH I WAS CERTAIN IT WOULD NEVER HAPPEN...
THE IDEA OF DISAPPOINTING HIM WAS UNACCEPTABLE.
YOU CLEAN UP WELL.
IF ONLY YOU COULD FIGHT AS GOOD AS YOU LOOK.
EXPLAIN SOMETHING TO ME, MARCOS...
HOW CAN SOMEONE BORN IINTO CHAOS--
BE SUCH AN AWFUL WARRIOR?
I DON'T KNOW.
I WAS--
AFRAID I GUESS.
AS YOU SHOULD BE STILL.
AFRAID??
WHERE THERE IS NO FEAR, THERE IS NO MAN.
COME... THERE'S SOMETHING I WANT YOU TO SEE.
WHAT DO YOU THINK?
THE MUSIC WAS MESMERIZING.
WHEN I WAS A BOY, I WOULD HIDE IN THE SHADOWS--
AND LISTEN WITH MY EYES CLOSED.
AND SOMEHOW IT MADE EVERYTHING A LITTLE BETTER.
AND MUCH LIKE ALI HAD INVITED MY FATHER--
YOUR BROTHER INVITED ME TO DANCE.

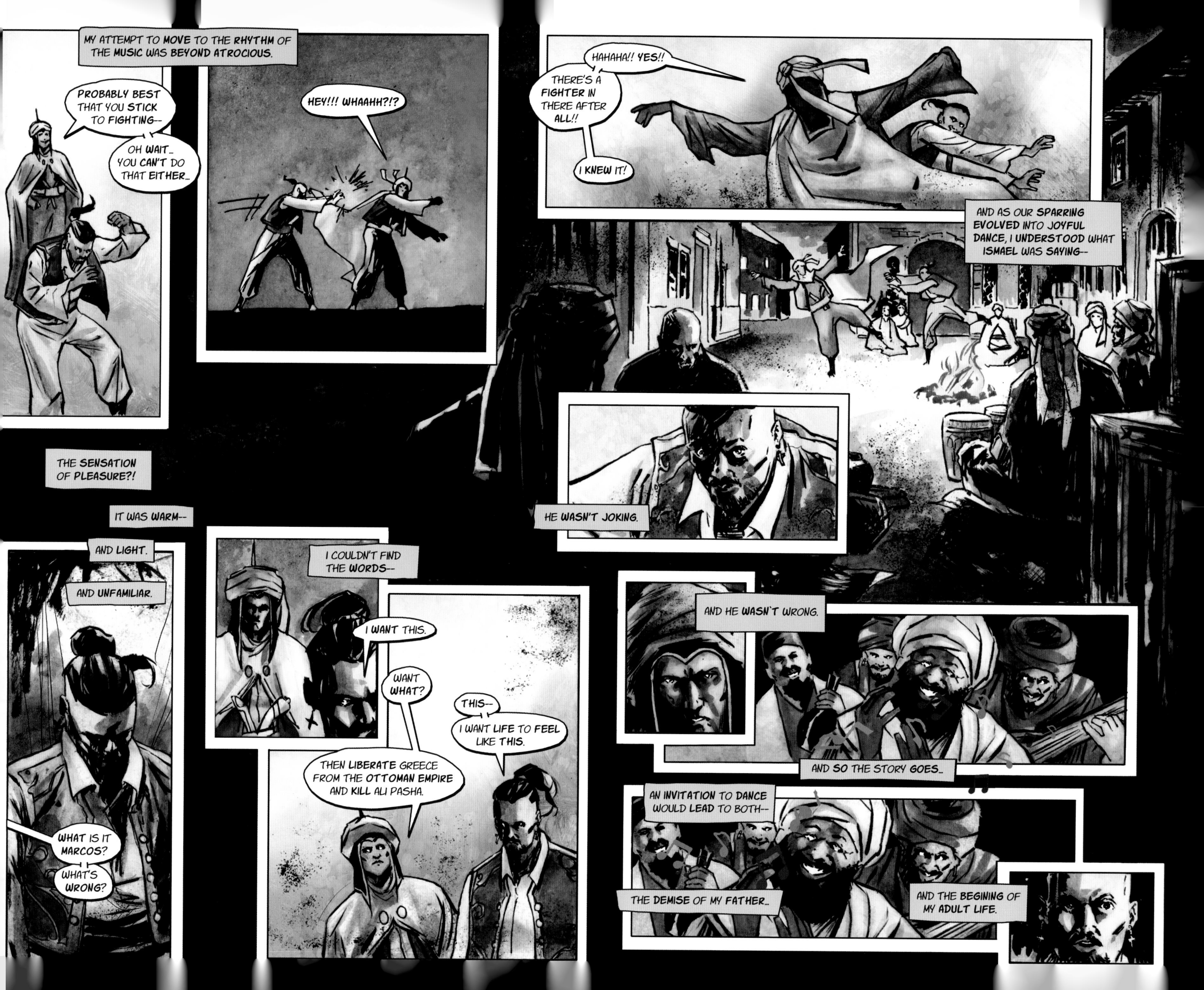
MY ATTEMPT TO MOVE TO THE RHYTHM OF THE MUSIC WAS BEYOND ATROCIOUS.
PROBABLY BEST THAT YOU STICK TO FIGHTING--
OH WAIT... YOU CAN'T DO THAT EITHER...
HEY!!! WHAAHH?!?
HAHAHA!! YES!!
THERE'S A FIGHTER IN THERE AFTER ALL!!
I KNEW IT!
AND AS OUR SPARRING EVOLVED INTO JOYFUL DANCE, I UNDERSTOOD WHAT ISMAEL WAS SAYING--
THE SENSATION OF PLEASURE?!
IT WAS WARM--
AND LIGHT.
AND UNFAMILIAR.
HE WASN'T JOKING.
WHAT IS IT MARCOS?
WHAT'S WRONG?
I COULDN'T FIND THE WORDS--
I WANT THIS.
WANT WHAT?
THIS--
I WANT LIFE TO FEEL LIKE THIS.
THEN LIBERATE GREECE FROM THE OTTOMAN EMPIRE AND KILL ALI PASHA.
AND HE WASN'T WRONG.
AND SO THE STORY GOES...
AN INVITATION TO DANCE WOULD LEAD TO BOTH--
THE DEMISE OF MY FATHER...
AND THE BEGINING OF MY ADULT LIFE.

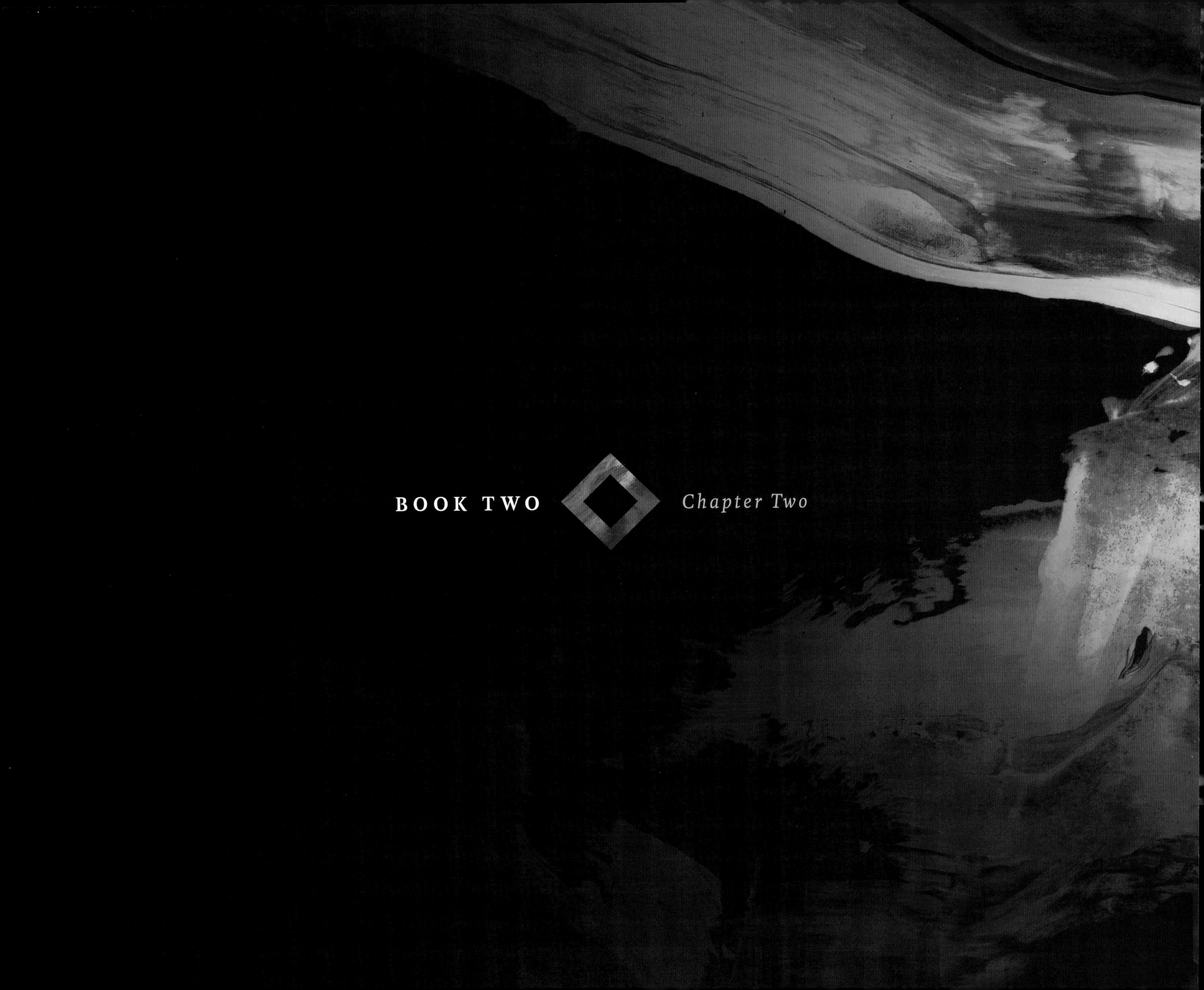

BOOK TWO

Chapter Two

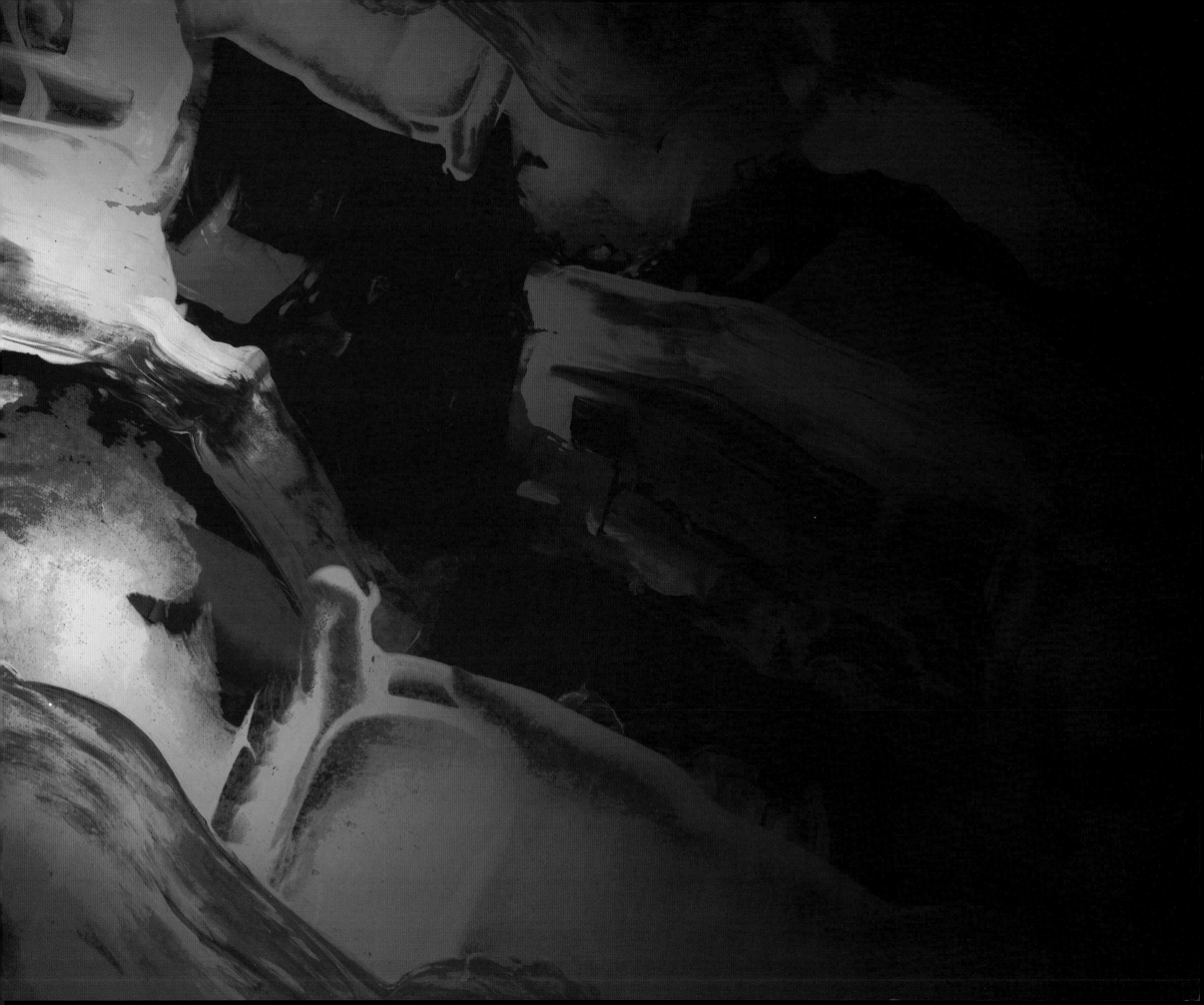

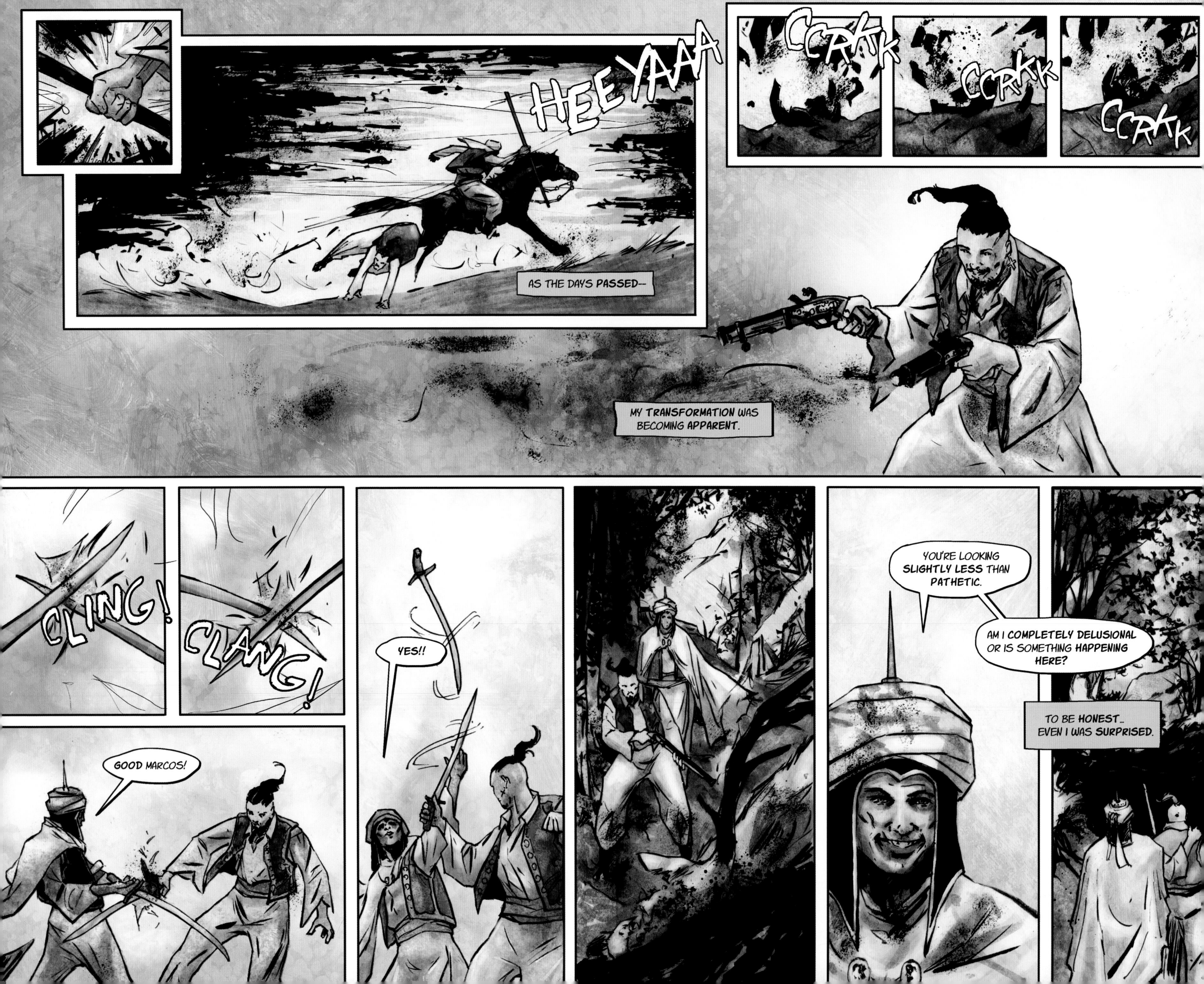
HEEYAAA
AS THE DAYS PASSED--
CCRAKK
CCRKK
CCRAKK
MY TRANSFORMATION WAS BECOMING APPARENT.
CLING!
CLANG!
GOOD MARCOS!
YES!!
YOU'RE LOOKING SLIGHTLY LESS THAN PATHETIC.
AM I COMPLETELY DELUSIONAL OR IS SOMETHING HAPPENING HERE?
TO BE HONEST... EVEN I WAS SURPRISED.

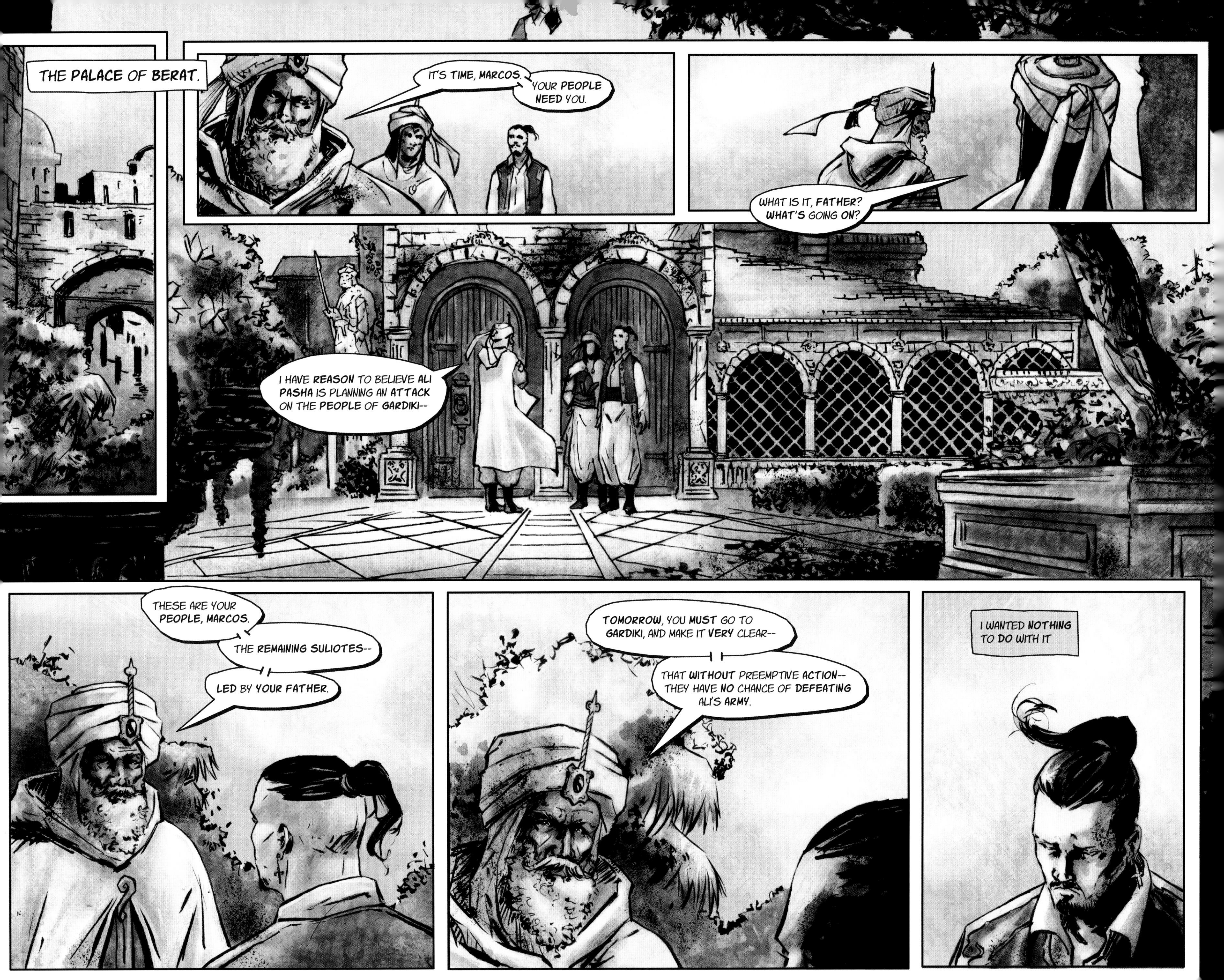
THE PALACE OF BERAT.
IT'S TIME, MARCOS.
YOUR PEOPLE NEED YOU.
WHAT IS IT, FATHER? WHAT'S GOING ON?
I HAVE REASON TO BELIEVE ALI PASHA IS PLANNING AN ATTACK ON THE PEOPLE OF GARDIKI--
THESE ARE YOUR PEOPLE, MARCOS.
THE REMAINING SULIOTES--
LED BY YOUR FATHER.
TOMORROW, YOU MUST GO TO GARDIKI, AND MAKE IT VERY CLEAR--
THAT WITHOUT PREEMPTIVE ACTION-- THEY HAVE NO CHANCE OF DEFEATING ALI'S ARMY.
I WANTED NOTHING TO DO WITH IT

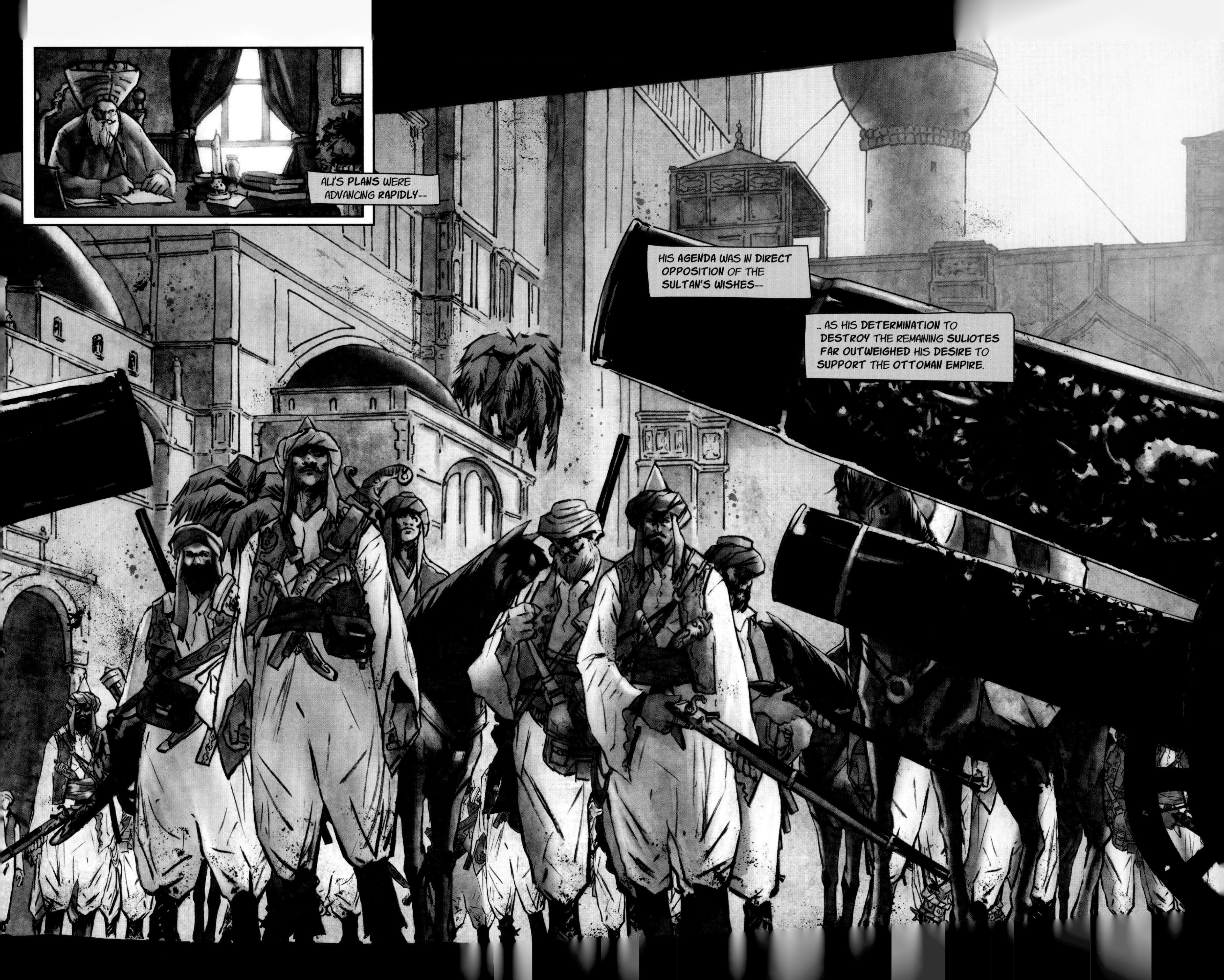
ALI'S PLANS WERE ADVANCING RAPIDLY--
HIS AGENDA WAS IN DIRECT OPPOSITION OF THE SULTAN'S WISHES--
... AS HIS DETERMINATION TO DESTROY THE REMAINING SULIOTES FAR OUTWEIGHED HIS DESIRE TO SUPPORT THE OTTOMAN EMPIRE.

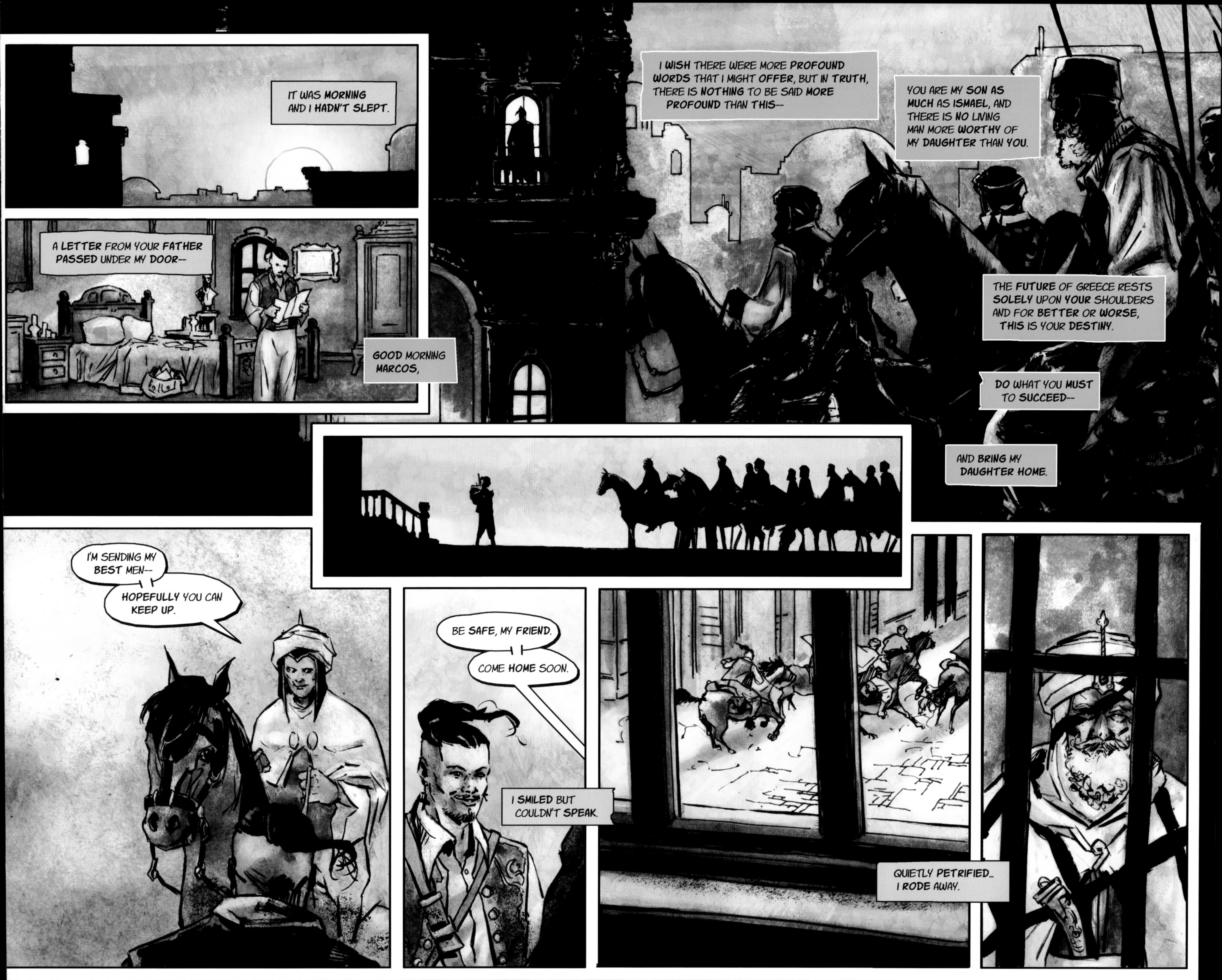
IT WAS MORNING AND I HADN'T SLEPT.
A LETTER FROM YOUR FATHER PASSED UNDER MY DOOR--
GOOD MORNING MARCOS,
I WISH THERE WERE MORE PROFOUND WORDS THAT I MIGHT OFFER, BUT IN TRUTH, THERE IS NOTHING TO BE SAID MORE PROFOUND THAN THIS--
YOU ARE MY SON AS MUCH AS ISMAEL, AND THERE IS NO LIVING MAN MORE WORTHY OF MY DAUGHTER THAN YOU.
THE FUTURE OF GREECE RESTS SOLELY UPON YOUR SHOULDERS AND FOR BETTER OR WORSE, THIS IS YOUR DESTINY.
DO WHAT YOU MUST TO SUCCEED--
AND BRING MY DAUGHTER HOME.
I'M SENDING MY BEST MEN--
HOPEFULLY YOU CAN KEEP UP.
BE SAFE, MY FRIEND.
COME HOME SOON.
I SMILED BUT COULDN'T SPEAK.
QUIETLY PETRIFIED... I RODE AWAY.

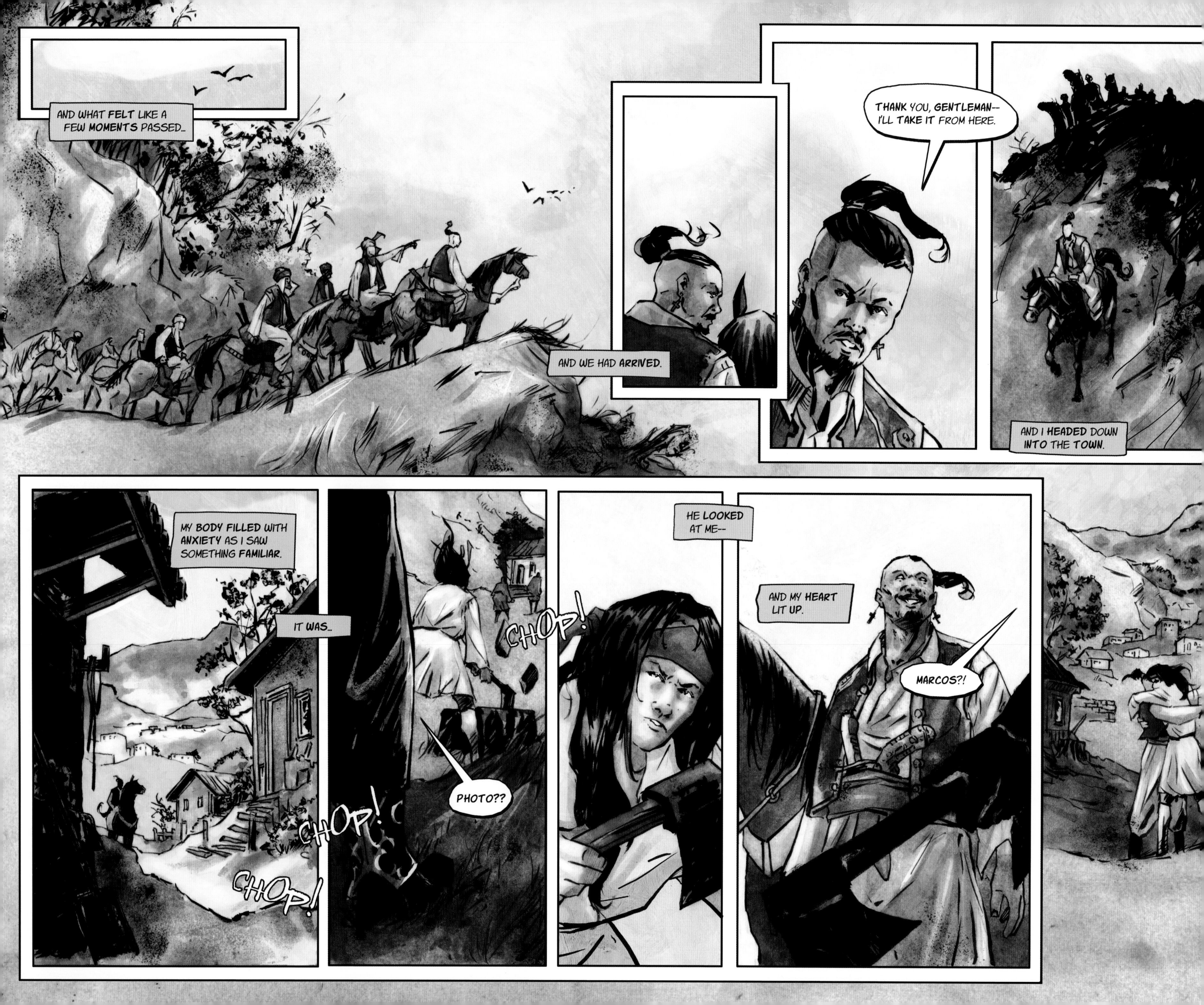
AND WHAT FELT LIKE A FEW MOMENTS PASSED...
AND WE HAD ARRIVED.
THANK YOU, GENTLEMAN-- I'LL TAKE IT FROM HERE.
AND I HEADED DOWN INTO THE TOWN.
MY BODY FILLED WITH ANXIETY AS I SAW SOMETHING FAMILIAR.
IT WAS...
CHOP!
CHOP!
CHOP!
PHOTO??
HE LOOKED AT ME--
AND MY HEART LIT UP.
MARCOS?!

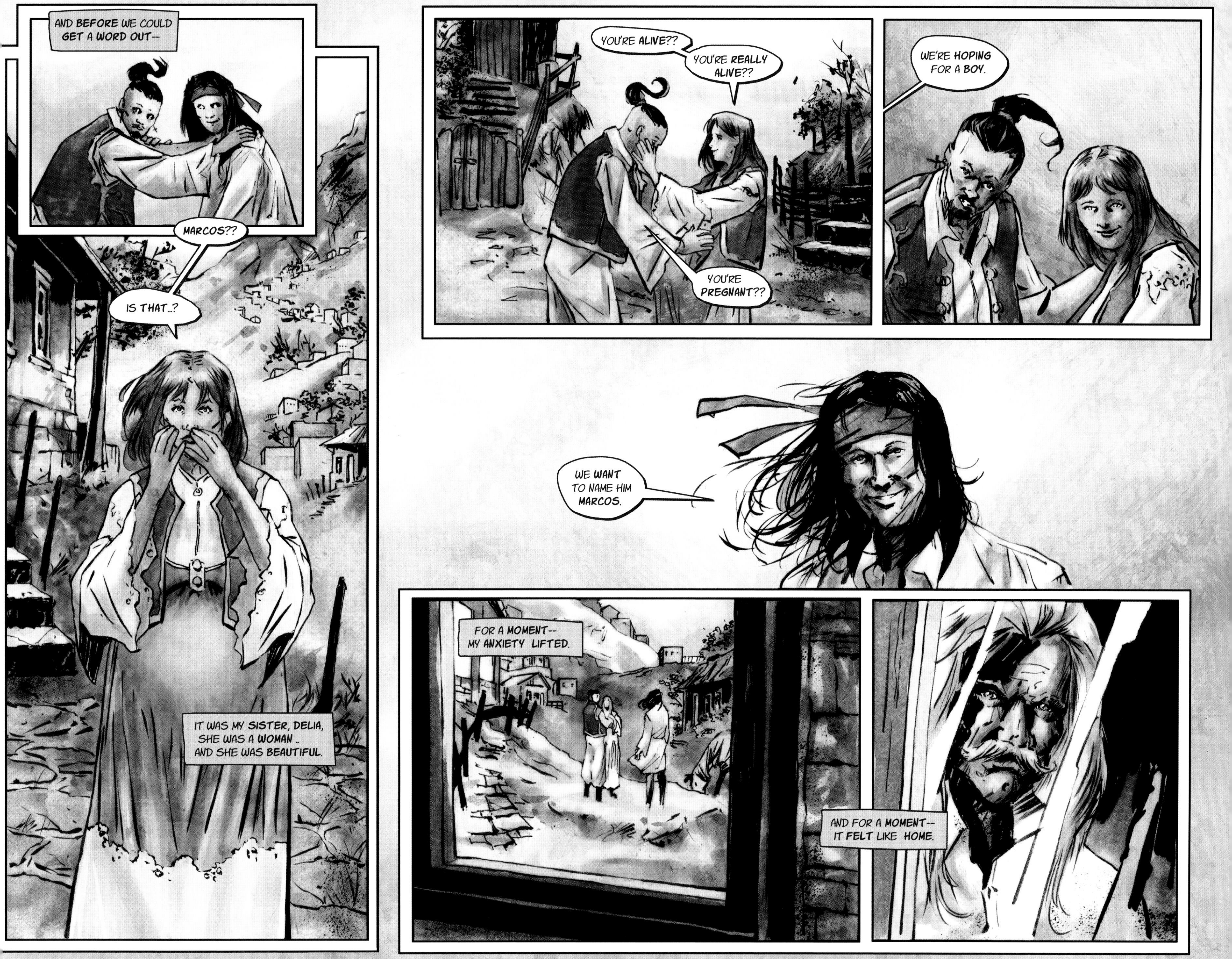
AND BEFORE WE COULD GET A WORD OUT--
MARCOS??
IS THAT...?
IT WAS MY SISTER, DELIA. SHE WAS A WOMAN .. AND SHE WAS BEAUTIFUL.
YOU'RE ALIVE??
YOU'RE REALLY ALIVE??
YOU'RE PREGNANT??
WE'RE HOPING FOR A BOY.
WE WANT TO NAME HIM MARCOS.
FOR A MOMENT-- MY ANXIETY LIFTED.
AND FOR A MOMENT-- IT FELT LIKE HOME.

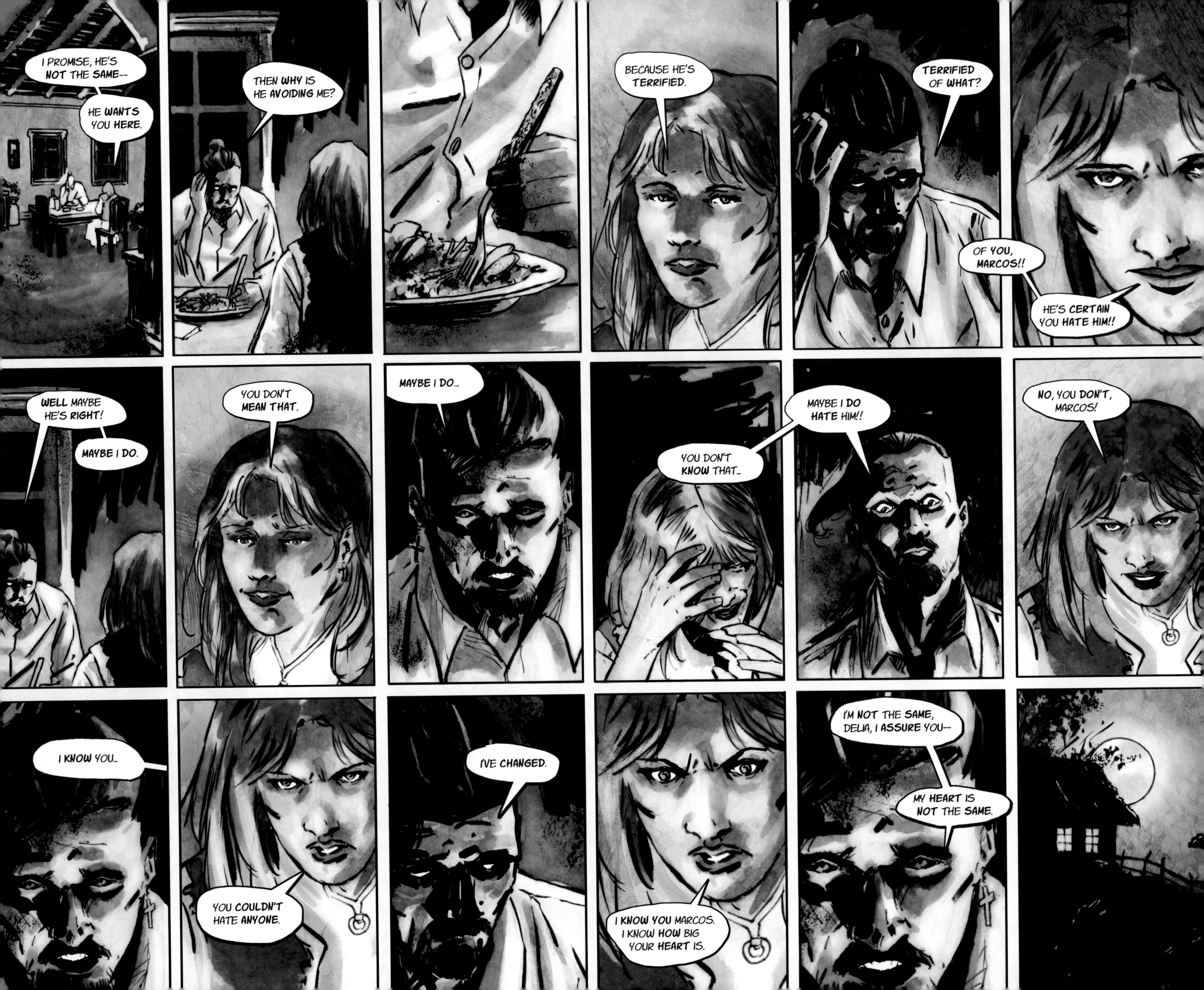
I PROMISE, HE'S NOT THE SAME--
HE WANTS YOU HERE.
THEN WHY IS HE AVOIDING ME?
BECAUSE HE'S TERRIFIED.
TERRIFIED OF WHAT?
OF YOU, MARCOS!!
HE'S CERTAIN YOU HATE HIM!!
WELL MAYBE HE'S RIGHT!
MAYBE I DO.
YOU DON'T MEAN THAT.
MAYBE I DO...
YOU DON'T KNOW THAT...
MAYBE I DO HATE HIM!!
NO, YOU DON'T, MARCOS!
I KNOW YOU...
YOU COULDN'T HATE ANYONE.
I'VE CHANGED.
I KNOW YOU MARCOS. I KNOW HOW BIG YOUR HEART IS.
I'M NOT THE SAME, DELIA, I ASSURE YOU--
MY HEART IS NOT THE SAME.

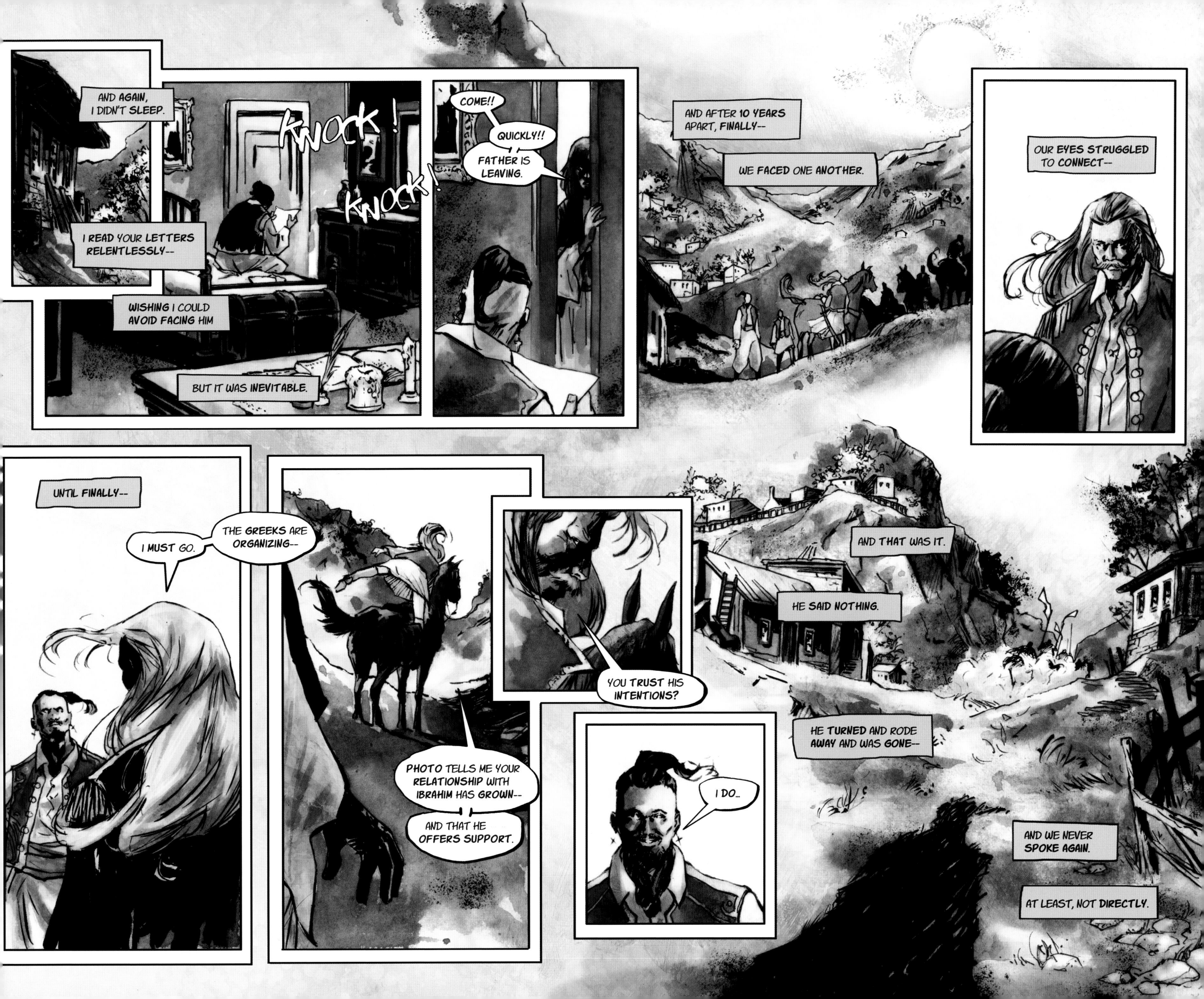

AND AGAIN, I DIDN'T SLEEP.
I READ YOUR LETTERS RELENTLESSLY--
WISHING I COULD AVOID FACING HIM
BUT IT WAS INEVITABLE.
KNOCK! KNOCK!
COME!!
QUICKLY!!
FATHER IS LEAVING.
AND AFTER 10 YEARS APART, FINALLY--
WE FACED ONE ANOTHER.
OUR EYES STRUGGLED TO CONNECT--
UNTIL FINALLY--
I MUST GO.
THE GREEKS ARE ORGANIZING--
PHOTO TELLS ME YOUR RELATIONSHIP WITH IBRAHIM HAS GROWN--
AND THAT HE OFFERS SUPPORT.
YOU TRUST HIS INTENTIONS?
I DO...
AND THAT WAS IT.
HE SAID NOTHING.
HE TURNED AND RODE AWAY AND WAS GONE--
AND WE NEVER SPOKE AGAIN.
AT LEAST, NOT DIRECTLY.

BOOK TWO ◇ *Chapter Three*

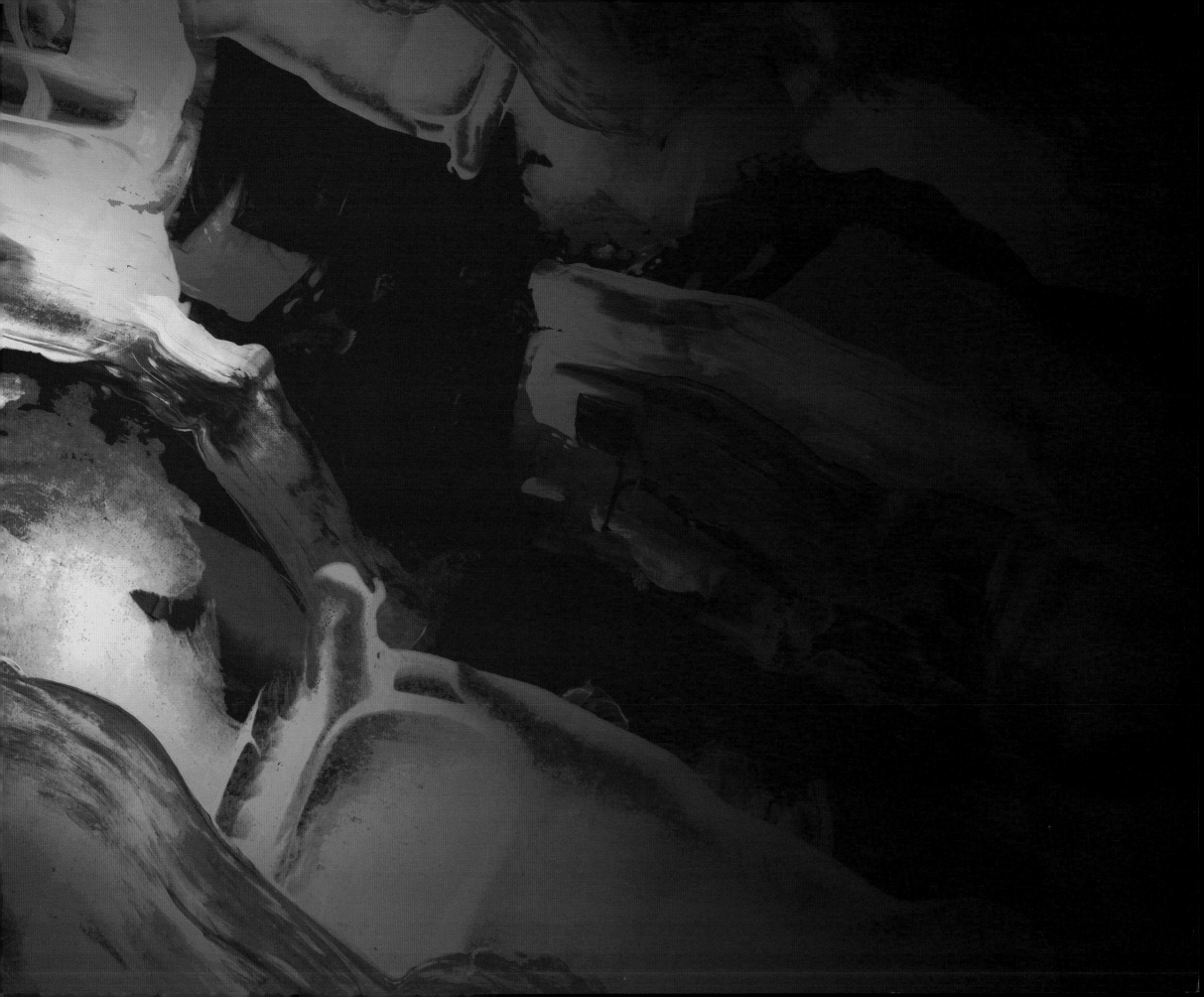

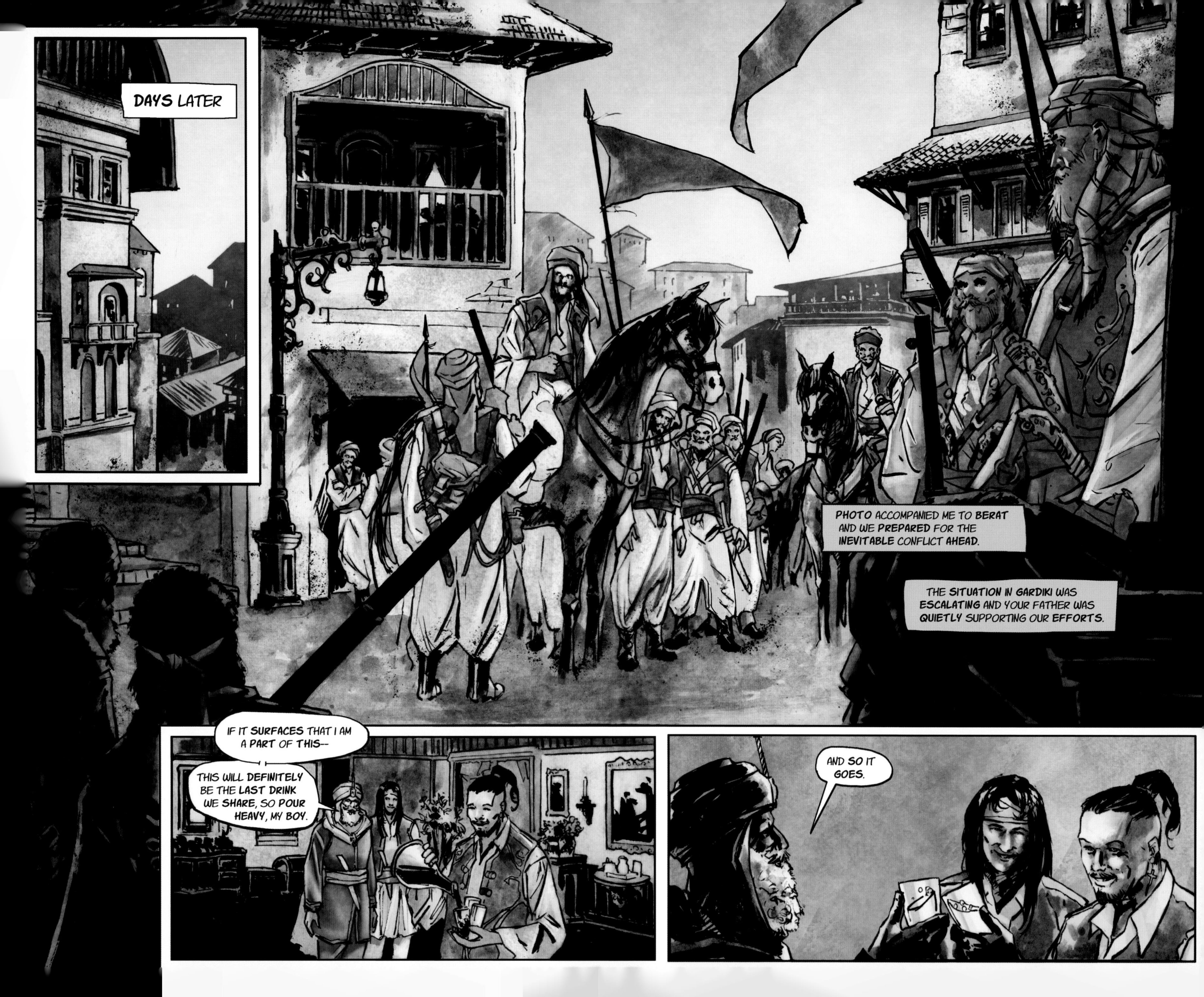

DAYS LATER
PHOTO ACCOMPANIED ME TO BERAT AND WE PREPARED FOR THE INEVITABLE CONFLICT AHEAD.
THE SITUATION IN GARDIKI WAS ESCALATING AND YOUR FATHER WAS QUIETLY SUPPORTING OUR EFFORTS.
IF IT SURFACES THAT I AM A PART OF THIS--
THIS WILL DEFINITELY BE THE LAST DRINK WE SHARE, SO POUR HEAVY, MY BOY.
AND SO IT GOES.

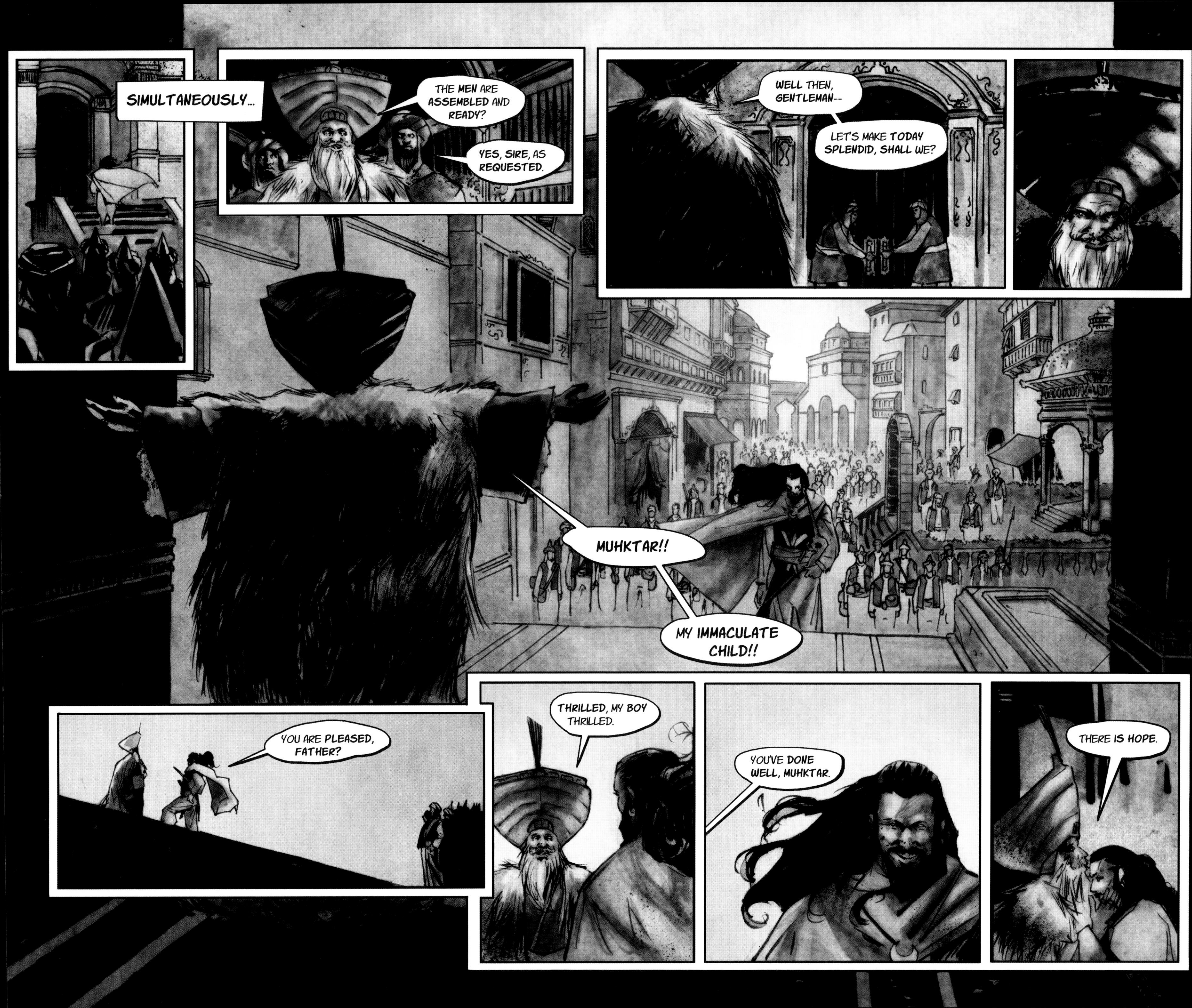
SIMULTANEOUSLY...
THE MEN ARE ASSEMBLED AND READY?
YES, SIRE, AS REQUESTED.
WELL THEN, GENTLEMAN--
LET'S MAKE TODAY SPLENDID, SHALL WE?
MUHKTAR!!
MY IMMACULATE CHILD!!
YOU ARE PLEASED, FATHER?
THRILLED, MY BOY THRILLED.
YOU'VE DONE WELL, MUHKTAR.
THERE IS HOPE.

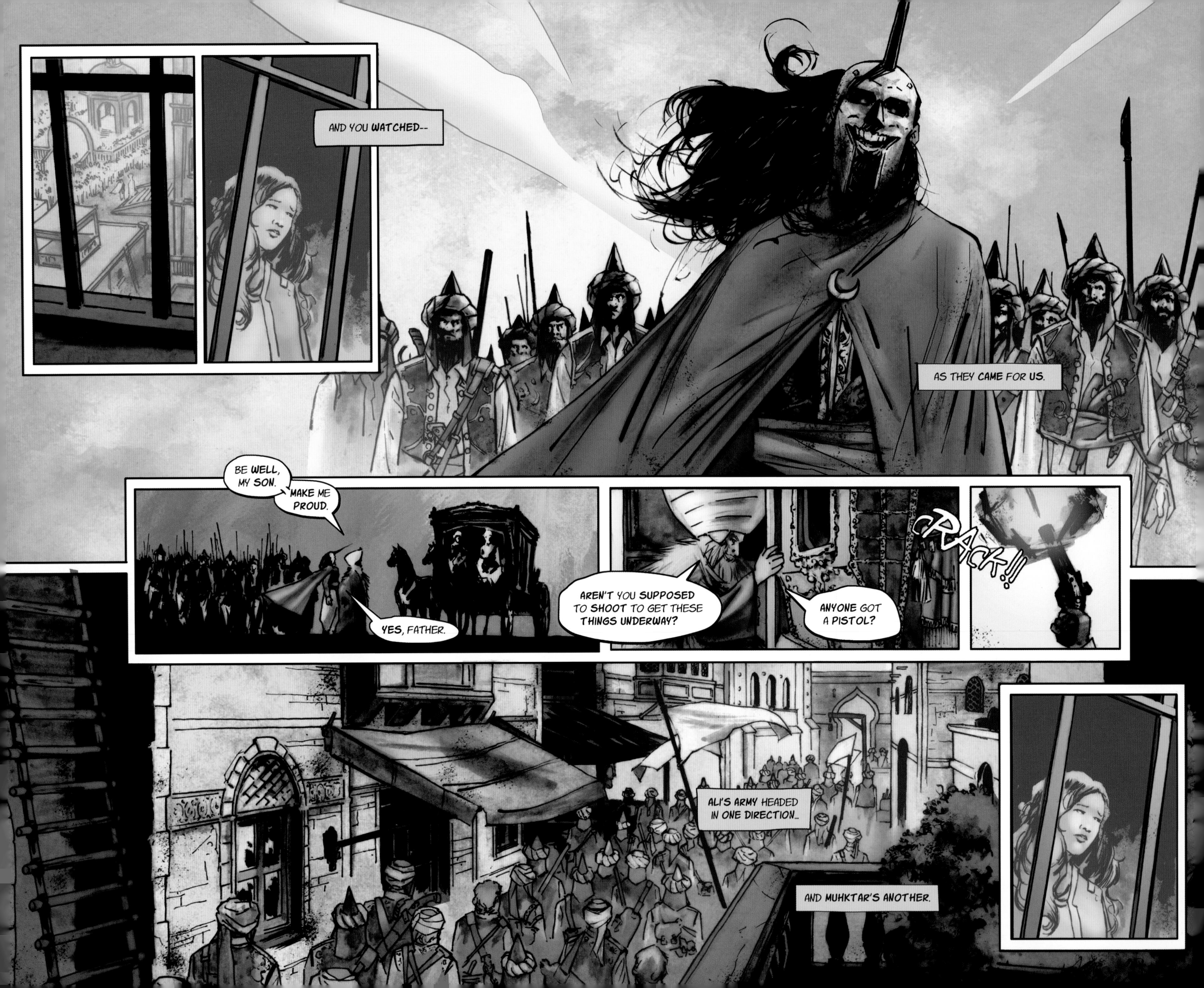
AND YOU WATCHED--
AS THEY CAME FOR US.
BE WELL, MY SON.
MAKE ME PROUD.
YES, FATHER.
AREN'T YOU SUPPOSED TO SHOOT TO GET THESE THINGS UNDERWAY?
ANYONE GOT A PISTOL?
CRACK!!
ALI'S ARMY HEADED IN ONE DIRECTION...
AND MUHKTAR'S ANOTHER.

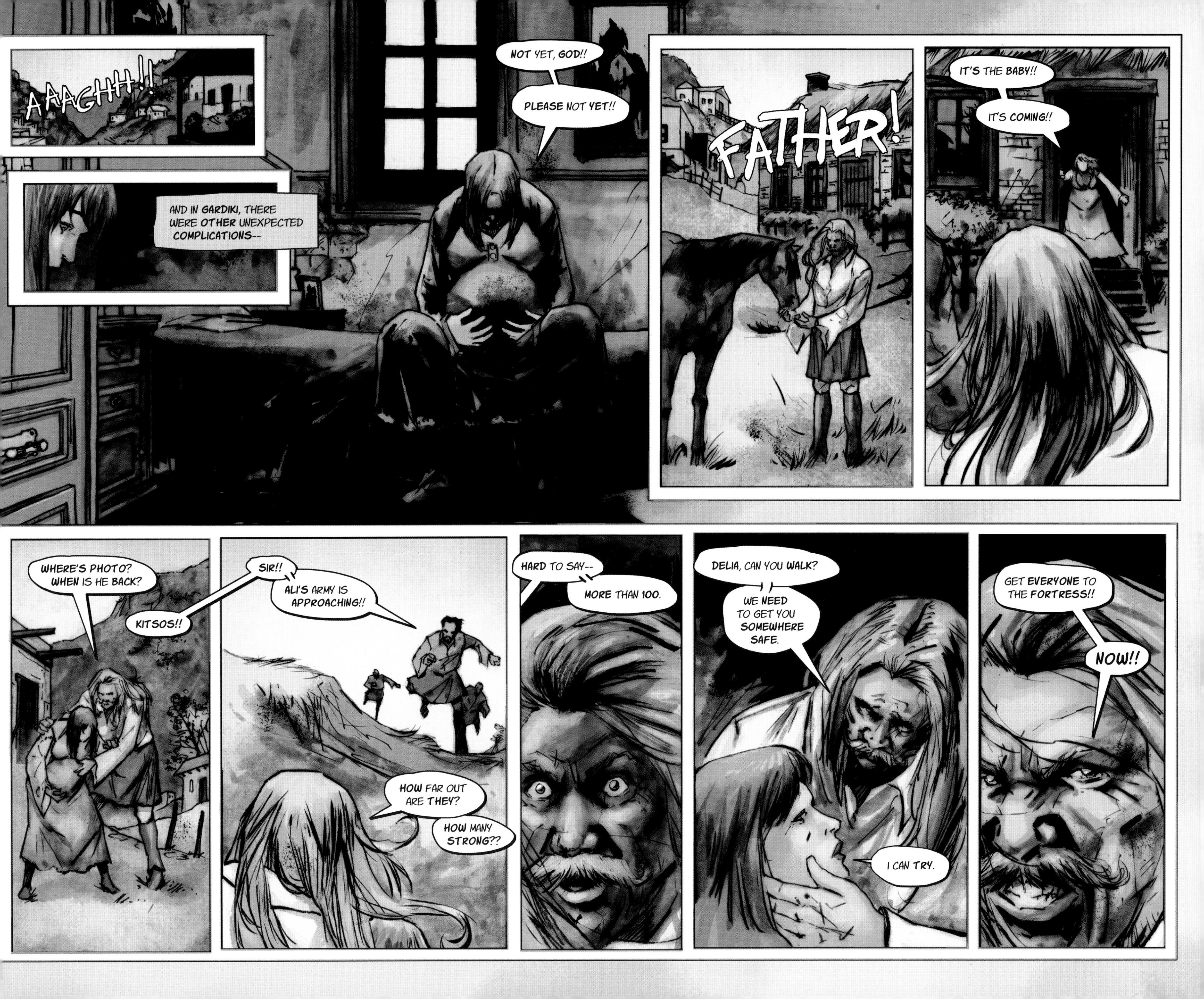
AAAGHH!!
AND IN GARDIKI, THERE WERE OTHER UNEXPECTED COMPLICATIONS--
NOT YET, GOD!!
PLEASE NOT YET!!
FATHER!
IT'S THE BABY!!
IT'S COMING!!
WHERE'S PHOTO? WHEN IS HE BACK?
KITSOS!!
SIR!!
ALI'S ARMY IS APPROACHING!!
HOW FAR OUT ARE THEY?
HOW MANY STRONG??
HARD TO SAY--
MORE THAN 100.
DELIA, CAN YOU WALK?
WE NEED TO GET YOU SOMEWHERE SAFE.
I CAN TRY.
GET EVERYONE TO THE FORTRESS!!
NOW!!

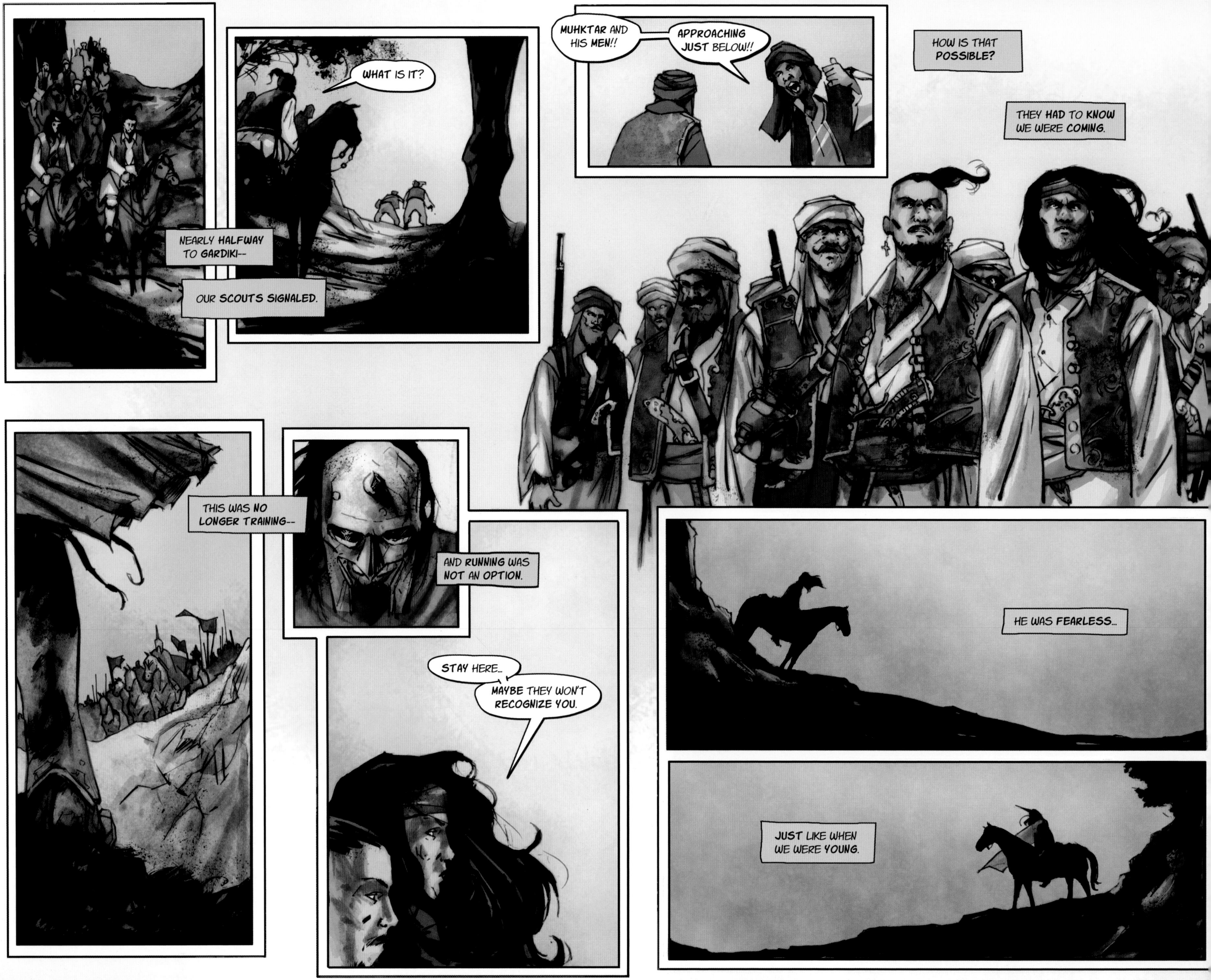
NEARLY HALFWAY TO GARDIKI--
OUR SCOUTS SIGNALED.
WHAT IS IT?
MUHKTAR AND HIS MEN!!
APPROACHING JUST BELOW!!
HOW IS THAT POSSIBLE?
THEY HAD TO KNOW WE WERE COMING.
THIS WAS NO LONGER TRAINING--
AND RUNNING WAS NOT AN OPTION.
STAY HERE...
MAYBE THEY WON'T RECOGNIZE YOU.
HE WAS FEARLESS...
JUST LIKE WHEN WE WERE YOUNG.

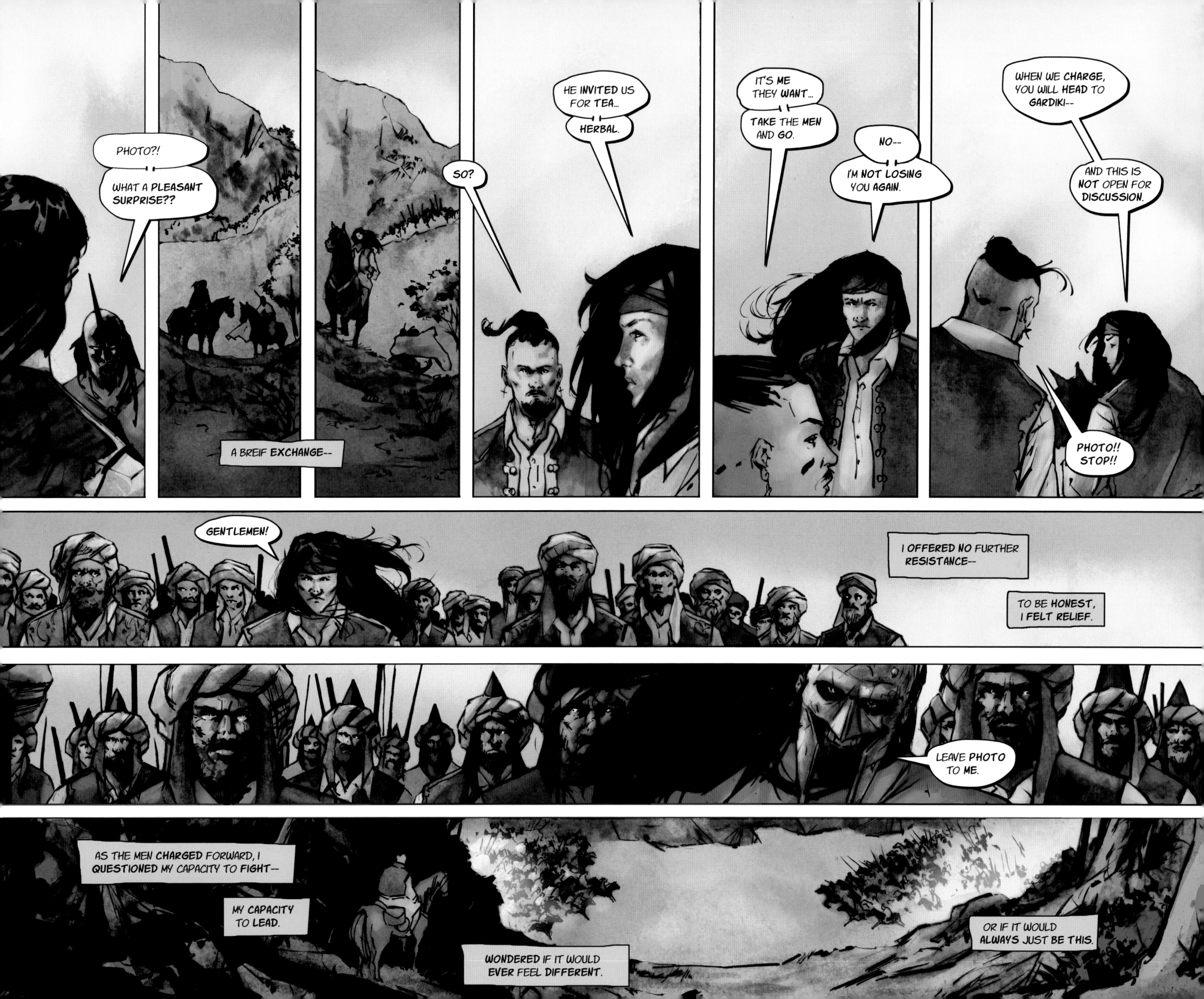
PHOTO?!
WHAT A PLEASANT SURPRISE??
A BREIF EXCHANGE--
SO?
HE INVITED US FOR TEA...
HERBAL.
IT'S ME THEY WANT...
TAKE THE MEN AND GO.
NO--
I'M NOT LOSING YOU AGAIN.
WHEN WE CHARGE, YOU WILL HEAD TO GARDIKI--
AND THIS IS NOT OPEN FOR DISCUSSION.
PHOTO!! STOP!!
GENTLEMEN!
I OFFERED NO FURTHER RESISTANCE--
TO BE HONEST, I FELT RELIEF.
LEAVE PHOTO TO ME.
AS THE MEN CHARGED FORWARD, I QUESTIONED MY CAPACITY TO FIGHT--
MY CAPACITY TO LEAD.
WONDERED IF IT WOULD EVER FEEL DIFFERENT.
OR IF IT WOULD ALWAYS JUST BE THIS.

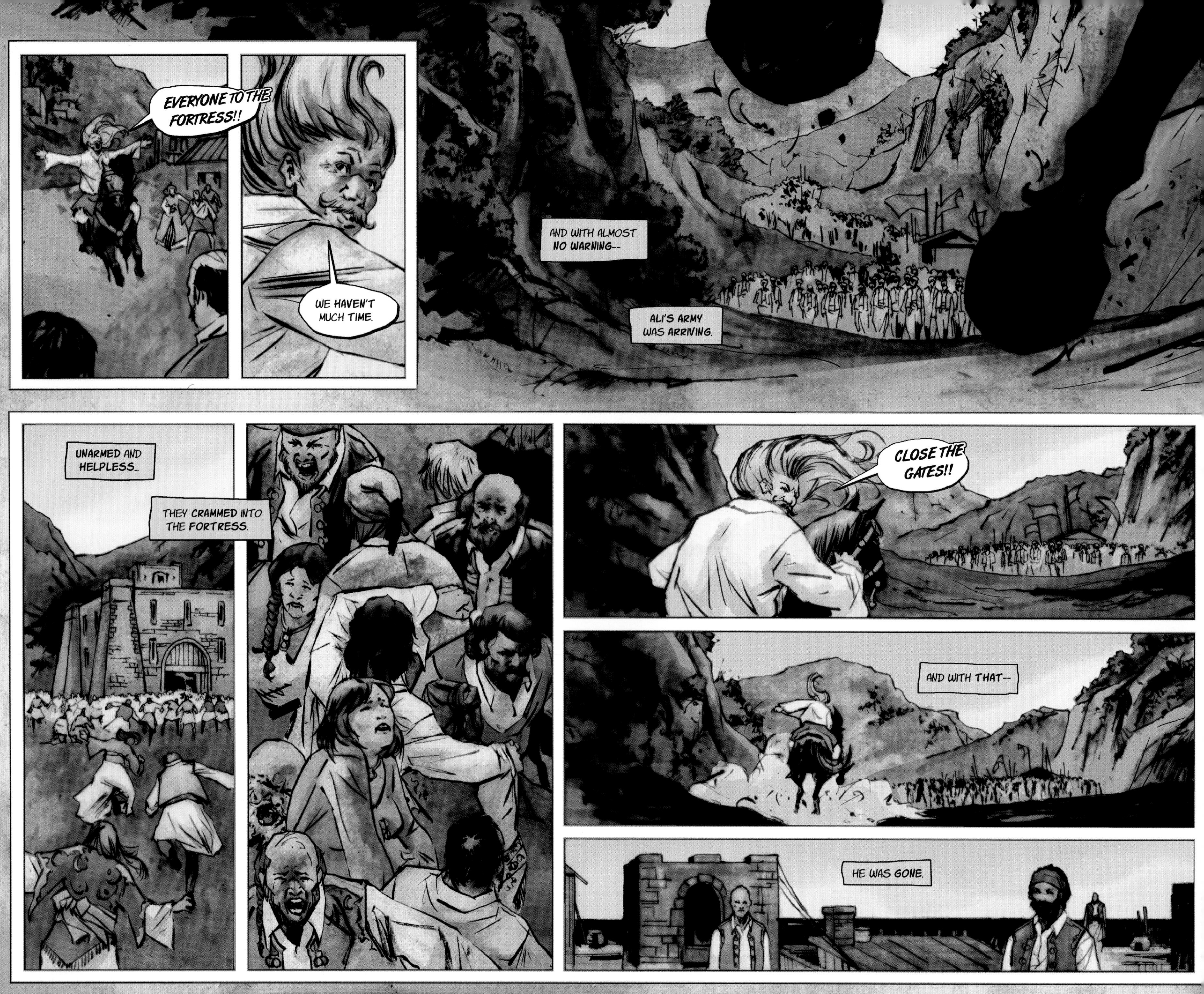
EVERYONE TO THE FORTRESS!!
WE HAVEN'T MUCH TIME.
AND WITH ALMOST NO WARNING--
ALI'S ARMY WAS ARRIVING.
UNARMED AND HELPLESS...
THEY CRAMMED INTO THE FORTRESS.
CLOSE THE GATES!!
AND WITH THAT--
HE WAS GONE.

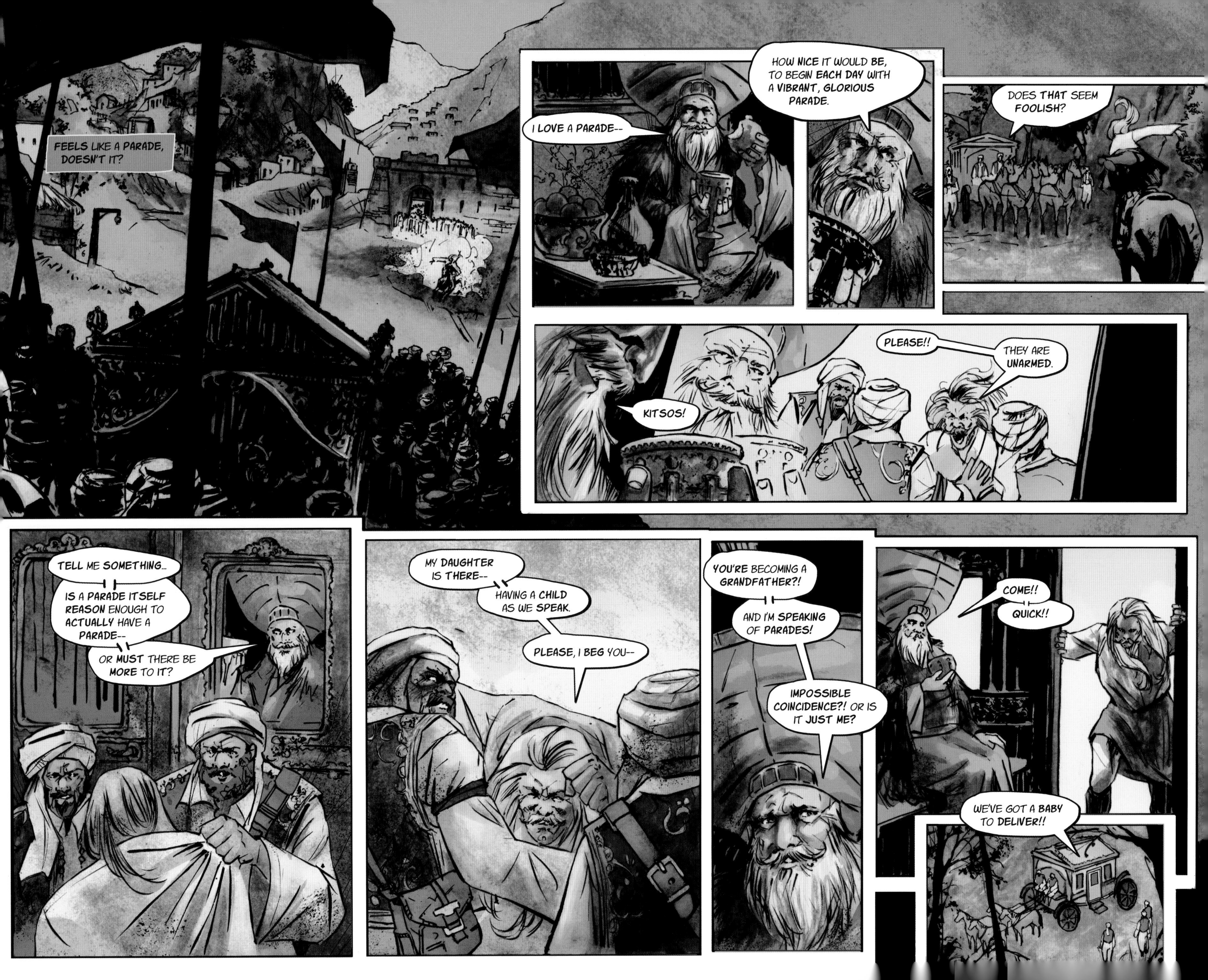
FEELS LIKE A PARADE, DOESN'T IT?
I LOVE A PARADE--
HOW NICE IT WOULD BE, TO BEGIN EACH DAY WITH A VIBRANT, GLORIOUS PARADE.
DOES THAT SEEM FOOLISH?
PLEASE!!
THEY ARE UNARMED.
KITSOS!
TELL ME SOMETHING...
IS A PARADE ITSELF REASON ENOUGH TO ACTUALLY HAVE A PARADE--
OR MUST THERE BE MORE TO IT?
MY DAUGHTER IS THERE--
HAVING A CHILD AS WE SPEAK.
PLEASE, I BEG YOU--
YOU'RE BECOMING A GRANDFATHER?!
AND I'M SPEAKING OF PARADES!
IMPOSSIBLE COINCIDENCE?! OR IS IT JUST ME?
COME!!
QUICK!!
WE'VE GOT A BABY TO DELIVER!!

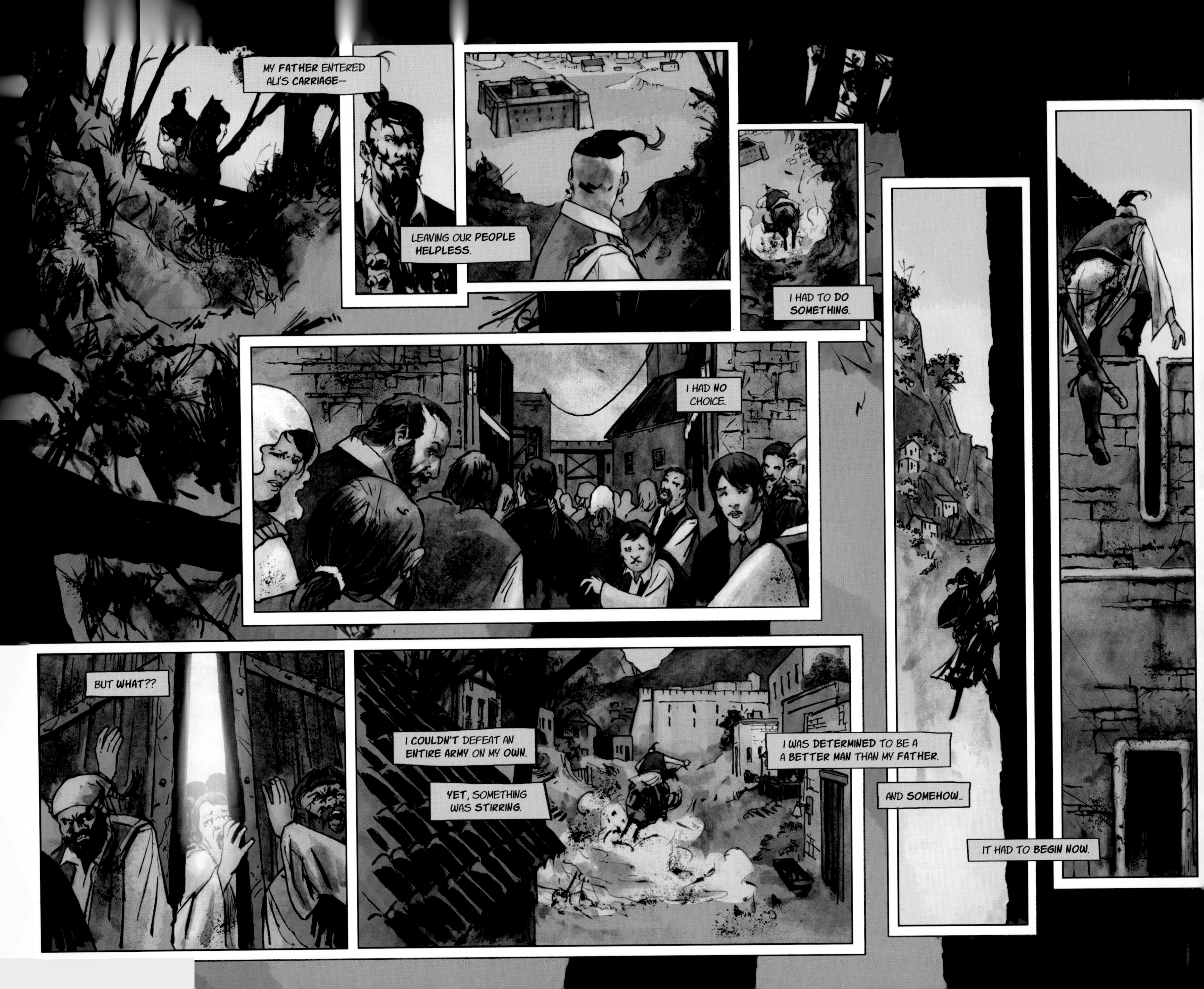
MY FATHER ENTERED ALI'S CARRIAGE--
LEAVING OUR PEOPLE HELPLESS.
I HAD TO DO SOMETHING.
I HAD NO CHOICE.
BUT WHAT??
I COULDN'T DEFEAT AN ENTIRE ARMY ON MY OWN.
YET, SOMETHING WAS STIRRING.
I WAS DETERMINED TO BE A BETTER MAN THAN MY FATHER.
AND SOMEHOW...
IT HAD TO BEGIN NOW.

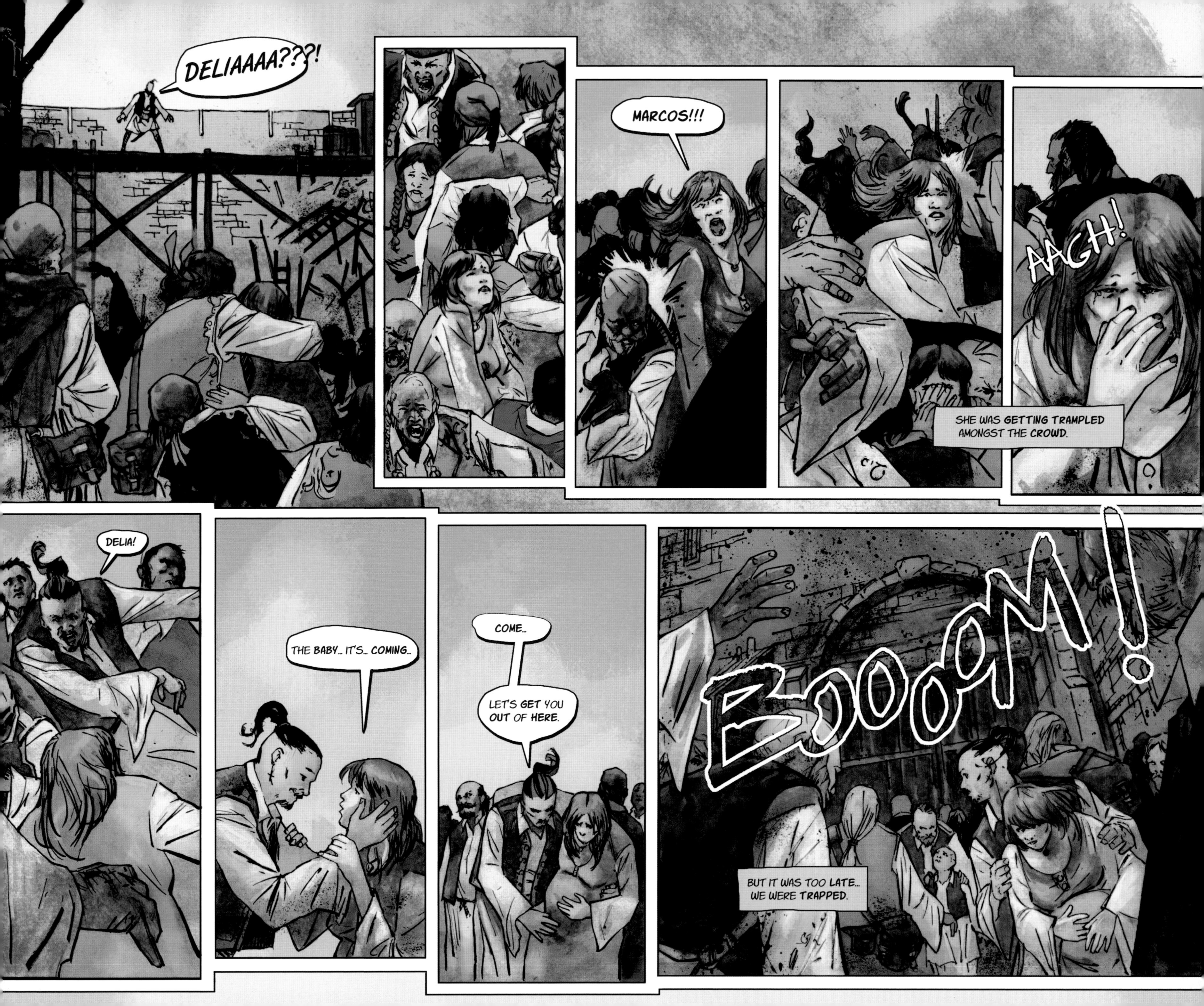
DELIAAAA???!
MARCOS!!!
AAGH!
SHE WAS GETTING TRAMPLED AMONGST THE CROWD.
DELIA!
THE BABY... IT'S... COMING...
COME...
LET'S GET YOU OUT OF HERE.
BOOOOM!
BUT IT WAS TOO LATE... WE WERE TRAPPED.

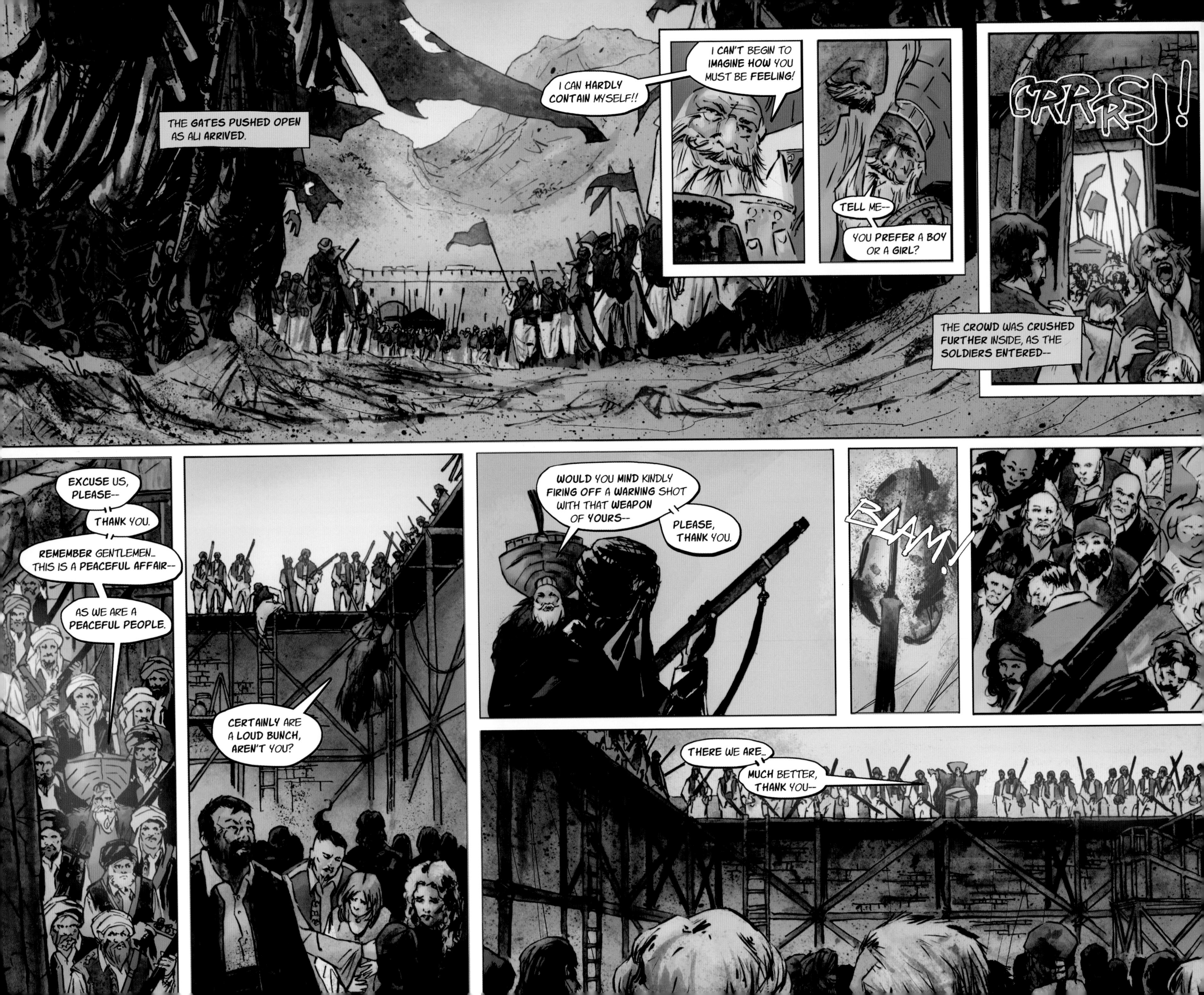
THE GATES PUSHED OPEN AS ALI ARRIVED.
I CAN HARDLY CONTAIN MYSELF!!
I CAN'T BEGIN TO IMAGINE HOW YOU MUST BE FEELING!
TELL ME--
YOU PREFER A BOY OR A GIRL?
CRRRSJ!
THE CROWD WAS CRUSHED FURTHER INSIDE, AS THE SOLDIERS ENTERED--
EXCUSE US, PLEASE--
THANK YOU.
REMEMBER GENTLEMEN... THIS IS A PEACEFUL AFFAIR--
AS WE ARE A PEACEFUL PEOPLE.
CERTAINLY ARE A LOUD BUNCH, AREN'T YOU?
WOULD YOU MIND KINDLY FIRING OFF A WARNING SHOT WITH THAT WEAPON OF YOURS--
PLEASE, THANK YOU.
BLAM!
THERE WE ARE...
MUCH BETTER, THANK YOU--

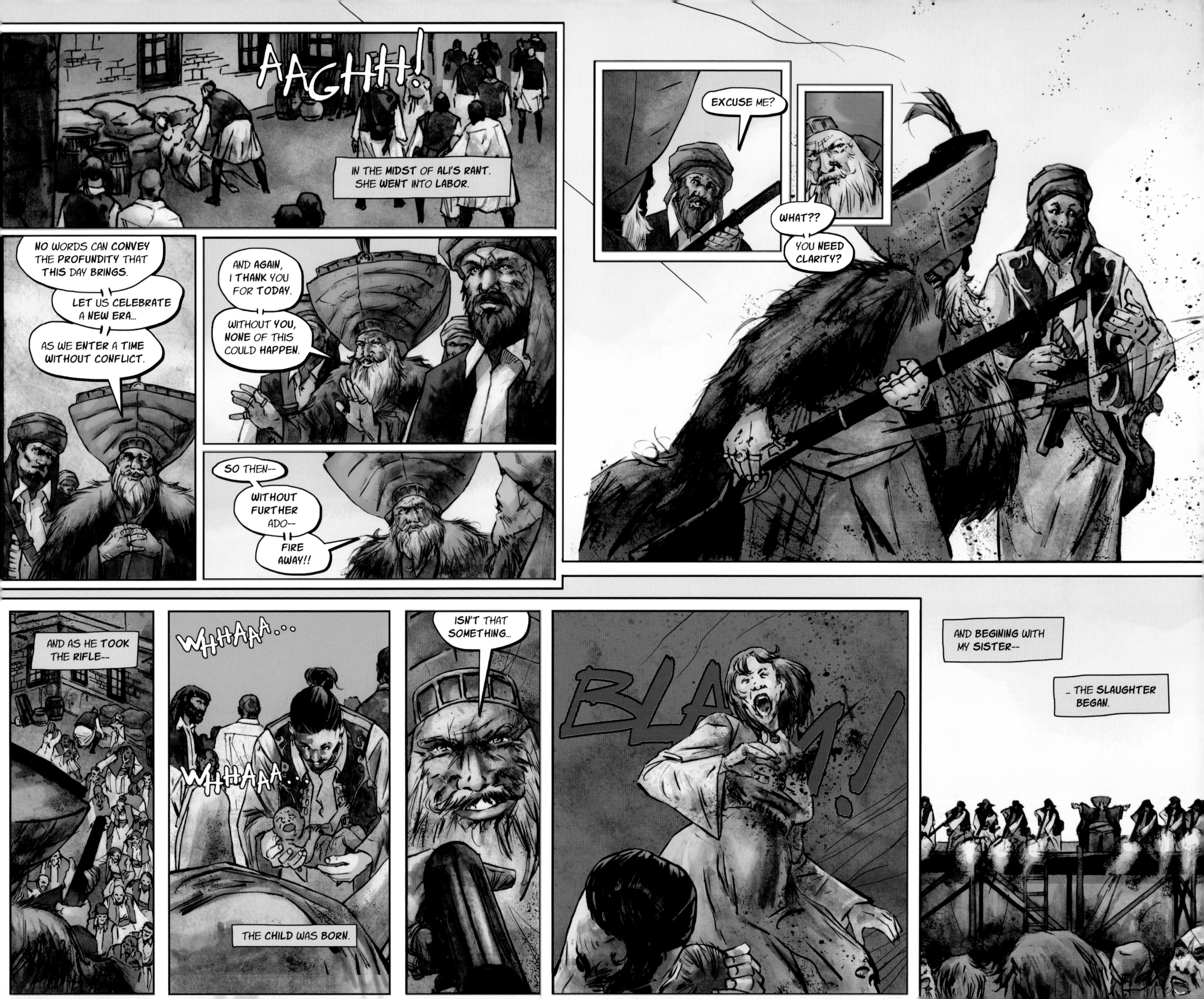
AAGHH!
IN THE MIDST OF ALI'S RANT. SHE WENT INTO LABOR.
NO WORDS CAN CONVEY THE PROFUNDITY THAT THIS DAY BRINGS.
LET US CELEBRATE A NEW ERA...
AS WE ENTER A TIME WITHOUT CONFLICT.
AND AGAIN, I THANK YOU FOR TODAY.
WITHOUT YOU, NONE OF THIS COULD HAPPEN.
SO THEN--
WITHOUT FURTHER ADO--
FIRE AWAY!!
EXCUSE ME?
WHAT??
YOU NEED CLARITY?
AND AS HE TOOK THE RIFLE--
WHHAAA...
WHHAAA...
THE CHILD WAS BORN.
ISN'T THAT SOMETHING...
BLAM!
AND BEGINING WITH MY SISTER--
...THE SLAUGHTER BEGAN.

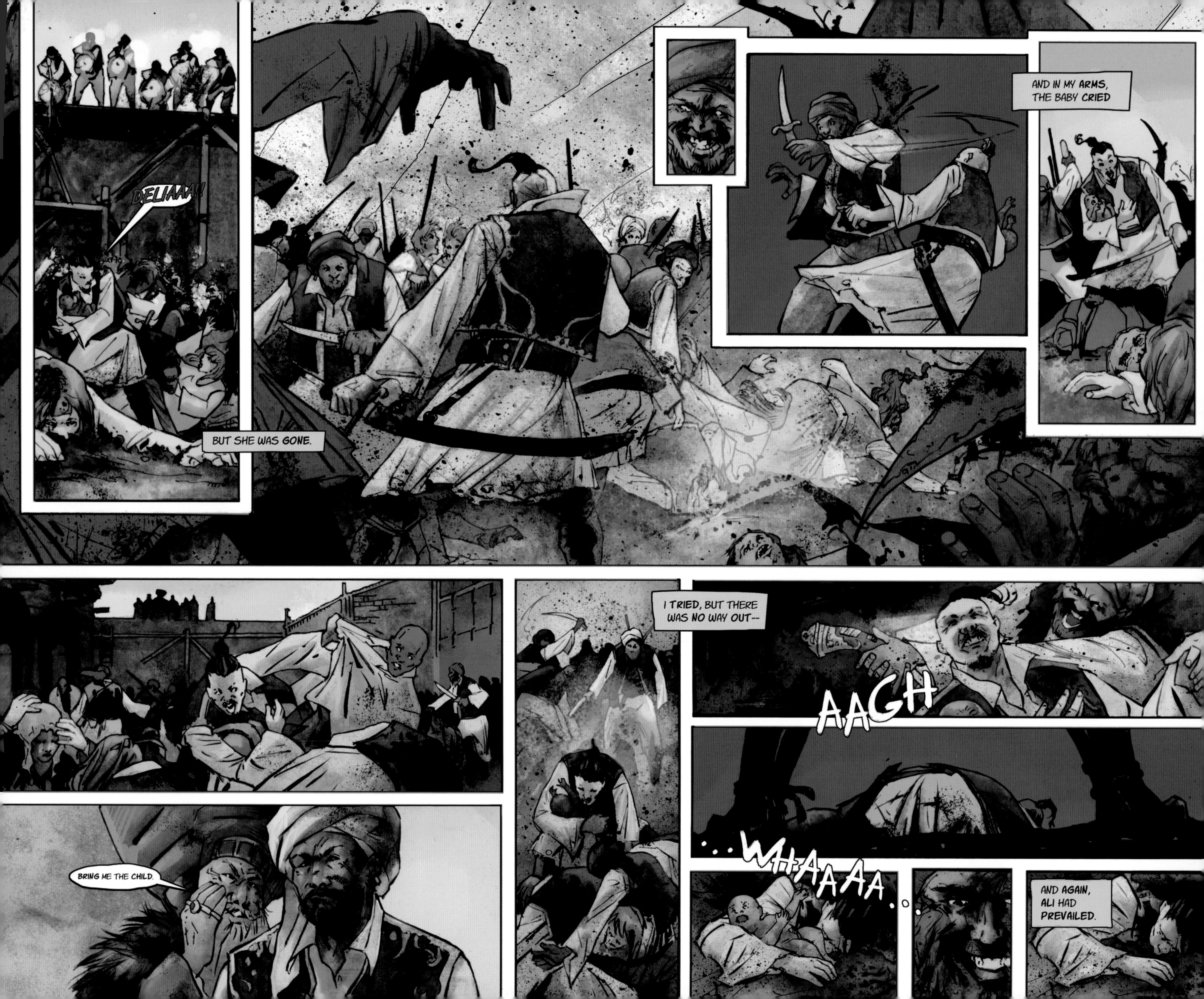
DELIAAA!!
BUT SHE WAS GONE.
AND IN MY ARMS, THE BABY CRIED
BRING ME THE CHILD.
I TRIED, BUT THERE WAS NO WAY OUT--
AAGH
...WHAAAAA...
AND AGAIN, ALI HAD PREVAILED.

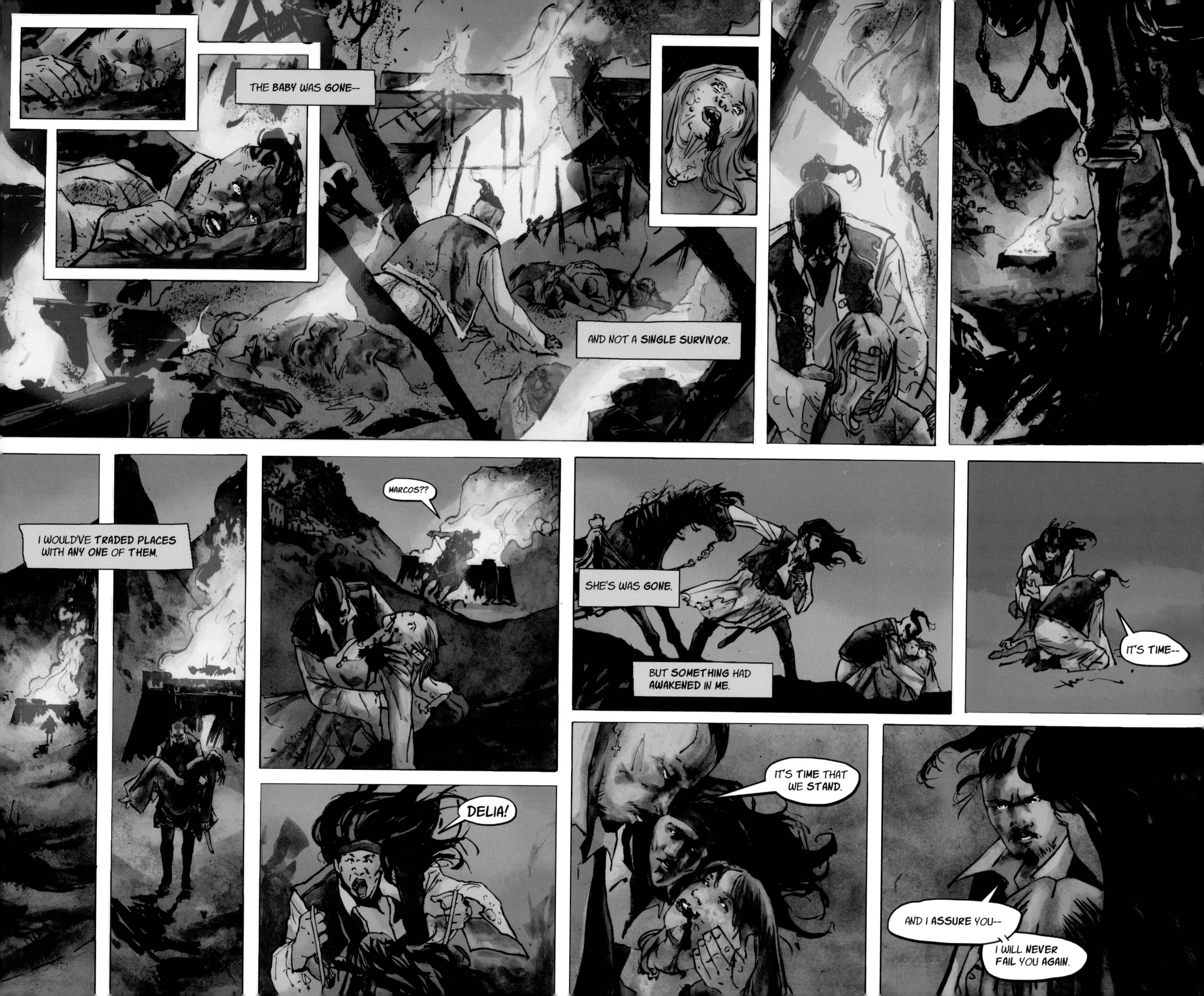
THE BABY WAS GONE--
AND NOT A SINGLE SURVIVOR.
I WOULD'VE TRADED PLACES WITH ANY ONE OF THEM.
MARCOS??
DELIA!
SHE'S WAS GONE.
BUT SOMETHING HAD AWAKENED IN ME.
IT'S TIME--
IT'S TIME THAT WE STAND.
AND I ASSURE YOU--
I WILL NEVER FAIL YOU AGAIN.

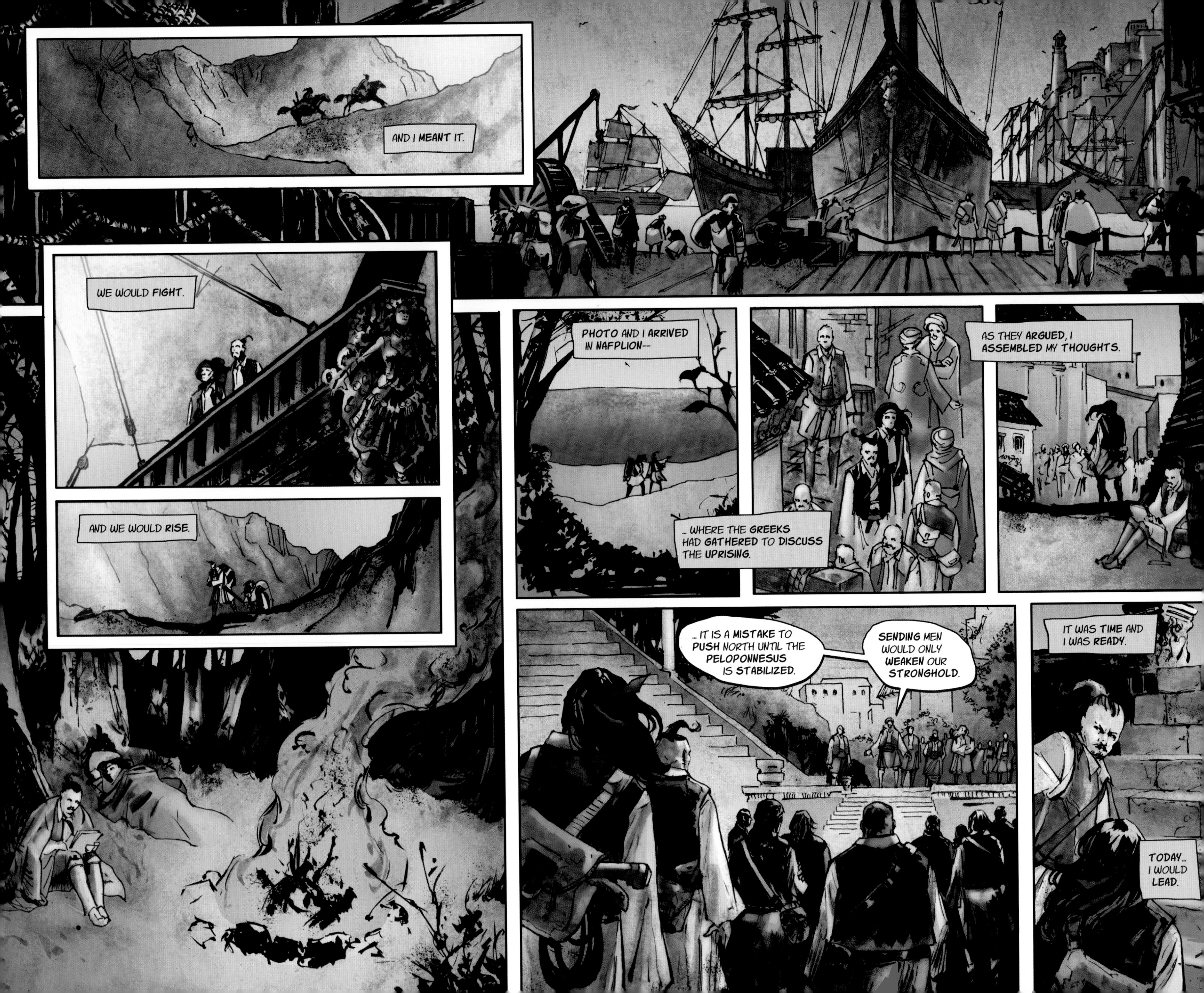

AND I MEANT IT.
WE WOULD FIGHT.
AND WE WOULD RISE.
PHOTO AND I ARRIVED IN NAFPLION--
... WHERE THE GREEKS HAD GATHERED TO DISCUSS THE UPRISING.
AS THEY ARGUED, I ASSEMBLED MY THOUGHTS.
... IT IS A MISTAKE TO PUSH NORTH UNTIL THE PELOPONNESUS IS STABILIZED.
SENDING MEN WOULD ONLY WEAKEN OUR STRONGHOLD.
IT WAS TIME AND I WAS READY.
TODAY... I WOULD LEAD.

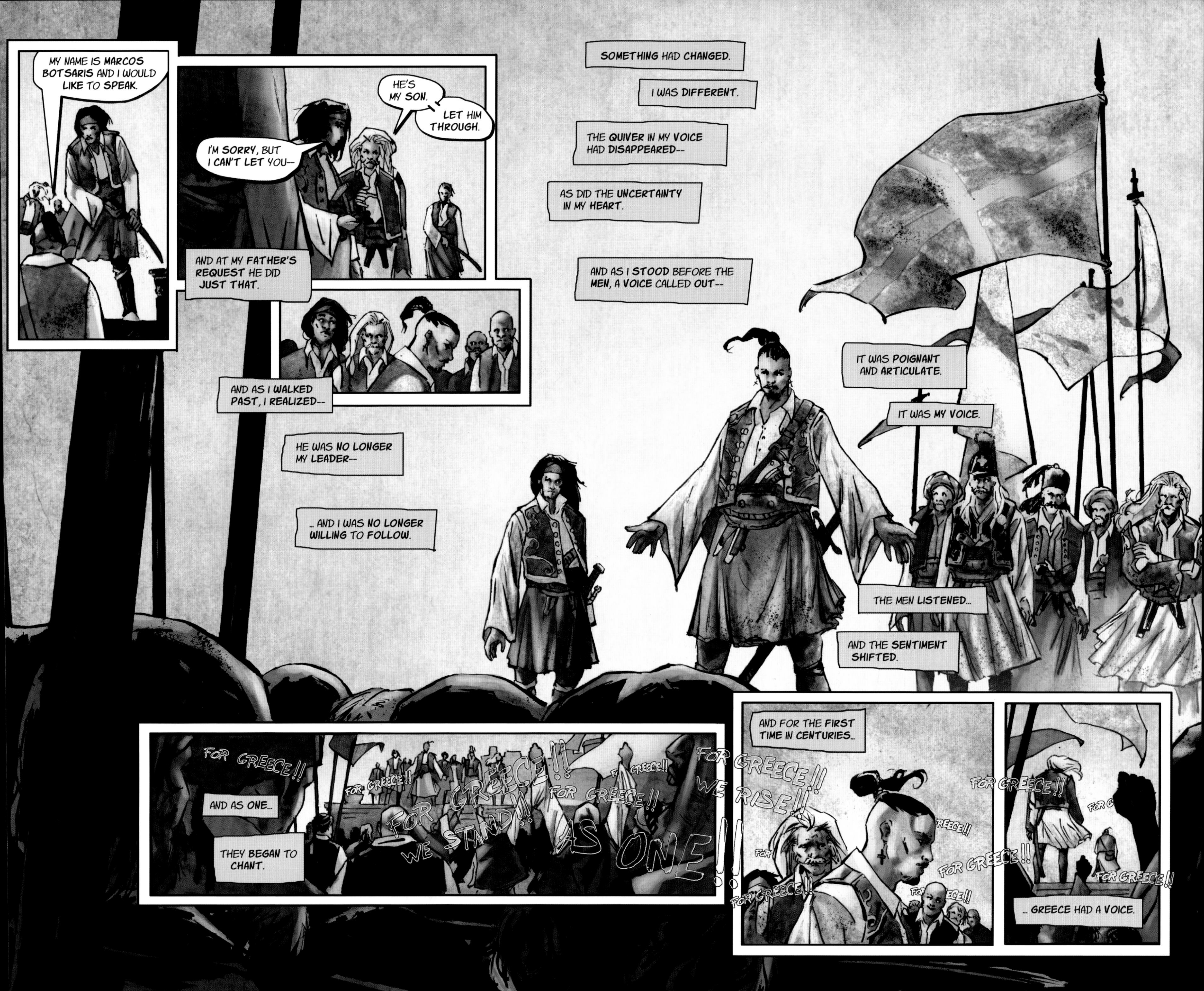
MY NAME IS MARCOS BOTSARIS AND I WOULD LIKE TO SPEAK.
I'M SORRY, BUT I CAN'T LET YOU--
HE'S MY SON.
LET HIM THROUGH.
AND AT MY FATHER'S REQUEST HE DID JUST THAT.
AND AS I WALKED PAST, I REALIZED--
HE WAS NO LONGER MY LEADER--
... AND I WAS NO LONGER WILLING TO FOLLOW.
SOMETHING HAD CHANGED.
I WAS DIFFERENT.
THE QUIVER IN MY VOICE HAD DISAPPEARED--
AS DID THE UNCERTAINTY IN MY HEART.
AND AS I STOOD BEFORE THE MEN, A VOICE CALLED OUT--
IT WAS POIGNANT AND ARTICULATE.
IT WAS MY VOICE.
THE MEN LISTENED...
AND THE SENTIMENT SHIFTED.
AND AS ONE...
THEY BEGAN TO CHANT.
FOR GREECE!!
FOR GREECE!!
FOR GREECE!!
FOR GREECE!!
WE STAND!!
AS ONE!!
FOR GREECE!!
WE RISE!!
AND FOR THE FIRST TIME IN CENTURIES...
FOR GREECE!!
FOR GREECE!!
FOR GREECE!!
FOR GREECE!!
... GREECE HAD A VOICE.

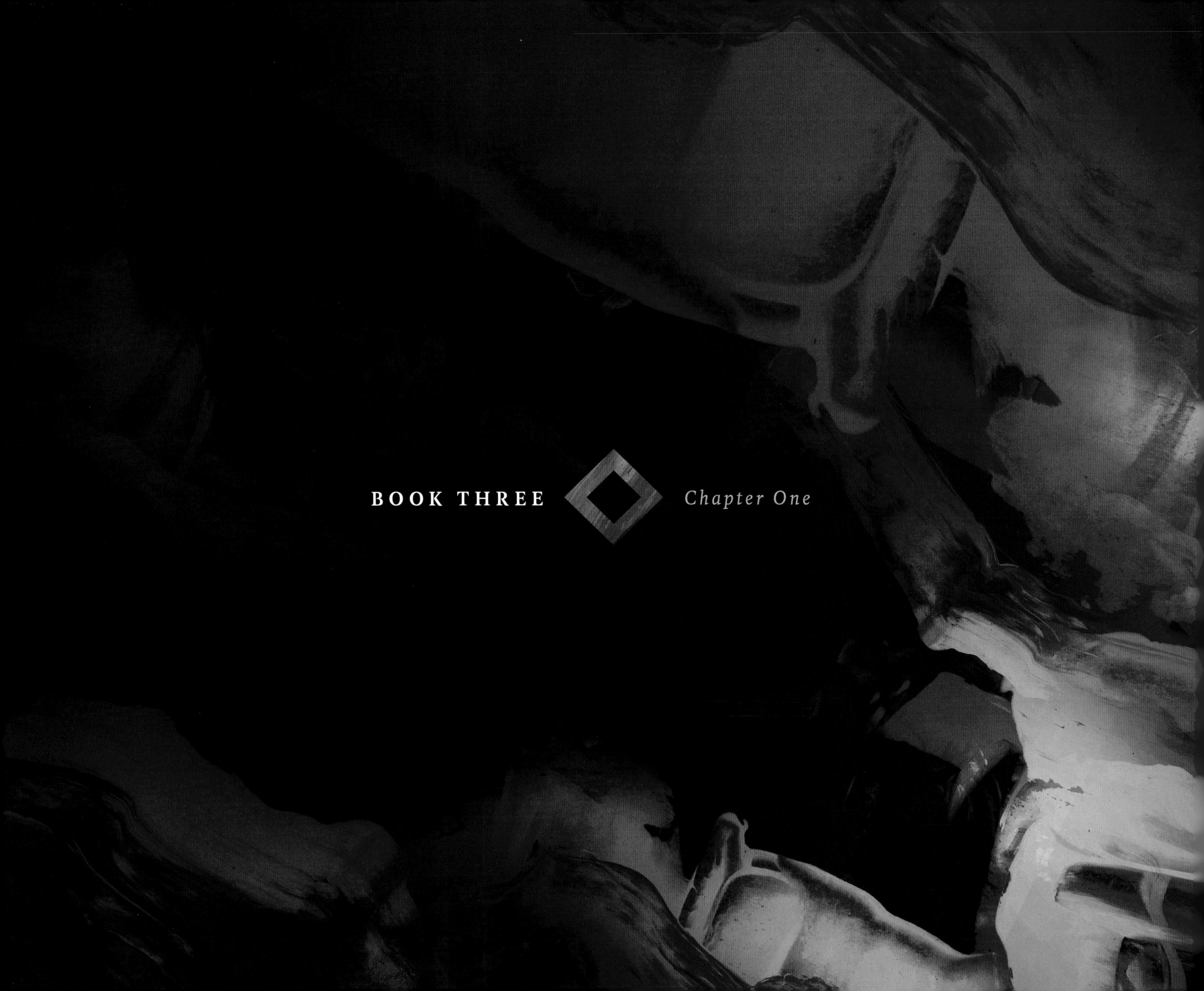

BOOK THREE

Chapter One

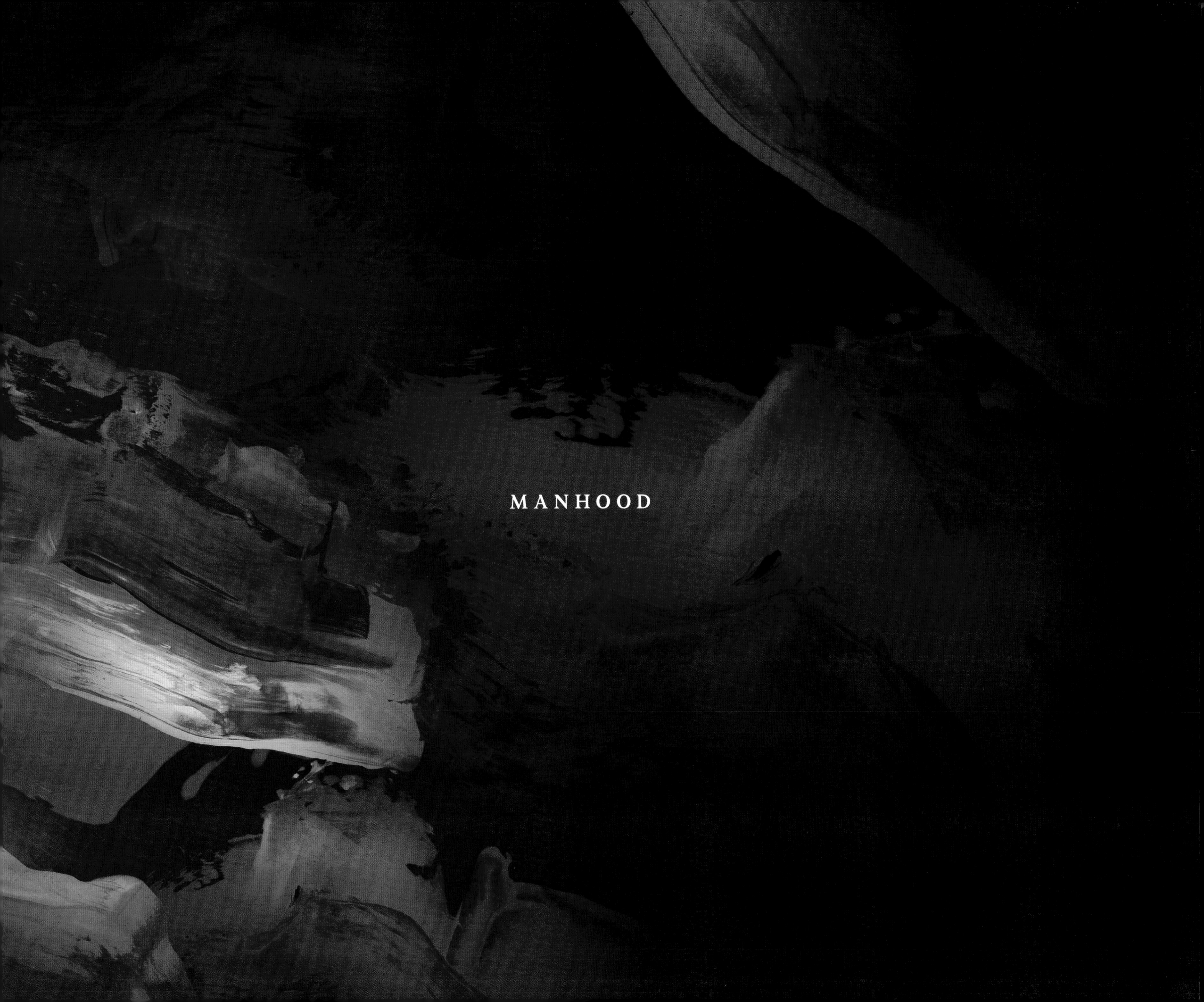

MANHOOD

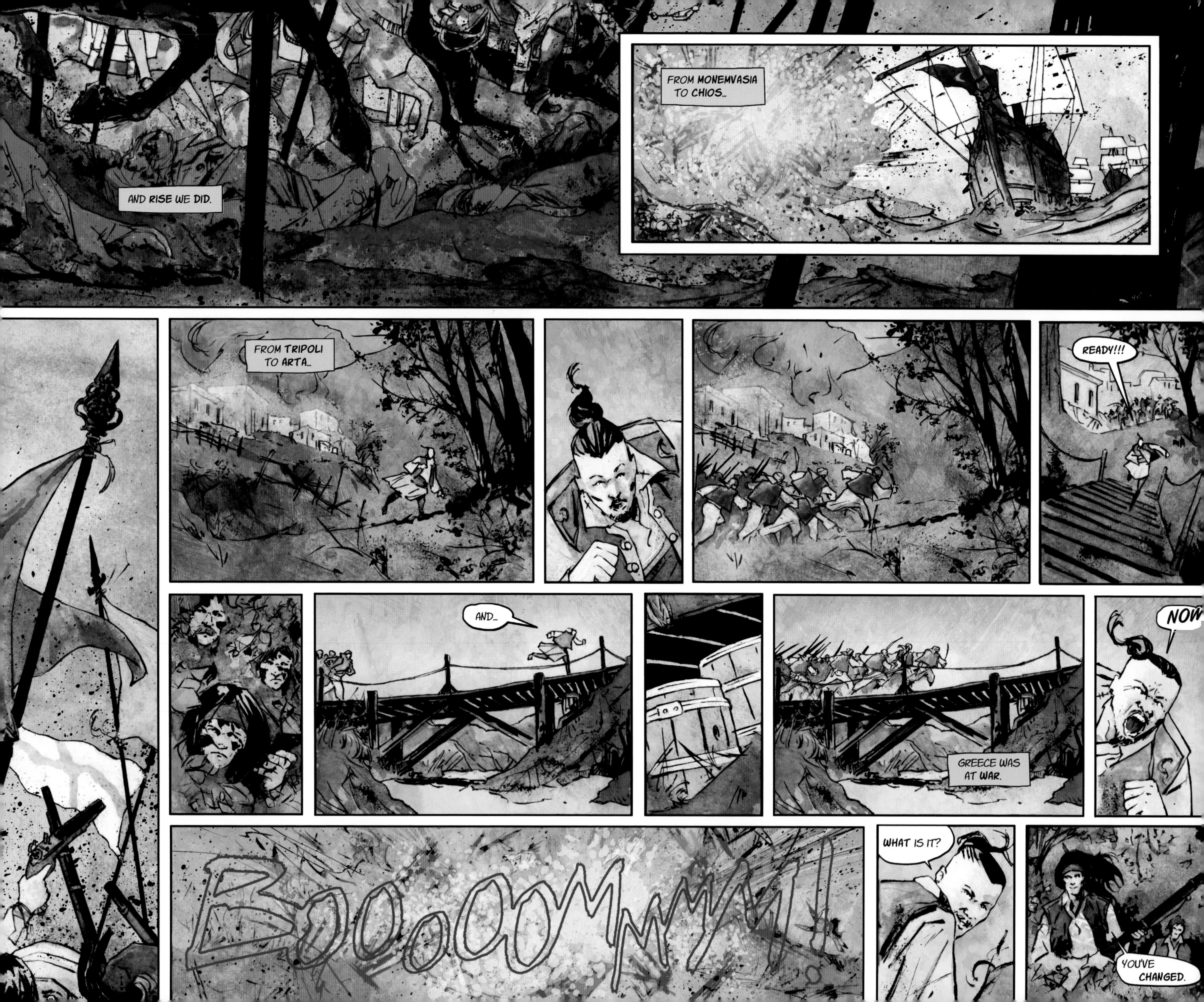
AND RISE WE DID.
FROM MONEMVASIA TO CHIOS...
FROM TRIPOLI TO ARTA...
READY!!!
AND...
GREECE WAS AT WAR.
NOW
BOOOOOMMM!
WHAT IS IT?
YOU'VE CHANGED.

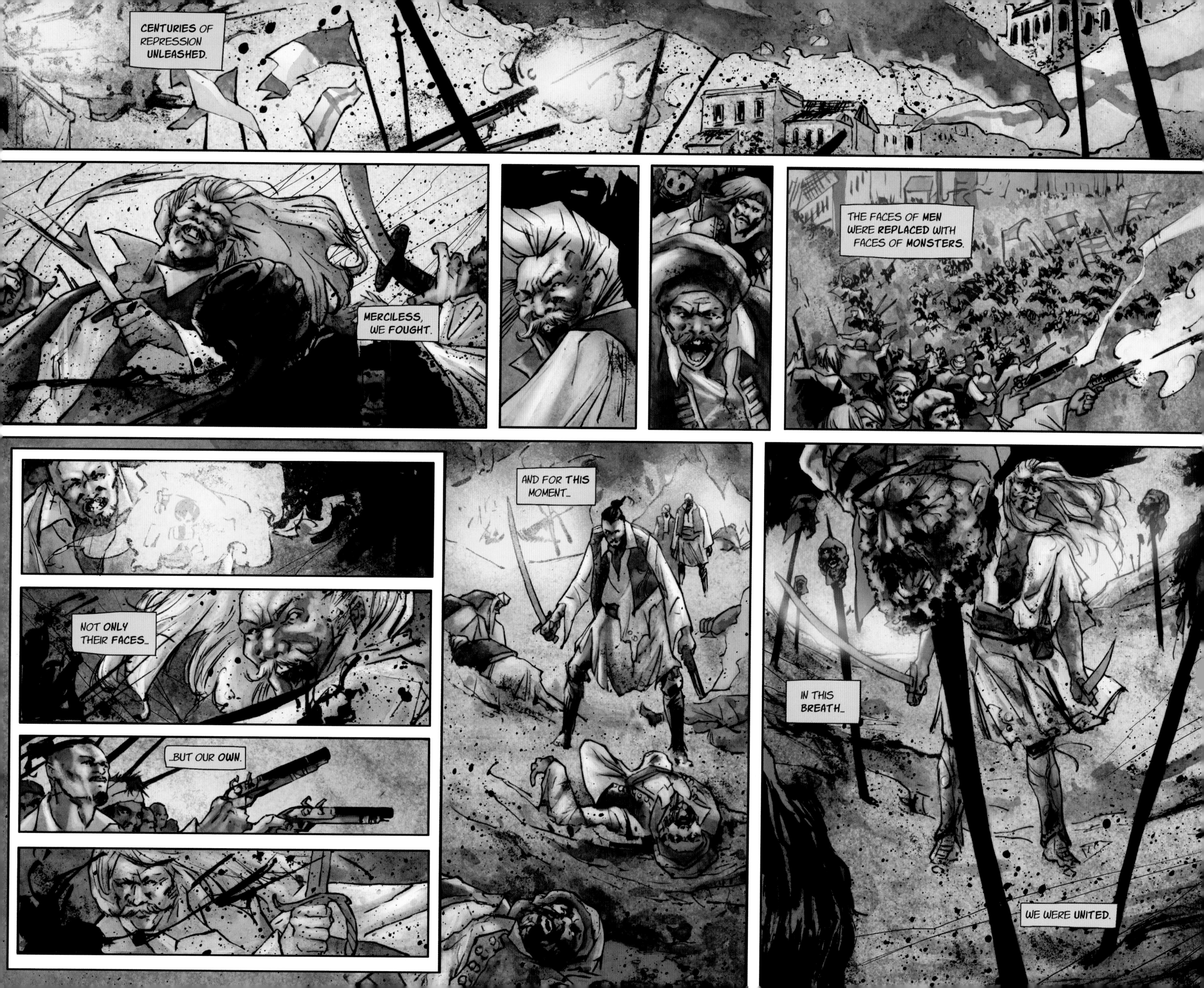
CENTURIES OF REPRESSION UNLEASHED.
MERCILESS, WE FOUGHT.
THE FACES OF MEN WERE REPLACED WITH FACES OF MONSTERS.
NOT ONLY THEIR FACES...
...BUT OUR OWN.
AND FOR THIS MOMENT...
IN THIS BREATH...
WE WERE UNITED.

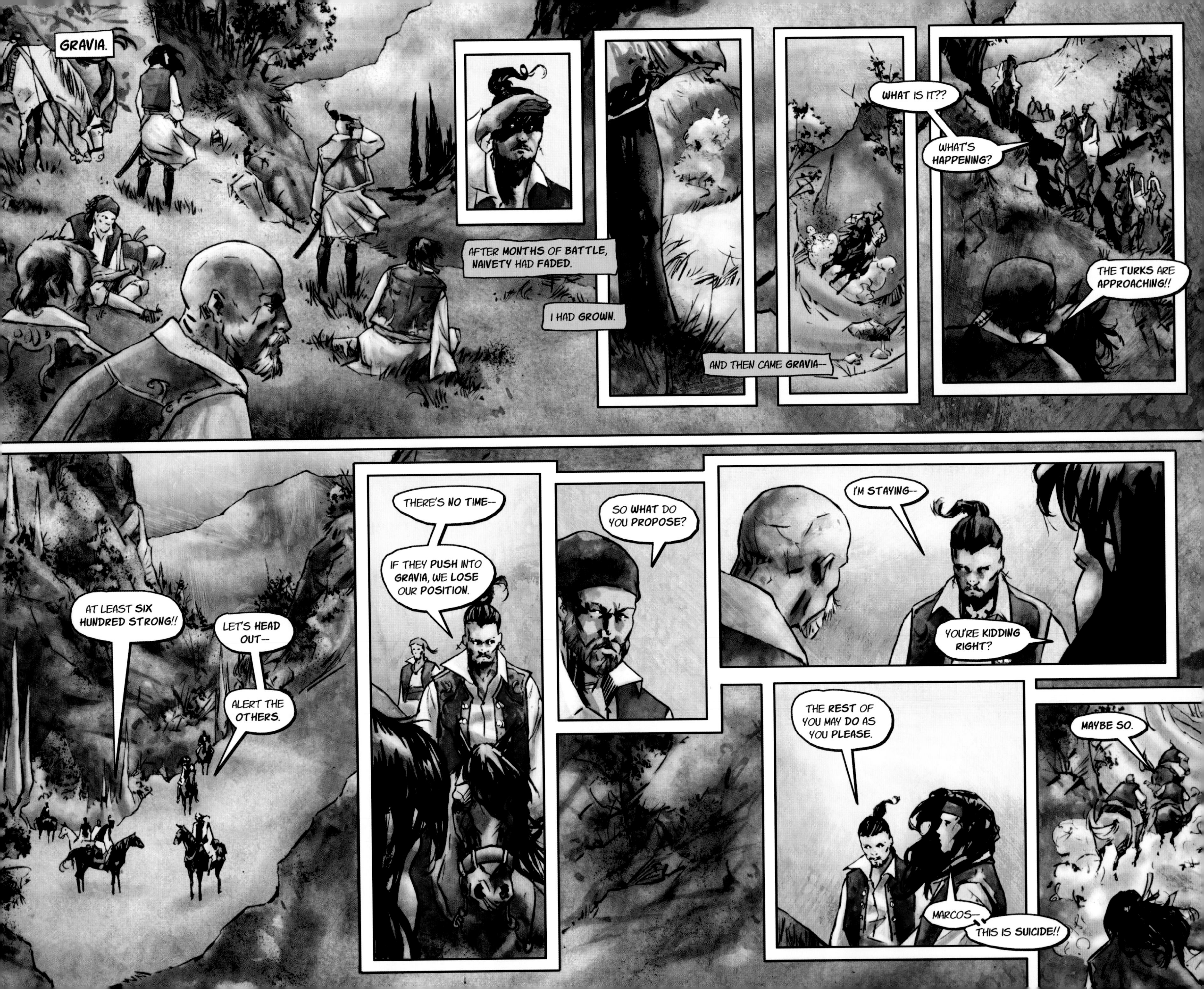
GRAVIA.
AFTER MONTHS OF BATTLE, NAIVETY HAD FADED.
I HAD GROWN.
AND THEN CAME GRAVIA--
WHAT IS IT??
WHAT'S HAPPENING?
THE TURKS ARE APPROACHING!!
AT LEAST SIX HUNDRED STRONG!!
LET'S HEAD OUT--
ALERT THE OTHERS.
THERE'S NO TIME--
IF THEY PUSH INTO GRAVIA, WE LOSE OUR POSITION.
SO WHAT DO YOU PROPOSE?
I'M STAYING--
YOU'RE KIDDING RIGHT?
THE REST OF YOU MAY DO AS YOU PLEASE.
MARCOS--
THIS IS SUICIDE!!
MAYBE SO.

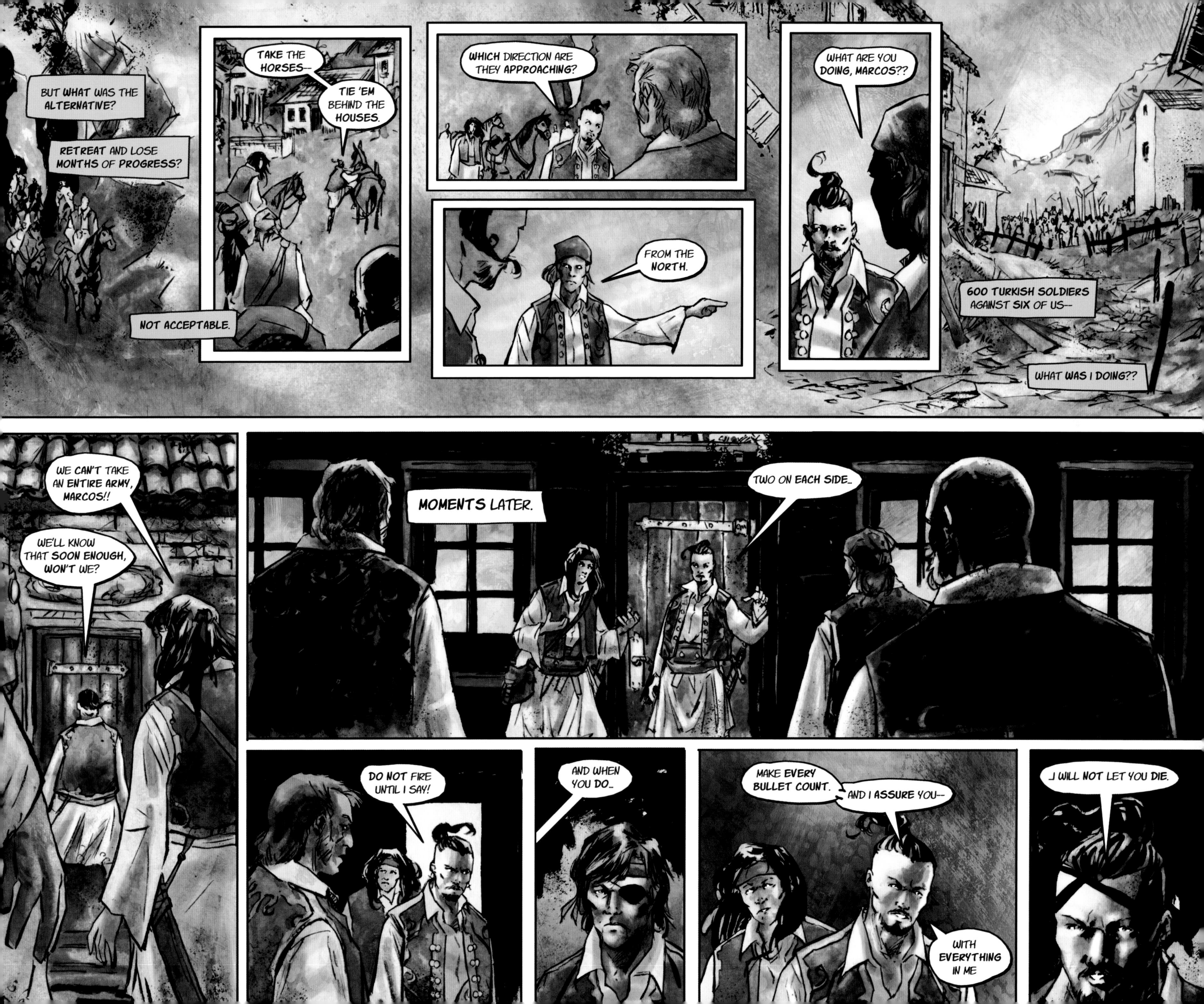
BUT WHAT WAS THE ALTERNATIVE?
RETREAT AND LOSE MONTHS OF PROGRESS?
NOT ACCEPTABLE.
TAKE THE HORSES--
TIE 'EM BEHIND THE HOUSES.
WHICH DIRECTION ARE THEY APPROACHING?
FROM THE NORTH.
WHAT ARE YOU DOING, MARCOS??
600 TURKISH SOLDIERS AGAINST SIX OF US--
WHAT WAS I DOING??
WE CAN'T TAKE AN ENTIRE ARMY, MARCOS!!
WE'LL KNOW THAT SOON ENOUGH, WON'T WE?
MOMENTS LATER.
TWO ON EACH SIDE...
DO NOT FIRE UNTIL I SAY!
AND WHEN YOU DO...
MAKE EVERY BULLET COUNT.
AND I ASSURE YOU--
WITH EVERYTHING IN ME
...I WILL NOT LET YOU DIE.

IOANNINA.

THE GREEKS ARE MOVING INTO ARTA AND DERVENAKIA--

AND THEY'VE TAKEN THE ENTIRE PELOPONNESUS.

AND THE SULTAN'S ARMY IS HEADED HERE?

YES, SIR.

HOW FAR OUT?

WITHIN DAYS

AND WITHIN THOSE DAYS...

THE SULTAN REQUESTS THAT YOU SEND YOUR ARMIES TO STAND AGAINST THE GREEKS AS THEY PUSH NORTH.

SORRY, SAY AGAIN--

I WENT SLIGHTLY UNCONSCIOUS WHILE YOU WERE SPEAKING.

AS YOU CAN SEE, I'M VERY ILL--

I DO APOLOGIZE.

I DO NOT WANT TO IMPOSE ON YOUR CONDITION, SIRE.

I AM ONLY EXPRESSING THE SULTAN'S WISHES.

COUGH!

COUGH!

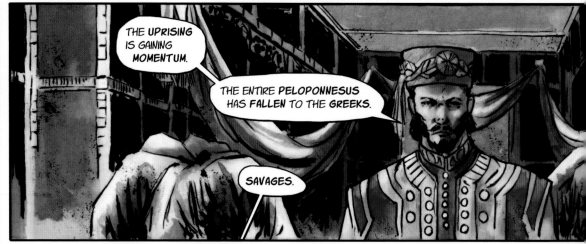

THE UPRISING IS GAINING MOMENTUM.

THE ENTIRE PELOPONNESUS HAS FALLEN TO THE GREEKS.

SAVAGES.

HICKUPP

UNTIL THESE DOCTORS ALLOW IT, I AM INCAPABLE OF LEADING AN ARMY

MY CONDITION IS QUITE CRITICAL APPARENTLY, HOWEVER...

BUURP

THE SULTAN CAN REST ASSUREDLY--

I WILL HAVE MY UNQUESTIONABLY COMPETENT SON TAKE CARE OF THE MATTER IMMEDIATELY.

THANK YOU, SIRE.

I FEAR I AM NOT LONG FOR THIS WORLD.

BUT AS LONG AS I AM ALIVE...

THE SULTAN HAS A COMMITTED SERVANT HERE IN IOANNINA.

THE SULTAN VALUES YOUR LOYALTY.

AS I VALUE HIS EXEMPLARY LEADERSHIP.

...BELCH...

HICKUPP

GOOD DAY TO YOU, SIRE.

A GOOD DAY TO YOU, MY FRIEND.

AND MAY THOSE INSOLENT GREEKS BE DAMNED ONCE AND FOR ALL...

HACK!

BUURP

THERE IS AN URGENT MATTER NEEDING YOUR ATTENTION, FATHER--

IS HE GONE?

HE'S GONE!

MY GOD--

I THOUGHT THEY WERE NEVER LEAVING!!

AAGHH... I'VE GOT NO FEELING IN MY LEG!!

OUCH!! OUCH!! OUCH!!

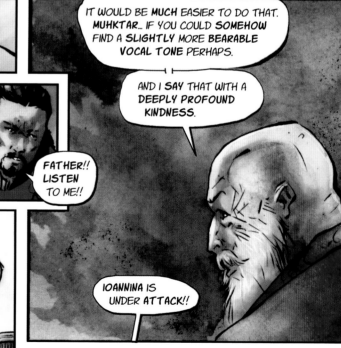

IT WOULD BE MUCH EASIER TO DO THAT, MUHKTAR... IF YOU COULD SOMEHOW FIND A SLIGHTLY MORE BEARABLE VOCAL TONE PERHAPS.

AND I SAY THAT WITH A DEEPLY PROFOUND KINDNESS.

FATHER!! LISTEN TO ME!!

IOANNINA IS UNDER ATTACK!!

AS IS YOUR LIKABILITY.

LIGHTEN UP.

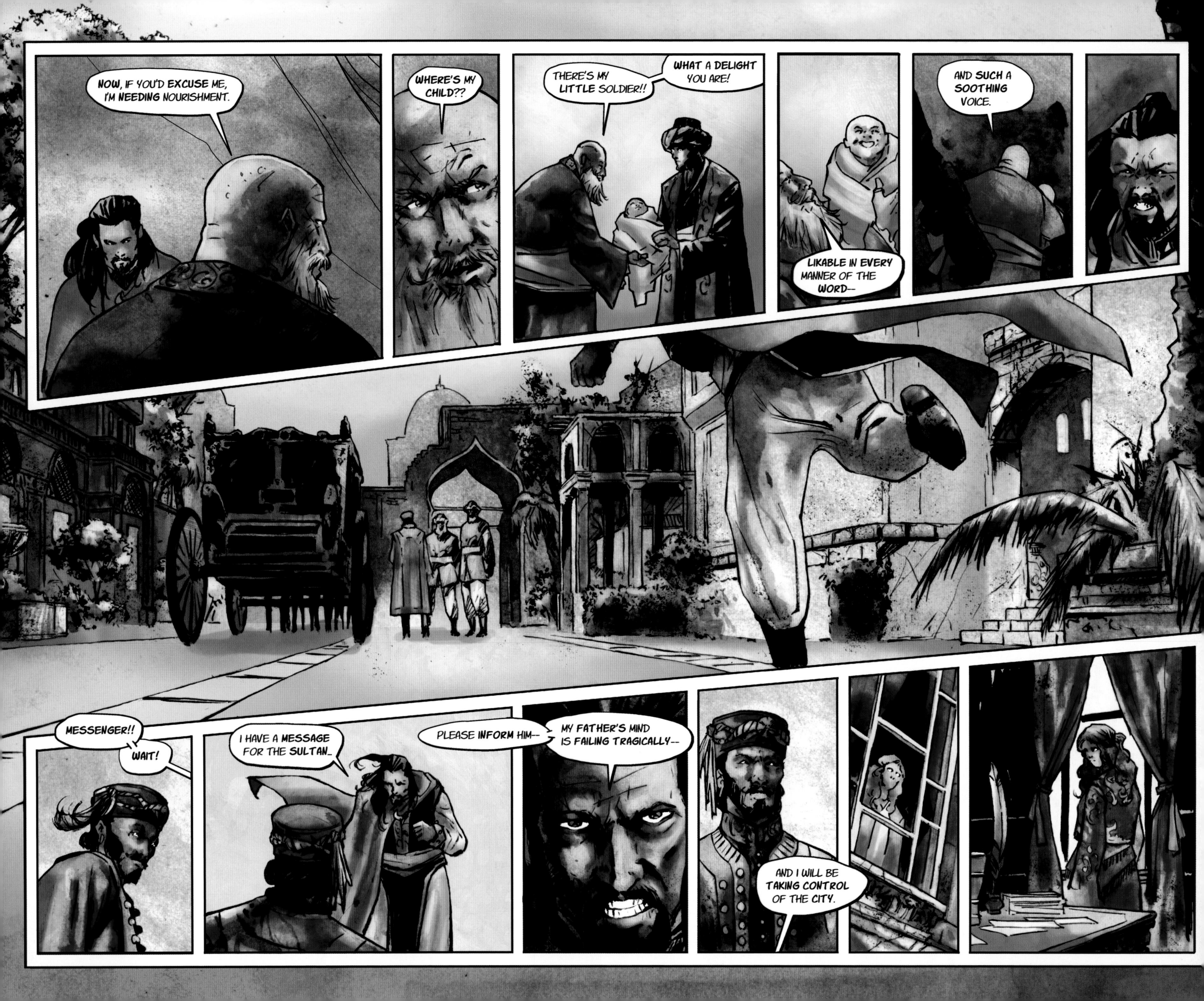
NOW, IF YOU'D EXCUSE ME, I'M NEEDING NOURISHMENT.
WHERE'S MY CHILD??
THERE'S MY LITTLE SOLDIER!!
WHAT A DELIGHT YOU ARE!
LIKABLE IN EVERY MANNER OF THE WORD--
AND SUCH A SOOTHING VOICE.
MESSENGER!!
WAIT!
I HAVE A MESSAGE FOR THE SULTAN..
PLEASE INFORM HIM--
MY FATHER'S MIND IS FAILING TRAGICALLY--
AND I WILL BE TAKING CONTROL OF THE CITY.

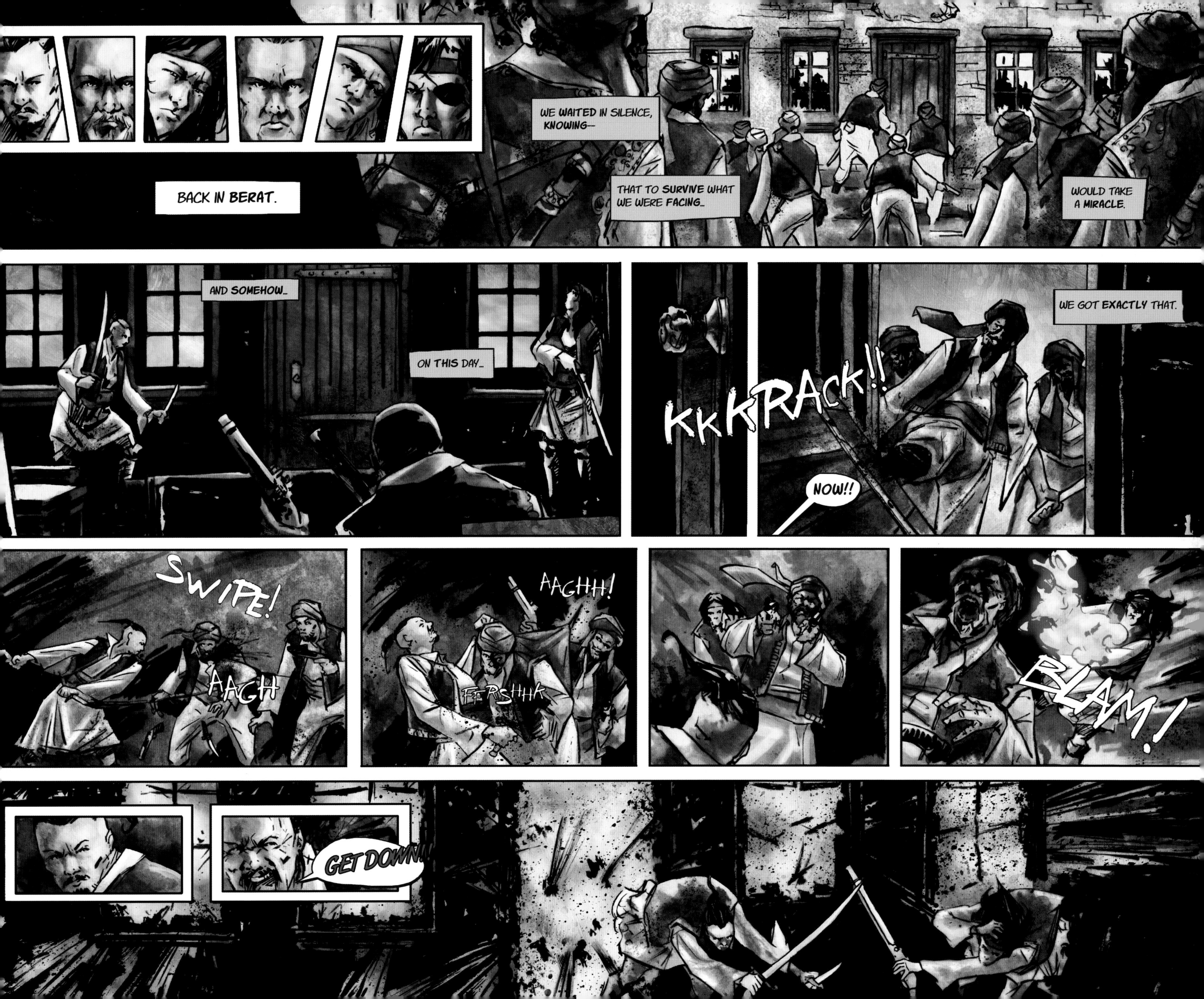
BACK IN BERAT.
WE WAITED IN SILENCE, KNOWING--
THAT TO SURVIVE WHAT WE WERE FACING...
WOULD TAKE A MIRACLE.
AND SOMEHOW...
ON THIS DAY...
KKKRACK!!
WE GOT EXACTLY THAT.
NOW!!
SWIPE!
AAGH
AAGHH!
FFRSHHK
BLAM!
GET DOWN!!

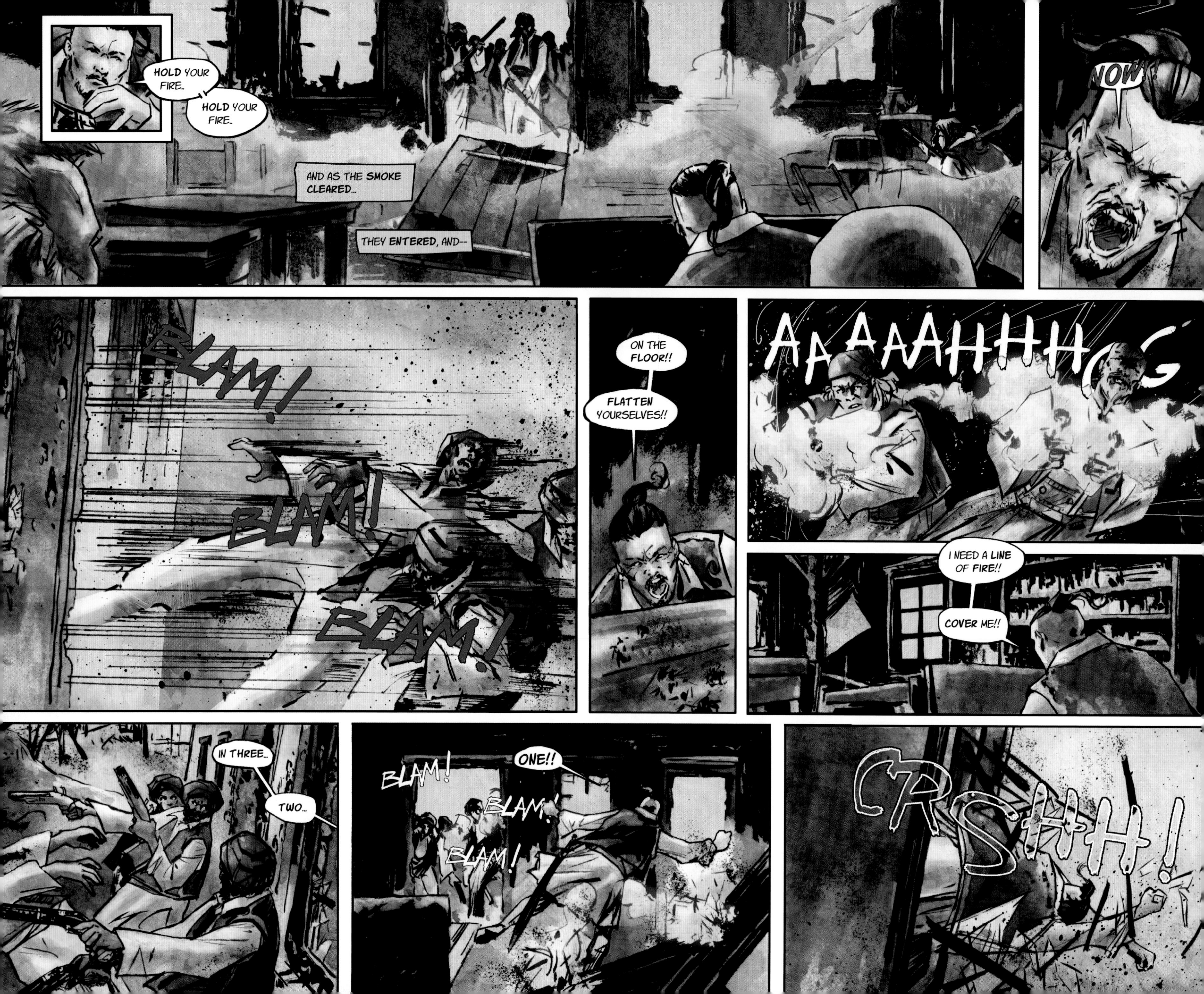
HOLD YOUR FIRE..
HOLD YOUR FIRE..
AND AS THE SMOKE CLEARED...
THEY ENTERED, AND--
NOW!
BLAM!
BLAM!
BLAM!
ON THE FLOOR!!
FLATTEN YOURSELVES!!
AAAAAHHHG
I NEED A LINE OF FIRE!!
COVER ME!!
IN THREE..
TWO...
ONE!!
BLAM!
BLAM!
BLAM!
CRSHH!

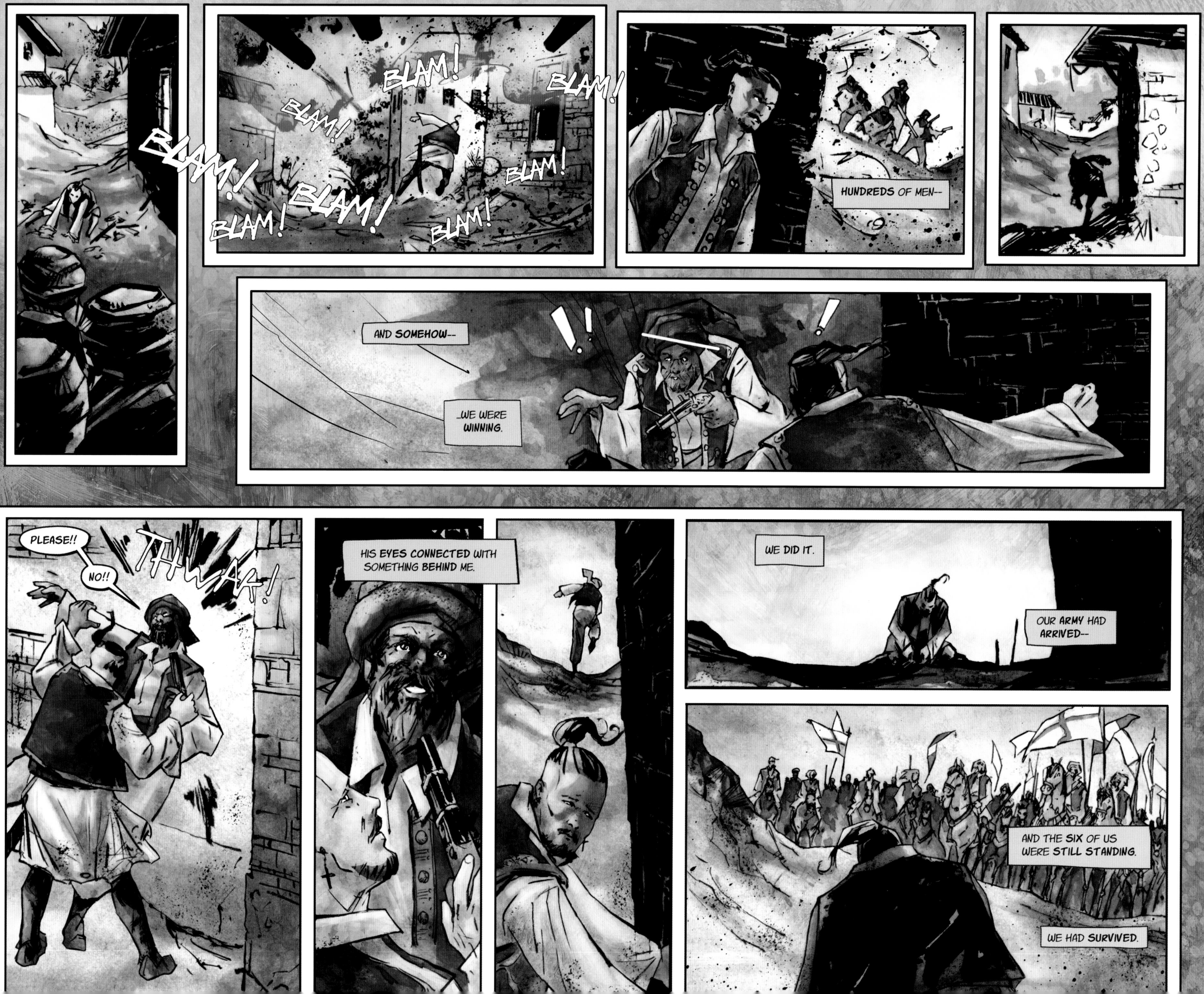
BLAM!
BLAM!
BLAM!
BLAM!
BLAM!
BLAM!
BLAM!
BLAM!
HUNDREDS OF MEN--
AND SOMEHOW--
!!
!
...WE WERE WINNING.
PLEASE!!
NO!!
THWAK!
HIS EYES CONNECTED WITH SOMETHING BEHIND ME.
WE DID IT.
OUR ARMY HAD ARRIVED--
AND THE SIX OF US WERE STILL STANDING.
WE HAD SURVIVED.

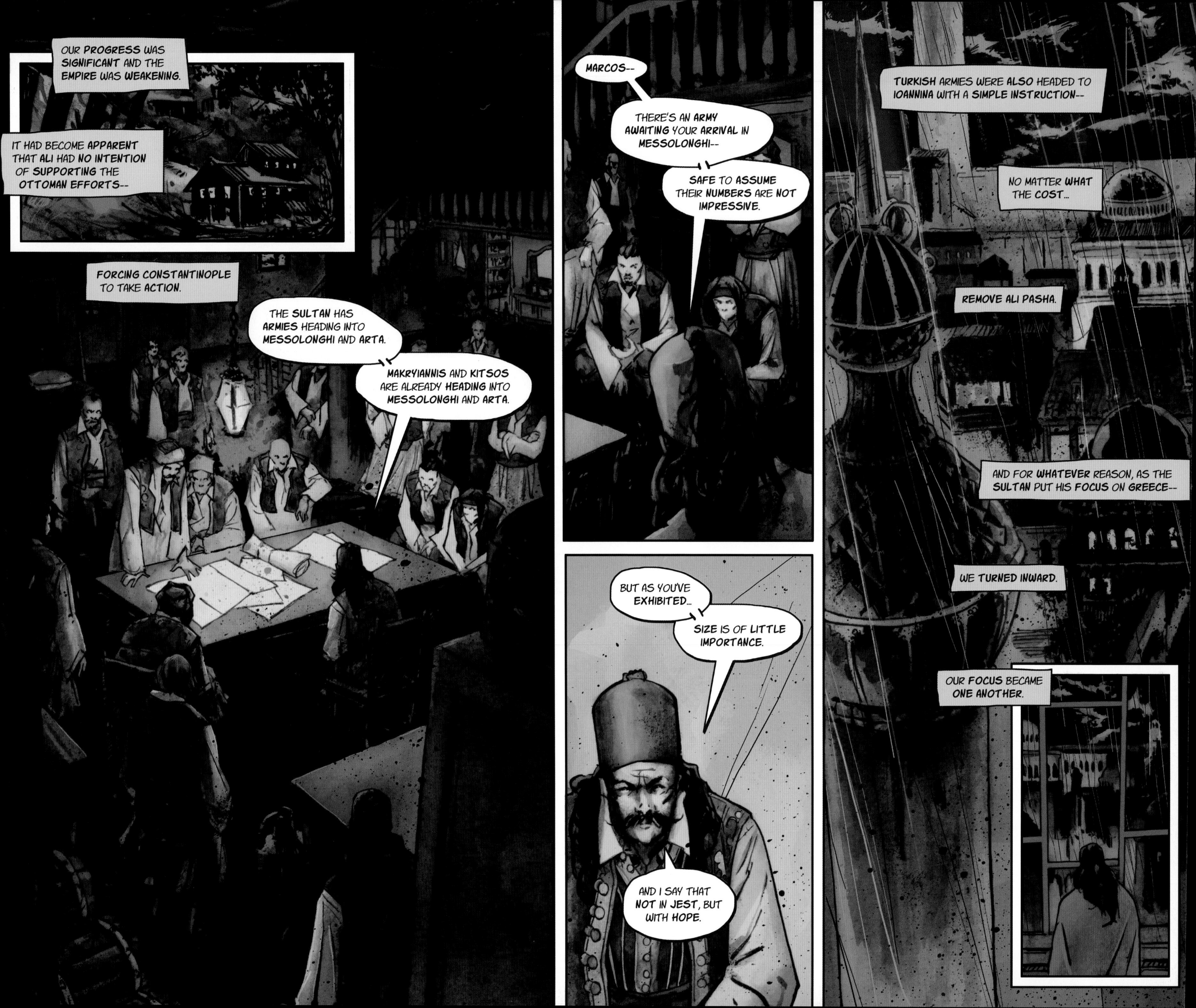
OUR PROGRESS WAS SIGNIFICANT AND THE EMPIRE WAS WEAKENING.
IT HAD BECOME APPARENT THAT ALI HAD NO INTENTION OF SUPPORTING THE OTTOMAN EFFORTS--
FORCING CONSTANTINOPLE TO TAKE ACTION.
THE SULTAN HAS ARMIES HEADING INTO MESSOLONGHI AND ARTA.
MAKRYIANNIS AND KITSOS ARE ALREADY HEADING INTO MESSOLONGHI AND ARTA.
MARCOS--
THERE'S AN ARMY AWAITING YOUR ARRIVAL IN MESSOLONGHI--
SAFE TO ASSUME THEIR NUMBERS ARE NOT IMPRESSIVE.
BUT AS YOU'VE EXHIBITED...
SIZE IS OF LITTLE IMPORTANCE.
AND I SAY THAT NOT IN JEST, BUT WITH HOPE.
TURKISH ARMIES WERE ALSO HEADED TO IOANNINA WITH A SIMPLE INSTRUCTION--
NO MATTER WHAT THE COST...
REMOVE ALI PASHA.
AND FOR WHATEVER REASON, AS THE SULTAN PUT HIS FOCUS ON GREECE--
WE TURNED INWARD.
OUR FOCUS BECAME ONE ANOTHER.

IBRAHIM PASHA!

COUGH COUGH

ALI HAD TAKEN YOUR FATHER PRISONER.

HE WASN'T WELL.

COME ON!! HE WANTS TO SEE YOU.

STILL WON'T EAT?!?

NO SIRE... WON'T TAKE FOOD WON'T TAKE WATER.

IBRAHIM PLEASE--

THIS IS HELPING NO ONE!!

YOU'RE FAMILY FOR GOODNESS SAKE--

AND FAMILY STICKS TOGETHER!!

COUGH COUGH

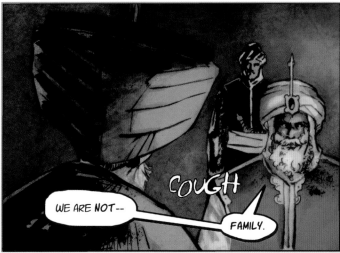

COUGH

WE ARE NOT--

FAMILY.

SOMEONE PLEASE--

BRING IN THE DOCTOR!!

I WOULD SOONER--

COUGH

COUGH

EXCUSE ME, SORRY--

WHAT WAS THAT?

I MISSED IT.

I SAID... I WOULD SOONER DIE--

COUGH

THAN BE YOUR FAMILY.

AAAHH, COME NOW--

YOU DON'T MEAN THAT.

THE DOCTOR HAS ARRIVED, SIRE.

AAAHH... VERY WELL, DOCTOR--

WOULD YOU MIND HAVING A LOOK AT MY FRIEND--

IT SEEMS SOMETHING IS BOTHERING HIM, RIGHT--

...IN THIS AREA HERE!!

SFFFSHH

AAGH

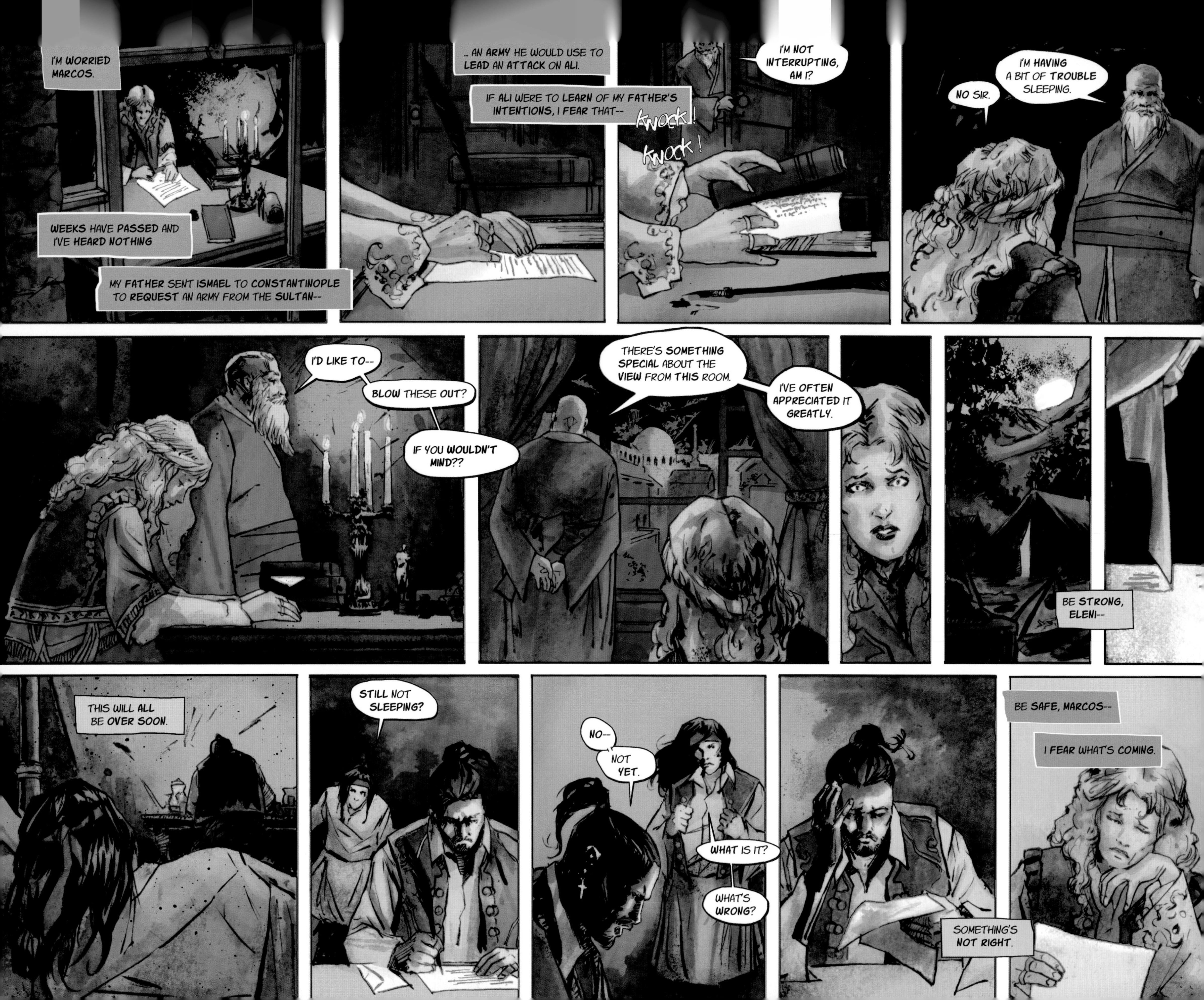
I'M WORRIED MARCOS.
WEEKS HAVE PASSED AND I'VE HEARD NOTHING
MY FATHER SENT ISMAEL TO CONSTANTINOPLE TO REQUEST AN ARMY FROM THE SULTAN--
... AN ARMY HE WOULD USE TO LEAD AN ATTACK ON ALI.
IF ALI WERE TO LEARN OF MY FATHER'S INTENTIONS, I FEAR THAT--
KNOCK!
KNOCK!
I'M NOT INTERRUPTING, AM I?
NO SIR.
I'M HAVING A BIT OF TROUBLE SLEEPING.
I'D LIKE TO--
BLOW THESE OUT?
IF YOU WOULDN'T MIND??
THERE'S SOMETHING SPECIAL ABOUT THE VIEW FROM THIS ROOM.
I'VE OFTEN APPRECIATED IT GREATLY.
BE STRONG, ELENI--
THIS WILL ALL BE OVER SOON.
STILL NOT SLEEPING?
NO--
NOT YET.
WHAT IS IT?
WHAT'S WRONG?
SOMETHING'S NOT RIGHT.
BE SAFE, MARCOS--
I FEAR WHAT'S COMING.

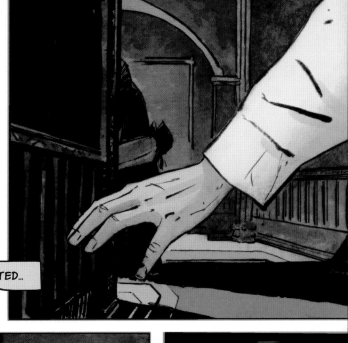

CCLLCK

HE WATCHED...

AND WAITED...

AND AS HE WENT AT HIS FATHER...

MMFF

LOOKING FOR A LATE NIGHT SNACK, ARE WE?

SWALLOW THIS-- MY LOVING CHILD!!

SWALLOW IT!!!

LOOK THERE... MY CHILD SEEMS TO BE SOMEWHAT SLEEPY.

GROWING BOY-- NEEDS HIS REST.

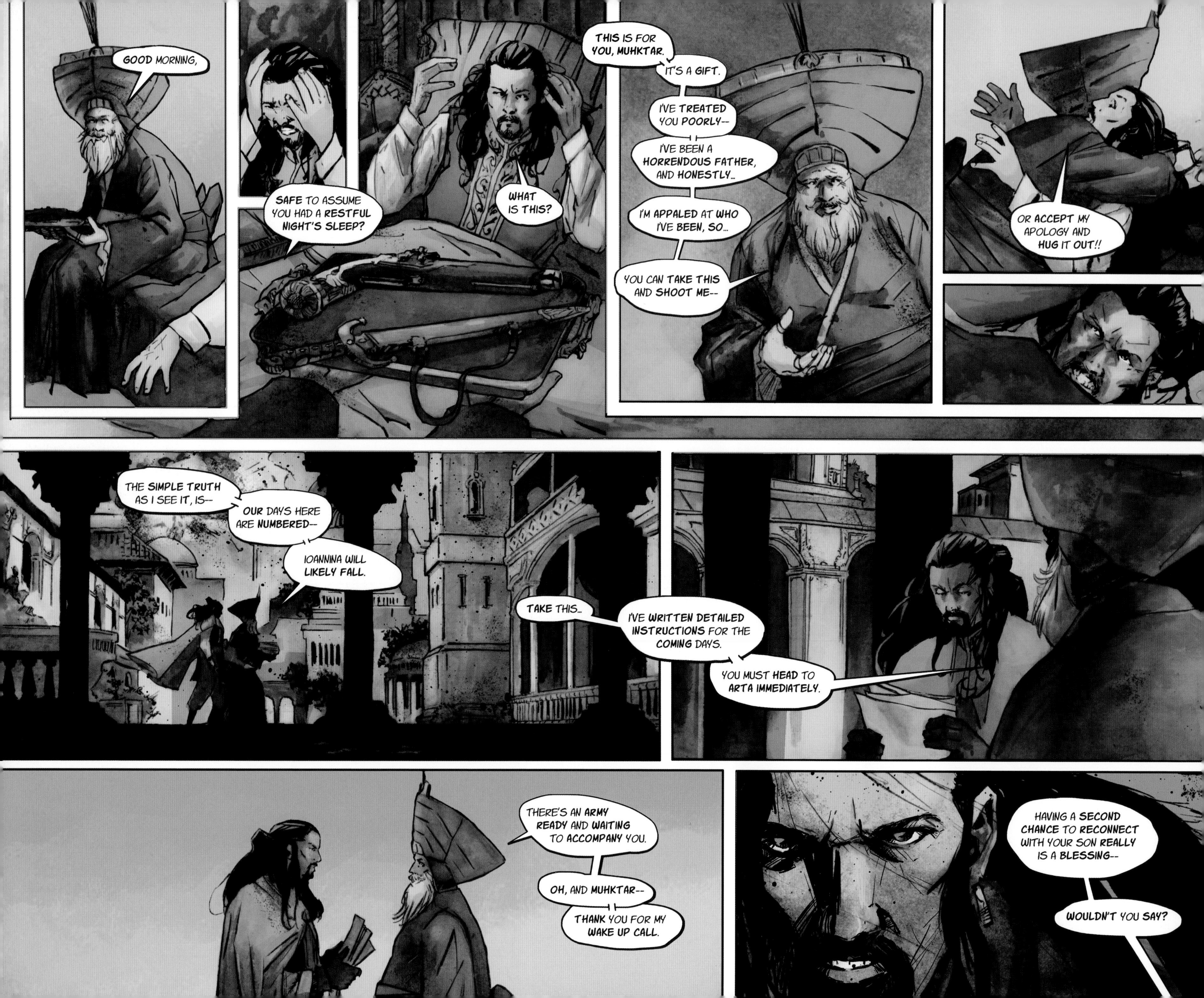
GOOD MORNING,
SAFE TO ASSUME YOU HAD A RESTFUL NIGHT'S SLEEP?
WHAT IS THIS?
THIS IS FOR YOU, MUHKTAR.
IT'S A GIFT.
I'VE TREATED YOU POORLY--
I'VE BEEN A HORRENDOUS FATHER, AND HONESTLY...
I'M APPALED AT WHO I'VE BEEN, SO...
YOU CAN TAKE THIS AND SHOOT ME--
OR ACCEPT MY APOLOGY AND HUG IT OUT!!
THE SIMPLE TRUTH AS I SEE IT, IS--
OUR DAYS HERE ARE NUMBERED--
IOANNINA WILL LIKELY FALL.
TAKE THIS...
I'VE WRITTEN DETAILED INSTRUCTIONS FOR THE COMING DAYS.
YOU MUST HEAD TO ARTA IMMEDIATELY.
THERE'S AN ARMY READY AND WAITING TO ACCOMPANY YOU.
OH, AND MUHKTAR--
THANK YOU FOR MY WAKE UP CALL.
HAVING A SECOND CHANCE TO RECONNECT WITH YOUR SON REALLY IS A BLESSING--
WOULDN'T YOU SAY?

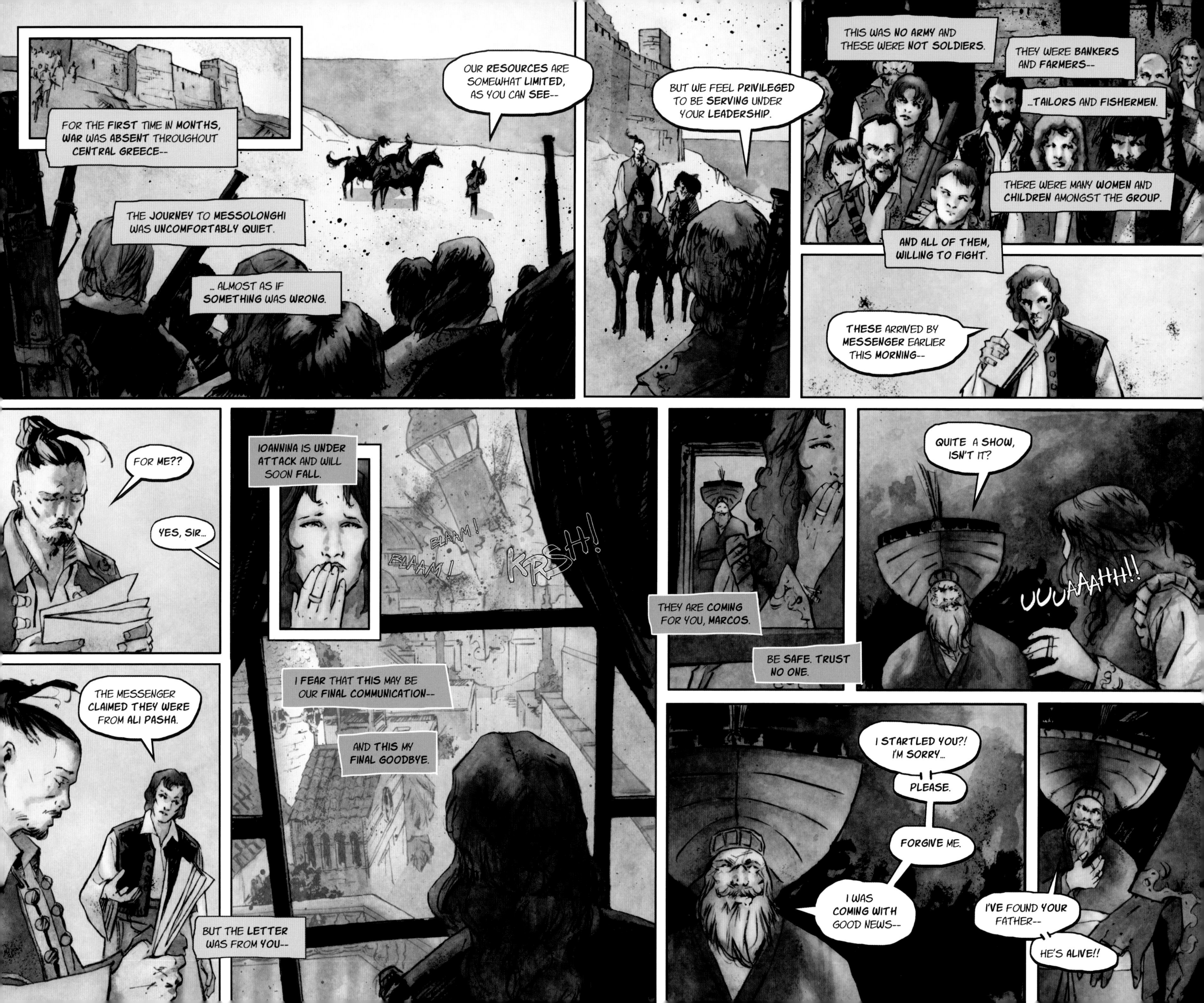

FOR THE FIRST TIME IN MONTHS, WAR WAS ABSENT THROUGHOUT CENTRAL GREECE--
THE JOURNEY TO MESSOLONGHI WAS UNCOMFORTABLY QUIET.
... ALMOST AS IF SOMETHING WAS WRONG.
OUR RESOURCES ARE SOMEWHAT LIMITED, AS YOU CAN SEE--
BUT WE FEEL PRIVILEGED TO BE SERVING UNDER YOUR LEADERSHIP.
THIS WAS NO ARMY AND THESE WERE NOT SOLDIERS.
THEY WERE BANKERS AND FARMERS--
...TAILORS AND FISHERMEN.
THERE WERE MANY WOMEN AND CHILDREN AMONGST THE GROUP.
AND ALL OF THEM, WILLING TO FIGHT.
THESE ARRIVED BY MESSENGER EARLIER THIS MORNING--
FOR ME??
YES, SIR...
THE MESSENGER CLAIMED THEY WERE FROM ALI PASHA.
BUT THE LETTER WAS FROM YOU--
IOANNINA IS UNDER ATTACK AND WILL SOON FALL.
BLAAM!
BLAAM!
KRSH!
I FEAR THAT THIS MAY BE OUR FINAL COMMUNICATION--
AND THIS MY FINAL GOODBYE.
THEY ARE COMING FOR YOU, MARCOS.
BE SAFE. TRUST NO ONE.
QUITE A SHOW, ISN'T IT?
UUUAAAHHH!!
I STARTLED YOU?! I'M SORRY...
PLEASE.
FORGIVE ME.
I WAS COMING WITH GOOD NEWS--
I'VE FOUND YOUR FATHER--
HE'S ALIVE!!

KITSOS.

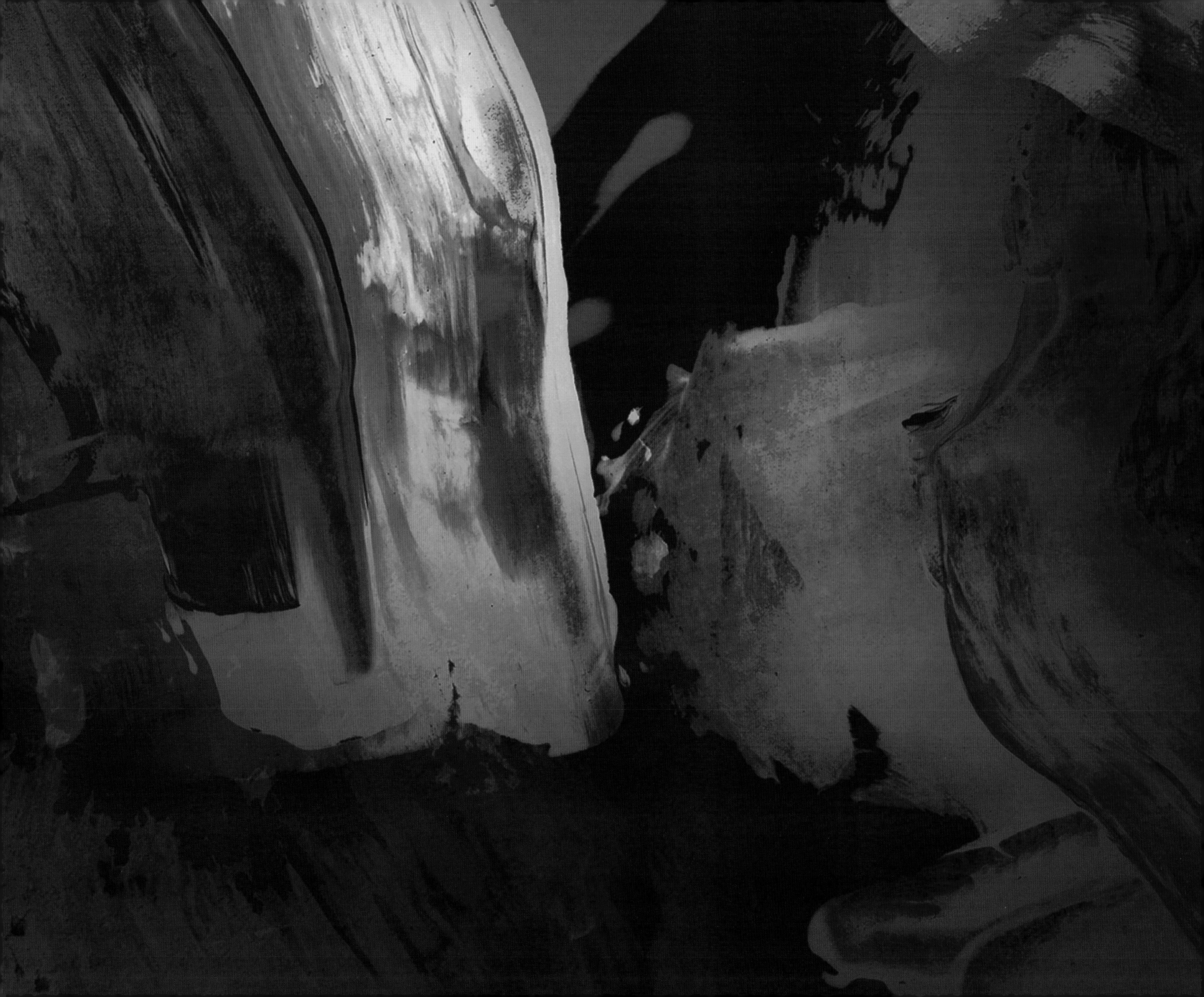

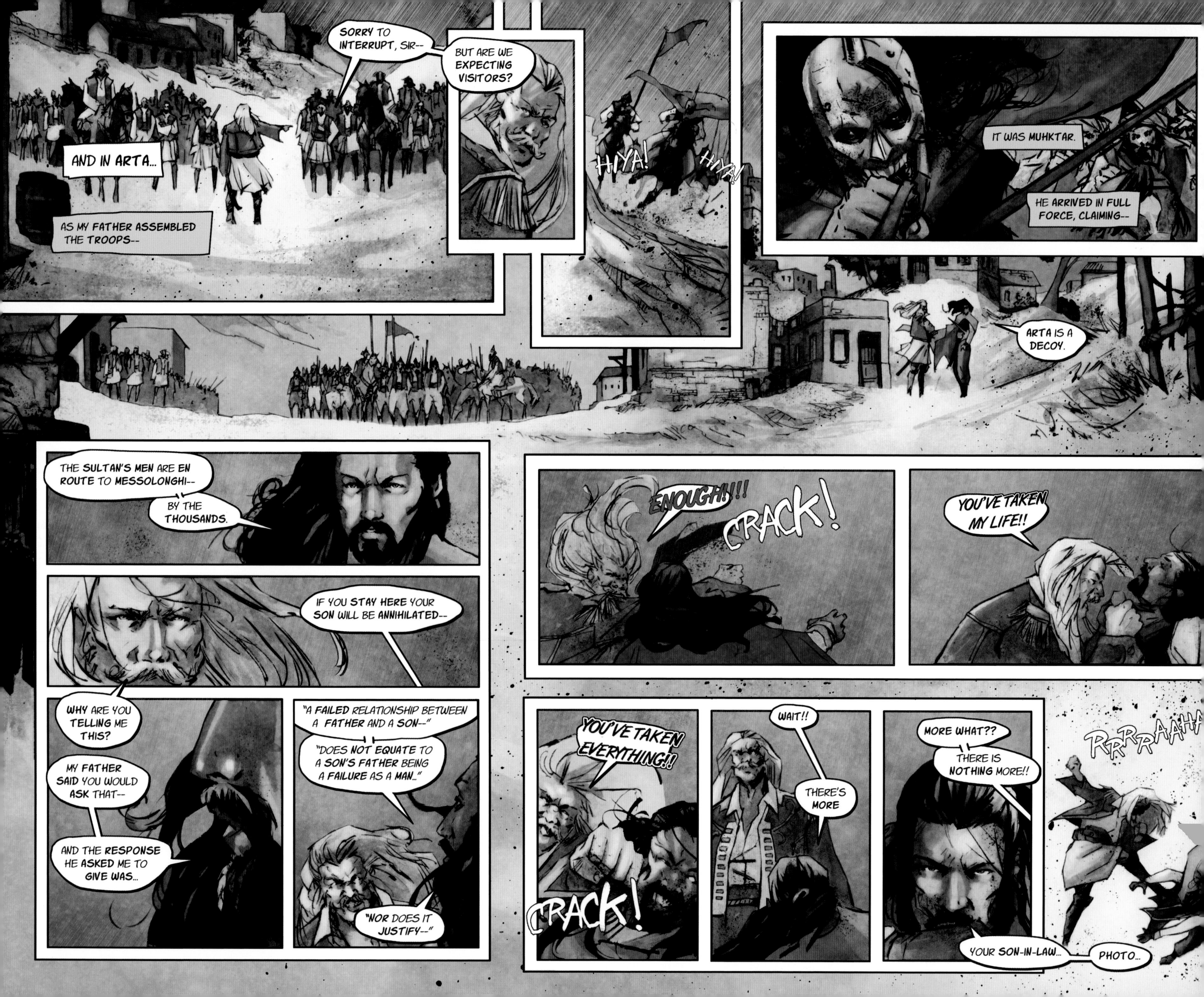
AND IN ARTA...
AS MY FATHER ASSEMBLED THE TROOPS--
SORRY TO INTERRUPT, SIR--
BUT ARE WE EXPECTING VISITORS?
HIYA!
HIYA!
IT WAS MUHKTAR.
HE ARRIVED IN FULL FORCE, CLAIMING--
ARTA IS A DECOY.
THE SULTAN'S MEN ARE EN ROUTE TO MESSOLONGHI--
BY THE THOUSANDS.
IF YOU STAY HERE YOUR SON WILL BE ANNIHILATED--
WHY ARE YOU TELLING ME THIS?
MY FATHER SAID YOU WOULD ASK THAT--
AND THE RESPONSE HE ASKED ME TO GIVE WAS...
"A FAILED RELATIONSHIP BETWEEN A FATHER AND A SON--"
"DOES NOT EQUATE TO A SON'S FATHER BEING A FAILURE AS A MAN..."
"NOR DOES IT JUSTIFY--"
ENOUGH!!!!
CRACK!
YOU'VE TAKEN MY LIFE!!
YOU'VE TAKEN EVERYTHING!!
CRACK!
WAIT!!
THERE'S MORE
MORE WHAT??
THERE IS NOTHING MORE!!
YOUR SON-IN-LAW...
PHOTO...
RRRRAAAHH

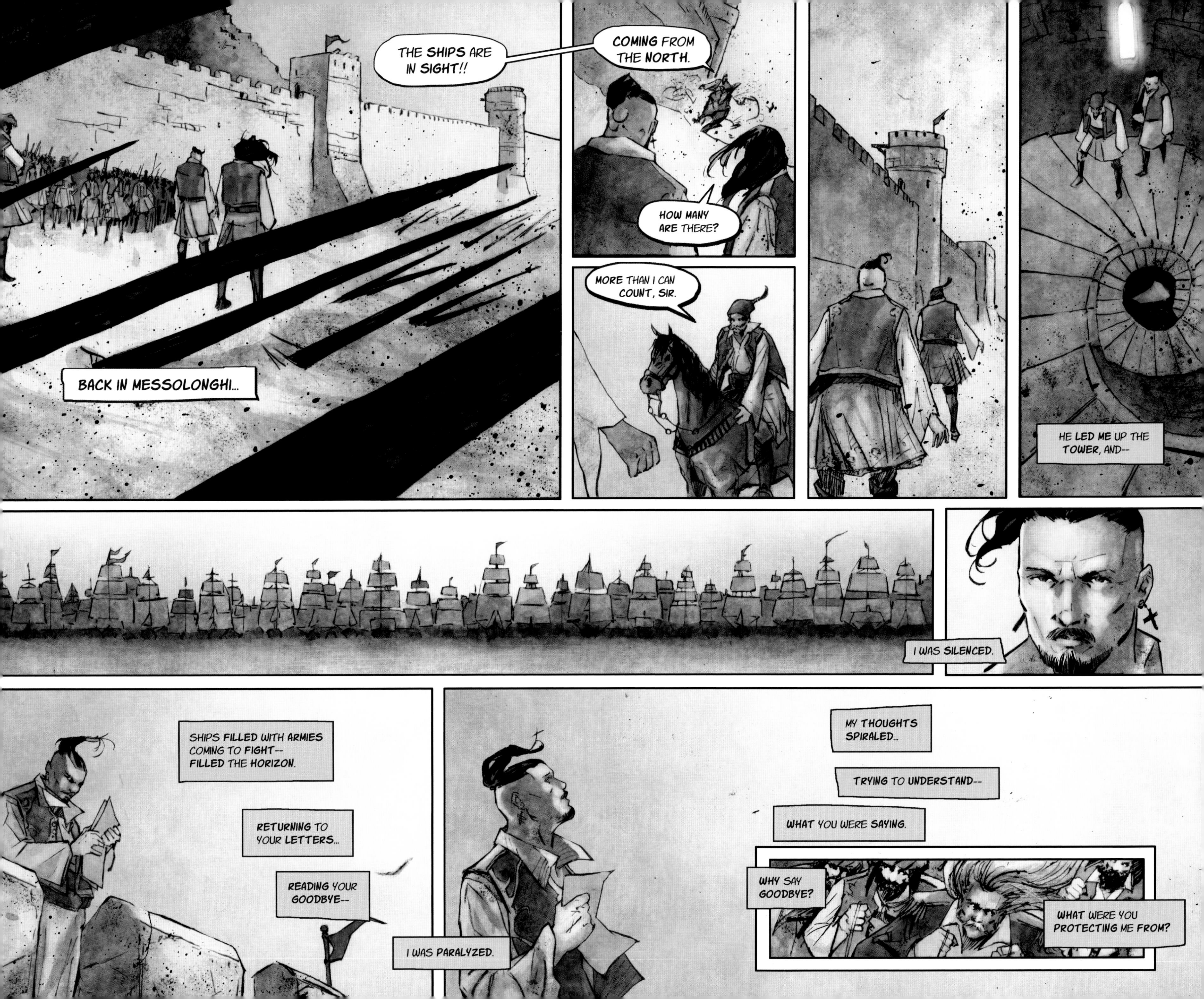
THE SHIPS ARE IN SIGHT!!
BACK IN MESSOLONGHI...
COMING FROM THE NORTH.
HOW MANY ARE THERE?
MORE THAN I CAN COUNT, SIR.
HE LED ME UP THE TOWER, AND--
I WAS SILENCED.
SHIPS FILLED WITH ARMIES COMING TO FIGHT-- FILLED THE HORIZON.
RETURNING TO YOUR LETTERS...
READING YOUR GOODBYE--
I WAS PARALYZED.
MY THOUGHTS SPIRALED...
TRYING TO UNDERSTAND--
WHAT YOU WERE SAYING.
WHY SAY GOODBYE?
WHAT WERE YOU PROTECTING ME FROM?

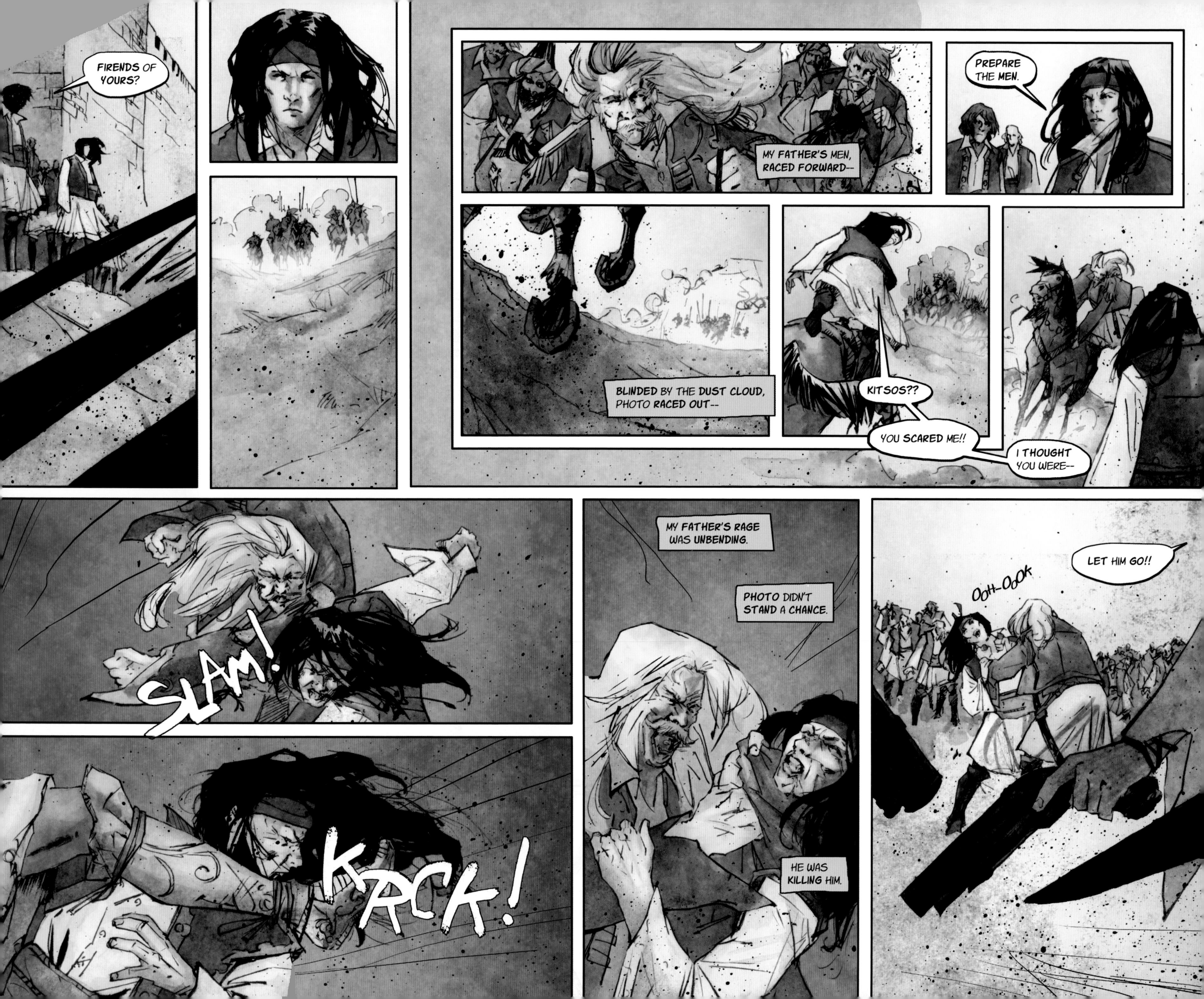

FIRENDS OF YOURS?
MY FATHER'S MEN, RACED FORWARD--
PREPARE THE MEN.
BLINDED BY THE DUST CLOUD, PHOTO RACED OUT--
KITSOS??
YOU SCARED ME!!
I THOUGHT YOU WERE--
SLAM!
KRCK!
MY FATHER'S RAGE WAS UNBENDING.
PHOTO DIDN'T STAND A CHANCE.
HE WAS KILLING HIM.
LET HIM GO!!
OOH-OOOK

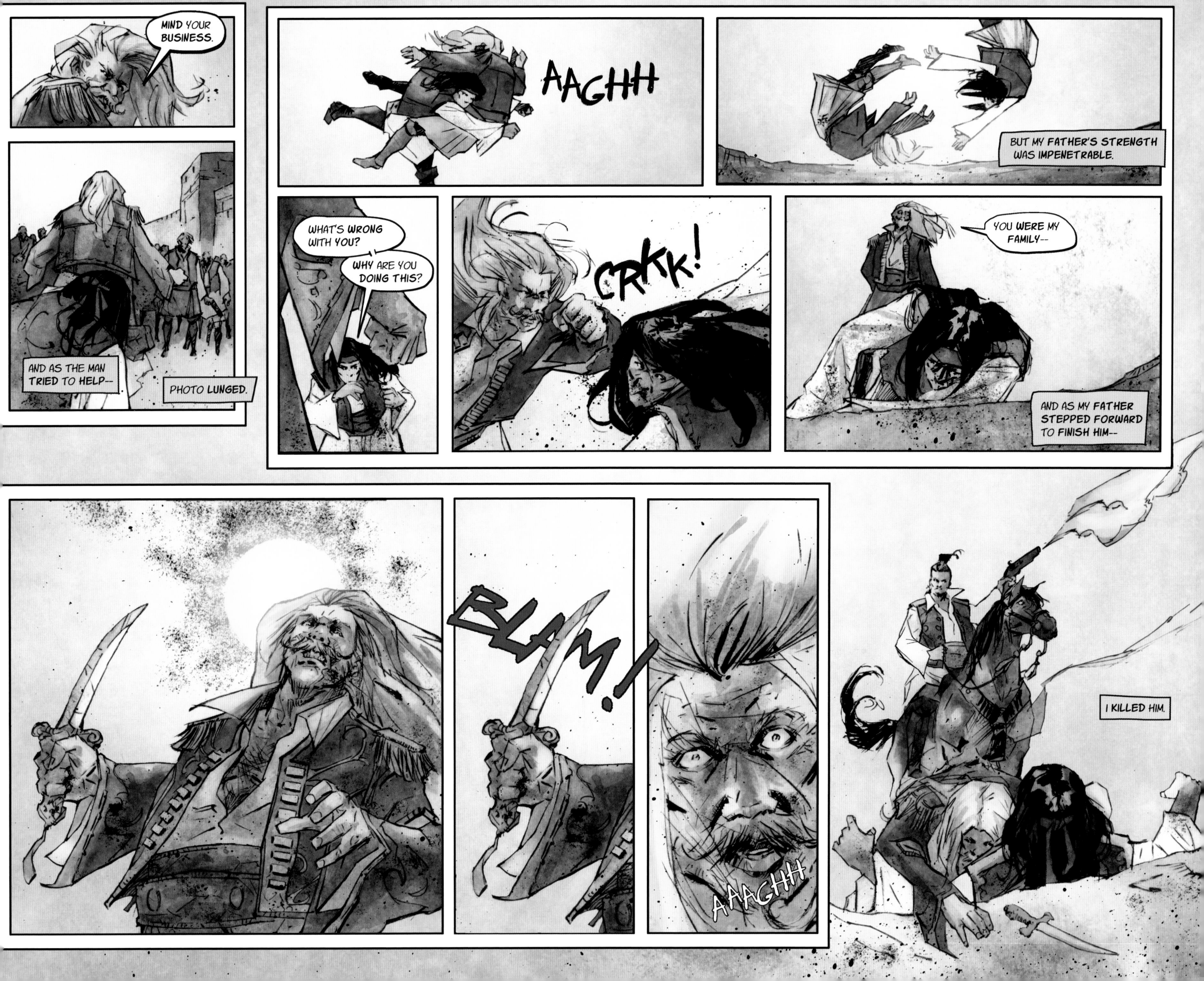

MIND YOUR BUSINESS.
AND AS THE MAN TRIED TO HELP--
PHOTO LUNGED.
AAGHH
BUT MY FATHER'S STRENGTH WAS IMPENETRABLE.
WHAT'S WRONG WITH YOU?
WHY ARE YOU DOING THIS?
CRKK!
YOU WERE MY FAMILY--
AND AS MY FATHER STEPPED FORWARD TO FINISH HIM--
BLAM!
AAAGHH
I KILLED HIM.

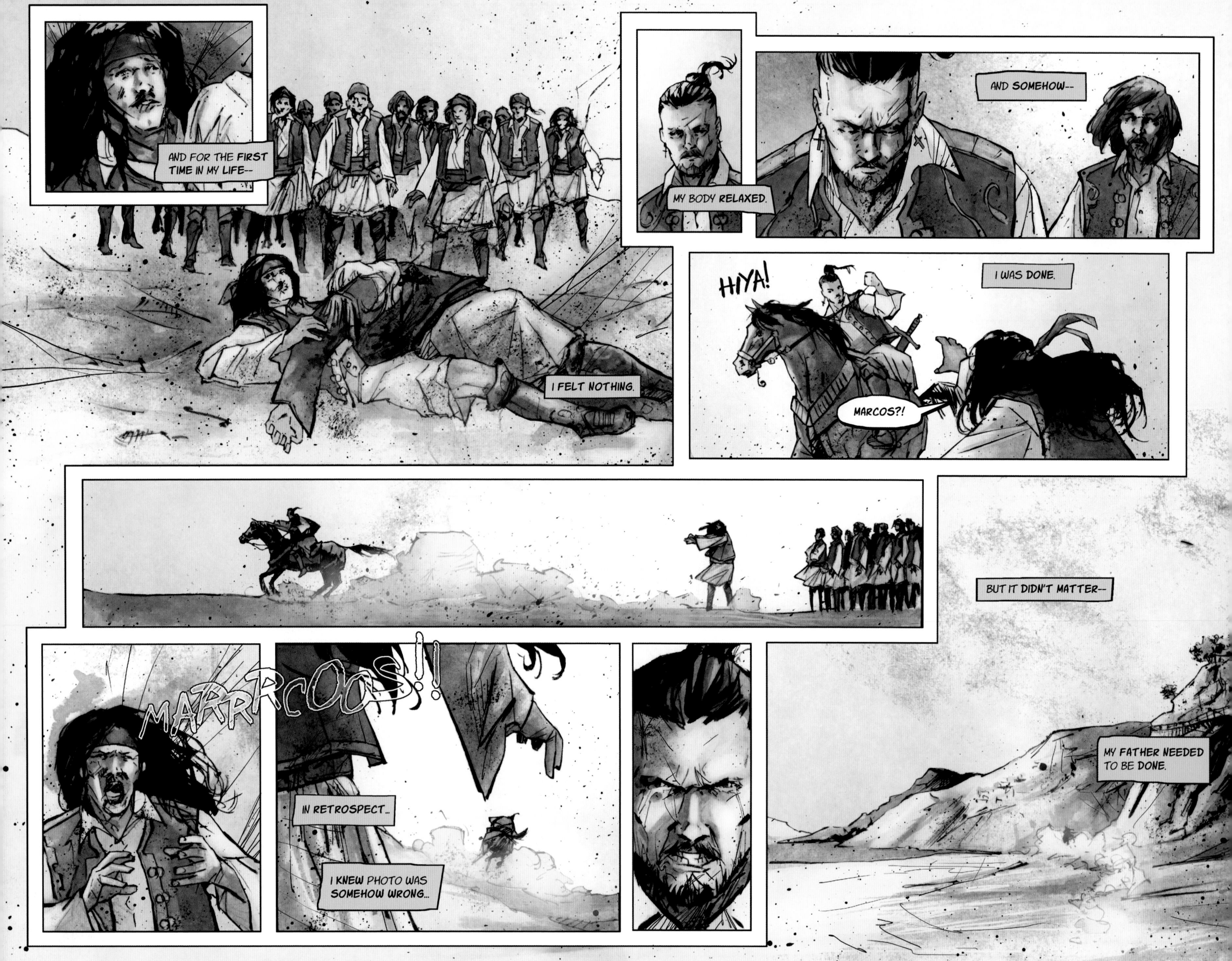
AND FOR THE FIRST TIME IN MY LIFE--
I FELT NOTHING.
MY BODY RELAXED.
AND SOMEHOW--
I WAS DONE.
HIYA!
MARCOS?!
BUT IT DIDN'T MATTER--
MARRRCOOS!!
IN RETROSPECT...
I KNEW PHOTO WAS SOMEHOW WRONG...
MY FATHER NEEDED TO BE DONE.

MUHKTAR.

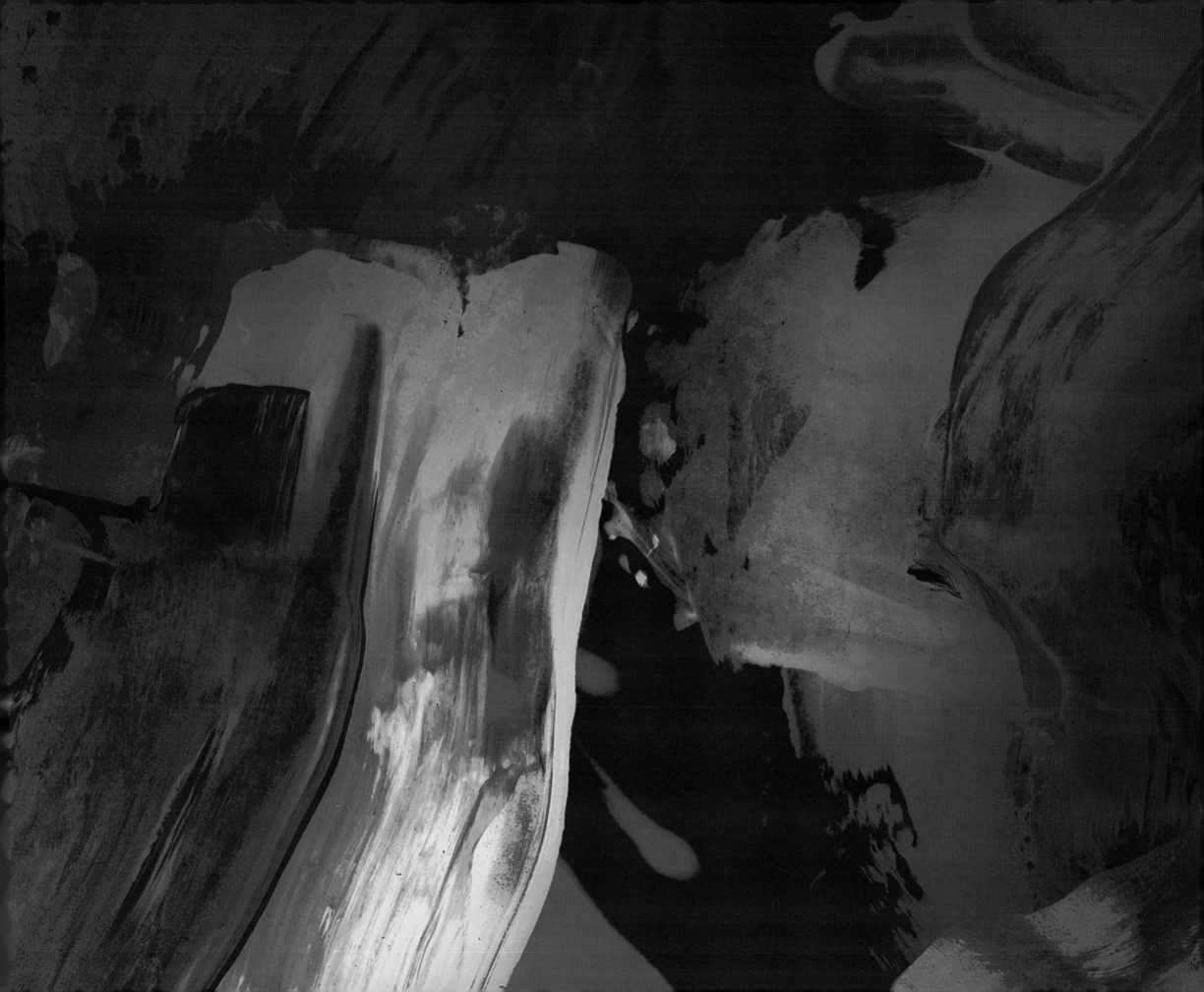

BOOK THREE ◇ *Chapter Two*

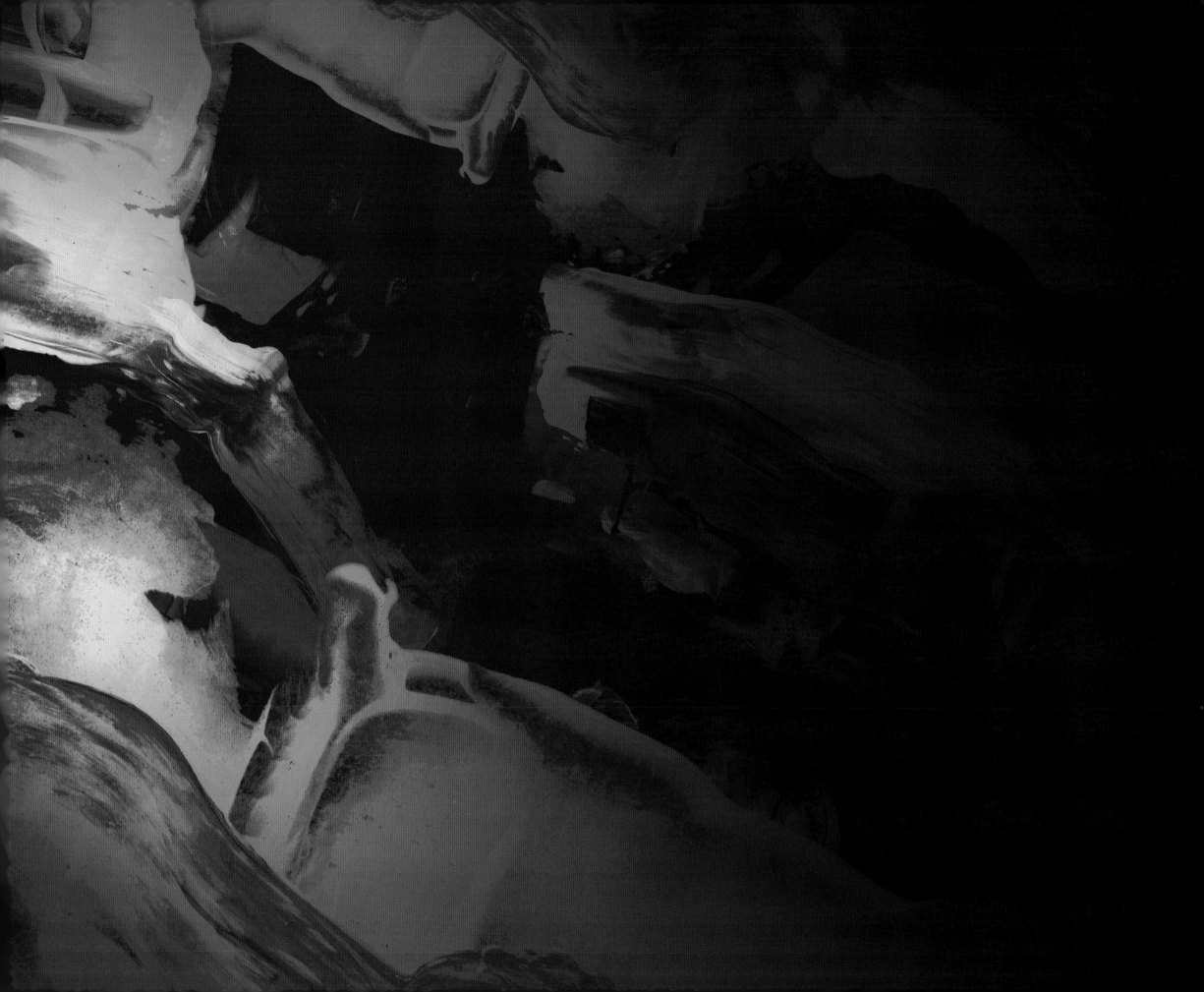

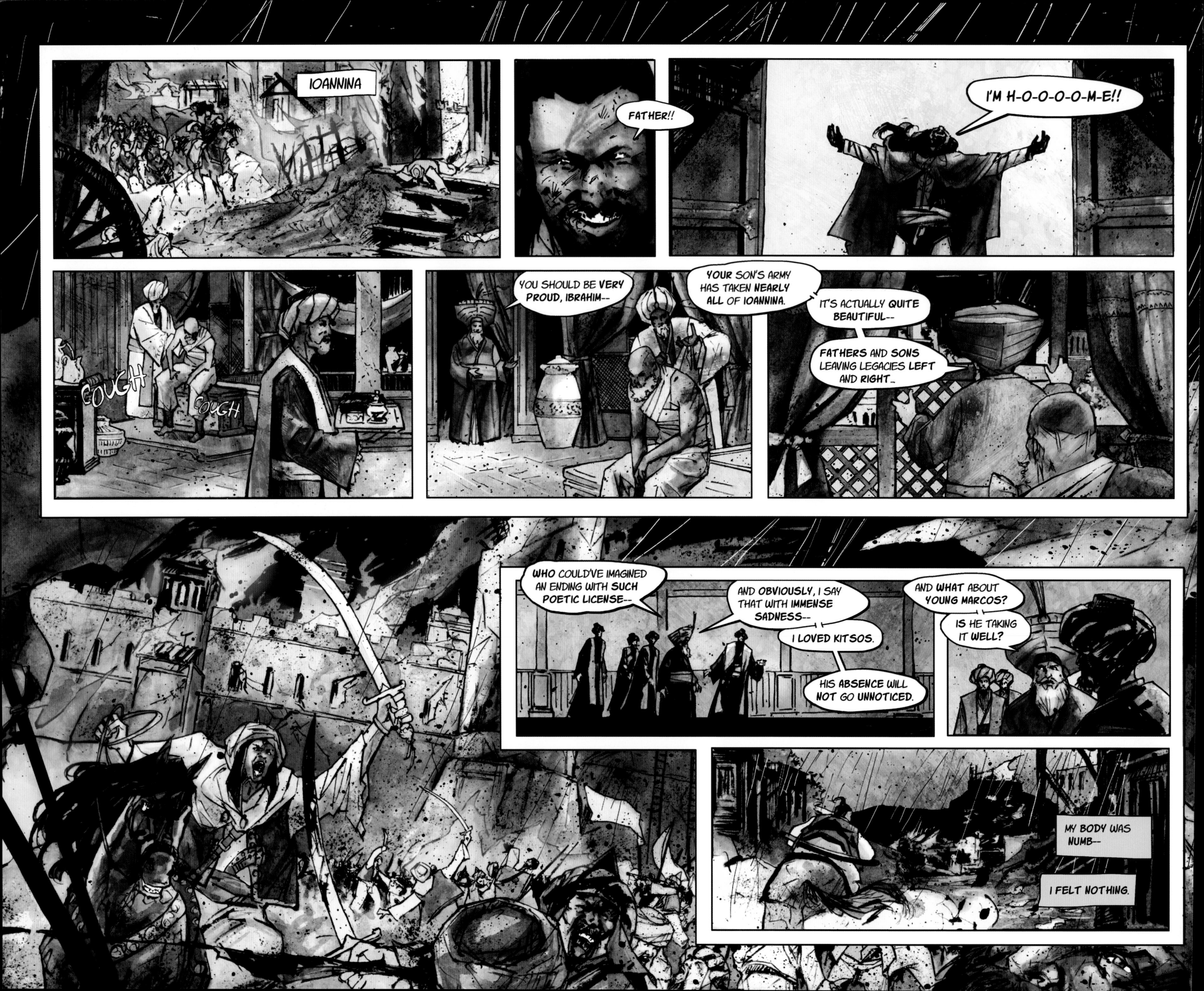
IOANNINA
FATHER!!
I'M H-O-O-O-O-M-E!!
COUGH
COUGH
YOU SHOULD BE VERY PROUD, IBRAHIM--
YOUR SON'S ARMY HAS TAKEN NEARLY ALL OF IOANNINA.
IT'S ACTUALLY QUITE BEAUTIFUL--
FATHERS AND SONS LEAVING LEGACIES LEFT AND RIGHT...
WHO COULD'VE IMAGINED AN ENDING WITH SUCH POETIC LICENSE--
AND OBVIOUSLY, I SAY THAT WITH IMMENSE SADNESS--
I LOVED KITSOS.
HIS ABSENCE WILL NOT GO UNNOTICED.
AND WHAT ABOUT YOUNG MARCOS?
IS HE TAKING IT WELL?
MY BODY WAS NUMB--
I FELT NOTHING.

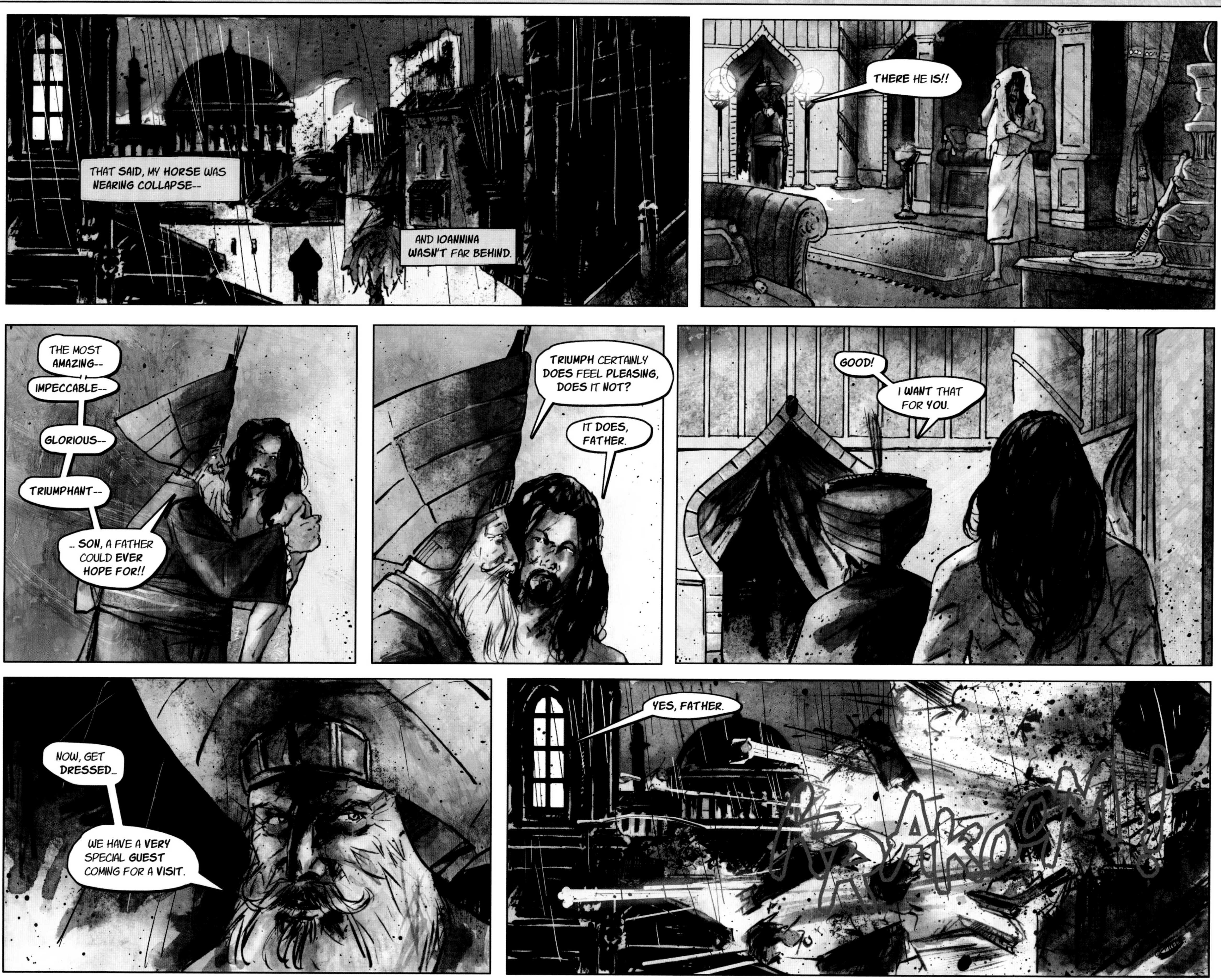

THAT SAID, MY HORSE WAS NEARING COLLAPSE--
AND IOANNINA WASN'T FAR BEHIND.
THERE HE IS!!
THE MOST AMAZING--
IMPECCABLE--
GLORIOUS--
TRIUMPHANT--
... SON, A FATHER COULD EVER HOPE FOR!!
TRIUMPH CERTAINLY DOES FEEL PLEASING, DOES IT NOT?
IT DOES, FATHER.
GOOD!
I WANT THAT FOR YOU.
NOW, GET DRESSED...
WE HAVE A VERY SPECIAL GUEST COMING FOR A VISIT.
YES, FATHER.
KRAKOOM!!

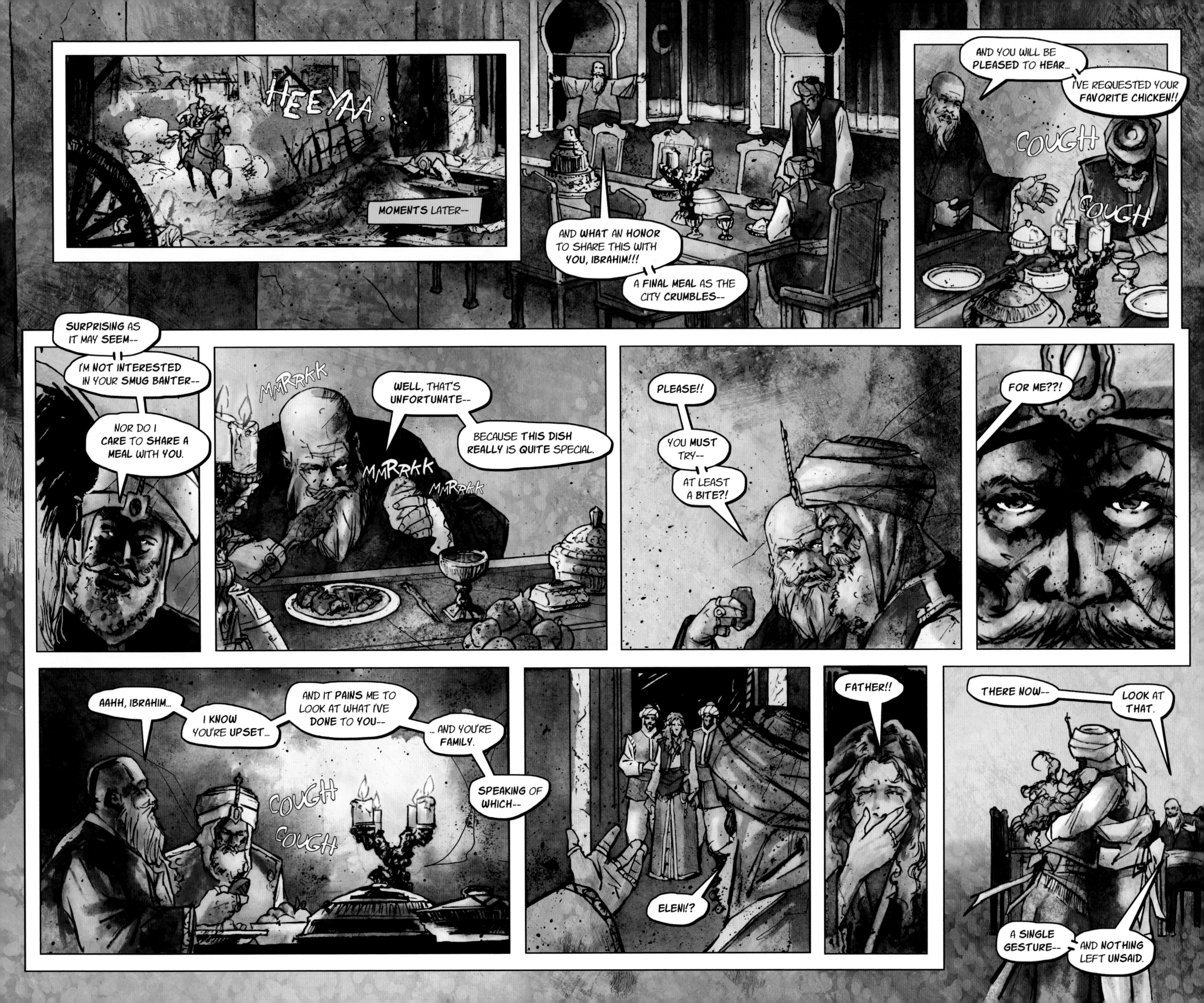
HEEYAA...
MOMENTS LATER--
AND WHAT AN HONOR TO SHARE THIS WITH YOU, IBRAHIM!!!
A FINAL MEAL AS THE CITY CRUMBLES--
AND YOU WILL BE PLEASED TO HEAR...
I'VE REQUESTED YOUR FAVORITE CHICKEN!!
COUGH
COUGH
SURPRISING AS IT MAY SEEM--
I'M NOT INTERESTED IN YOUR SMUG BANTER--
NOR DO I CARE TO SHARE A MEAL WITH YOU.
MMRRAKK
WELL, THAT'S UNFORTUNATE--
BECAUSE THIS DISH REALLY IS QUITE SPECIAL.
MMRRAKK
MMRRAKK
PLEASE!!
YOU MUST TRY--
AT LEAST A BITE?!
FOR ME??!
AAHH, IBRAHIM...
I KNOW YOU'RE UPSET...
AND IT PAINS ME TO LOOK AT WHAT I'VE DONE TO YOU--
... AND YOU'RE FAMILY.
SPEAKING OF WHICH--
COUGH
COUGH
ELENI!?
FATHER!!
THERE NOW--
LOOK AT THAT.
A SINGLE GESTURE--
AND NOTHING LEFT UNSAID.

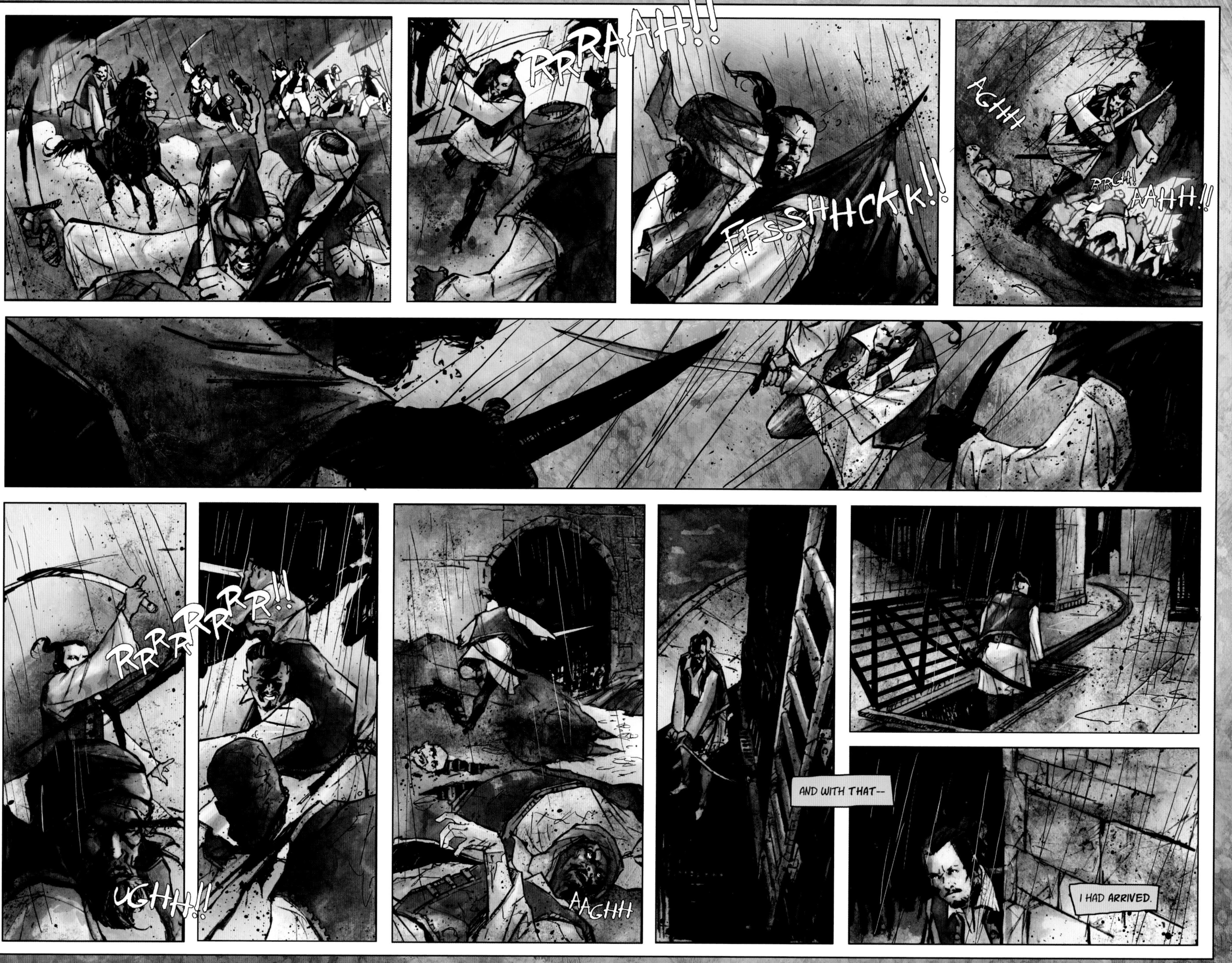

RRRAAAH!!
FFSSHHCKKK!!
AGHH
RRGH!
AAHH!!
RRRRRRRRR!!
UGHH!!
AAGHH
AND WITH THAT--
I HAD ARRIVED.

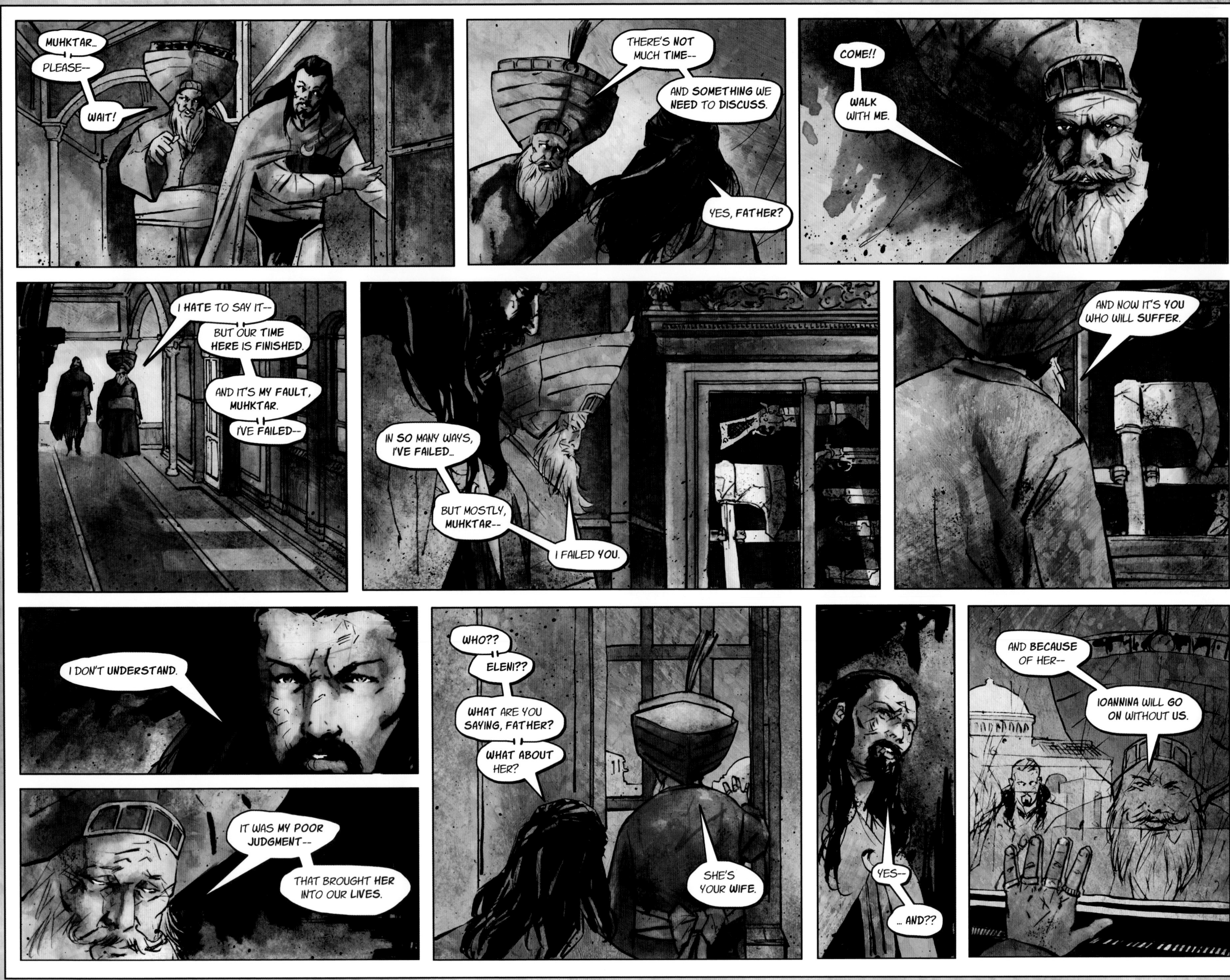
MUHKTAR...
PLEASE--
WAIT!
THERE'S NOT MUCH TIME--
AND SOMETHING WE NEED TO DISCUSS.
YES, FATHER?
COME!!
WALK WITH ME.
I HATE TO SAY IT--
BUT OUR TIME HERE IS FINISHED.
AND IT'S MY FAULT, MUHKTAR.
I'VE FAILED--
IN SO MANY WAYS, I'VE FAILED...
BUT MOSTLY, MUHKTAR--
I FAILED YOU.
AND NOW IT'S YOU WHO WILL SUFFER.
I DON'T UNDERSTAND.
IT WAS MY POOR JUDGMENT--
THAT BROUGHT HER INTO OUR LIVES.
WHO??
ELENI??
WHAT ARE YOU SAYING, FATHER?
WHAT ABOUT HER?
SHE'S YOUR WIFE.
YES--
... AND??
AND BECAUSE OF HER--
IOANNINA WILL GO ON WITHOUT US.

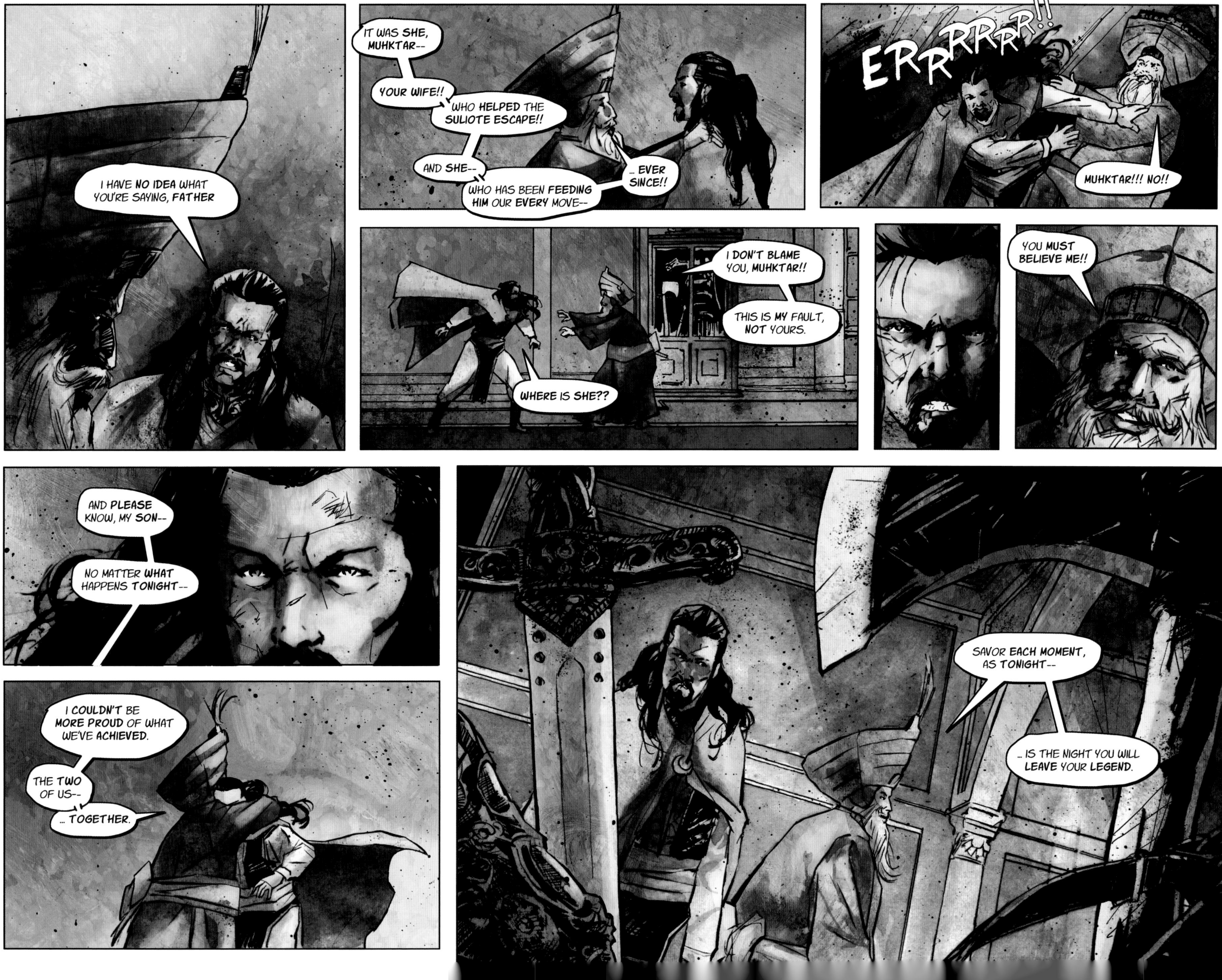
I HAVE NO IDEA WHAT YOU'RE SAYING, FATHER
IT WAS SHE, MUHKTAR--
YOUR WIFE!!
WHO HELPED THE SULIOTE ESCAPE!!
AND SHE--
WHO HAS BEEN FEEDING HIM OUR EVERY MOVE--
... EVER SINCE!!
ERRRRRRR!!
MUHKTAR!!! NO!!
WHERE IS SHE??
I DON'T BLAME YOU, MUHKTAR!!
THIS IS MY FAULT, NOT YOURS.
YOU MUST BELIEVE ME!!
AND PLEASE KNOW, MY SON--
NO MATTER WHAT HAPPENS TONIGHT--
I COULDN'T BE MORE PROUD OF WHAT WE'VE ACHIEVED.
THE TWO OF US--
... TOGETHER.
SAVOR EACH MOMENT, AS TONIGHT--
... IS THE NIGHT YOU WILL LEAVE YOUR LEGEND.

OR MAYBE THERE WOULD BE NO LEGEND.

MAYBE IN DEATH, MUHKTAR WOULD LIVE IN SHADOWS--

. JUST AS HE DID IN LIFE.

BUT AS OF NOW, NONE OF THAT MATTERED...

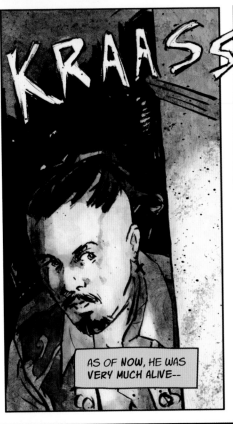

KRAASSSHH

AS OF NOW, HE WAS VERY MUCH ALIVE--

... AND I WAS COMING TO CHANGE THAT.

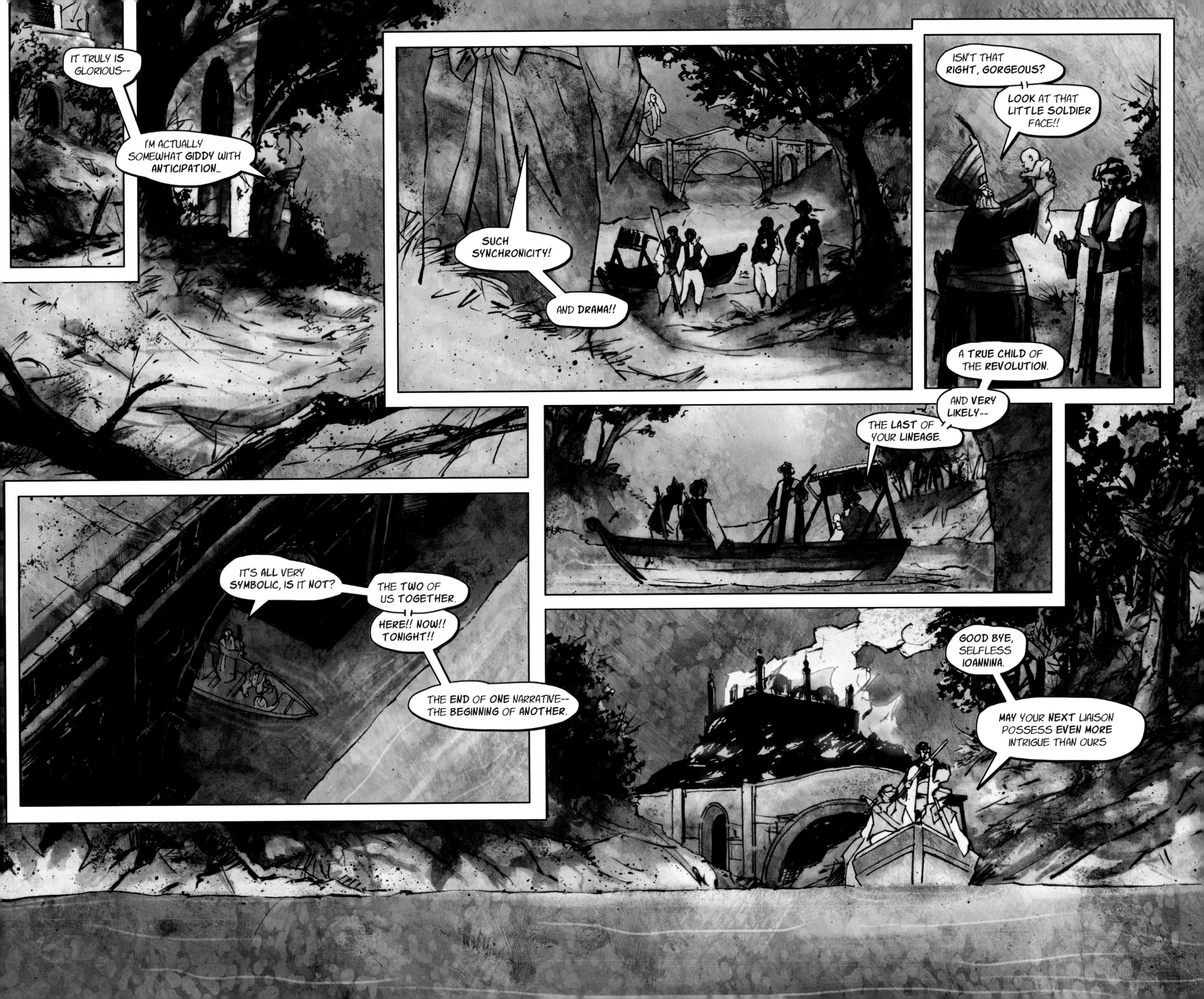
IT TRULY IS GLORIOUS--
I'M ACTUALLY SOMEWHAT GIDDY WITH ANTICIPATION...
SUCH SYNCHRONICITY!
AND DRAMA!!
ISN'T THAT RIGHT, GORGEOUS?
LOOK AT THAT LITTLE SOLDIER FACE!!
A TRUE CHILD OF THE REVOLUTION.
AND VERY LIKELY--
THE LAST OF YOUR LINEAGE.
IT'S ALL VERY SYMBOLIC, IS IT NOT?
THE TWO OF US TOGETHER.
HERE!! NOW!! TONIGHT!!
THE END OF ONE NARRATIVE-- THE BEGINNING OF ANOTHER.
GOOD BYE, SELFLESS IOANNINA.
MAY YOUR NEXT LIAISON POSSESS EVEN MORE INTRIGUE THAN OURS

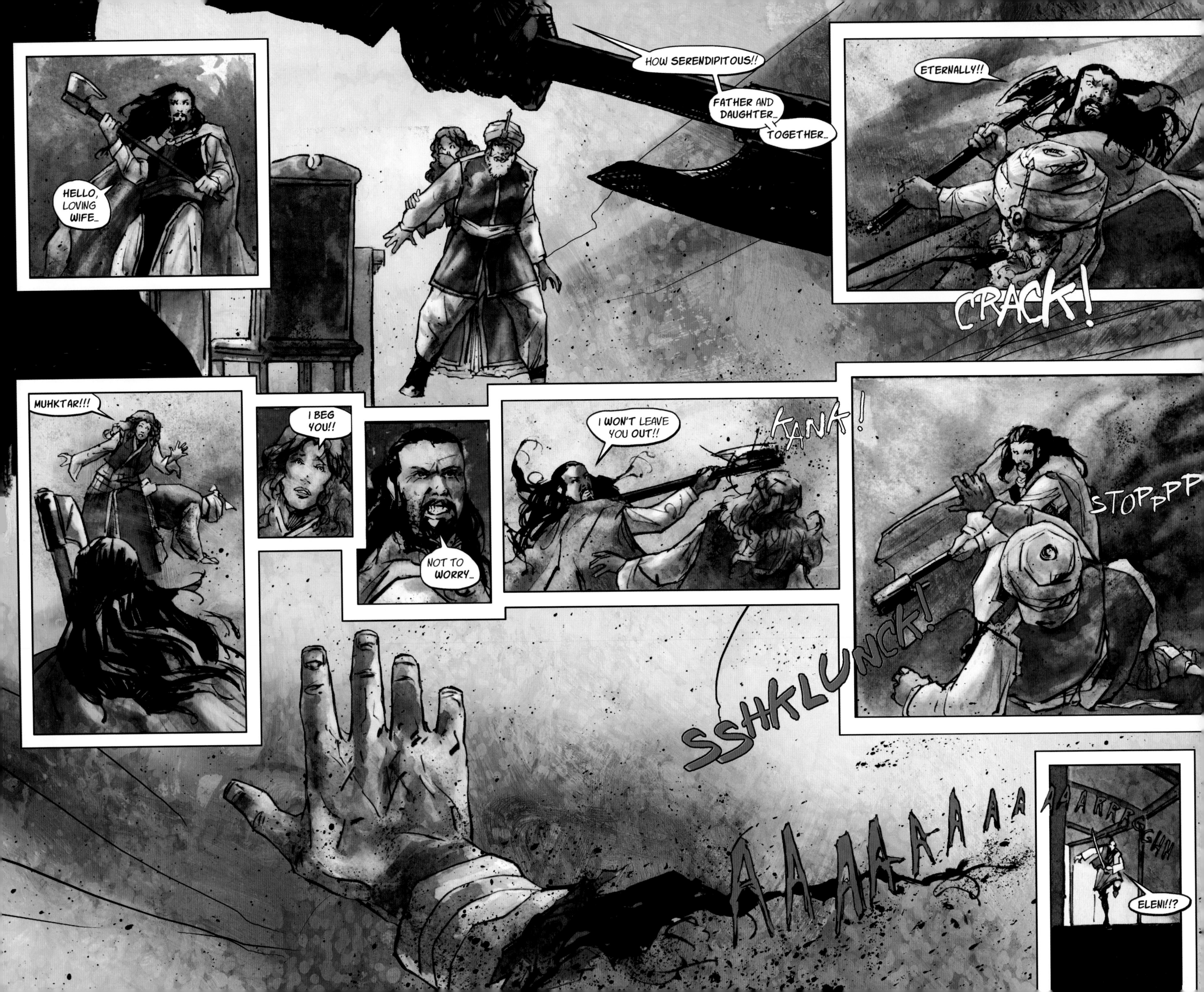
HELLO, LOVING WIFE...
HOW SERENDIPITOUS!!
FATHER AND DAUGHTER...
TOGETHER...
ETERNALLY!!
CRACK!
MUHKTAR!!!
I BEG YOU!!
NOT TO WORRY...
I WON'T LEAVE YOU OUT!!
KANK!
STOPPPP
SSHKLUNCK!
AAAAAAAAAARRRGHH
ELENI!!?

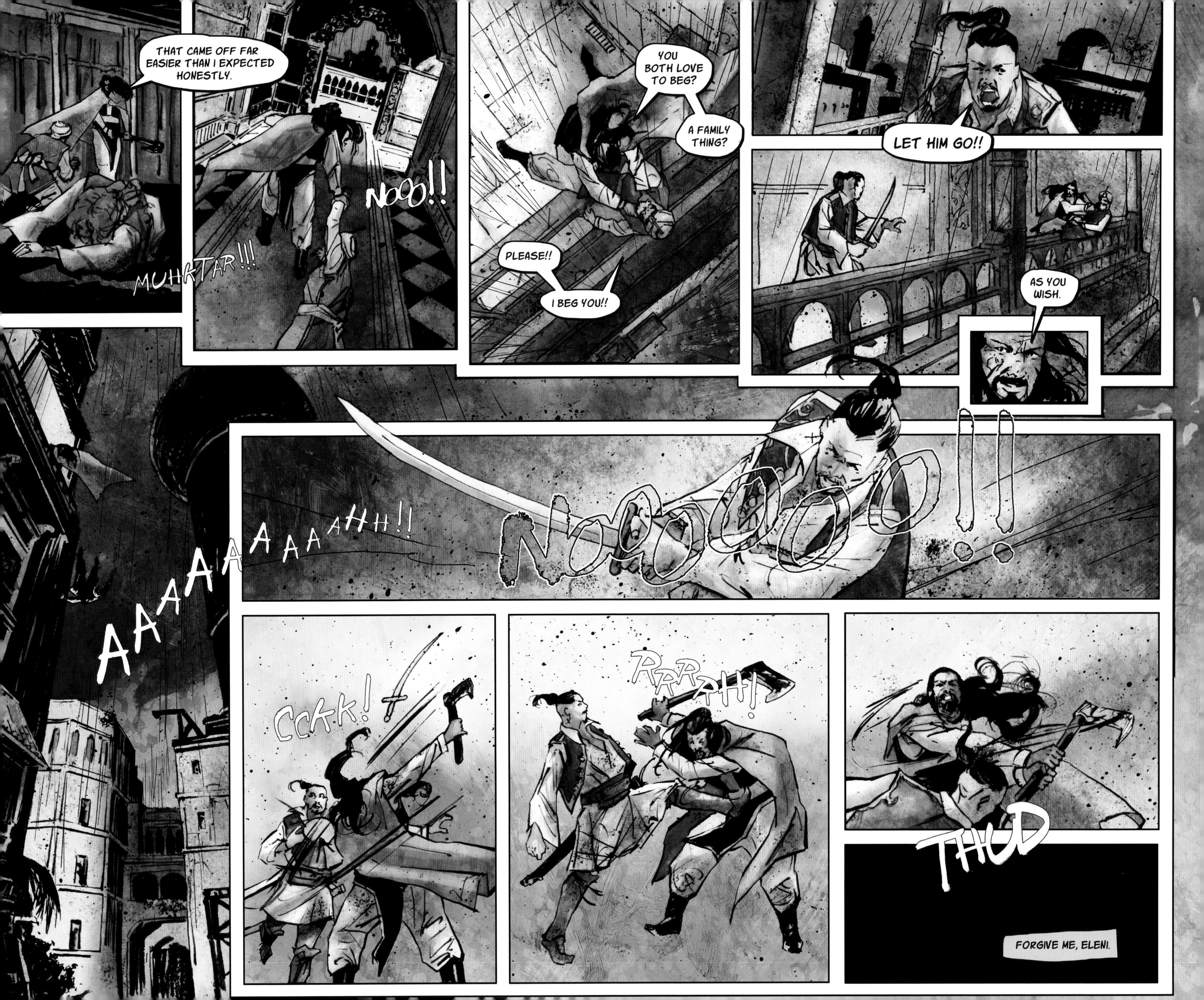
THAT CAME OFF FAR EASIER THAN I EXPECTED HONESTLY.
MUHRTAR!!!
NOOO!!
YOU BOTH LOVE TO BEG?
A FAMILY THING?
PLEASE!!
I BEG YOU!!
LET HIM GO!!
AS YOU WISH.
AAAAAAAAAAHH!!
NOOOOOOO!!
CCKK!
RRRAH!
THUD
FORGIVE ME, ELENI.

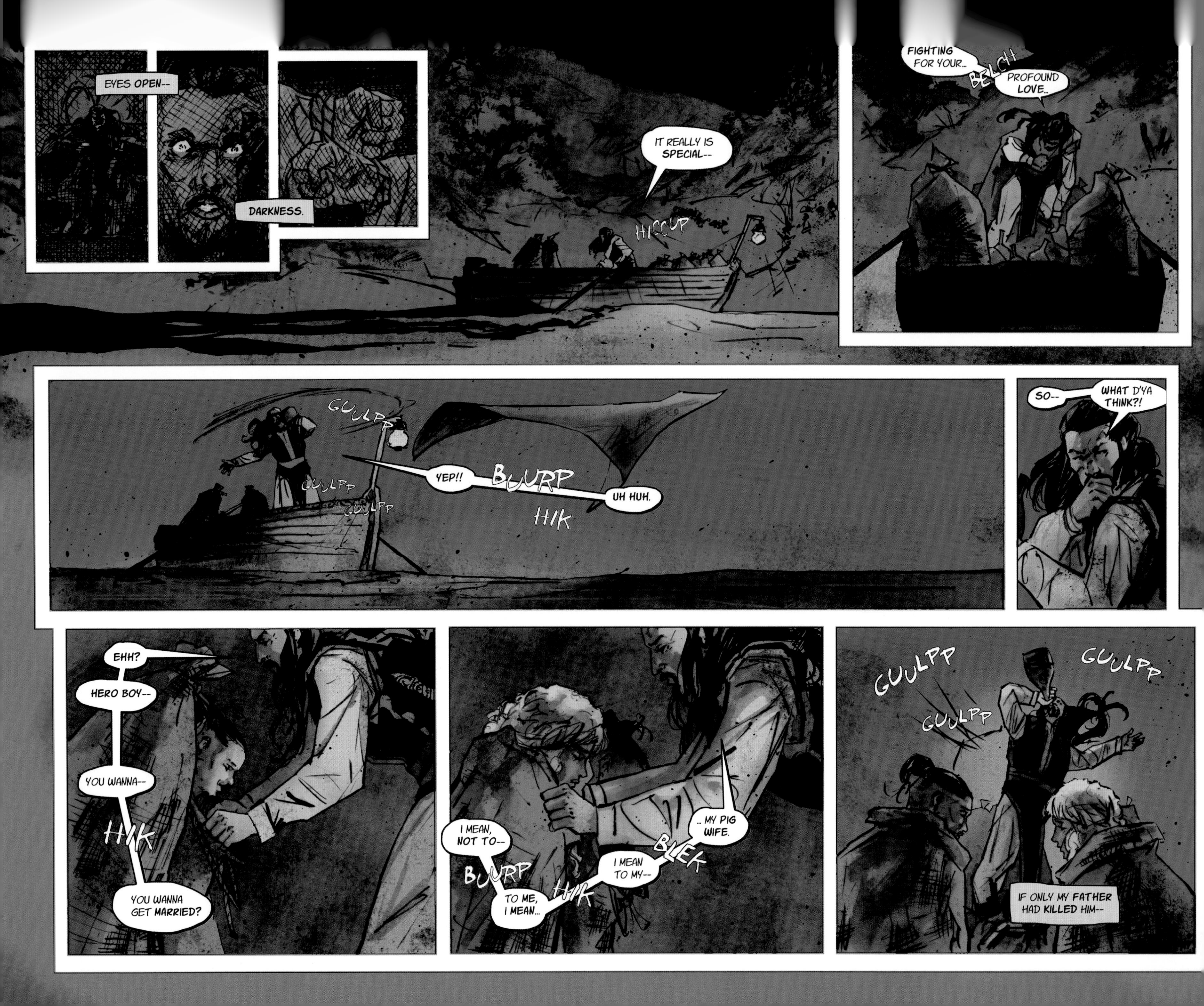
EYES OPEN--
DARKNESS.
IT REALLY IS SPECIAL--
HICCUP
FIGHTING FOR YOUR...
BELCH
PROFOUND LOVE...
GUULPP
GUULPP
GUULPP
YEP!!
BUURP
UH HUH.
HIK
SO--
WHAT D'YA THINK?!
EHH?
HERO BOY--
YOU WANNA--
HIK
YOU WANNA GET MARRIED?
I MEAN, NOT TO--
BUURP
TO ME, I MEAN...
HIK
I MEAN TO MY--
BLEK
... MY PIG WIFE.
GUULPP
GUULPP
GUULPP
IF ONLY MY FATHER HAD KILLED HIM--

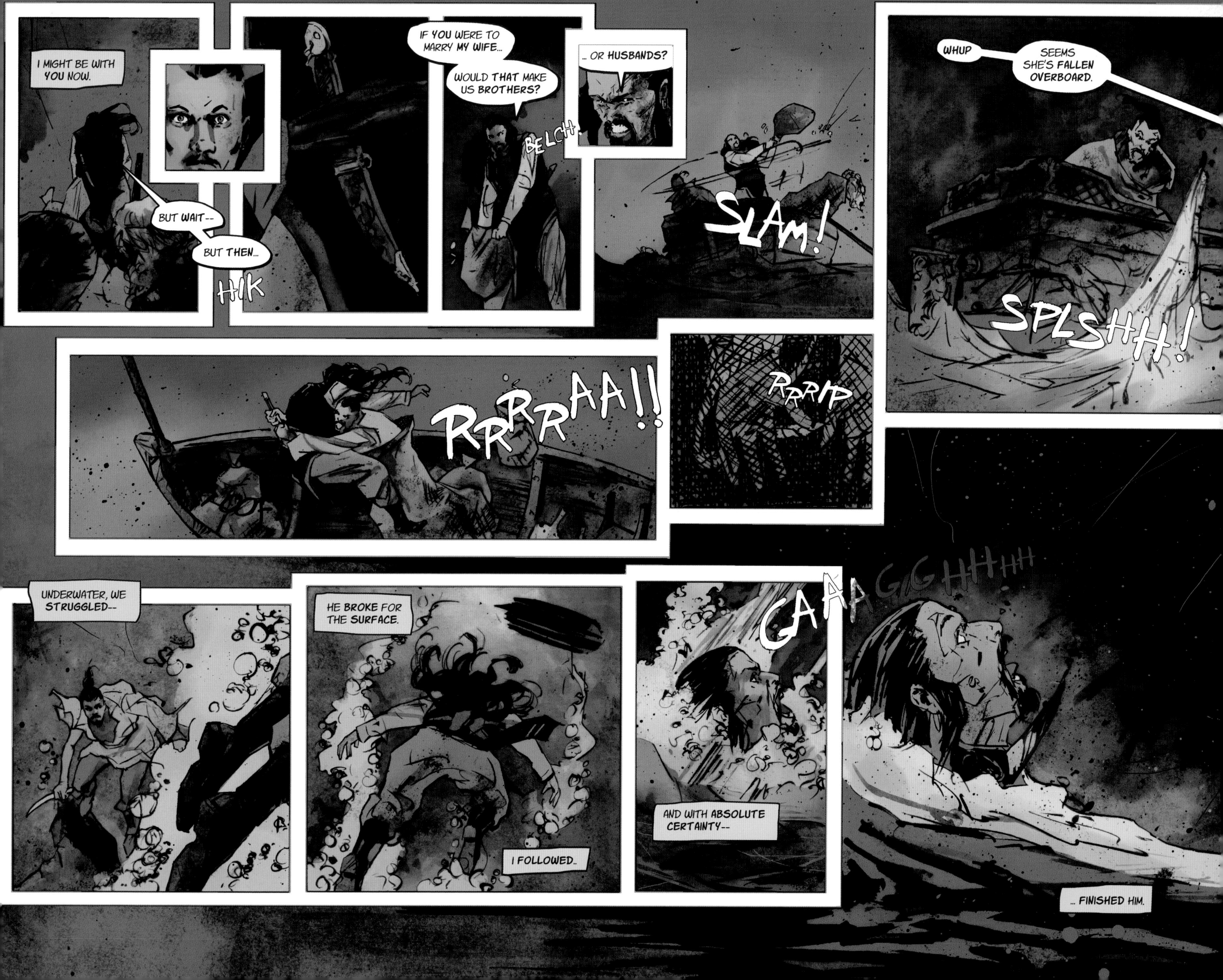
I MIGHT BE WITH YOU NOW.
BUT WAIT--
BUT THEN...
HIK
IF YOU WERE TO MARRY MY WIFE...
WOULD THAT MAKE US BROTHERS?
BELCH
... OR HUSBANDS?
SLAM!
WHUP
SEEMS SHE'S FALLEN OVERBOARD.
SPLSHHH!
RRRRAA!!
RRRIP
UNDERWATER, WE STRUGGLED--
HE BROKE FOR THE SURFACE.
I FOLLOWED..
AND WITH ABSOLUTE CERTAINTY--
GAAAGGHHHH
... FINISHED HIM.

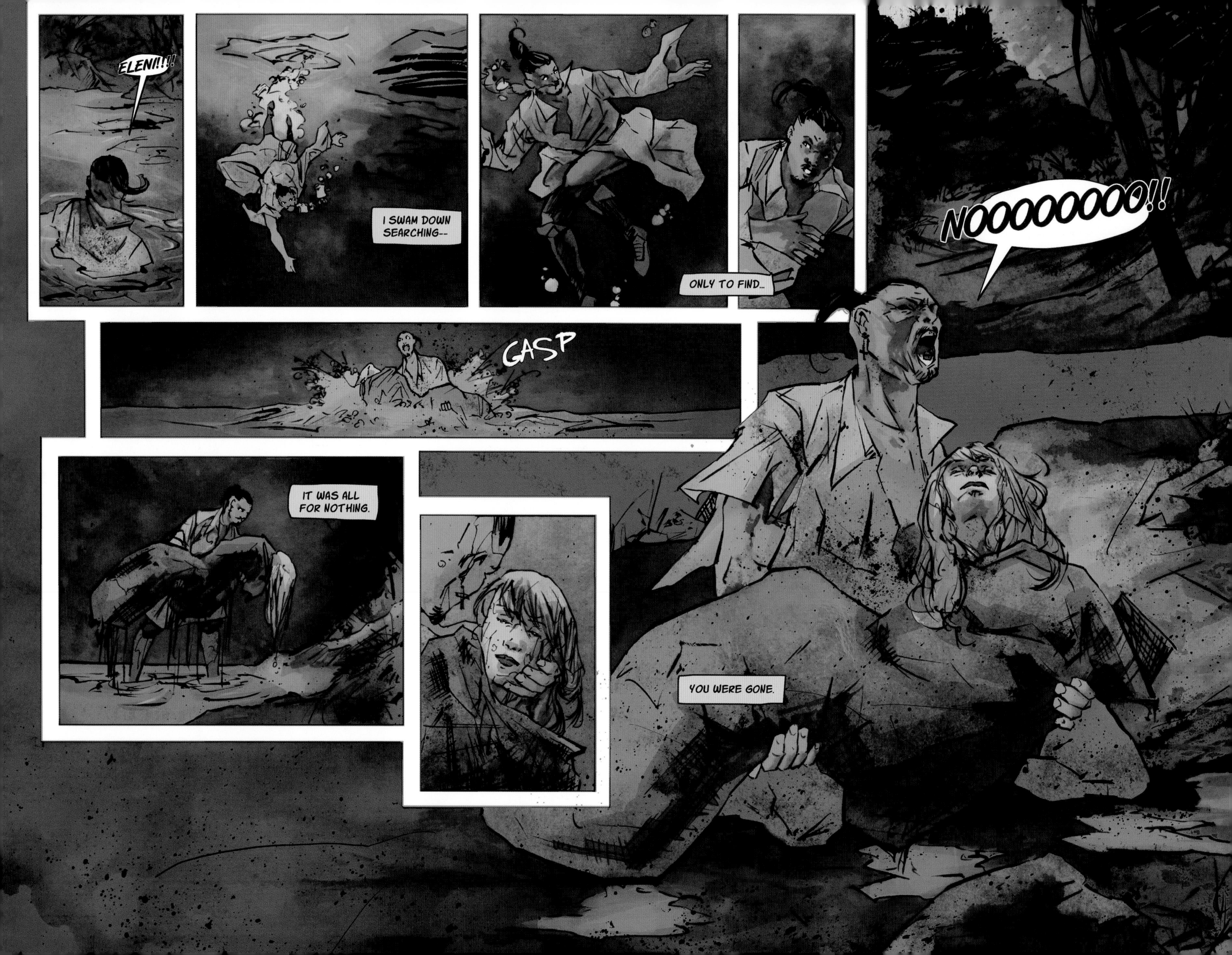
ELENI!!!!
I SWAM DOWN SEARCHING--
ONLY TO FIND...
GASP
IT WAS ALL FOR NOTHING.
YOU WERE GONE.
NOOOOOOOO!!

AND ◇ NOW...

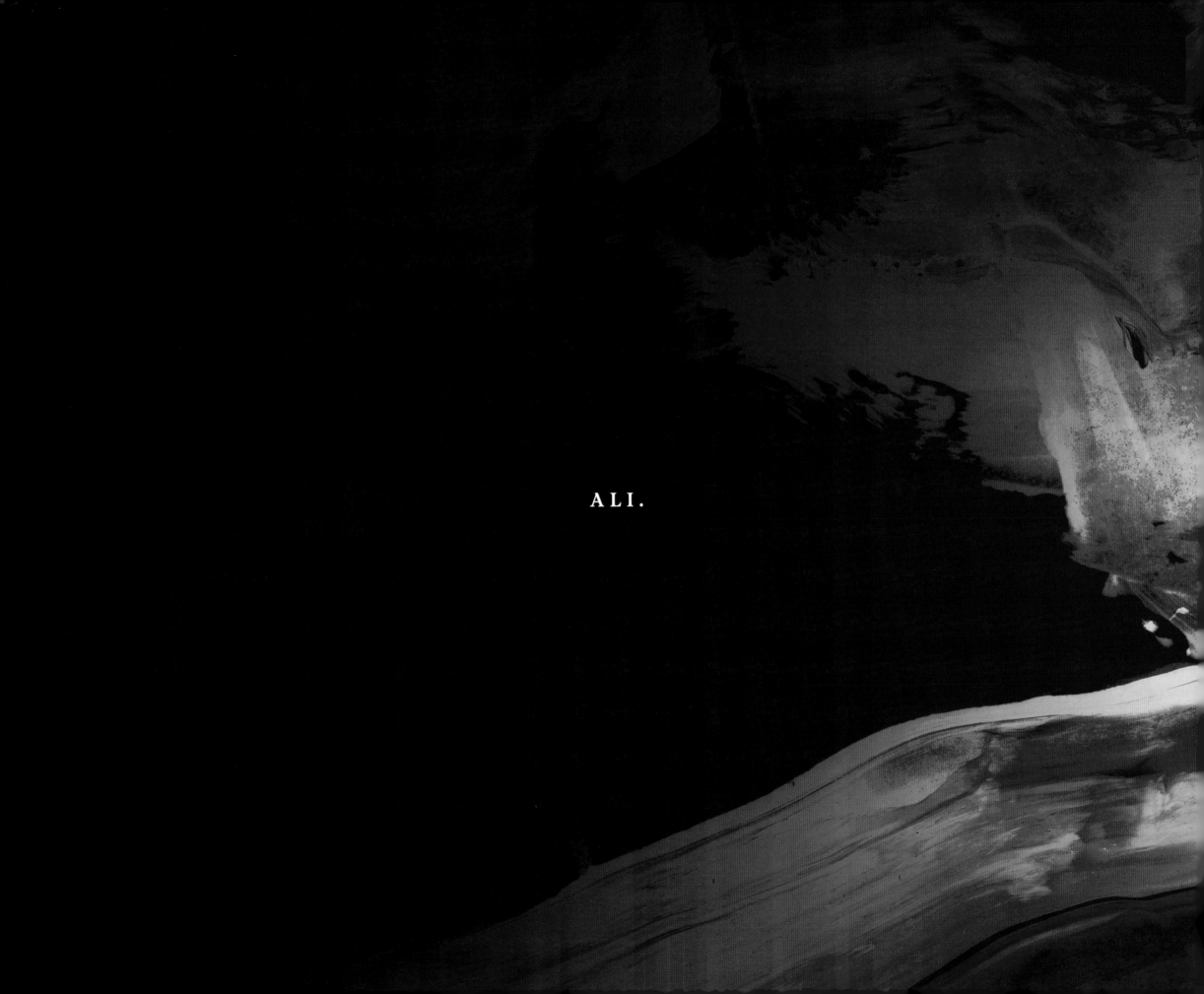

ALI.

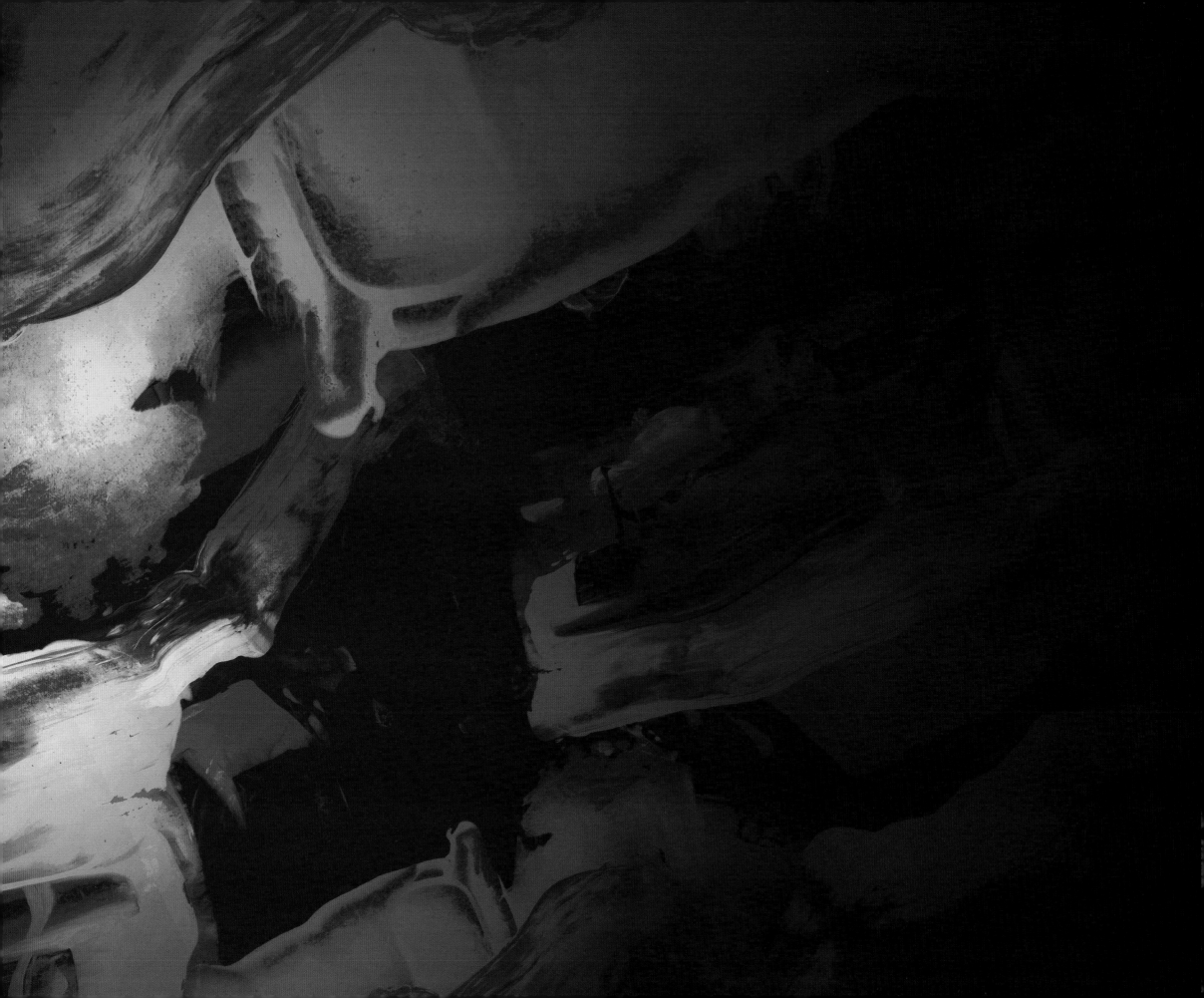

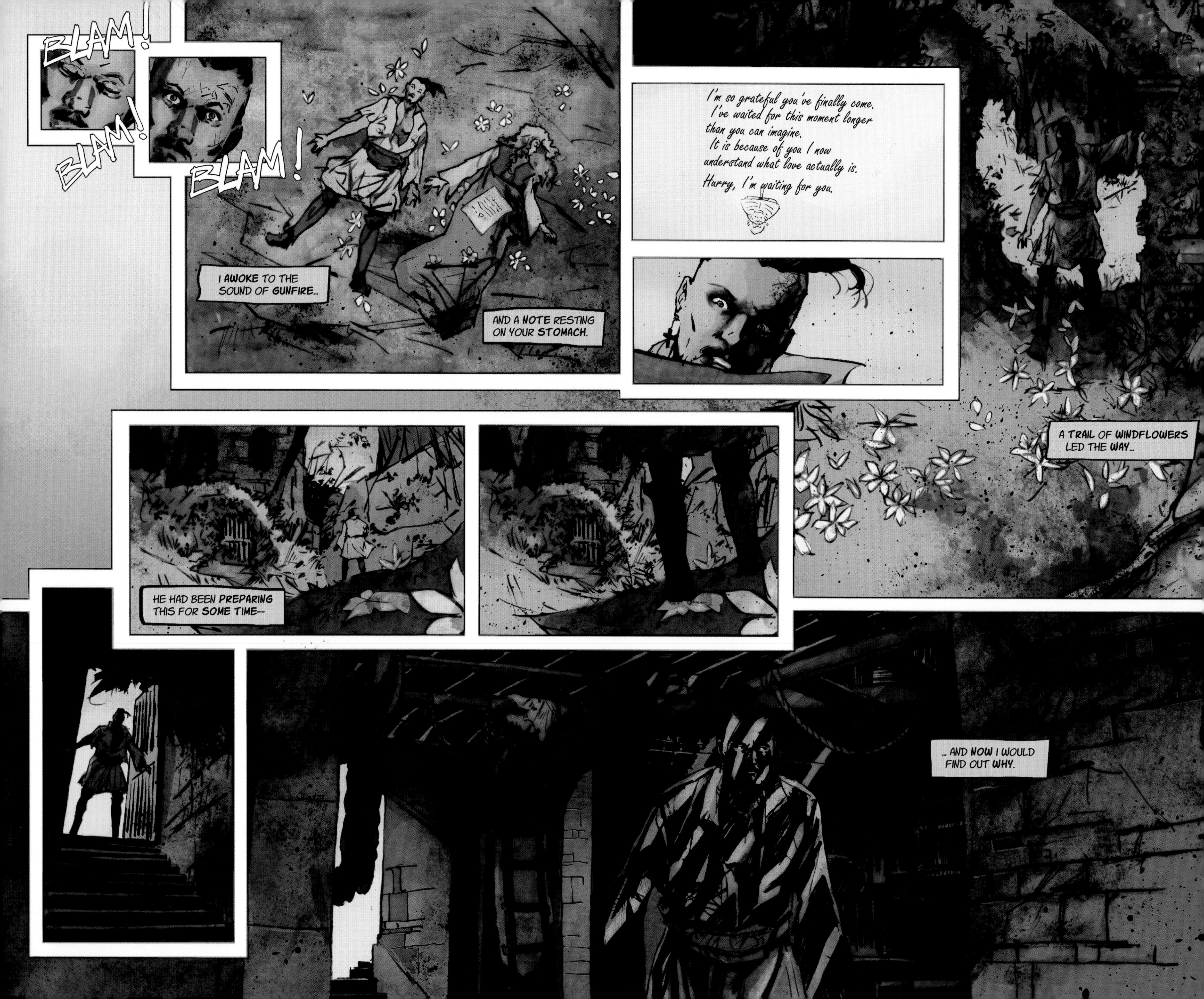
BLAM!
BLAM!
BLAM!
I AWOKE TO THE SOUND OF GUNFIRE...
AND A NOTE RESTING ON YOUR STOMACH.
I'm so grateful you've finally come. I've waited for this moment longer than you can imagine. It is because of you I now understand what love actually is.
Hurry, I'm waiting for you.
A TRAIL OF WINDFLOWERS LED THE WAY...
HE HAD BEEN PREPARING THIS FOR SOME TIME--
...AND NOW I WOULD FIND OUT WHY.

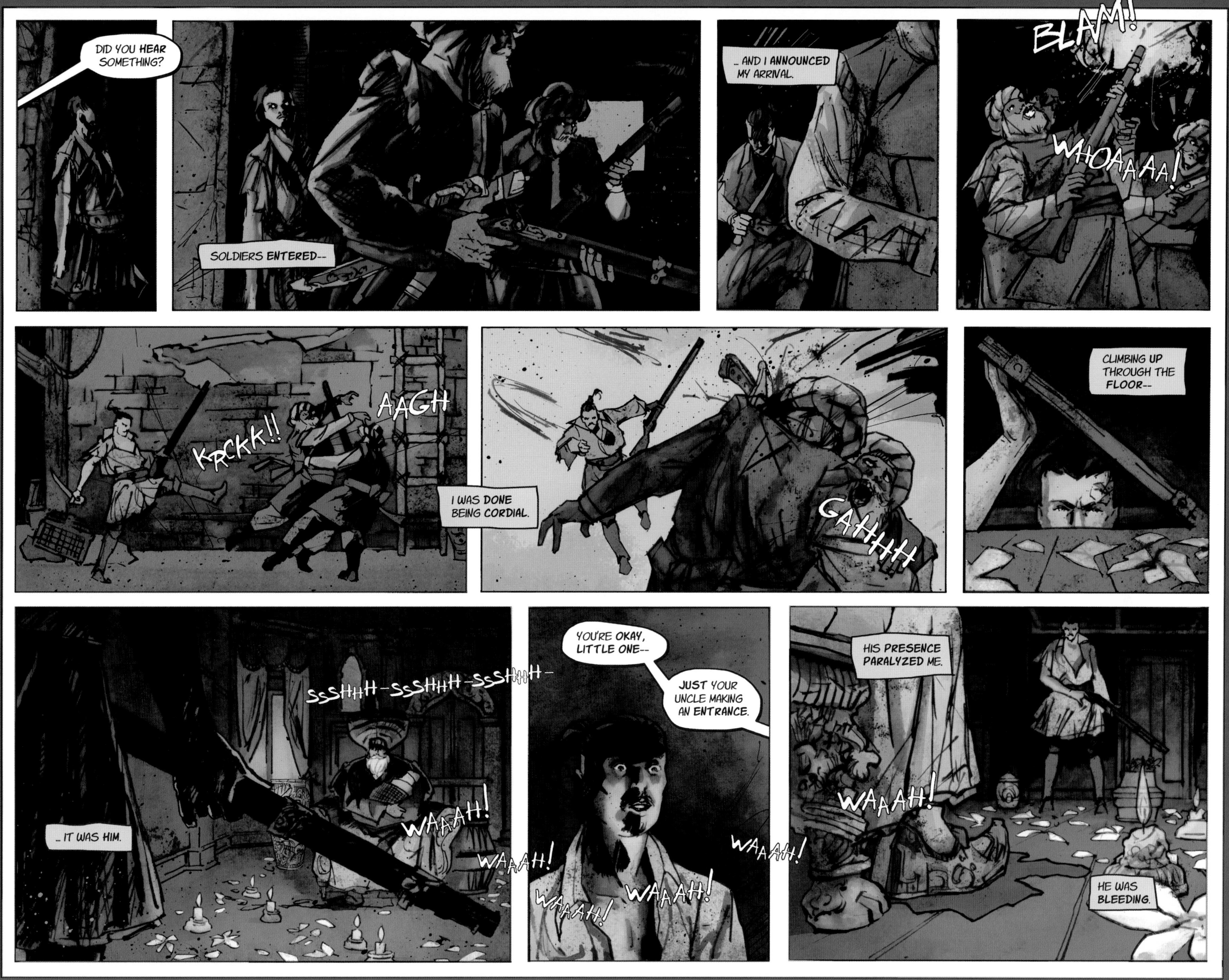
DID YOU HEAR SOMETHING?
SOLDIERS ENTERED--
...AND I ANNOUNCED MY ARRIVAL.
BLAM!
WHOAAAAA!
KRCKK!!
AAGH
I WAS DONE BEING CORDIAL.
GAHHHH
CLIMBING UP THROUGH THE FLOOR--
SSSHHH-SSSHHH-SSSHHH-
...IT WAS HIM.
WAAAH!
WAAAH!
YOU'RE OKAY, LITTLE ONE--
JUST YOUR UNCLE MAKING AN ENTRANCE.
WAAAH!
WAAAH!
WAAAH!
HIS PRESENCE PARALYZED ME.
WAAAH!
HE WAS BLEEDING.

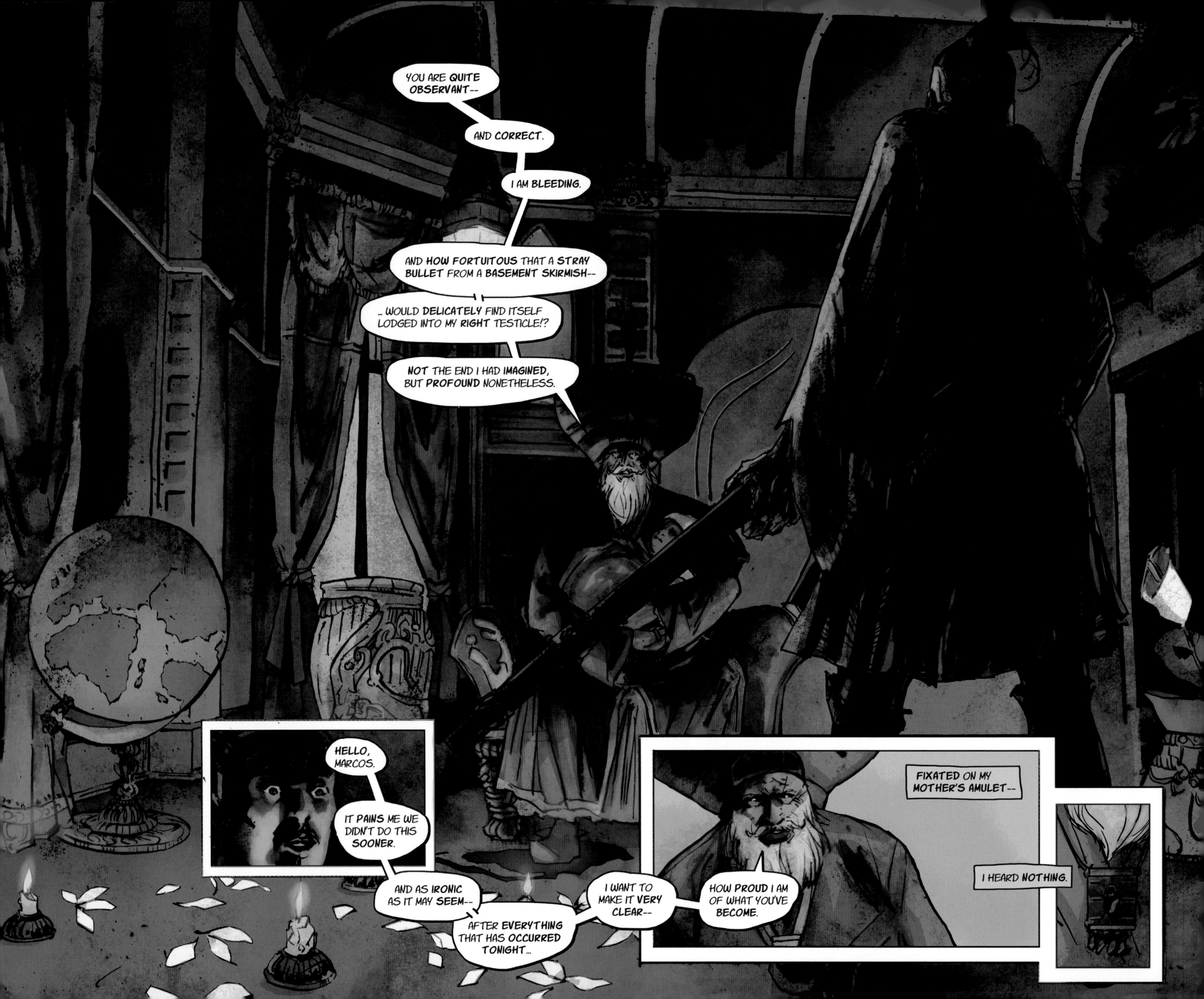
YOU ARE QUITE OBSERVANT--
AND CORRECT.
I AM BLEEDING.
AND HOW FORTUITOUS THAT A STRAY BULLET FROM A BASEMENT SKIRMISH--
.. WOULD DELICATELY FIND ITSELF LODGED INTO MY RIGHT TESTICLE!?
NOT THE END I HAD IMAGINED, BUT PROFOUND NONETHELESS.
HELLO, MARCOS.
IT PAINS ME WE DIDN'T DO THIS SOONER.
AND AS IRONIC AS IT MAY SEEM--
AFTER EVERYTHING THAT HAS OCCURRED TONIGHT...
I WANT TO MAKE IT VERY CLEAR--
HOW PROUD I AM OF WHAT YOU'VE BECOME.
FIXATED ON MY MOTHER'S AMULET--
I HEARD NOTHING.

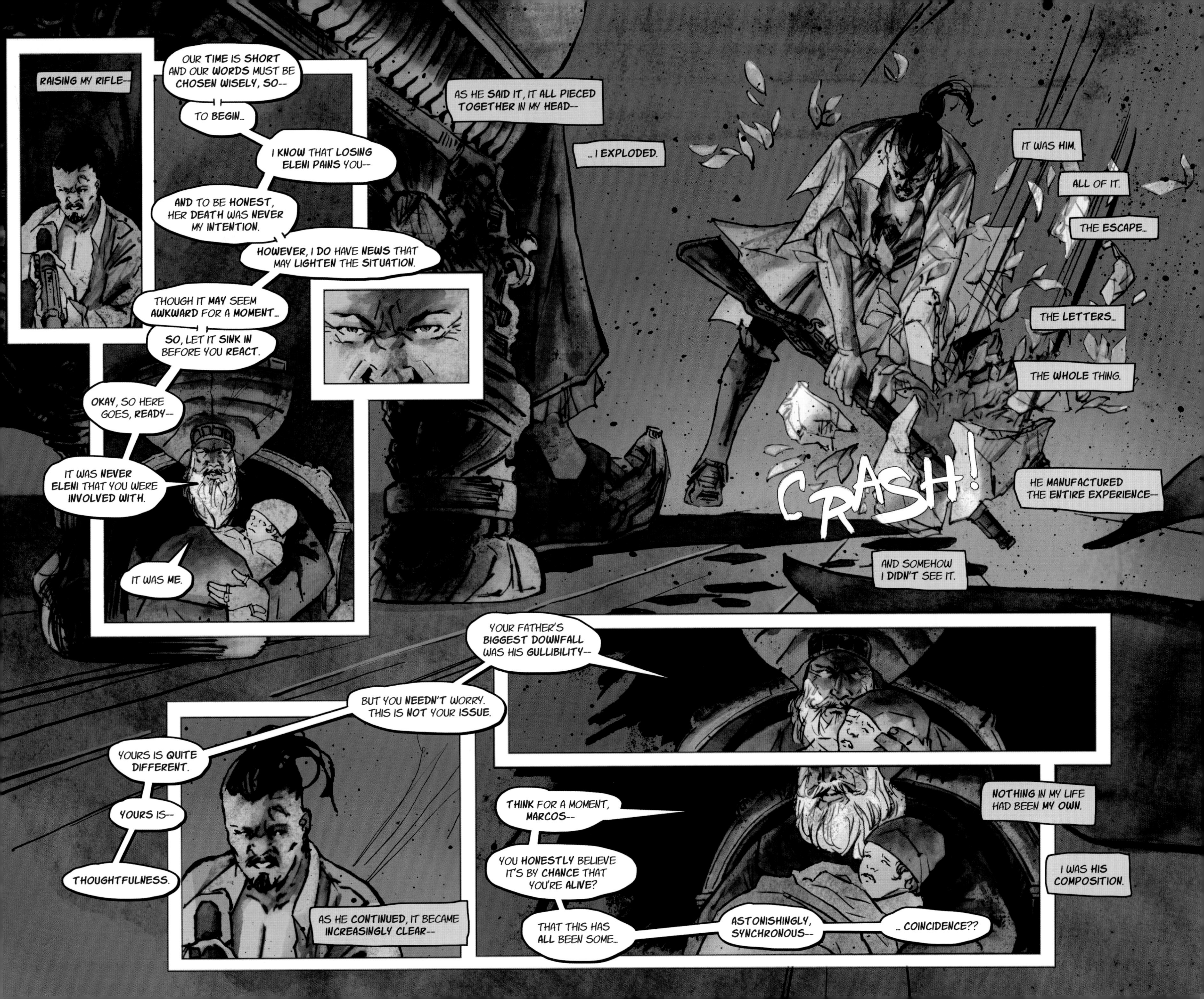
RAISING MY RIFLE--
OUR TIME IS SHORT AND OUR WORDS MUST BE CHOSEN WISELY, SO--
TO BEGIN...
I KNOW THAT LOSING ELENI PAINS YOU--
AND TO BE HONEST, HER DEATH WAS NEVER MY INTENTION.
HOWEVER, I DO HAVE NEWS THAT MAY LIGHTEN THE SITUATION.
THOUGH IT MAY SEEM AWKWARD FOR A MOMENT...
SO, LET IT SINK IN BEFORE YOU REACT.
OKAY, SO HERE GOES, READY--
IT WAS NEVER ELENI THAT YOU WERE INVOLVED WITH.
IT WAS ME.
AS HE SAID IT, IT ALL PIECED TOGETHER IN MY HEAD--
... I EXPLODED.
IT WAS HIM.
ALL OF IT.
THE ESCAPE...
THE LETTERS...
THE WHOLE THING.
CRASH!
HE MANUFACTURED THE ENTIRE EXPERIENCE--
AND SOMEHOW I DIDN'T SEE IT.
YOUR FATHER'S BIGGEST DOWNFALL WAS HIS GULLIBILITY--
BUT YOU NEEDN'T WORRY. THIS IS NOT YOUR ISSUE.
YOURS IS QUITE DIFFERENT.
YOURS IS--
THOUGHTFULNESS.
AS HE CONTINUED, IT BECAME INCREASINGLY CLEAR--
THINK FOR A MOMENT, MARCOS--
YOU HONESTLY BELIEVE IT'S BY CHANCE THAT YOU'RE ALIVE?
THAT THIS HAS ALL BEEN SOME...
ASTONISHINGLY, SYNCHRONOUS--
... COINCIDENCE??
NOTHING IN MY LIFE HAD BEEN MY OWN.
I WAS HIS COMPOSITION.

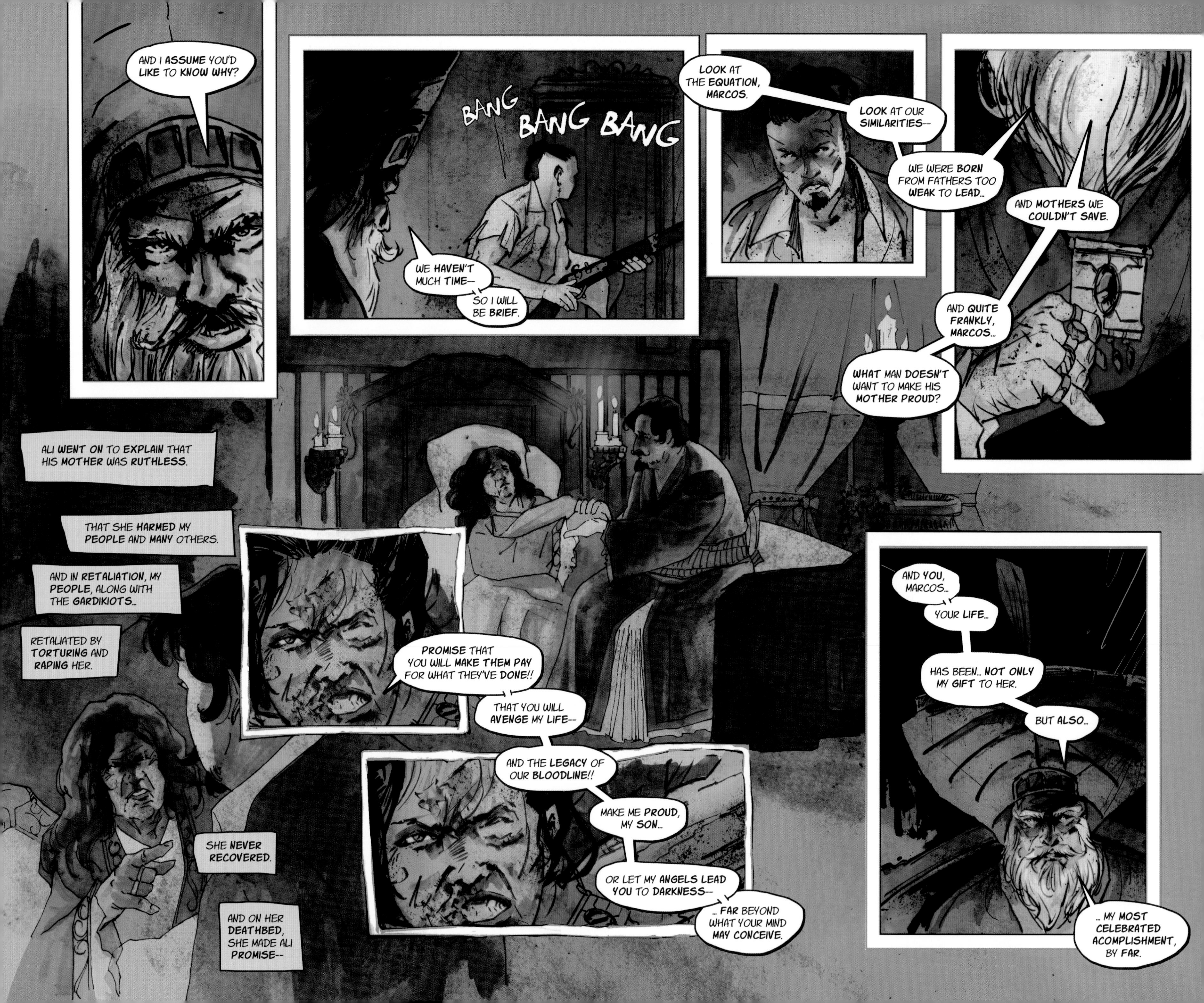
AND I ASSUME YOU'D LIKE TO KNOW WHY?
BANG BANG BANG
WE HAVEN'T MUCH TIME--
SO I WILL BE BRIEF.
LOOK AT THE EQUATION, MARCOS.
LOOK AT OUR SIMILARITIES--
WE WERE BORN FROM FATHERS TOO WEAK TO LEAD...
AND MOTHERS WE COULDN'T SAVE.
AND QUITE FRANKLY, MARCOS...
WHAT MAN DOESN'T WANT TO MAKE HIS MOTHER PROUD?
ALI WENT ON TO EXPLAIN THAT HIS MOTHER WAS RUTHLESS.
THAT SHE HARMED MY PEOPLE AND MANY OTHERS.
AND IN RETALIATION, MY PEOPLE, ALONG WITH THE GARDIKIOTS...
RETALIATED BY TORTURING AND RAPING HER.
SHE NEVER RECOVERED.
AND ON HER DEATHBED, SHE MADE ALI PROMISE--
PROMISE THAT YOU WILL MAKE THEM PAY FOR WHAT THEY'VE DONE!!
THAT YOU WILL AVENGE MY LIFE--
AND THE LEGACY OF OUR BLOODLINE!!
MAKE ME PROUD, MY SON...
OR LET MY ANGELS LEAD YOU TO DARKNESS--
... FAR BEYOND WHAT YOUR MIND MAY CONCEIVE.
AND YOU, MARCOS...
YOUR LIFE...
HAS BEEN... NOT ONLY MY GIFT TO HER.
BUT ALSO...
... MY MOST CELEBRATED ACOMPLISHMENT, BY FAR.

WAAA

RRRHH

I'M ETERNALLY IN YOUR DEBT.

I WAS DONE LISTENING.

BUT HE KEPT GOING...

WAAA!! WAAA!! WAAA!! WAAA!! WAAA!!

WAAA!!

ANYONE CAN DESTROY VILLAGES—

BUT TO EMBODY THE MIND...

TO ERADICATE CERTAINTY...

AND PUPPETEER THE LIVES OF YOUR ENEMY'S FAMILY—

WAAA!! WAAA!! WAAA!!

TO POSSESS THE INNER WORKINGS OF YOUR ENEMY'S CHILD!!

IS QUITE AN ACHIEVEMENT, YOU MUST ADMIT!!

AND THAT'S NOT EVEN THE BEST PART.

KRRCK!

CCRACK!!

ALONG THE WAY...

I BUILT YOU—

TAUGHT YOU TO THINK...

TO TRUST NO ONE—

TO FEAR NOTHING—

BEAT DOWN YOUR VULNERABILITY—

I MADE YOU A LEADER, MARCOS...

THWAK!

THE LEADER YOUR FATHER WISHED HE COULD BE...

THE MAN WHO KILLED ALI PASHA.

THAT'S YOU, MARCOS.

YOU ARE THAT MAN, MARCOS.

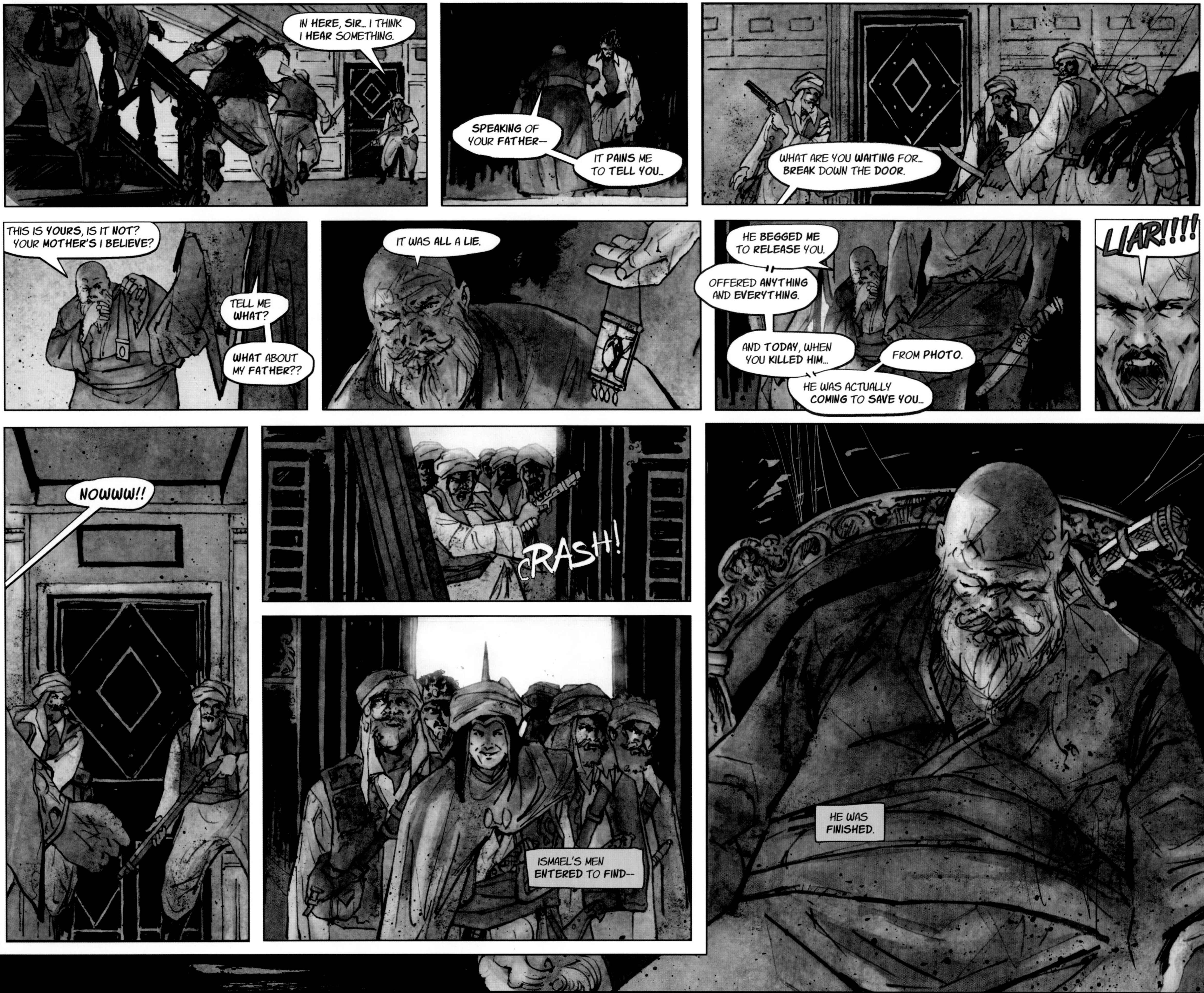
IN HERE, SIR... I THINK I HEAR SOMETHING.
SPEAKING OF YOUR FATHER--
IT PAINS ME TO TELL YOU...
WHAT ARE YOU WAITING FOR... BREAK DOWN THE DOOR.
THIS IS YOURS, IS IT NOT? YOUR MOTHER'S I BELIEVE?
TELL ME WHAT?
WHAT ABOUT MY FATHER??
IT WAS ALL A LIE.
HE BEGGED ME TO RELEASE YOU.
OFFERED ANYTHING AND EVERYTHING.
AND TODAY, WHEN YOU KILLED HIM...
HE WAS ACTUALLY COMING TO SAVE YOU...
FROM PHOTO.
LIAR!!!!
NOWWW!!
CRASH!
ISMAEL'S MEN ENTERED TO FIND--
HE WAS FINISHED.

AND I WOULD ◇ SOON FOLLOW.

BOOK THREE ◇ *Chapter Three*

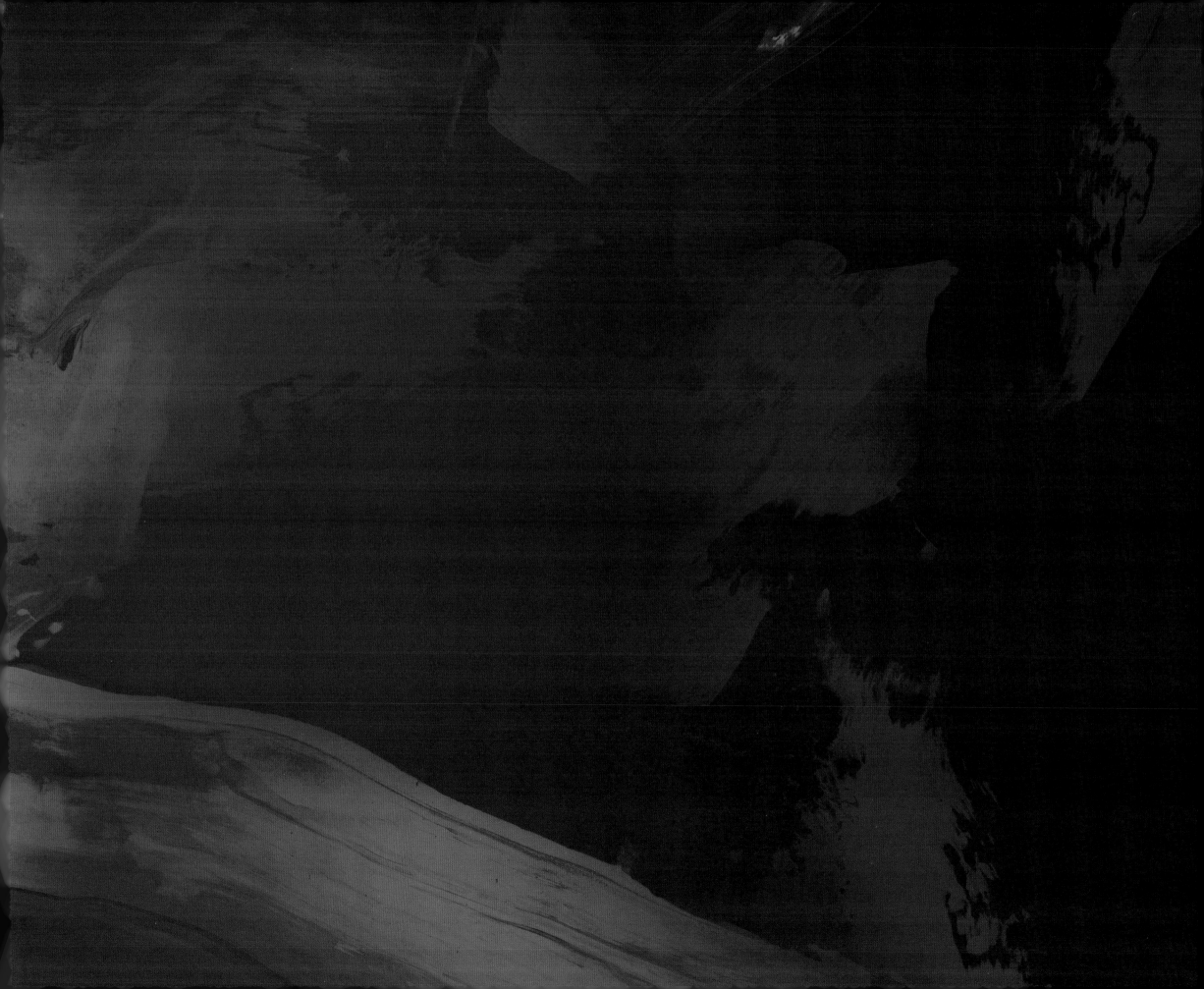

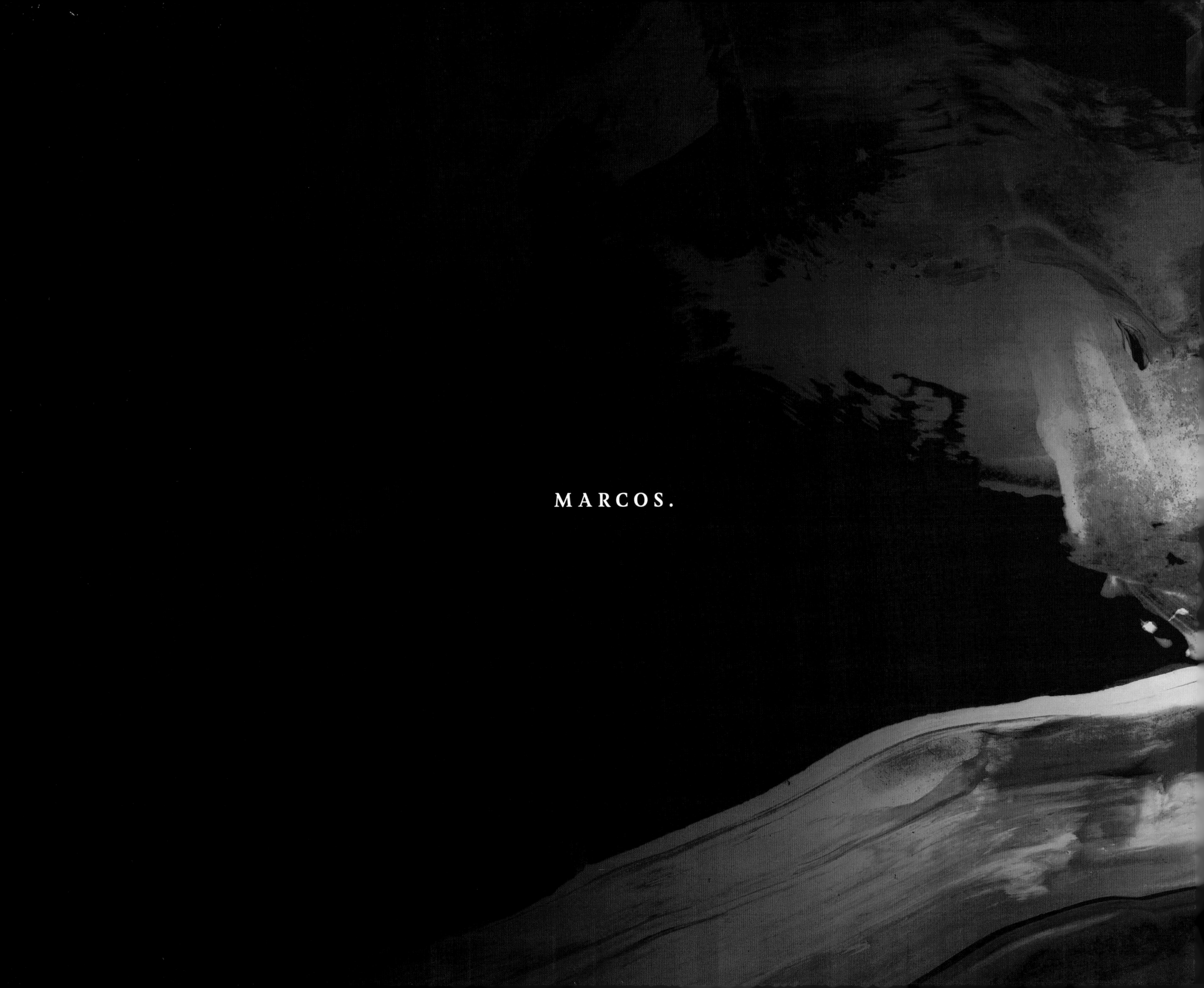

MARCOS.

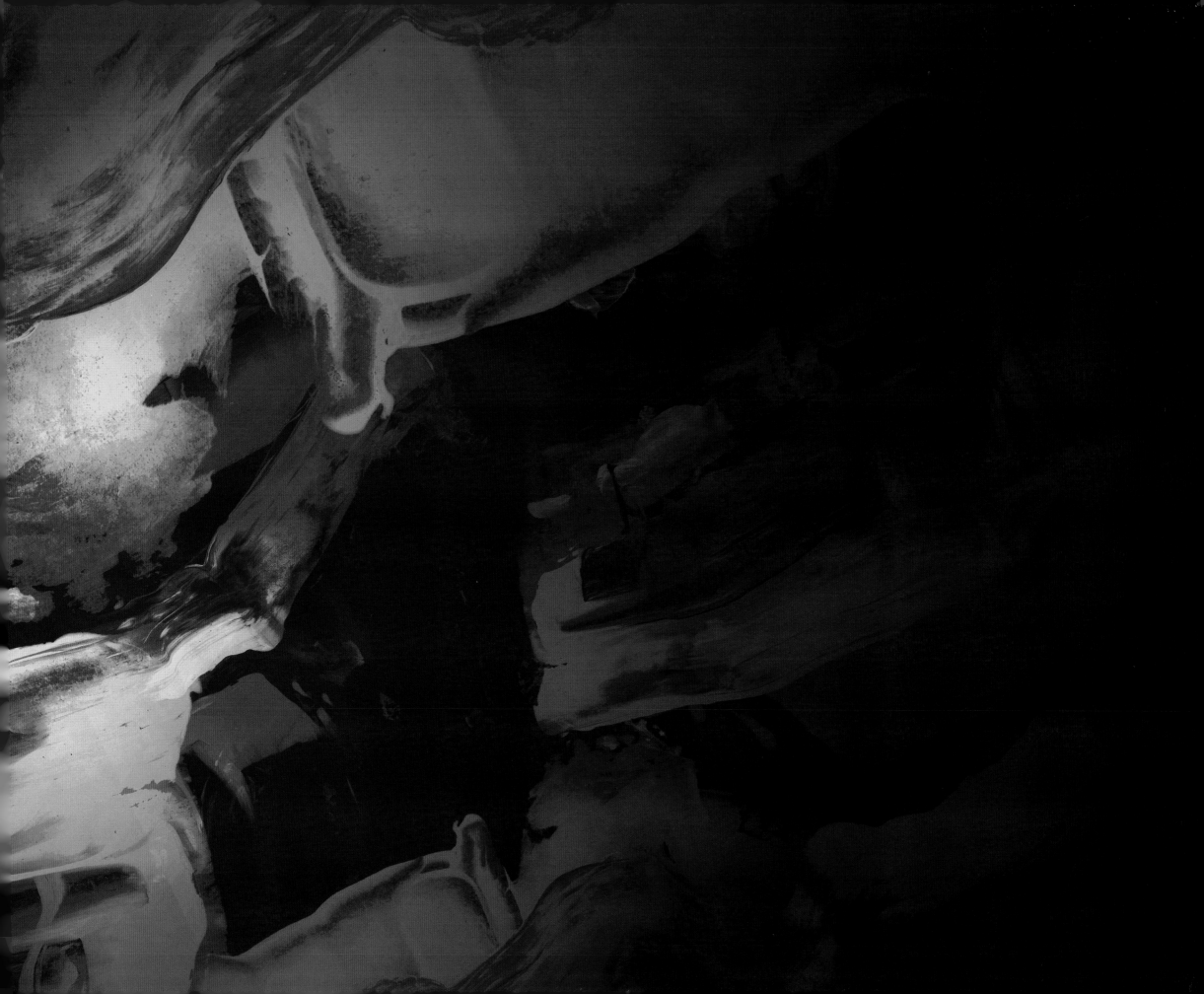

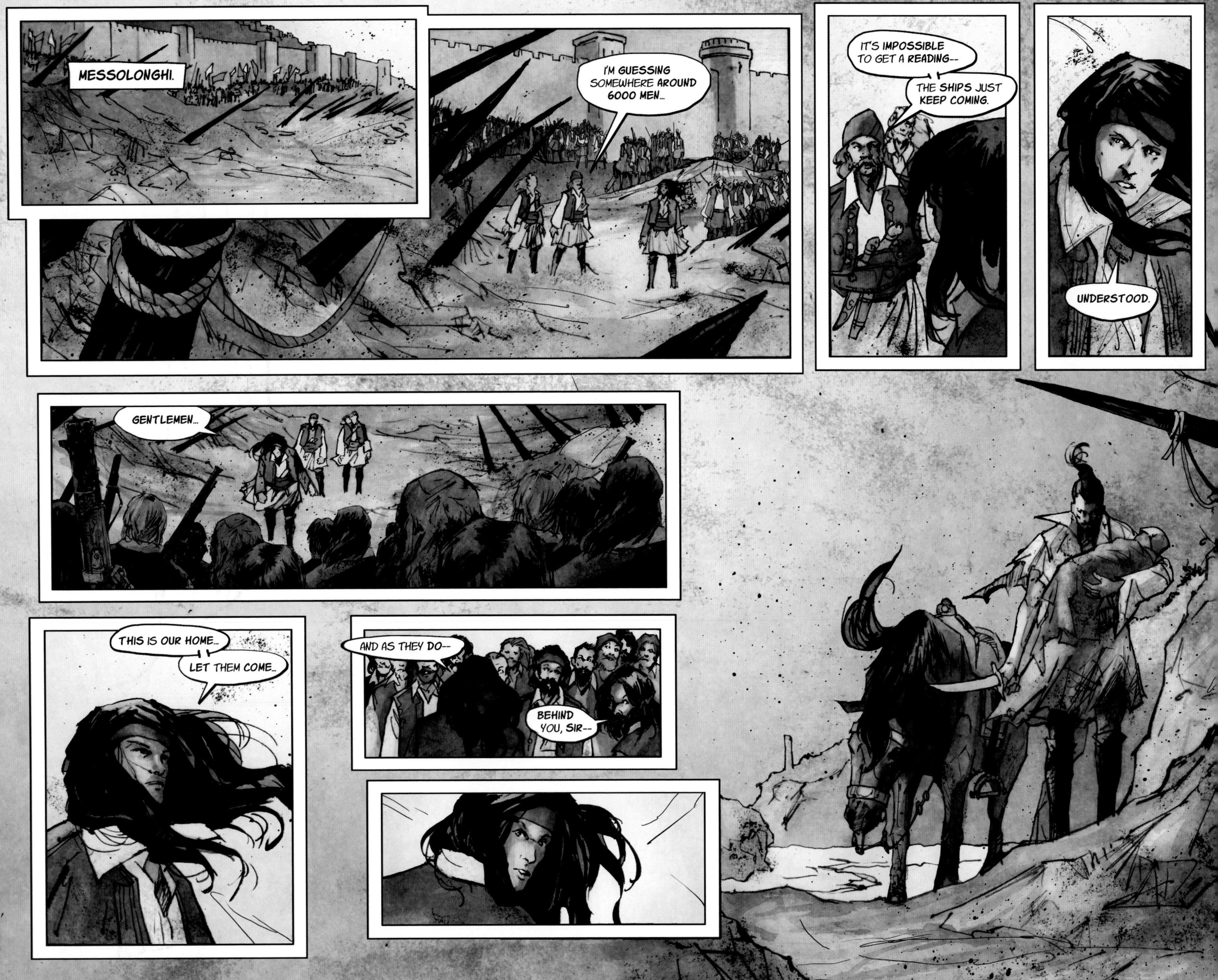
MESSOLONGHI.
I'M GUESSING SOMEWHERE AROUND 6000 MEN...
IT'S IMPOSSIBLE TO GET A READING--
THE SHIPS JUST KEEP COMING.
UNDERSTOOD.
GENTLEMEN...
THIS IS OUR HOME...
LET THEM COME...
AND AS THEY DO--
BEHIND YOU, SIR--

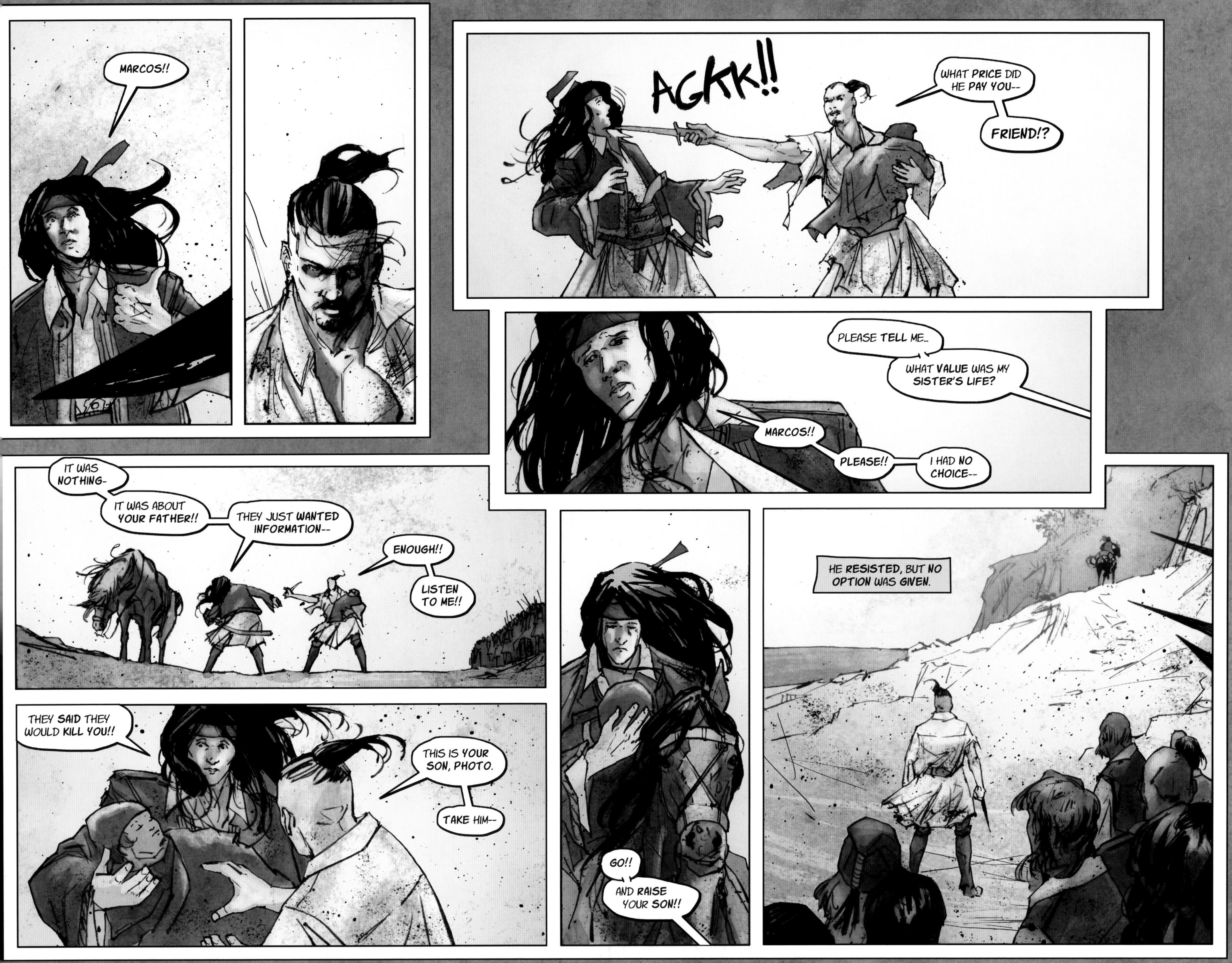

MARCOS!!
AGKK!!
WHAT PRICE DID HE PAY YOU--
FRIEND!?
PLEASE TELL ME...
WHAT VALUE WAS MY SISTER'S LIFE?
MARCOS!!
PLEASE!!
I HAD NO CHOICE--
IT WAS NOTHING-
IT WAS ABOUT YOUR FATHER!!
THEY JUST WANTED INFORMATION--
ENOUGH!!
LISTEN TO ME!!
THEY SAID THEY WOULD KILL YOU!!
THIS IS YOUR SON, PHOTO.
TAKE HIM--
GO!!
AND RAISE YOUR SON!!
HE RESISTED, BUT NO OPTION WAS GIVEN.

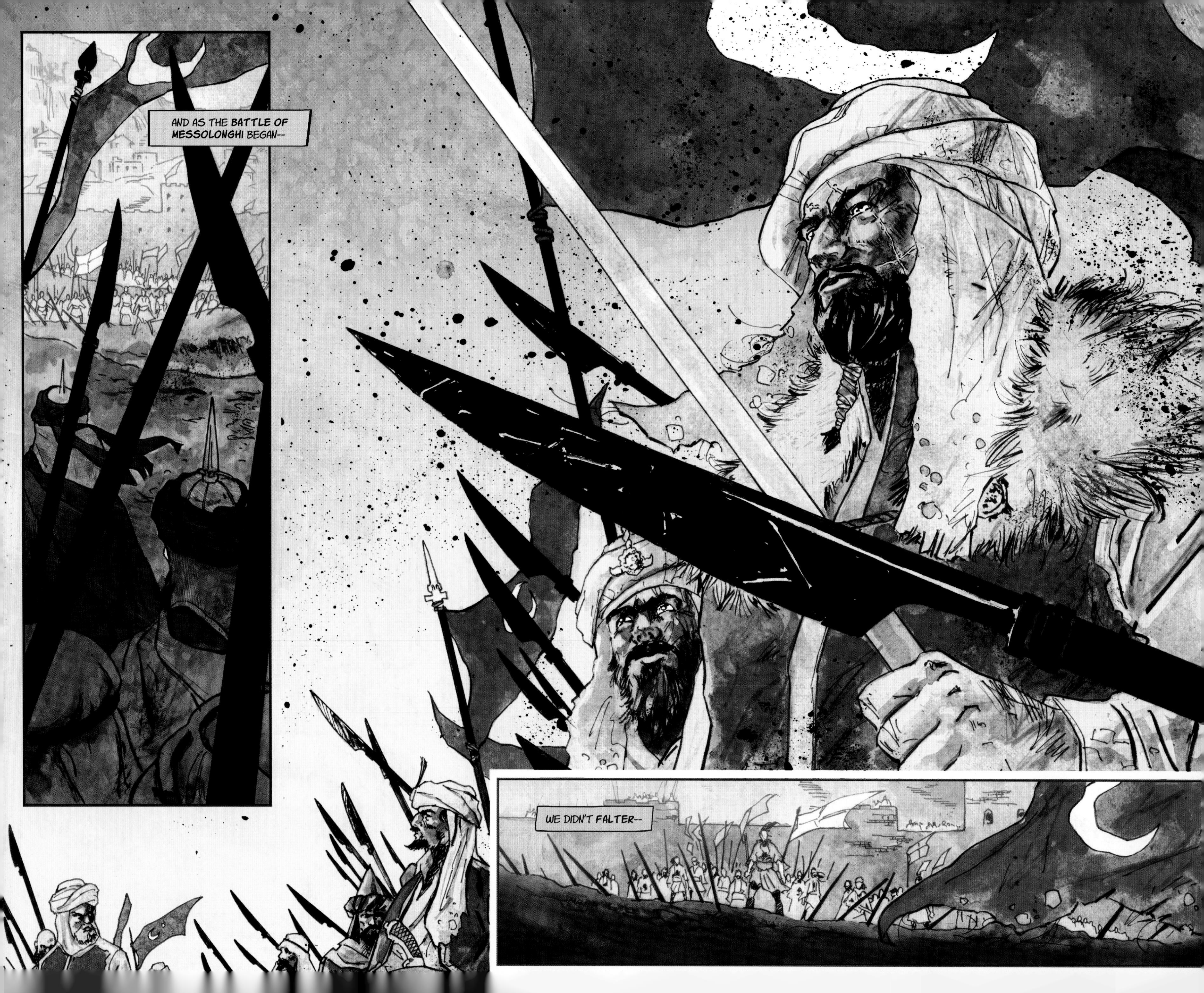
AND AS THE BATTLE OF MESSOLONGHI BEGAN--
WE DIDN'T FALTER--

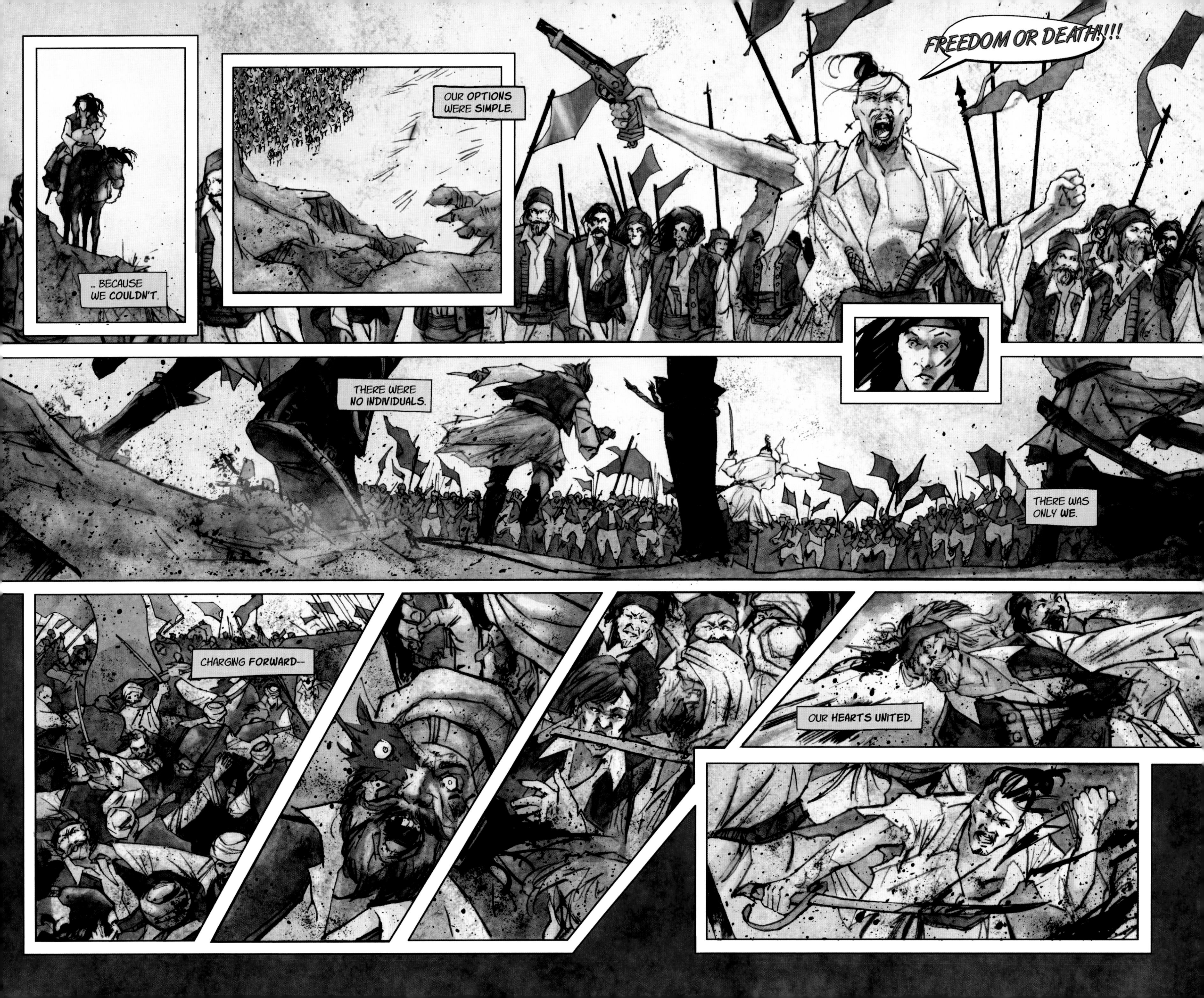

... BECAUSE WE COULDN'T.
OUR OPTIONS WERE SIMPLE.
FREEDOM OR DEATH!!!!
THERE WERE NO INDIVIDUALS.
THERE WAS ONLY WE.
CHARGING FORWARD--
OUR HEARTS UNITED.

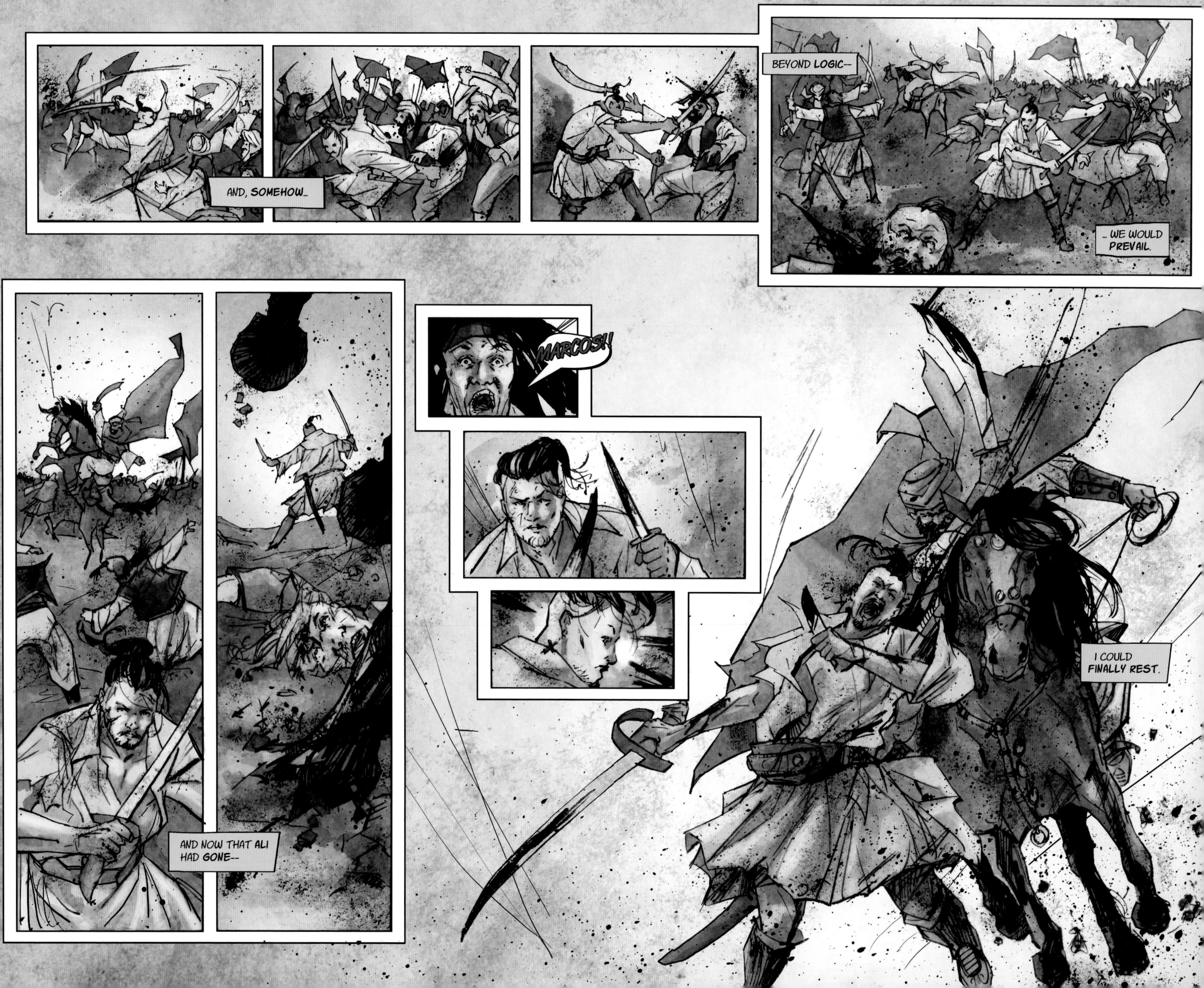
AND, SOMEHOW...
BEYOND LOGIC--
...WE WOULD PREVAIL.
AND NOW THAT ALI HAD GONE--
MARCOS!!
I COULD FINALLY REST.

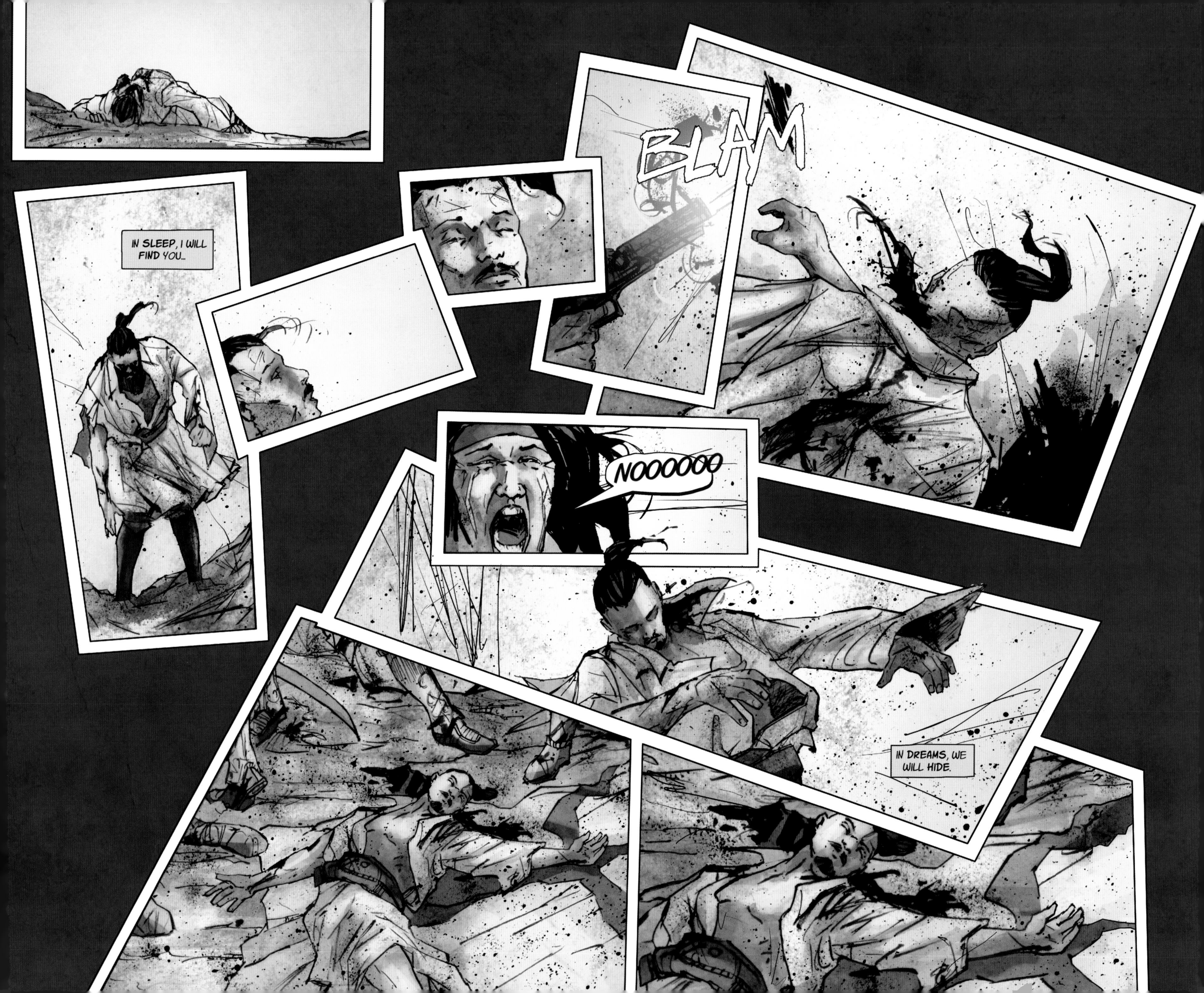
IN SLEEP, I WILL FIND YOU...
BLAM
NOOOOOO
IN DREAMS, WE WILL HIDE.

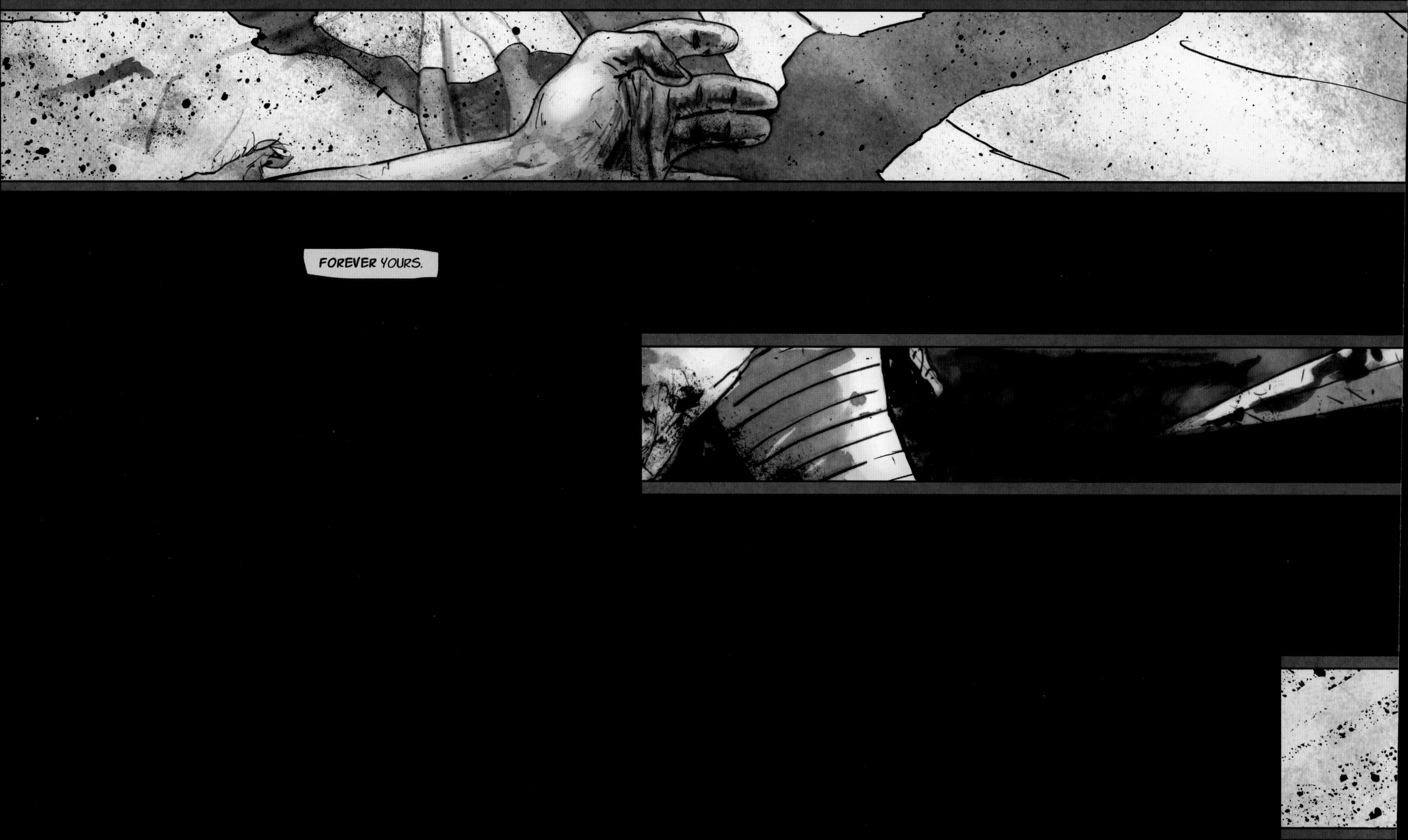
FOREVER YOURS.

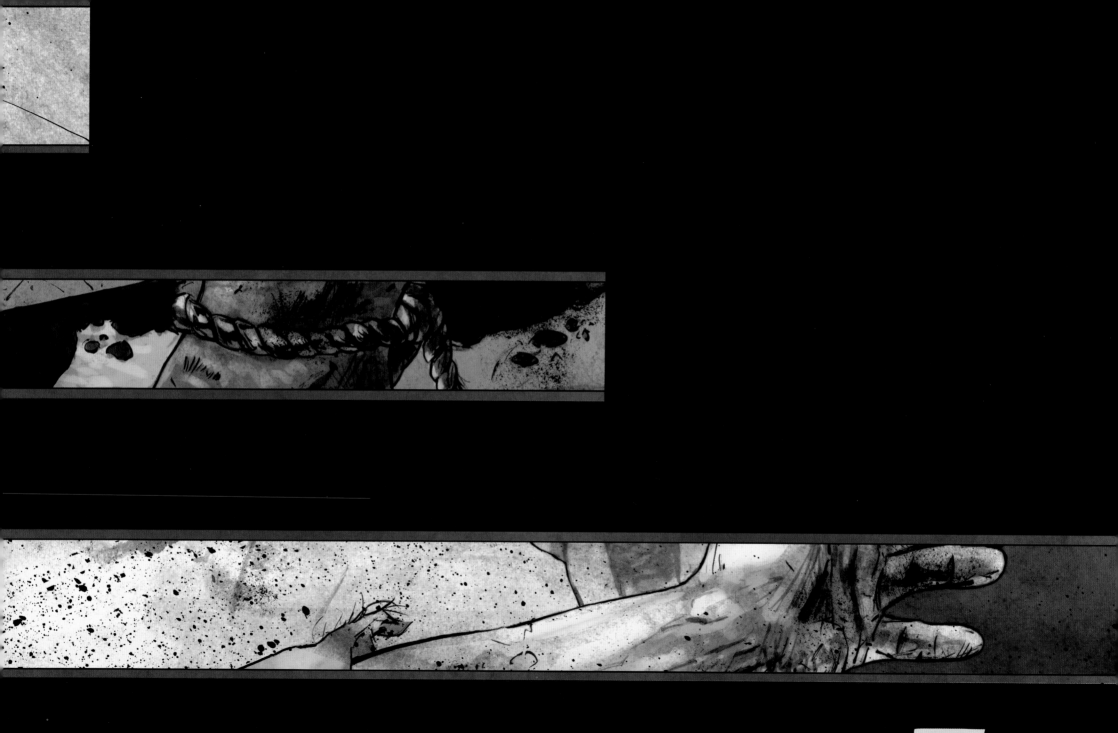

... MARCOS.

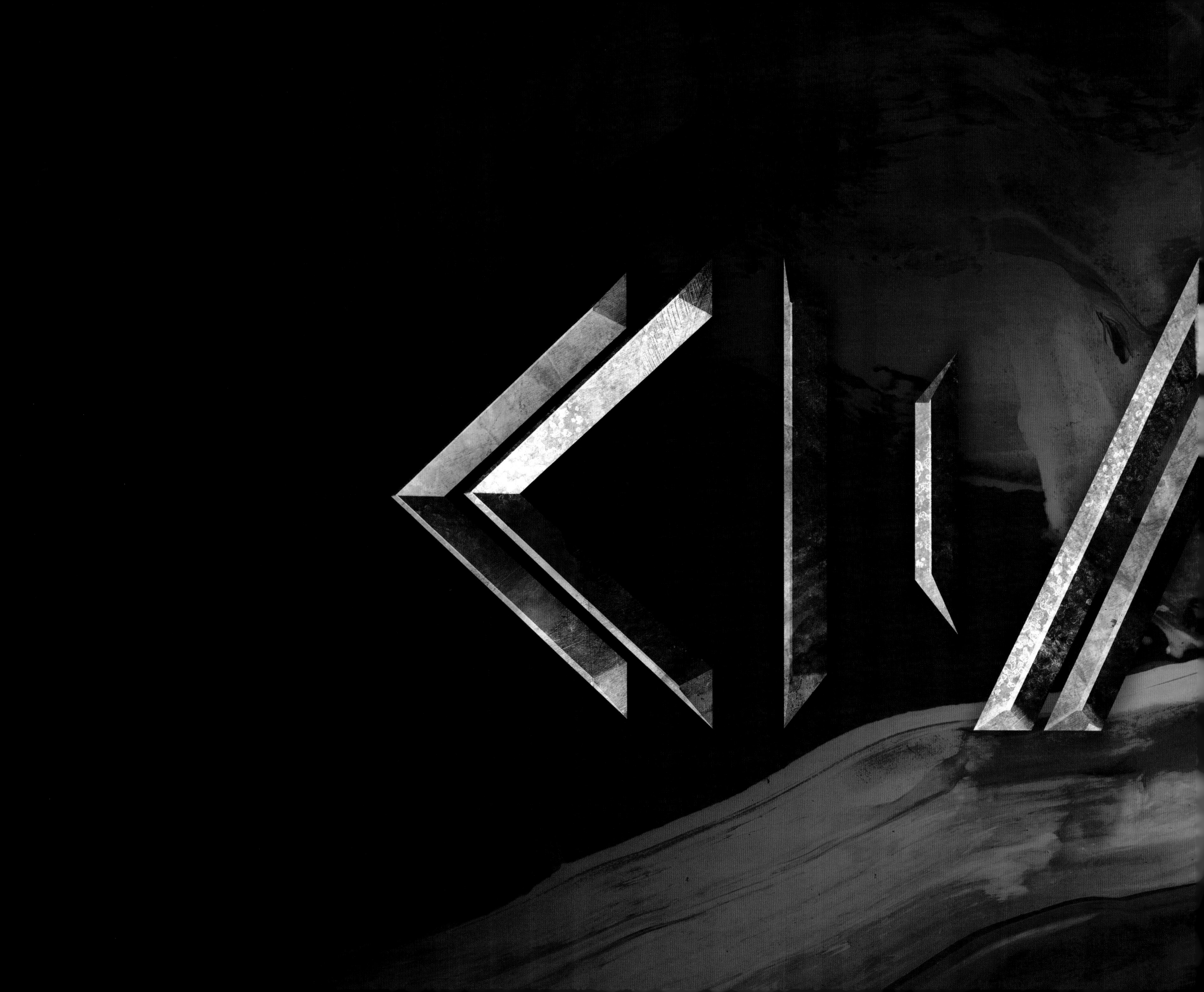

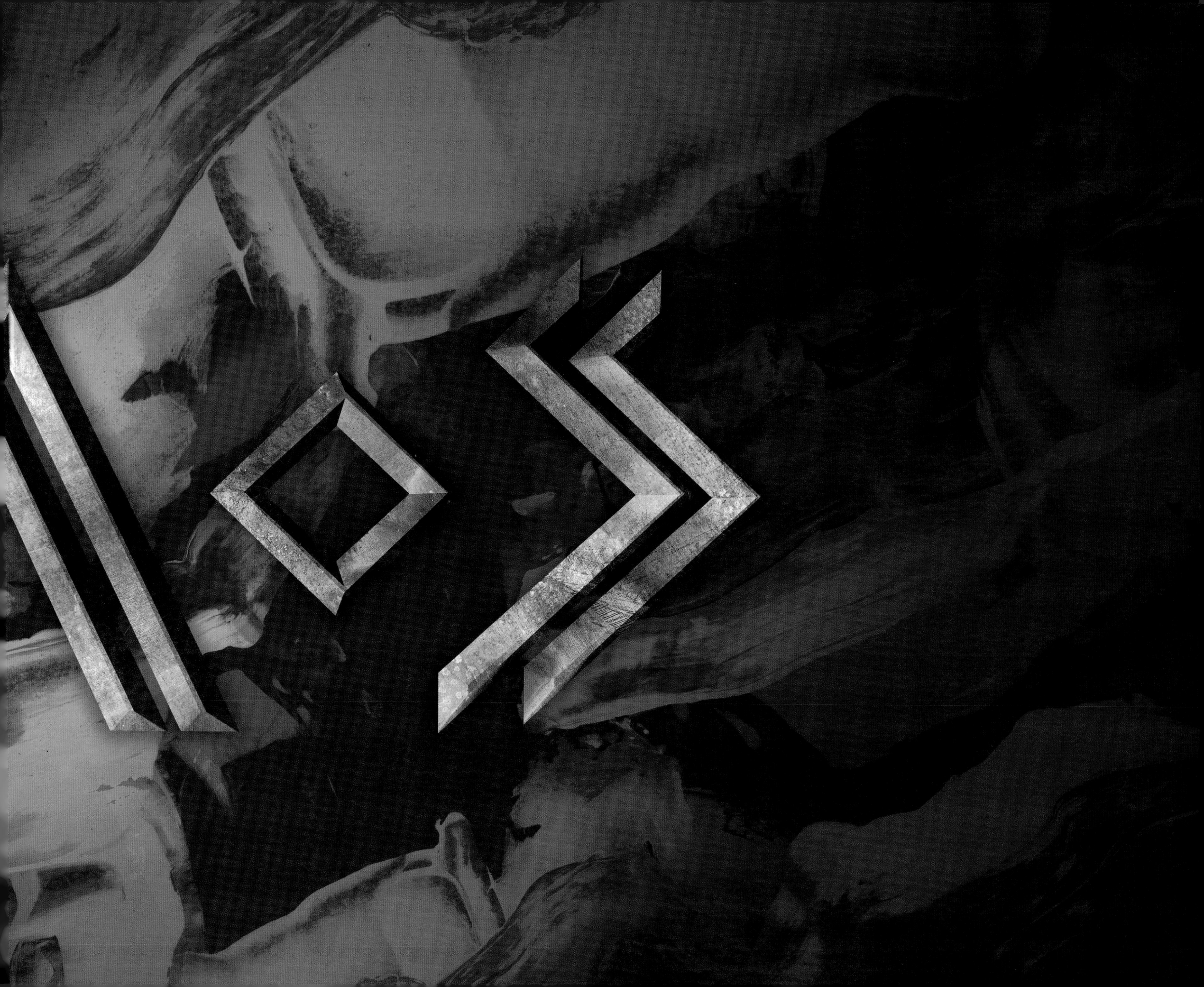

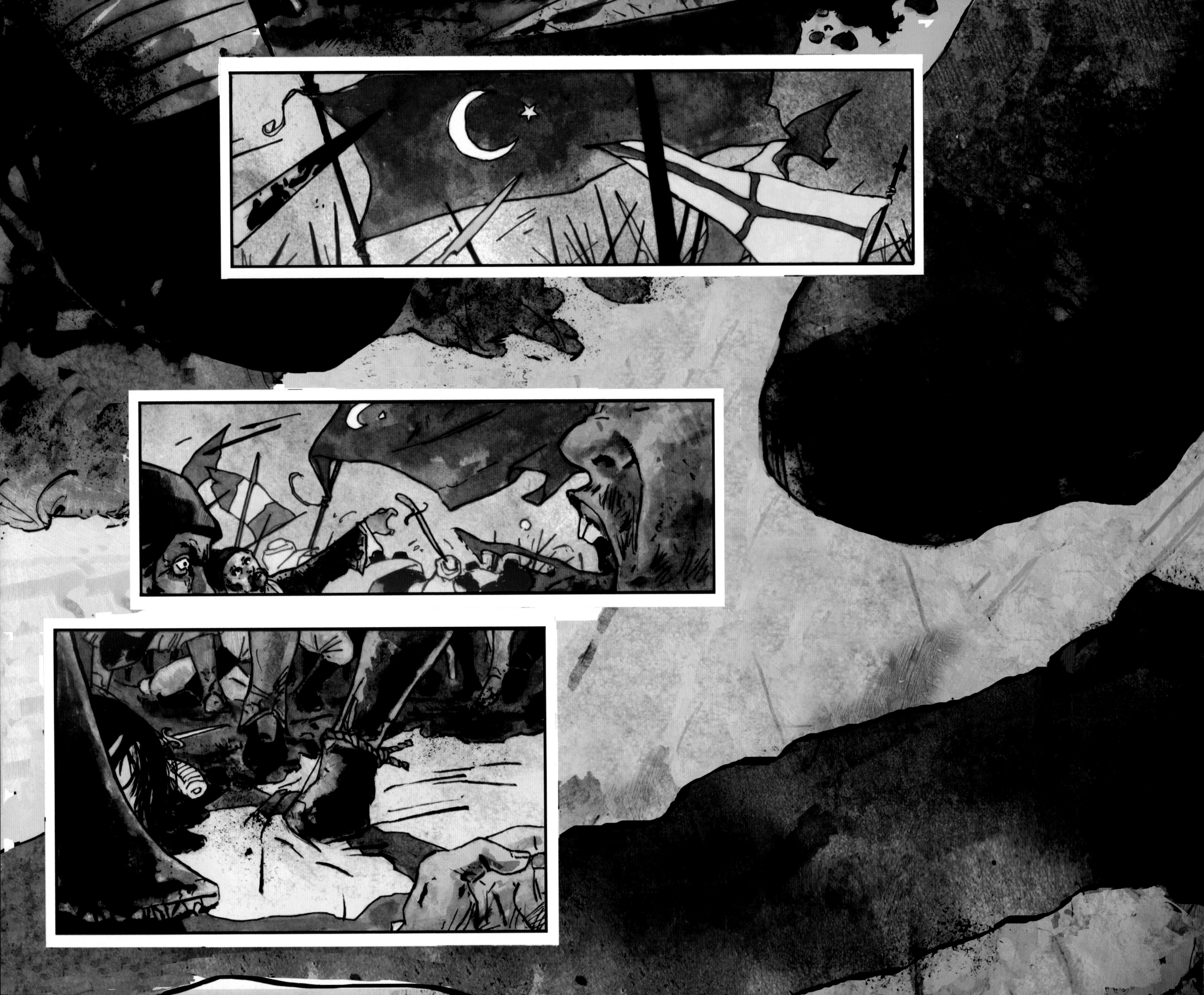

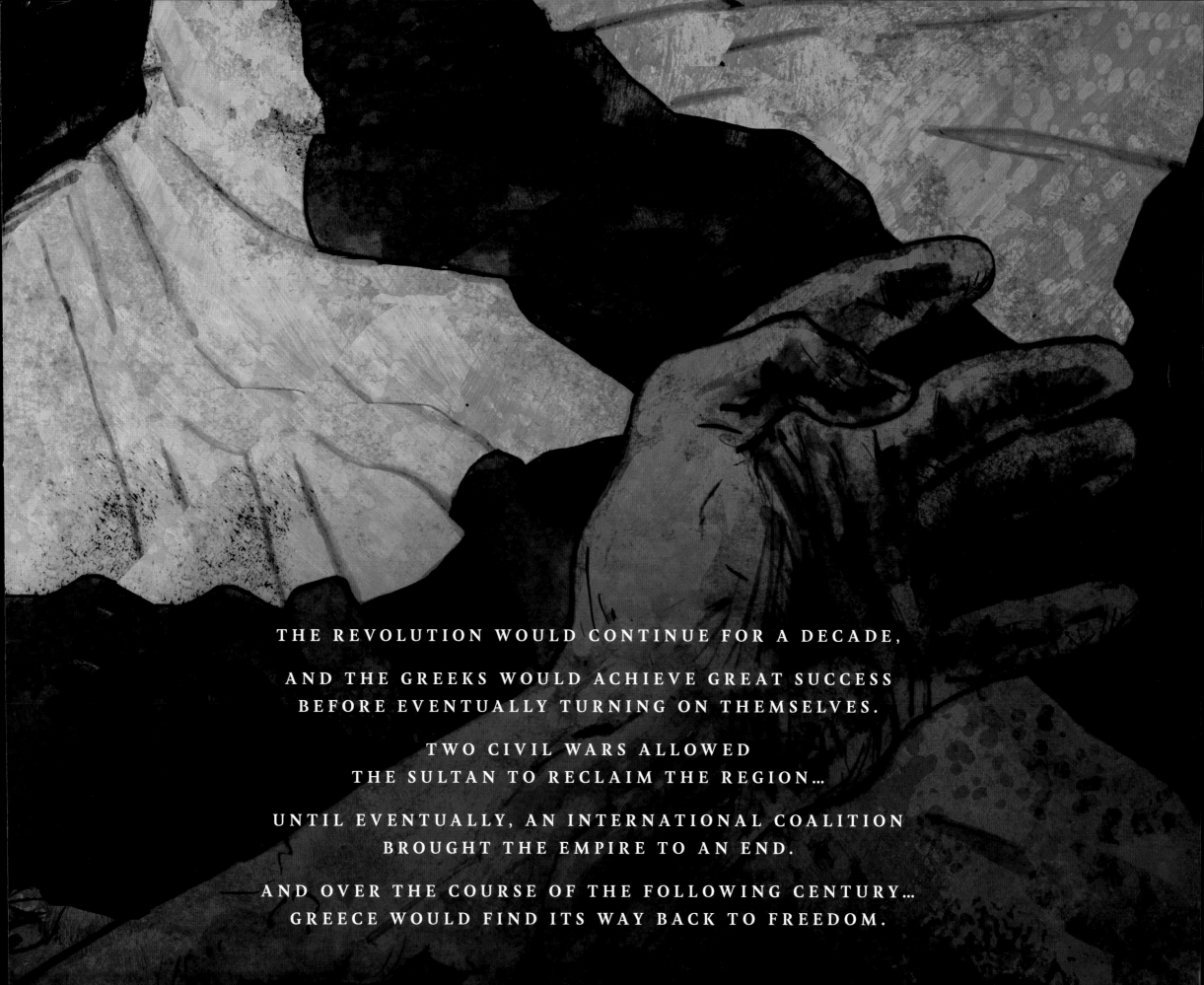

THE REVOLUTION WOULD CONTINUE FOR A DECADE,

AND THE GREEKS WOULD ACHIEVE GREAT SUCCESS
BEFORE EVENTUALLY TURNING ON THEMSELVES.

TWO CIVIL WARS ALLOWED
THE SULTAN TO RECLAIM THE REGION...

UNTIL EVENTUALLY, AN INTERNATIONAL COALITION
BROUGHT THE EMPIRE TO AN END.

AND OVER THE COURSE OF THE FOLLOWING CENTURY...
GREECE WOULD FIND ITS WAY BACK TO FREEDOM.

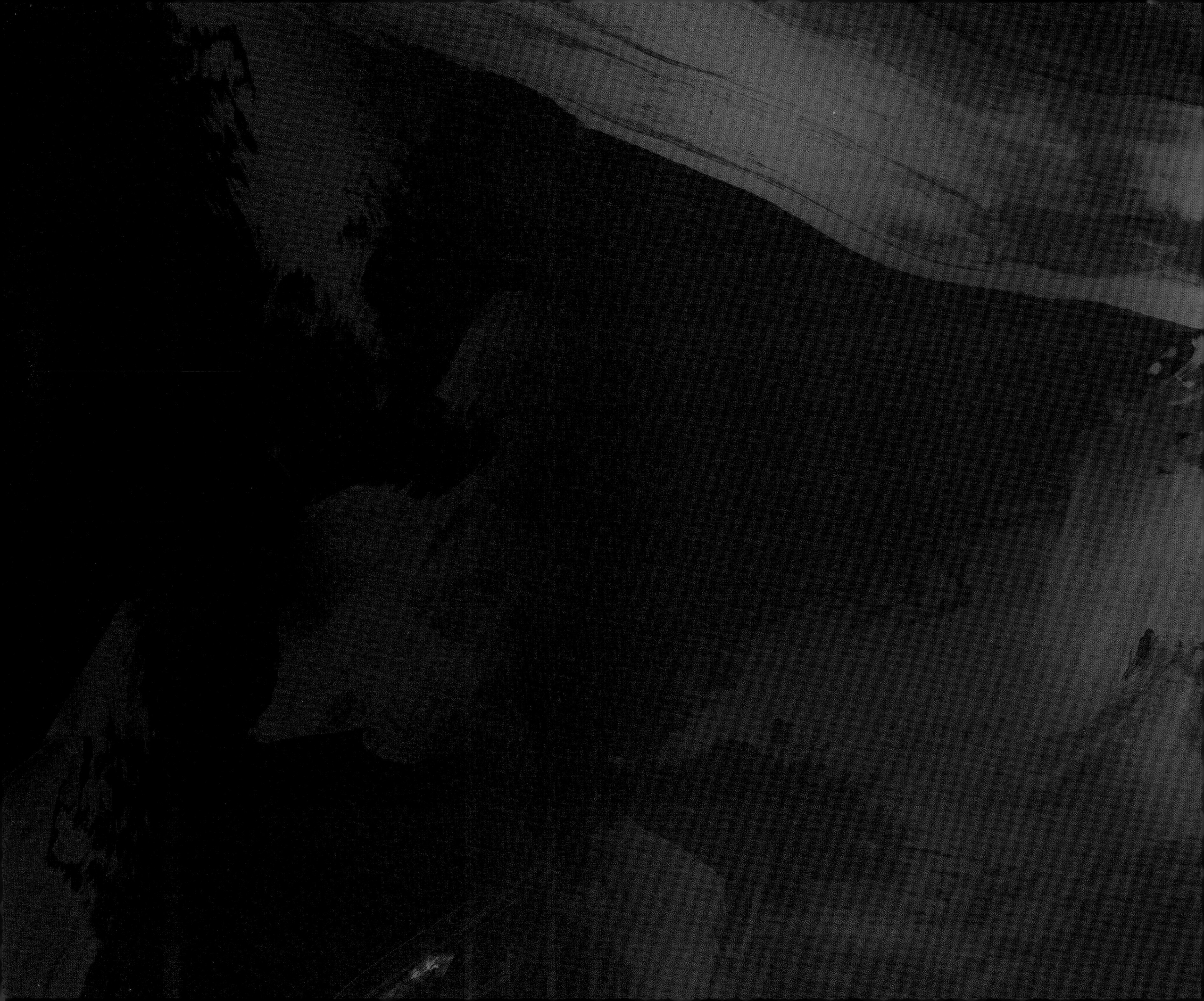

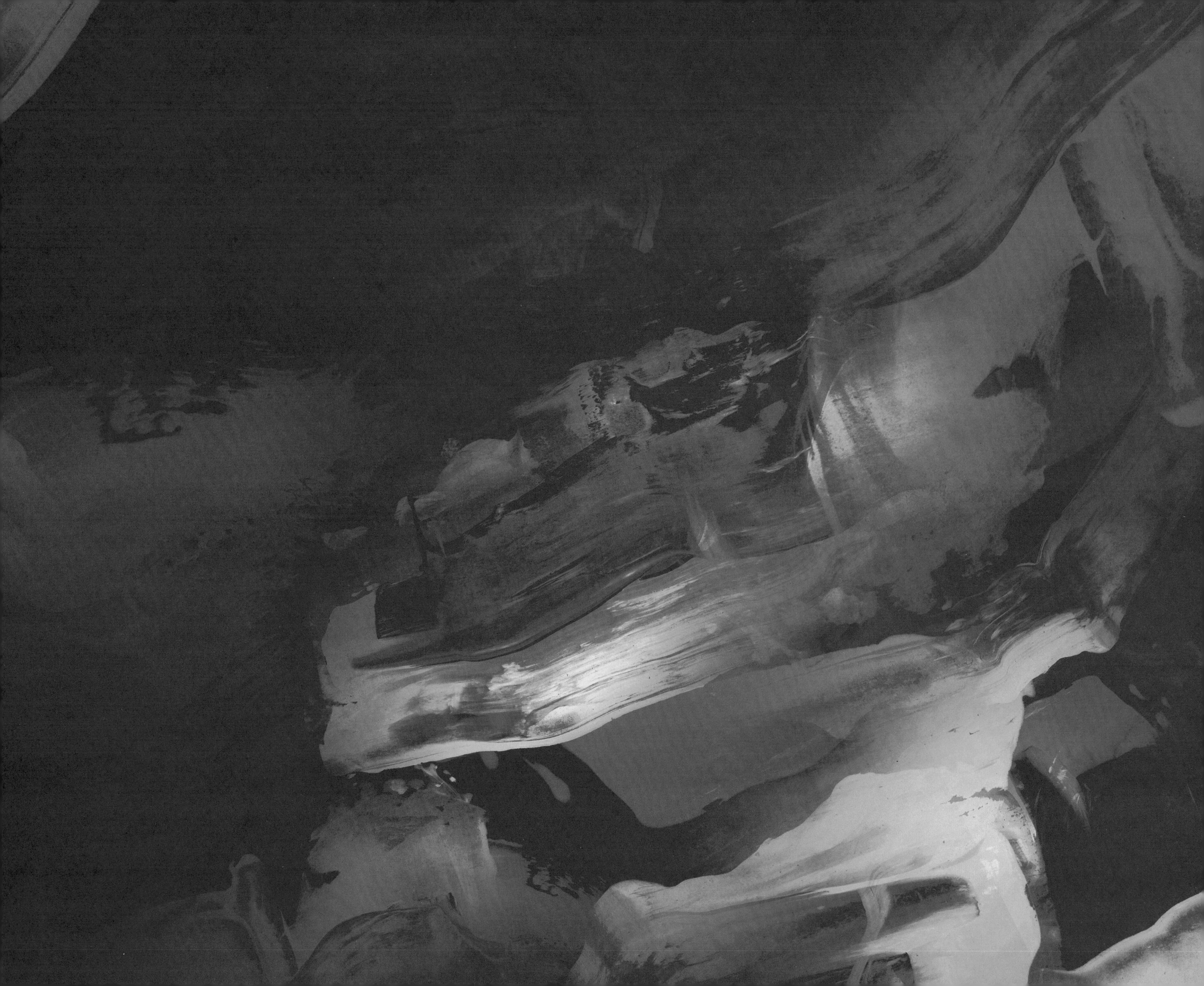

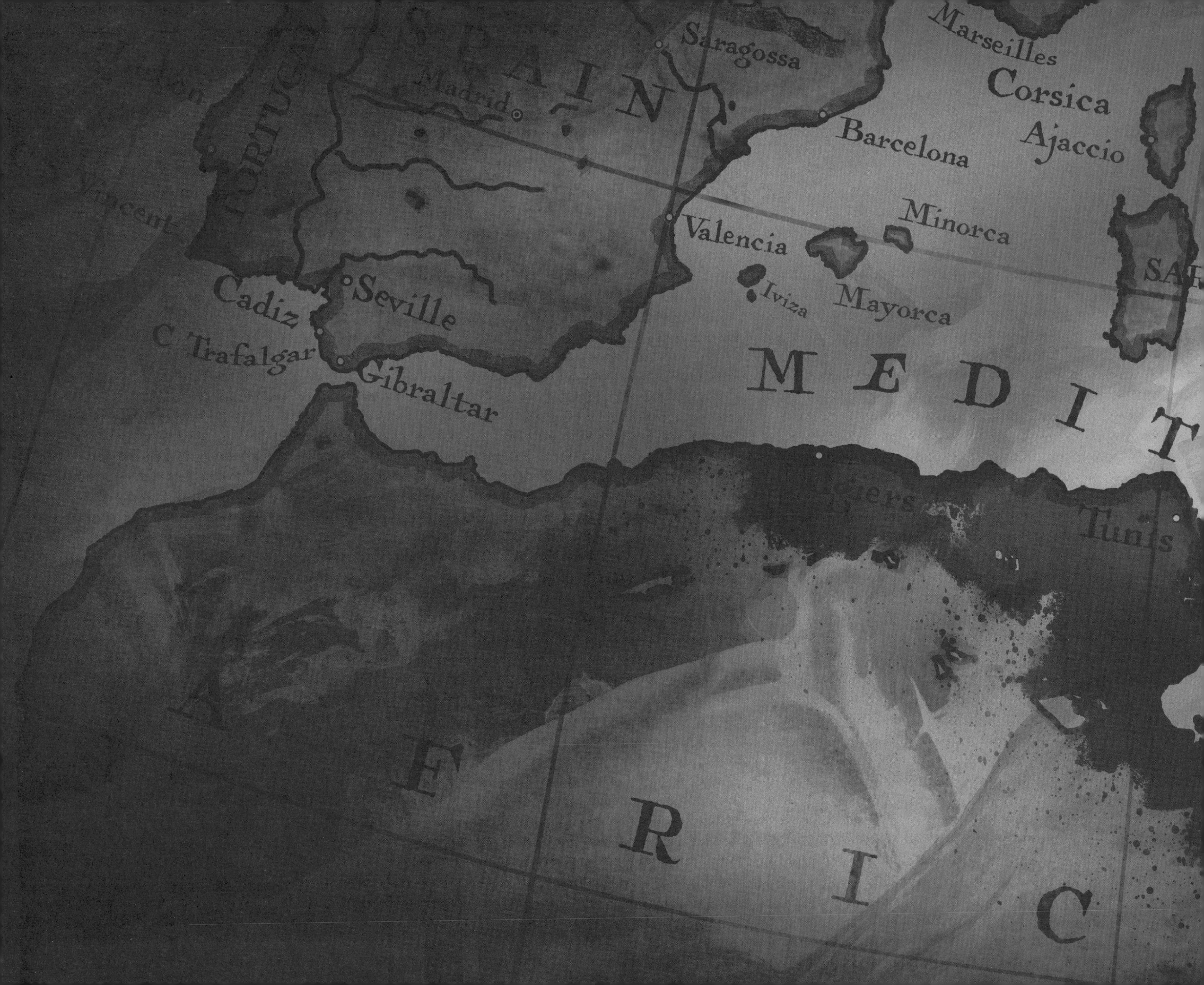

SPAIN
Saragossa
Marseilles
Corsica
Madrid
Barcelona
Ajaccio
Minorca
Valencia
Mayorca
Iviza
Vincent
Cadiz
Seville
C Trafalgar
Gibraltar
MEDIT
Tunis
A F R I C